OUT OF CARDS

OUT OF CARDS

KNIGHTS OF LOVELEN
Book One

ALLISON ALDRIDGE

Out of Cards
Paperback Edition

Love N. Books Press
An Imprint of Wolfpack Publishing
1707 E. Diana Street
Tampa, FL 33610

www.lovenbookspress.com

Cover design by Jennilynn Wyer Designs
Edited by My Brother's Editor

Paperback ISBN 979-8-89567-759-9
Ebook ISBN 979-8-89567-758-2
LCCN

For those who inherited burdens instead of choices and still managed to carve a name beyond the roles written for them.

content warnings

Explicit sexual content, alcohol, blood, gore, dead bodies, burned bodies, burns, broken bones, car accident, poison, gangs, mention of human trafficking, death, choking, drugging, domestic violence, mentions of child abuse not explicit, panic attacks, death of a parent, drug overdose

If you have any questions or concerns regarding these trigger warnings, please reach out at https://www.allisonaldridge.com/contact.

playlist

"Dear Reader" by Taylor Swift
"Just One Yesterday" by Fall Out Boy
"Silence" by Marshmello, Khalid
"The Albatross" by Taylor Swift
"Poker Face" by Lady Gaga
"Favorite Crime" by Olivia Rodrigo
"If You Want Love" by NF
"While You're At It" by Jessie Murph
"Devil's in the Backseat" by Lostboycrow
"Lucky" by Dermot Kennedy
"Like I Do" by Tate McRae
"Champagne Problems" by Taylor Swift
"Collide" by Justine Skye, Tyga
"Gone Forever" by Three Days Grace
"Raging on a Sunday" by Bohnes
"oh god" by MOTHICA

Check out the full *Out of Cards* Playlist on Spotify.

OUT OF CARDS

CHAPTER ONE

acelynn

RED SPECKLED dots stained my hands, dried and dark against my skin. The sharp bite of cuffs dug into the sensitive flesh of my wrists as I shifted, trying to find a more comfortable position on the cold, reflective surface of the interrogation table. A greenish glow from the overhead light cast ominous shadows against the concrete walls, shrinking the already cramped room and increasing my panicked heartbeat.

Opposite me, a two-way mirror taunted me. The sensation of unwanted eyes on me behind the glass made the hairs on the back of my neck stand up straight. I glared into the panel, hoping my stare might remind whatever officer watching me who I was—what my family had been.

The door slammed open, and two men entered. The first looked barely twenty-five with a baby face that might've charmed me on another day, maybe from across a bar with music so loud you could barely hear your own thoughts and the smell of cheap whiskey in the air. His chestnut hair was trimmed short, each strand carefully gelled into place. Warm brown eyes locked on mine, shining with something like pity. That was his first mistake.

Then there was the other one. Older, smug, the kind of man who thought his mediocre detective career made him untouchable. Gray streaked his black hair just enough to make him think he resembled a certain beloved TV doctor, but I would be the one to break it to him that even with all the primping he did on it, he would never come close to McDreamy. The smirk on his face told me he didn't think I would be much of a challenge for him and his partner.

"Well, well," the older one spoke, his voice slow and cocky.

The screech of metal against cement echoed off the stone walls as he yanked the chair out. With all the flair of a bad detective drama, he spun the chair around and straddled it backward, folding his arms across the backrest like he owned the entire precinct. His gaze pinned me in place.

"Seems like you've landed yourself in quite a mess, sweetheart."

"Seems so," I replied coolly, tilting my head with a mocking curiosity I knew would get under his skin. If he wanted to play this game, we could, but I would win in the end. "Though I would say the cuffs are a bit dramatic, Detective..."

"Parsons," he replied evenly. "And that is Detective Watson."

I smiled a bright, full-tooth grin at the young Detective Watson, causing him to shrink slightly into himself. At least I intimidated one of them.

"The cuffs stay," Parsons's voice pulled my attention back to him. He reached over to tighten them a notch.

I winced, hissing as the metal bit deeper. The chain

clinked against the table as I jerked back. Parsons just laughed at my reaction.

Out of the corner of my eye, I saw Watson finally take his seat next to his partner. He shifted awkwardly, nerves practically bleeding off him. This had to be one of his first cases, maybe even *the* first.

"First time, Watson?" I asked sweetly, voice sugary sweet.

He swallowed hard, Adam's apple bobbing against his throat.

I leaned forward, watching him through lowered lashes. "Don't worry. I'll be gentle."

He cleared his throat, fumbling with his invisible nerves as I leaned back in my chair, waiting for one of them to begin the questioning.

Parsons slammed a thick manila folder onto the table. It burst open at the edges—papers, photos, and a single name scrawled across the tab: *Spade.*

My family's name.

Years of criminal activity were reduced to ink on printed paper. And this was only what they *knew* about. What they could prove had been carried out by the Death Dealers.

"The Spade family," Parsons sneered, jabbing a finger into the folder. The dirty yellow material of the folder bent inward with the pressure of his touch. "One of the top three crime syndicates in the state of Arizona. Claimed the Holbeck Valley just north of Lovelen. Charming little town."

I bit my tongue. The Death Dealers held far more land than just Holbeck, but none of it mattered now. Everything we built, every club asset, every sliver of territory—it would all be handed over to the Knights of Lovelen on a silver platter. To *Kaius Mordred.* The man who had struck the match that had burned down my entire world.

"And tonight," Parsons went on, voice thick with mockery. "Your whole family was slaughtered at their estate."

The comment ignited something inside me—anger so hot it made my blood boil.

"How did you pull this off, Ms. Spade?" he continued. "You were barely involved in the club—shipped off to private school, far from the influence of the family business, when you were barely able to read. Not much time to learn the trade from states away."

"You think I killed them?" I hissed. "I didn't orchestrate this attack."

Parsons leaned back and hummed, taunting me to give up anything that could incriminate myself. I knew better than to continue this without a lawyer present, but who was I going to call now that the club was gone? And I sure as hell didn't trust a public defender against Parsons. All that I would get was a plea deal that pinned me as the monster in the Spade line.

He cocked his head to the side. "You're the only Spade left standing. We found you over your brother's body, leaving you the heir to everything. And you want us to believe that's a coincidence? You're the only one who would benefit from his death."

His dark chuckle echoed like slow drumbeats in my ears. I lunged forward, the cuffs yanking me back hard. My voice cracked as I screamed, "There were *children* in that house! You think I could kill my own blood? The family my father built from the ground up? I didn't put that bullet in my brother's head. And I didn't light that fire. He was already dead when I got there!"

"Then what happened?" Watson asked softly. "That is all we want to know, Ms. Spade."

His voice pulled me back from the edge like a smooth

hand resting on my shoulder. I turned toward him, the calm in his gaze quieting the storm raging in my mind just long enough for me to breathe. There was empathy in those eyes —real, honest empathy that wasn't manufactured in a training room.

So I told them.

Told them every moment, every choice I regretted, every second that led me to the ruins of my home. I gave them everything.

When I finally finished, the silence around the three of us felt heavier than the chains holding me in place. My head bowed, and for the first time tonight, hot tears spilled down my cheeks. They hit the metal table with soft, explosive drops that echoed like bombs in my chest.

"The Knights of Lovelen destroyed the only good thing in my world," I whispered. My heart beat so loudly it felt like it might tear out of my chest. In the dark of my memory, I saw them—those cold, merciless green eyes I had met just before the end.

Kaius Mordred, King of Lovelen.

I lifted my gaze and stared directly at Watson. "If given the chance, I would burn this entire city to the ground just for them to feel a fraction of what I feel right now."

CHAPTER TWO

acelynn

TWO MONTHS LATER

EVERYTHING ABOUT ME WAS A LIE.

From the jet-black box dye hastily applied over my bleached hair in the dim bathroom of a police station, to the fake ID tucked securely in my wallet, there wasn't a trace of my real identity left—except for the necklace. The only piece of my former life I was allowed to keep.

A thin silver chain hid beneath my shirt, and at the end of it dangled a single deadly charm—a black ace of spades. My fingers brushed against the familiar outline, comforted by the cold metal pressing into my skin. A reminder. A warning.

Acelynn Thorton.

The name was acid in my mouth, a sick joke courtesy of the smug detective who had arranged this whole charade. He knew exactly what he was doing—picking a name that would twist the knife every time I spoke it. An ode to the mighty Spade family, which had fallen so far from grace. I had no doubt that kind of cruelty would be a regular occurrence every time we spoke from here on out.

The soft chime of the Cactus & Chrome Diner's front door broke me out of my thoughts. It was just past three in the morning. The usual drunk crowd had trickled out, leaving behind an exhausted waitress, a couple in the corner, and me—waiting.

I didn't spare the others a glance.

Because *she* had just arrived.

Astoria Mordred, darling of Lovelen and my one-way ticket to getting close enough to her brother to kill him. Even if that wasn't my official assignment, it was the one I was after. I would feel the King of Lovelen's blood pool between my fingers by the end of this.

The girl entered the diner like she owned the night—head held high, confidence radiating off her with every step, and a smile on her lips as if the world revolved solely around her. And maybe it did. Dark jeans clung like paint to her long, slender legs, and the orange halter top made her sun-kissed skin glow under the flickering diner lights.

"Come on, Tor," a man's voice broke through the silence as he stepped up next to her. He threw a possessive arm around her shoulders. His dark hair flopped perfectly into his face as he beamed at her like she was the only girl left on earth. "Let me stay."

Astoria rolled her eyes, trying to shrug him off. "Don't call me that, Nolan. You *know* the rules."

Nolan grinned, a slow, arrogant curve of his mouth that should've melted her on the spot. "Remind me again, pretty girl."

She didn't even blink. Astoria Mordred was immune to his charm, and Nolan was trying too hard to get her to spare him a glance.

A glint of gold flashed on his left hand as he twirled a strand of her honey-blonde hair around his fingers. My eyes narrowed at the symbol engraved into the ring.

The Knights of Lovelen insignia.

It shimmered in the hard diner lights. A simple piece at first glance, but it was unmistakable. A holy grail that was cracked clean down the middle, with a crooked crown dangling from the rim. Around the base of the cup, delicate flowers bloomed.

Not decorative.

Not innocent.

Hemlock.

One of the Knights' signature methods of disposing of obstacles that threatened them in any way. If I hadn't studied the symbol like a scripture, I might have missed the entire meaning. Might have thought they were just a pretty accent to an ominous symbol. But I knew better.

I'd made a deal with the devil. Stepped into their Eden willingly. And I promised to be the serpent in the garden.

Now the game had begun.

CHAPTER THREE

acelynn

STEAM DRIFTED *from the coffee set before me, curling lazily into the stale air. The dark liquid resembled sludge more than anything drinkable, but that didn't stop Parsons from knocking his back like it was a fine roast. Across the table, the low-rank rent-a-cop assigned to serve us smirked.*

"See something you like?" I shot a glare up at the balding officer.

He grinned, flashing yellowed teeth as he reached for the necklace resting at my collarbone. It had been a gift from my brother on my eighth birthday. His grimy fingers brushed the charm, and I jerked away, but the cuffs locked me to the table.

"What'd you do to get yourself locked up in here, little Ace?" he asked, voice thick with a Southern drawl. His breath hit my cheek, hot and stale. He leaned in like he was admiring the spade charm, but we both knew he was trying to get a peek down my shirt.

I batted my lashes, voice dry. "A little bit of everything, judging by the charges."

He let the necklace fall back into place and gave my chin a condescending tweak. I snapped at his retreating hand, teeth just missing skin.

Parsons chuckled under his breath. "I like that nickname. What do you think, Ace?"

"I think you should either tell me what you want or charge me already. It's been a long night. I'd like to get some rest before I face a judge." I watched the officer exit the room with a mocking wave before turning back to Parsons.

He let the silence linger, probably thinking it would rattle me. It didn't. I'd learned long ago how to deal with men who thought power was a permanent thing...and how to turn their illusions upside down with a few calculated words.

My gaze drifted to Watson. He was hunched over a stack of papers, casually marking them with a pen every so often. He must've felt my eyes because he looked up. I smiled sweetly. "Or you could just tell me why I was brought in, Watson."

"I..." Watson stammered, glancing helplessly at Parsons.

Parsons tilted his head, clearly weighing his next move. "Have you ever met Kaius Mordred?"

I frowned. "Maybe as a child, but I saw a lot of people pass through my father's doors. They never paid me much attention."

He studied me like a bug he was getting ready to squash. "So he wouldn't remember you if he had seen you?"

"No, I doubt it. But he'd know my name if you gave it to him."

"That can be changed," Watson muttered, scribbling something on his papers.

I wrinkled my nose. "Change my name? Why bother if I'm going to prison?"

Parsons leaned back in his chair, arms folding across his chest. "Or you could work with us—help take down the Knights of Lovelen."

I raised an eyebrow but said nothing.

"Become an informant," he continued. "We'll dismiss all charges. You get your revenge, and we get to clean up the streets of Lovelen."

I leaned forward, letting my elbows rest on the cold metal table. "What's the catch?"

"No catch," Parsons said, lifting his hands in mock innocence. "Bring down the Knights, and you walk."

"And if I don't agree to this suicide mission?"

"Then you'll rot away in prison. For the rest of your miserable life."

With the mountain of charges stacked against me, I didn't have the luxury of choice. The deal was the only thing keeping me from a life sentence—or worse. Parsons, with his superior ego, thought this plan was foolproof. But he was blind to the obvious. If the Knights discovered me, I would be returning to him in a body bag, not with club secrets to bring them to justice he was so hell-bent on. If there was anyone who deserved justice from them, it was me. Infiltrating Lovelen's most dangerous criminal empire wasn't a mission. It was a death wish.

Not that they cared.

The department had backed me so far into a corner I could barely breathe, let alone escape. And now, with the possibility of gathering intel on the city's most feared gang, they were more than willing to feed me to the coyotes.

I tore my eyes from the gold ring glinting on Nolan's finger and refocused on my target. Astoria. She gave an exaggerated roll of her emerald eyes before swatting Nolan Bedivere's hand away from her hair and sweeping past him. But not before glancing back and fluttering her long, dark lashes just enough to keep him twisted around her pretty little finger.

I raised my glass of water to my lips, watching from

behind the rim as Nolan ran a hand down his face, struggling not to race after her. Every muscle in his back was pulled so tight, his leather jacket strained at the seams as his restraint wore thin.

Then Astoria turned, her voice smooth as velvet and sharp as a blade. “You’d better run back to my brother.”

She licked her pink lips with deliberate ease. “We both know how he gets when you keep him waiting.”

Nolan only lingered in the doorway for a heartbeat longer, watching as Astoria disappeared behind a teal-painted restroom door. Then, with a shove that sent the glass door rattling against the frame, he stepped out into the darkness of the desert night.

I stood from my booth and moved casually through the near-empty diner, weaving between the faded vinyl chairs that stuck out from the chipped tables until I reached the bathroom.

The moment I stepped inside, I could tell this place hadn’t been renovated since the ’80s. Once baby blue, the walls were now dull and peeling. The overhead light buzzed faintly, casting a sickly yellow hue over everything, making the bubblegum pink stall doors look even more awful than they already were.

My gaze caught my reflection in the mirror, and I had to mask the startled look on my face as I looked into the hazel contact lenses staring back at me. It was like looking at a stranger. Another sacrifice to who I was. Another piece of me stripped away in the name of survival. I leaned forward, pretending to fix a smudge in my lipstick just as Astoria emerged from the far stall, eyes glued to her phone, completely unaware she was no longer alone.

She stepped up beside me, slipping the phone into her back pocket and flicking the faucet on. I kept my act up, adjusting my shirt just enough for the silver chain around my neck to slip free. The ace of spades pendant caught the flickering light, glinting in the mirror like the beacon of destruction it once was.

Astoria's eyes snapped to it.

"Pretty necklace," she said with a smile. But her tone was a blade wrapped in silk—soft on the surface but razor sharp underneath. A warning. This was the Knights of Lovelen's territory. And opposing clubs' symbols weren't welcome here. Not unless you were family. And mine was dead.

I straightened slowly, matching her stance. She had a few inches on me in her heeled boots, but the height didn't rattle me like she intended it to.

"Thanks," I said smoothly. "My grandmother gave it to me when I was little."

The lie felt like ash in my mouth. I touched the charm, letting my fingers linger on the familiar curve of the spade. "She thought she was being clever."

Astoria tilted her head, eyes still fixed on the necklace. "Clever?"

"Yeah." I let out a breathy laugh. "My name's Acelynn. Every gift she ever gave had this damn thing on it. Some kids learn to bake from their grandparents. Mine taught me how to cheat at poker."

That earned a genuine laugh from her. Astoria's soft bubble of amusement echoed off the bathroom tiles.

"You're funny," she said through her laughter. "I might have to bribe one of the guys at the bar to sneak you onto the poker night roster just to see if you could clean my brother out. He could use a little humbling every once in a while."

"Name the time and place." I shot her a wink, letting the chain fall back against its home on my chest.

Astoria's gaze sharpened slightly. "You must be new if

you don't know that wearing that out in the open could get you killed in Lovelen."

There was curiosity in her voice, but not alarm. Maybe she believed my story. Or maybe she was just good at playing along. When you grow up around criminal activity, you learn how to chameleon yourself to be what people want to either take advantage of them or get out of trouble. Either way, her posture had relaxed—and for now, that was a win.

I shrugged before turning toward the door and began to exit the bathroom. "Just moved here. Didn't realize I had landed in a place where a simple playing card symbol could cause anarchy."

"Oh," she said with a smirk as she held the door open with one hand. "You have no idea."

The click of her boots rang out behind me as we exited into the diner once again. I slid back into my booth. Astoria helped herself to the seat across from mine, no invitation needed. I guess when your family owns the entire town, you don't need to ask for permission for much of anything.

"So, Acelynn..." She trailed off, fishing for a last name.

"Acelynn Thorton," I said casually, offering my hand to her.

She took it in her own. The cool kiss of her metal rings brushed against my heated skin as she shook it firmly.

"Astoria Mordred." She grinned, dropping my hand before leaning back into the booth. "What brings you to Lovelen, Arizona? Unless you are a fan of jumping chollas and the unrelenting sun, there is not much here for newcomers."

I let out a snort of amusement. "I inherited a property from a distant relative. I had to come out here anyway to meet with her lawyer, so I figured I would stay awhile. Wasn't leaving much behind in Raleigh."

"Running from something?" Astoria's smile dipped into a devious one that I could tell only meant trouble for anyone who came in contact with it.

"Running, relocating...same thing to me." I lifted my glass and took a long drink. "And when this opportunity fell into my lap, I couldn't help but jump at the chance."

Astoria's lips parted to respond, but the sharp crack of gunfire split through the air. The front windows exploded inward, sending shards of glass spraying like shrapnel across the diner. Astoria shrieked and ducked beneath the table. I followed without hesitation, heart hammering against my chest as more bullets tore through the space. My ears rang, but I could still hear the distant, angry shouts of men growing closer.

I locked eyes with Astoria, signaling that we needed to move. Now.

Her eyes widened with realization, but it was too late.

A hand fisted in my hair, yanking me violently back from under the table. I screamed as my assailant dragged me across the broken glass, the sharp edges slicing into my arms, my legs, my side. I kicked out, twisting and turning to try to break free, but my attacker only tightened their grip, dragging me across the diner floor like I was nothing.

We suddenly stopped. Their hand jerked my head by the roots, wrenching my neck at an awkward angle until my spine arched.

The man above me leaned in close. He was in his mid-forties with graying, thinning hair. A jagged scar ran across his throat like someone had tried to slit it a long time ago but failed to get the job done. His skin was pale, almost a sickly shade, and his eyes...

Dark. Familiar. Evil.

Recognition hit me like a freight train. And I knew with icy certainty that I had met this man before.

But the question was, did he know who I really was? If the answer was yes, then I was already dead.

CHAPTER FOUR

kaius

FEW THINGS SATISFIED me more than the sound of a man begging for his life when he knew he was mere inches away from death. Some found it sick that just the reminder of the whimpers could brighten my day. Nolan, my second, always joked that there was no other sound that could do it for me, and on most days, I agreed.

My knuckles cracked against bone, splitting skin and sending a fresh spray of blood across the cold concrete. The man slumped back into the chair, groaning in half-conscious misery, each breath a shallow, pitiful gasp.

"There is only one way this ends, Joshua," I said, my voice steady as I sneered down at him.

He coughed, blood dripping from his lips. "Please...I told you. I don't know how the Muze is coming into the city. All I have been told is it was being traded near the border. Somewhere near the old mill. I swear to god, that's everything I know!"

I bent at the knee to come eye level with him. "You're lying."

Without looking, I held out my hand. Vincent leaned against the wall behind me with all the patience of a bored cat, flicking a butterfly knife open and closed before dropping it into my waiting palm. I flipped it open with a fluid snap, the blade catching the dim light with a wink. I turned the knife side to side to admire its beauty.

Joshua recoiled instinctively, but the ropes binding him to the folding chair held him in place. His voice rose, a scrambled mess of stuttering pleas spilling from his lips, but I didn't bother to acknowledge them.

"Nolan," I called out calmly.

From the shadows, Nolan stepped forward, locking one arm around Joshua's throat and the other across his forehead, holding him in place for me.

I stood, pressing my fingers against Joshua's cheeks to force his mouth open. The man's eyes widened in panic as I snatched his tongue between my thumb and forefinger, pulling it toward me with a harsh tug. Before Joshua even realized what I was doing, his severed tongue was hanging limply in front of him.

His screams came out as a gurgle as blood poured down his chin and over Nolan's arm. The bright red color soaked into Joshua's shirt, pooling beneath the surface onto his collarbones. The severed tongue hit the floor with a wet slap as I let it go. Joshua's body began to spasm as he choked on the gush of blood flooding his throat.

I turned toward Vincent once again. He held out a small vial—delicate glass cradling dried petals and leaves the color of ash and jade. I handed back his knife and took the vial, holding it up to the overhead light.

"She is beautiful, isn't she?" I said to no one in particular, admiring the flecks of white blooms in the mix. "Most mistake her for parsley, you know. Harmless little thing... until she's not."

I pulled the stopper with a soft pop, pinching the batch out of its glass.

"Hemlock," I continued on my lesson, letting a dark chuckle roll off my lips. "Slows your heart. Paralyzes you from the inside out while your nervous system begins to shut down. Sometimes, if you are lucky, this little beauty will plague its victim with hallucinations."

Vincent always ensured the dose was a deadly one unless we wanted to play with our target for a little longer. Wanted to draw out their death for our own sick pleasure. There was only one time recently that I had the desire to use that method of torture. The images of what occurred in that house on the night of the Death Dealers' massacre still clawed their way into my dreams.

Joshua had stopped struggling, his head lolling slightly. Blood leaked in long, slow trails from the corners of his mouth. I moved closer to the man.

"The thing is, she doesn't bite me anymore," I whispered, my smirk returning. "I've grown immune. My father made sure of it, said we all needed to know our poison of choice. Explained we should become it if we wanted to survive our world."

In one swift motion, I seized forward and shoved the hemlock into the man's throat. He choked, convulsed, but I made sure the plant went down—every vein in his neck standing out almost black as his skin lost color. His eyes rolled back in his head, and Nolan finally released him. We stood and watched as his body twitched for a few more moments before going still.

Joshua's eyes stared blankly, glassy and vacant, up at the ceiling, all signs of life gone from him.

"She's a nasty little thing." I cracked a grin, tossing the empty vial back to Vincent. "Just how I like them."

CHAPTER FIVE

acelynn

DOMINIC VIRELLI, the leader of the Iron Serpents, loomed over me with a sneer. "Well, you're not the sweet girl I was hoping to speak to, but you'll do just fine to send a message."

I spat at his boots in defiance. "Do I look like a fucking mailman to you? Deliver the message yourself."

He clicked his tongue, yanking my head back so hard I cried out. The sound died in my throat as he wrapped his hand around it, squeezing until my airway shriveled beneath the pressure. My nails clawed against his hold as dark spots began to dance across my vision.

Dominic leaned in, his hot breath against my ear, voice dipping into a venomous whisper only I could hear. "The massacre should've taken you out, little queen. But if you deliver this message for me, I'll keep your identity our little secret until I want a favor from you. No one has to know who you really are behind that bad dye job and new eye color."

I stared at him, eyes frantically trying to convey that I

would agree to anything he wanted in this moment to not give myself away.

He must have gotten the message because he continued on, "Tell the Knights that our trade deal is off. We found a new Muze dealer that is willing to pay us double for our runs."

Dominic dropped his hold on me, letting my limp body slam against the tile floor. I gulped in the air my lungs so desperately needed as he started out of the diner, boots crunching against the shattered glass.

"You good?" Astoria's voice called out to me as she maneuvered herself out from under our booth.

I nodded a few times, still not sure if I could talk. The distant wails of sirens rang out in the night air as the cops began to make their way to the scene of this crime.

Panic rushed into me, sharp and sudden, as the adrenaline that once settled there wore off. My body ached in a thousand places, but I knew we couldn't stay here for much longer.

"We need to move," Astoria spoke my thoughts as she helped me to my feet. I winced as my muscles strained to just stand. She nodded toward the back, throwing one arm around me to help guide me toward the back of the diner. "This way. I know a shortcut through the kitchen. The cops won't start back there."

"Not a fan of them?" I asked, voice hoarse with each word. We slipped into an abandoned kitchen. Dirty dishes were still littered on the steel countertop, and a pot of burning goo was bubbling over onto a burner.

"Let's just say..." She shot me a sly grin, releasing me from her hold and venturing further into the kitchen. "The law enforcement of Lovelen aren't huge fans of my family either. What we do isn't exactly...legal, per se."

I hobbled after her. "I am guessing it has something to do with those Knight people that guy wants me to deliver a message to?"

Astoria stiffened but gave a short nod in acknowledgment. She reached into her back jeans pocket, pulling out her phone before tapping in a number with practiced speed. It rang only once before a man picked up on the other line.

"I need you to come get me." She paused once, shooting me a look quickly before continuing. "And a friend."

The voice on the other end was loud enough I could hear the irritation from here. Astoria rolled her eyes at them, voice snappy in response to their attitude. "Nolan, just shut up and get over here. Calvin went back on his deal with us, and the Serpents hit the diner. Cops are about to be crawling all over this place."

She ended the call before he could argue more. Turning back to me with a sigh, "There is an old park behind the diner. He will bitch the whole way, but he'll come."

Nolan took less than ten minutes to get there. Astoria and I were sitting on a pair of rickety swings, both of them creaking quietly in the dark, when his truck screeched into the parking lot. The man was across the grassy area in front of Astoria, examining her for any injuries, before I could stand fully.

She swatted at his hands as they ran down her arms once more. "Quit fussing. I am fine."

"Tori," he said through gritted teeth, earning him a glare from the girl for the nickname. "I told you I should've stayed. But no, you had to be stubborn and think that you could take on the world on your own. Now look—"

"You're being a mother hen," I cut in, arms crossing over my chest.

Nolan whirled to face me, an icy glare that I was sure scared most people, directed at me.

I smiled sweetly, setting the bait I practically begged him to take. "They didn't touch a hair on her head."

"Her, on the other hand..." Astoria cringed as her eyes swept over me. "But she is kind of a badass the way she spoke to Dom."

"Dominic was there?" Nolan's voice dropped into a growl. Rage surged behind his eyes as he realized what could have happened if I hadn't been there tonight. He ran a hand down his face, then turned back toward the truck. "Let's go before your brother finds out and throws my ass in the basement for the night."

A flicker of something dark caught my eye, a rust color, maybe blood, on the collar of his white T-shirt. My stomach turned, and I suddenly had no doubt what going down into the basement entailed. The Knights had their own ways of torture, and they had to have a place to enact those horrors without alerting the entire town.

"Acelynn is coming with us," Astoria called after Nolan.

He halted mid-step, whirling around to point one finger at her. "He said no more strays, Astoria."

"She doesn't count as a stray," she countered his point. "One, she saved my life tonight, so I think you at least owe her a drink. And two, Dominic gave her a message for the Knights, which is probably something *he* would like to be informed of."

"This is your funeral, Tor." Nolan threw his hands up in the air at her before mumbling, "Kaius is going to murder her, and then I am going to have to murder my best friend since I was six."

The drive wasn't long, and before I knew it, a bar came into view like a relic of a forgotten world. A sign that read "The Queen's Table" was barely visible in the dark. All its marquee lights were shut off for the night.

Nolan was the first out of the truck. He slammed his door, rattling the entire truck before rounding the front of the vehicle and stalking into the bar's entrance.

"Excuse his lack of charm and hospitality," Astoria muttered, climbing out after him.

I followed close behind and barely made it to the door as she swung it open. Nolan positioned himself in the doorway, blocking the way in.

Astoria tried to push past him. "Move. Before I start screaming, and you know how much everyone in the club enjoys hearing my tantrums."

"He wants to speak to her. They are at the roundtable." Nolan held his ground.

She cursed under her breath but didn't argue any further. Nolan motioned to me, placing a firm hand on my back and leading me in. He guided us toward a pair of deep wood doors. Golden handles adorned each of them, and I watched Nolan slowly push them open, forcing us both inside.

Heat hit me like a punch to the chest. A massive, gleaming white round table dominated the room. The crimson insignia of the Knights of Lovelen bled across its center like a wound. Men sat on either side of the table in large, upholstered chairs, but only one mattered.

Images of fire and carnage piled up flashed across my mind as the devil himself, the man who burned my life to ash, sat inches from me.

Kaius Mordred.

His impossibly green eyes tacked me with lazy intent. It took every bit of self-control not to lunge across the table and choke the life out of the King of Lovelen. Not that I would get anywhere near him with Nolan standing behind me, but the attempt would soothe some of the burning anger crawling through my veins at the moment.

"It appears my sister may have brought home a useful stray for once in her life." His voice was like smoke and aged whiskey. It filled me with a dangerous warmth in the pit of my stomach that I shouldn't be feeling.

"I am not a plaything for the lot of you to toy with," I growled out, taking a step forward until my hips stood even with the table.

His gaze dragged down my body like a brand. I leaned forward, placing both hands on the smooth wooden surface, spade necklace swinging between us like a threat. His eyes darkened at the symbol.

A playful smirk crossed my lips. "Like what you see, pretty boy?"

Kaius dragged his gaze back up to my face, eyes unblinking. "You're no different from any of the other strays that my darling sister drags through those doors daily."

I narrowed my eyes at him, studying his appearance for the first time since the massacre. His blond hair hung just past his sharp cheekbones, strands pushed back haphazardly. Even with half of his face being covered by the shadows of the room, I could see the light scruff that covered his jaw. His green eyes were sharp and piercing, a glint of mischief shining through them as he stared me down. His skin was weathered, kissed by the Arizona sun and the wind, giving him a natural tan. The charm was almost worse than the cruelty that he wielded. A deadly combination that I wanted to explore more. Maybe I would have let myself if it weren't for the fact that he found a sick delight in torturing the ones I loved.

A low cough of warning sounded from beside me, but I kept my gaze locked on Kaius. Settling back in his chair, he brought his left hand up to run over his bottom lip. His ring gleamed in a taunting motion that begged me to continue this game.

"But, kitten, don't you know that whatever information you gained tonight will determine your fate?" Kaius said, voice dark as silk. "And then you'll be whatever I decide you are."

CHAPTER SIX

kaius

THE KITTEN MY sister had dragged into the lion's den had just shown her claws. And I couldn't decide if I wanted to rip them out one by one or let her mark me as her favorite prey. I tilted my head, examining the woman at the other end of the table. Dark hair curtained part of her face, but the glimpse I saw made me more than intrigued. Hazel eyes locked onto mine, the hint of challenge glinting in them had my cock hardening.

If it weren't for the little symbol hanging around her throat, I'd have cleared the room and had her on her knees, looking up at me with those defiant, storm-filled eyes.

"What did that man, Dominic, I think he said his name was, call you tonight? The King of Lovelen?" she growled out, words full of fire that were setting heat to my blood. "You are fucked in the head if you think I will ever bow to you or any of your little Knights."

Nolan let out a sharp laugh from behind her. "You have no idea how accurate your observation is, sweets."

I tossed him a dry look, which was only responded to

with a shrug. A collection of muffled laughs traveled around the table. This little kitten had balls, and every Knight in this room felt that raw, untamed thing in her. Most who came to the roundtable succumbed to the power surrounding them immediately upon entering, but this woman reveled in it.

A true queen without a throne to claim.

"You saved my sister tonight," I said flatly.

It wasn't a question, and the entire room knew it. The woman straightened, hands still planted firmly on the table that held more blood-soaked history than she could even begin to understand. She wasn't as tall as Astoria, but what she lacked in height she made up for in attitude that matched a seven-foot man. "I wanted to thank you personally for that..."

"Acelynn," she said, voice clipped. "Acelynn Thorton."

I gave her a single nod. She shifted uncomfortably, clearly thrown by the civility in my tone. The necklace shifted again, catching the light and my attention.

"Got any family around here?" I asked.

"No." Her jaw clenched. A flash of something overtook her features. A mix of rage and regret crossed her face so fast that only someone trained to notice would have caught it. "The last of my mother's family died recently. I inherited their estate here in Lovelen. I don't speak to my father anymore."

Acelynn brought the left side of her bottom lip between her teeth, chewing lightly as her nerves began to bleed through the cracks. She was hiding something. But as long as it didn't have to do with a Spade, there was no reason to pry any further into a random girl's personal life. She would be gone soon enough once she saw what the Knights were. It was one of the reasons Astoria resented the club. She never had a "normal" friend stick around.

"Does this have to do with that rival club that attacked the diner tonight?" Acelynn looked down as she spoke. "Or maybe the one with the spade symbol?"

She peered up at me through her lashes, shoulders sagging in defeat. "Astoria already grilled me about it."

"The Spades are dead." Vincent's voice was deep and gravelly as he spoke.

Acelynn's eyes snapped to him without hesitation, watching the man to my right with a healthy amount of caution. Most made it a point to not even look at the man if they could avoid it, but Acelynn didn't even bat an eye at him. Whether that was from boldness or sheer stupidity was yet to be determined.

Vincent was a man of very few words, but they always made their point. He was the epitome of the stereotypical biker club member, with his unruly dark hair, beard, and tattoos covering almost every inch of his skin from the neck down.

"Well..." Acelynn wet her lips once. "That sounds unfortunate for them."

Vincent watched her for any deception, then grunted once in response to her comment. That was as close as anyone got to impressing him.

I rolled my eyes at him and downed the last of my whiskey. The burn of the liquor grounded me as I muttered, "You done testing the stray?"

Another grunt passed through him, and I knew he wouldn't be saying anything else for the rest of the meeting. Moody bastard.

"Nolan said Dominic gave you a message for me," I said, pulling the conversation back to the main topic at hand.

Acelynn gulped at the mention of the leader of the Iron Serpents. I could see the purple bruises and light pink cuts that were scattered across her skin from the fight she must have put up against the man. The sight had something deep inside me pulsing with rage.

"Yes," she whispered. It took her another beat before she spoke again. "Dominic said to tell the Knights that your trade deal was off. They found a new Muze dealer who is willing to pay them double for the runs."

I ground my teeth together. If Joshua had spilled more tonight, this might have been avoided. But I had a feeling this new dealer wasn't a stranger who had just happened upon Muze. No, there was a lone Spade left who was now continuing their trade route in hopes of salvaging what hadn't burned with their club.

"Thank you," I ground out, the tension in the room growing as the Knights all looked toward me for answers I had not come up with yet. Drumming my fingers against the table, I continued, "Do you have a place to stay tonight?"

She raised a brow at me in accusation. I cut her off before whatever snarky comment she was going to say could be heard.

"That was not an invitation to my bed."

"That was not what I was going to say," she snapped, arms crossing tight over her chest. The motion did dangerous things to her neckline, breasts pooling further out of the top of the dark top she was wearing. I fought the urge to groan.

The smirk playing on her lips said she knew exactly what she had just done. "I am staying at the old motel on Davis Street."

"That place is only good for two things." Nolan chuckled. "Drug deals and pay-by-the-hour hookups."

"I'll be sure to lay out a towel before passing out," Acelynn quipped, rolling her eyes at his comment.

"You can stay in one of the dorms with Astoria for the night," I offered.

Her gaze snapped back to mine, trying to pick apart my motive.

"With the mess at the diner, it is a safe bet Dom's men are still looking for the two of you. The Canyon View Motel will be one of the first places they will look for a new face in town. Stay here. At least until you find something more permanent."

"Wouldn't want to ruin this pretty face any more tonight, would we?" Nolan tossed an arm over Acelynn's shoulder.

She rolled her eyes at him again, but didn't swat him away. The smug look he was shooting me told me he was proud of himself for winning over the girl.

Nolan had a soft spot for strays. Always had, which made sense. He had been one himself once. A half-starved, angry kid I had dragged home to my father when we were six. Luckily for both of us, my father had decided to allow the boy to stay and treated him like one of his own. It had been hard on my best friend, considering that he had a heart like my sister's when it came to how he cared for others. That heart had almost gotten him killed more times than he would like to admit.

Acelynn sighed, running a hand over her face. She flinched as her fingers graced the splotchy purple finger marks blooming across her jaw.

"Fine," she muttered. "Just show me to the bed farthest from his, Nolan, so I can get some damn sleep."

CHAPTER SEVEN

acelynn

WARM DESERT AIR *threaded through the ends of my hair as I rolled down my car's windows, letting the familiar scent of rain drift through the space. The cracked and peeling "Welcome to Holbeck Valley" sign passed on my right, the once vibrant coloring now bleached by the sun. I let out a soft laugh as it swayed in the wind, barely keeping upright. Still, the sight brought a quiet bittersweet ache to my chest.*

Home.

After more than a decade of coming and going, I was finally home. Permanently. My parents had done what they thought was best—"raising" me from a distance to ensure I was far away from the Death Dealers. Away from the violence and the drugs that came entangled in club life. They wanted me to have a future. A normal life.

But holidays and short visits never satisfied the desperate need to be in this town. My soul was in a perpetual state of feeling homesick.

I had just wrapped up my final semester of university and told the school to mail the diploma to my parents' address. No walking a stage. No beaming photos. No need to sit in a room full of silver-spooned legacies whose lives had been laid out for them since birth. My business degree was nothing more than a peace offering to my parents, and it would sit in the back of my closet gathering dust.

As I pulled up to the mechanic shop my father owned, the low rumble of motorcycle engines echoed in my memory as I scanned the empty lot. Spade Auto Repair looked a little worse for wear than I had remembered it. The sign out front, once bold in blue and orange, was now sun-faded and flaking off in random places.

I placed the car in park and stepped out of it, waiting for the familiar tune of an old radio station floating around the shop to fill my ears. But no one was outside, and the doors to all the mechanic bays were locked down like we were closed for business. But it was just past two, one of the busiest times of the shop most days.

A pit of dread filled my stomach. My brother was always the first to greet me—usually in some dramatic, over-the-top way that included a speech about his baby sister being home. But this time? Silence.

The crunch of gravel under my boots echoed in the quiet as I made my way over to the shop's entrance. I pulled against it, fully expecting it to be locked, but it opened, the little bell dinging as I stepped through the entryway. It was dark, the fluorescent lights not burning my eyes as I entered. No clang of metal, engines roaring to life, or laughter filtered through the space. Just eerie stillness.

Something was off.

My eyebrows pulled together as I scanned the space, waiting for someone to jump out from the dark and admit this was all some weird joke the boys were playing on me. But as the seconds ticked by, I knew I was alone. The blaring ring of the phone shattered the quiet.

I flinched, heart skipping a beat as it continued to ring. My eyes locked on the red blinking light that signaled that the call had been sent to voicemail, but then it rang again. And again. This cycle continued for the next few minutes. Me standing, watching the device, and it angrily ringing back at me. When it rang for a fourth time, I finally moved forward, reaching over the top of the counter and grabbing the receiver, bringing it up to my ear to answer the insistent caller.

"Spade Auto Repair," I said, voice tight.

There was a pause before the sound of heavy breathing answered me.

"Hello?" I asked, a tremor sneaking into my voice.

"Hey doll, it's been a while," a familiar voice responded.

My stomach plummeted, shaky hands almost dropping the phone from my ear. My father and brother had assured me that the man on the other end of the call had been taken care of. So why was he coming back to haunt me from his shallow grave? Taunting me the moment my foot hit Holbeck soil for the first time in years.

"Logan?" My voice cracked in fear.

"You're looking real nice, Em." His voice purred, and I wanted to throw up.

Scrambling around the countertop, I watched the front windows of the shop, but the painted panels obscured the outside view. My eyes watched for any movement, but there was none. Just an endless desert stretching on for miles.

And then I saw it. Up in the corner of the waiting room was a camera someone had haphazardly hung. I slowly raised my head to look at the device as the mechanical whizzing sound of the lens pushing in and out as it focused on my figure flowed through the space. Gulping down the bile rising in my throat, I tried to compose myself as Logan's dark and cold chuckle filled my ear.

"I'll see you real soon, pretty little Spade. And then, we can pick up where we left off."

The line went dead. I slammed the receiver down, stumbling back on shaky legs before launching myself toward the exit. My feet slammed against the linoleum floor. The bell went off again as I hit my palms against the door. It crashed against the outside wall, resulting in the entire window shaking violently inside it. My heel caught on the curb, and I flew forward into the gravel. Tiny rocks bit into my knees, blood beginning to soak through my jeans. A hiss of pain escaped me as I pulled myself onto my hands and knees, crawling toward where my car was parked.

Fumbling with the door handle, I finally got my sweat-slicked hand around it and yanked it open. Tumbling into the safety of my vehicle, I searched my pockets for the keys. My hands shook as I tried to place the key into the ignition, cursing every time it missed, and I had to start the process over again. Finally, after the third time, I managed to shove the metal home and turned it. The engine roared to life in response. I jammed my finger against the locks, letting the click of them soothe me for a moment.

My forehead slammed into the steering wheel as I tried to suck in a few breaths and reminded myself Logan wouldn't be stupid enough to enter Death Dealers territory. Not when he was supposed to be a dead man. He was probably hours away, getting off on my fear as he toyed with me.

"Shit." I breathed out through my nose once.

My eyes caught the movement in the back seat, but it was already too late as a gloved hand snaked around the headrest, silencing the scream that spilled from my lips. I fought against my attacker's hold, only making them grip down hard on my face, holding my head in place against the seat.

"Oh, how I've missed the sound of you screaming for me, doll."

I bolted upright in bed, gasping for air. My heart hammered violently in my chest. It was just a dream.

Another goddamn nightmare. I pressed a hand to my throat, trying to will away the lingering panic.

Astoria shifted beside me, her breathing slow and even as she slept. The safety of her presence was enough to calm me. I lay back again, my eyes watching the shadows of the early morning waver on the ceiling.

The memories that haunted my dreams were trying to tell me something. Begging me to piece together the truth behind the massacre, behind the lies I had been fed my entire life. But so far, all they gave me were more questions than ever.

I pulled at a loose thread in the cream sheets, letting the repetitive motion calm my fraying nerves. Even in the safest place in Lovelen, I couldn't outrun the ghosts. Not awake. Not asleep. And certainly not from him.

The sharp clatter of dishes dragged me from sleep. Thin rays of sunlight filtered through the blinds, slicing the room into pale strips of gold and shadow. Astoria's side of the bed was empty, the sheets tangled and cold.

My eyes burned slightly from the contacts that had dried up during the night on my eyes. I blinked a few times, hoping the sensation would dissipate, but unfortunately for me, I think I was stuck with the feeling until I could remove them or get my hands on some eyedrops.

I swung my legs off the mattress, the concrete floor biting into the soles of my feet. The oversized black T-shirt Astoria had thrown at me last night skimmed my thighs, the hem brushing the tops of the borrowed sleep shorts beneath. A bloodred queen chess piece in mid-checkmate with a white king piece was printed across the front. "The

Queen's Table" was written in stark bold letters beneath it.

Even though the fabric of the shorts hid it, I tugged the shirt lower to cover the thin scar that curved along the top of my hip bone as I stood. Some things weren't meant for curious eyes or careless questions. Especially not *his*.

I padded out of the room, following the low murmur of voices and the soft chime of shifting cups down the hall. The bar was dim, but not lifeless. It appeared to be the kind of place that came alive only after dark and always had secrets buried deep beneath the floorboards.

Astoria leaned against the back counter, her long legs tucked beneath her as she clutched a steaming mug of coffee in both hands. Nolan sat opposite her on one of the tall stools, one elbow propped on the bar top, the other cradling his own mug of dark liquid.

The place was plainer than the flashy bars I had experienced in my college town. All sharp angles and muted color, except for the red-and-black chessboard dance floor and velvet U-shaped booth that sat in the back corner. It looked like some sort of forgotten relic from the '70s. The only other seating was the line of black wooden stools that ran along the bar.

But the bar itself was something else.

It was an L-shaped slab wide enough to comfortably walk across, and a polished pole at the corner stood tall like an unspoken challenge. Running across the full length of the bar top was an industrial metal bar, and if you were tall enough, you could probably pull yourself up until you were dangling over it. Spotlights hung low, begging for someone to climb up and command the room. It wasn't just a bar. It was a stage.

"Morning," Nolan's voice cut through the haze.

Astoria lifted the coffee pot without a word, her brows arched in a silent question. I nodded gratefully and slid onto the stool beside Nolan as she poured. Laid out across the sleek black surface were multiple different résumés. Each was accompanied by a headshot that showed off what the girls thought were their best angles. I lifted the mug of coffee to my lips, eyes scanning over the experience of each candidate. None looked that impressive just from a glance.

"Did you sleep well?" Nolan asked, his tone light and teasing.

Tearing my eyes from the pair, I glared at him while taking another large drink of my coffee. "*Well* is a relative term," I muttered, hugging the warm mug closer to my body.

The coffee was scalding and pulled me further from the fog of my nightmares. Nolan chuckled loudly enough to echo, earning a dramatic glare from Astoria.

"I think she might be more quippy than you, Tor." He smirked.

Astoria rolled her eyes dramatically, but the corner of her mouth twitched upward into a smile. "What have I told you about calling me that?"

"You secretly love it. Admit it," he shot back, and she didn't deny it.

Suddenly, I felt caught in a moment that felt very intimate between them as they stared each other down with a burning desire that I had never witnessed two people have for each other. It made the green monster inside me spark alive. But as soon as it began to rear its ugly head in my mind, Astoria tore her eyes away from Nolan and met mine again.

"So..." She turned her body toward me, cutting Nolan off from the conversation. "Any plans today?"

"Lawyer," I said, setting the mug down on top of a

picture of a blonde girl who had painted her lids with purple shadow and overlined her lips with red lipstick that made it borderline clown territory. "Estate stuff."

"I'll drive you if you want," Astoria offered without hesitation.

I paused. Not because I didn't need the ride, but because I didn't deserve her kindness. Still, I nodded once, trying to ignore the guilt rotting in my gut like a slow leak of poison.

Astoria clapped her hands lightly on the bar. "Great. I'll find you some decent clothes to wear. Maybe something with fewer bloodstains than the ones you had on last night."

She winked and turned toward the hallway, but before she could get far, I called after her, "Astoria."

She turned on her heel, blonde hair swaying around her face. "Yeah?"

"Thanks," I said, the word landing heavy in the quiet surrounding us.

Astoria's smile softened into something raw and real. "Of course. Even though I drag in strays all the time, I think you might actually stick this time. My brother seemed... intrigued."

Heat burned my cheeks instantly. I didn't need the reminder of the way Kaius Mordred's stare had burned through me last night. And how I enjoyed being the center of his attention.

Then, right on cue, the devil himself appeared.

Kaius strolled out of the door that sat on the right side of the hallway. He was dressed in a black long-sleeve shirt that clung to his frame. The sleeves were rolled up to his elbows, showing off the deep ink that marked his skin. Dark jeans slung low on his hips, and I wanted him to turn just slightly so I could fully admire how they hugged his butt.

A girl followed behind him—tall, bleached blonde, and

trying too hard to look like she wasn't hanging on Kaius's every word. She wore a bright-blue club dress that cut down in the front until it reached her belly button. Her heels clacked against the checkered floor as Kaius walked her out.

A deep, bubbling rage began to prickle at my skin as I watched him place a hand on the small of her back. It didn't make sense. I shouldn't care who Kaius was with, let alone how he touched them. I hated the man. But for some reason, something deep inside of me wanted nothing more than to wipe the little smirk off the bottle blonde Barbie that was standing next to him. I might as well piss on him at this point just to really drive the point home.

"Heather wants to bartend," Kaius said with mild amusement, nodding toward the girl. "But I told her we don't hire anyone who can't not only serve behind the bar but also do the routines on it."

"Well, if she wants the job so bad, she can jump up right now and give us a taste of what she can do." Nolan's lips dipped into a devilish grin as he spoke. He was baiting the poor girl, and I was going to enjoy every minute of it.

"Is that a challenge, Nolan?" Heather asked, and it was so painfully obvious she was trying to sound sexy.

I bit my tongue watching as the blonde clumsily maneuvered herself onto the bar like a wet fish out of the water. Astoria stepped back into the room, turning toward a screen on the wall behind the bar. She pressed a few buttons, and then a pop song began to blare out of the speakers.

I almost spit out my coffee when she started to dance, if that is even what you could call what she was doing. She flailed around like she was being electrocuted, hips moving entirely off beat, arms running up and down her body in a motion I could tell she thought was sexy. Her eyes looked directly into Kaius's bored ones, squinting and winking as she thrashed about.

Nolan coughed into his cup, which caught Heather's attention. He choked down his laughter and gave her an awkward two thumbs up. I bit my lip so hard I could taste blood as she dropped onto all fours and began to crawl toward Nolan, her hands and knees crunching the résumés as she trampled them. When she finally got close enough to the man, she began to whip her head around, blonde locks smacking Nolan in the face. Astoria had to turn into the wall as one of Heather's extensions sailed through the air, landing just in front of her feet.

When the music finally faded out, Heather whipped her head up and then leaned back on her legs, spreading them slightly so we could all see she wasn't wearing anything under her dress.

I flicked my eyes toward Kaius, but he just stood there, unimpressed, arms crossed over his chest, but I could see a faint smirk ghosting his lips.

Nolan looked petrified of the woman, and I think this was the only time in his life he was rendered speechless. Astoria began to clap, coming around the bar and helping Heather off it.

"You're hired!" Astoria exclaimed.

Heather squealed in joy, listening to Astoria's clear instructions to be here for her shift next Monday night at eight. Heather thanked her once before skipping out of the bar, one hand tracing Kaius's chest as she went. I clenched my teeth, turning to a shocked Nolan as he looked toward Astoria.

"What the hell, Tor?" Nolan sputtered out.

Astoria looked at him once before bursting out laughing.

Her hands fell to her knees as she hunched over, trying to catch her breath.

He glared at her. "Oh, so you think it is funny that you just hired someone who is going to have customers running out of here as fast as they can?"

"I'm sorry," she said through her remaining giggles. Astoria straightened, swiping away the tears that were falling from her eyes. "I just thought you might actually get laid if she came back and seduced you again. You seemed really into it."

"She even left you a gift to remember her by," I said into my coffee mug, eyes staring at the blonde hair extension on the ground.

This sent Astoria sprawling out onto the bar floor, clutching her stomach as she howled out laughter.

"It's fine. I am sure our stray here knows how to pour a good drink." Kaius spoke over his sister's laughing, eyes scanning over my body. "When that girl doesn't work out, you'll be our new bartender, won't you, kitten?"

Astoria stopped laughing. "Absolutely not. Every bartender we have ever had besides me and Josie, you have fucked. Acelynn is off limits. No sticking your dick in places it doesn't belong!"

"Over my dead body would I fuck your brother, Astoria." I sneered at him, but the idea of being dominated by the man in front of me had me clenching my thighs together.

Kaius shot me a wink. "Over a dead body? That's a new one for me, but I'm down to try anything at least once, kitten."

"You are a pig," Astoria screeched, reaching down to remove her flip-flop and chuck it at her brother's head.

He dodged it easily and rolled his eyes at his sister's words.

I turned fully around on the barstool, staring him down with a challenge. "I'll make you a deal. When that girl ultimately fails at this, I will bartend for you. But only bartend, I am not getting up on that bar and shaking my ass for every man who waltzes through that door."

Kaius's gaze flicked to mine, sharp and unreadable. "I require all my bartenders to be able to dance."

"I never said I couldn't dance, just that I wouldn't."

He cocked his head to the side, smirking at me. "One dance a night. That is all. The rest of the time, you can spend your nights making drinks."

And just like that, the game between the two of us had begun. I reached out a hand. "Deal."

CHAPTER EIGHT

acelynn

ASTORIA DROPPED me off in front of an aging brick building nestled in the heart of downtown Lovelen. The town's main street was barely a mile long, a sleepy strip of timeworn storefronts, weathered signage, and fading paint adding to the character of the small town. On either side, law offices and small businesses sagged under the weight of the desert heat and decades of dust.

I waved toward Astoria, smiling brightly to mask the feeling of a thousand knives lodging themselves in my gut. Only once she turned the corner and vanished from view did I pivot away from the law office and quickly walk two doors down to the police station.

The lobby was dead quiet. It was just past noon, and it looked like the place had already given up on the day. A long admin desk sat in the space's front, a girl no older than twenty-one sitting behind it. Her light red hair was knotted into a bun on the top of her head, and she'd ditched her blazer in favor of just wearing the cream-colored blouse that had lain underneath. Two buttons at the top were undone, causing the shirt's material to lie open against her sweaty skin. A small desk fan buzzed lightly as it spun on high speed, sending hot air through the space, but all anyone cared about during the Arizona heat was the illusion of it helping.

She looked up from the book she was reading as I made my way further into the waiting room, brows lifting in question.

"Can I help you?" Her voice was light and airy as she asked the question.

"Tell Detective Parsons his midday appointment is here to see him." I smiled sweetly.

Her eyes widened before she shot to her feet so fast the chair squeaked and nearly toppled over. Without another word, the girl rushed down the dim hallway.

My smile faded as soon as she disappeared. The fear she radiated—pure, stifling, and far too familiar—twisted something deep in my stomach. Parsons had a talent for breaking people down, especially the ones just trying to hold their heads above water. If I had my way, I'd force him into early retirement with a fistful of evidence and a one-way ticket to hell. Muffled voices carried from the back of the station. A door slammed hard against a wall, and heavy boots stomped toward the front.

"Penelope, how many goddamn times do I have to say I don't take midday appointments!" Parson bellowed as he rounded the corner, the young girl trailing behind him with her head bowed, jaw opening and closing to respond.

My arms folded one over the other as I leaned casually against the doorframe, clearing my throat to get his attention away from her. Parsons whipped toward me, an agitated sigh slipping from his lips. "Ms. Thorton, I forgot we were meeting today."

"Detective," I said with ice in my voice. "Do you always scream at your employees, or is that treatment only reserved for the sheriff's daughter?"

Penelope's face was tinged a light shade of pink at the comment, but it wasn't from embarrassment. No, the look she shot me was pure venom. If Parsons weren't standing between us, I had no doubt she would lunge.

The detective's gaze snapped to me, and the irritation in his eyes was evident. He stepped aside, placing one hand out to gesture for me to lead the way down the hall. I pushed off the frame, sauntering past Penelope and ignoring the glare drilling into the back of my skull.

I knew the way to his office by heart now—same grimy hallway, same cracked blue-checkered linoleum flooring as before. The air in the station was always stale and clung to the space like ghosts of every dirty secret Parsons had ever buried here.

His office was barely larger than a closet. An oversized oak desk dominated the space. A full map of the city of Lovelen adorned the white wall behind it. Little pins scattered the landscape like bullet holes. On both sides of the map, there were two overstuffed filing cabinets that never completely closed because of the numerous papers Parsons had crammed inside. I took my usual seat in the uncomfortable, curved wooden chair. It was cool against my bare legs, sending a slight shiver down my spine.

Parsons closed the door with a sharp *click*, then turned on me like a vulture ready to descend on its next meal. "You're not supposed to show up here unannounced, Acelynn. What if someone from the Knights saw you? How would you explain that away?"

"I wouldn't, I would be dead." I didn't even flinch. "But I'm not. And you're going to forge the paperwork for the estate transfer for me, so it looks like everything's set when the papers get sent to the law office down the street to obtain my dear old, estranged aunt's house."

"You don't give me orders," Parsons snapped. "I'm the one who decides how this operation runs, and I will make the calls as I see fit. If you don't like it, I can toss your ass in a cell and let you rot."

I smiled slowly and stood. "Guess that means you don't want to hear about my appearance at the roundtable last night?"

That stopped him cold.

"Sit. Down," he growled out. I obliged, reclining casually in the chair as he stalked around the desk to lean back against it in front of me. He waved his hand once in annoyance for me to continue.

"Patience, Parsons." I swirled my finger around the charm on my necklace—the spade pendant that nearly got me killed. "The diner incident this morning. Club-related. I just happened to step in and saved the Knights' darling girl in the process."

I paused my motion, plucking the charm up between two fingers, holding it up for him to see. "And this was apparently enough to put a target on my back. Think maybe it would have been smart for someone in this department to tell me that my family's symbol would cause not one but both of the Mordred siblings to question me about it?"

"No." Parsons's lips quirked up at the corners. "Your ability to keep yourself alive is not my concern."

"Of course it's not," I muttered, slouching lower in the seat.

"Stop pouting." He scowled at me, annoyance sharpening his words. "Next time, use the burner to give us a heads up on your arrival. That's what it's for."

The burner phone he had mentioned was shoved in a duffel that I had dumped at the temporary house I was using as my "aunt's home." There was no way I was walking around with that loaded bomb in my pocket. Not when I was so close to the Knights. If I was going to use the device, it would be the only time it was used, and then Parsons would be replacing it, which I assumed he would get tired of rather quickly.

The detective narrowed his eyes at me when I didn't continue quickly enough for him. "That all? You spoke to the Knights about a charm? That doesn't build a case against them."

"Not quite," I said, lips spreading into a devious grin. "I got a job."

Parsons blinked slowly at me. "A job?"

"At *the Queen's Table*," I said nonchalantly, as if it was the most normal thing for me to utter in this situation. "Behind the bar."

"You are bartending at the Knights' bar? Just steps away from where they conduct their club dealings?" His jaw tightened as if he were unhappy with this progress. Which didn't make any sense, considering Parsons was the one who had pushed so hard for me to get something on the club.

I nodded once. "Astoria hired me this morning. Said I had the fire that they could use behind the bar, and Nolan vouched for me. So...I'm in."

I smiled at him, letting him believe that was what had occurred in the bar. Parsons didn't need to know that Kaius was the one who had offered me the job. It would make him too eager. And I didn't need him breathing down my neck just yet.

"That's dangerous."

"Thought you didn't care about my safety," I said,

narrowing my eyes at the man. Parsons stared at me, like he couldn't quite decide if I was brilliant or if I had a death wish. Probably both.

He snapped out of his trance, a smirk toying at his lips. "You're going to make that man fall in love with you so you can unravel all of the Knights' secrets, aren't you?"

I licked my canines slowly, letting the fantasy of Kaius being at my mercy bloom in my mind. "Even better. I am going to make the King of Lovelen beg me to love him...and then I'll put a bullet between his eyes."

CHAPTER NINE

acelynn

COTTON CANDY HUES streaked across the desert sky. My back pressed against the shingle rooftop, watching the sunset bleed into molten gold over the cactus-studded horizon. The cool kiss of my beer touched my lips, a sharp contrast to the heat clinging to the day.

Nothing compared to an Arizona sunset.

My thoughts drift back to a time before Logan, before everything went up in flames. Back to when he and I would sneak up onto a random roof with a handle of whatever cheap liquor we could scrounge, trading secrets for stars until the bottle ran dry.

A dull ache twisted in my chest, stealing the breath from my lungs. I blinked fast, swallowing the burn that was creeping up my throat. I would not cry for that bastard—not after everything he had done. Logan should've been dead, yet somehow, he still haunted me. No matter how many times I buried him, his corpse kept crawling back out of its shallow grave to haunt me.

My phone buzzed against my chest. Only two people had

this number, Parsons and Watson, and both were stored under fake aliases.

I glanced down, coming upon the bright, bold letters of Astoria's name. She must have snagged the phone and put her number in when I was in the shower this morning, making sure to add the flamingo emoji next to it to differentiate her from every other Astoria in it, obviously.

I sighed, torn between my goal of revenge and the guilt eating away at my heart. Answering meant another step toward dismantling her brother and the Knights—but Astoria had been kind to me. Too kind. My brother used to say I felt everything way too deeply, and that was partly why I was grateful to have grown up away from the club. It made it easier to pretend my family was just auto mechanics when people from school asked me about them.

Swiping right, I brought the phone to my ear. "Hello."

"Hey bitch," Astoria's cheery voice sounded over the rock music blaring in the background. "Are you dressed?"

"Uh..." I glanced down at my worn AC/DC shirt and cutoff shorts. "Define your version of dressed?"

"Someth—hold on," Astoria grumbled before her voice became distant. "Give me a damn second, Vincent. I will be out there when I am ready."

A gruff man's voice snapped back at her, but I couldn't make out what was being said. Astoria mimicked him in a high-pitched tone for a moment before coming back to the phone. "Sorry about that, Acelynn. I swear these men don't know how to properly listen. Anyway, as I was saying, change into something sexy. You are coming to the bar tonight."

I let out a sarcastic laugh. "Yeah, no thanks."

"Come onnnnn," Astoria whined. "It'll be fun! I can show you the lay of the land behind the bar before you start a real shift, and you can get the vibe of how the bar is. I only have to work for an hour tops tonight. Josie and Karli are already here. Thursdays are dead, just regulars and club boys. And I want to dance!"

I tilted my head back, letting out a groan. The last thing I wanted to do was interact with people tonight, but maybe a drink or two with Astoria would do me some good. I used to love dancing in college. There was something so exhilarating about letting myself feel the beat of the music in the pit of my stomach with a stranger who I would forget about in the next hour.

"Fine," I relented.

Astoria let out an earsplitting squeal, which had me pulling the device away from my ear. I stood up from the slanted roof and climbed back through the open window, phone wedged between my ear and shoulder.

"How long do I have to get ready?"

She hummed. "An hour? I'll be done with anything the girls might need behind the bar by then, and then I will be all yours!"

"Lucky me," I replied.

Astoria just let out a laugh in reply, which made me smile. There were very few people in my life who had ever gotten my dry, sarcastic tone. Most just thought I was being a bitch who needed an attitude adjustment.

"I'll see you in an hour, Tori."

"I'll have a shot waiting for you, Ace."

The Queen's Table was packed.

Lights pulsed through the parking lot in time with the blaring music coming from inside. A wall of people crowded the bar's entrance, making it impossible to see where the door was actually located. I placed the car in park before stepping from the driver's seat, eyes wide with amazement at the spectacle that was happening before me.

A girl in a green leather skirt and halter top strutted, taking a drag from a fruit-scented vape. The smoke swirled behind her like a neon ghost. As I scanned the crowd, I realized that most of the women around me were dressed similarly to her. Suddenly, I felt out of place in the outfit I had chosen. The light denim cutoffs and black cropped turtleneck with a keyhole cutout made me immediately wish I had dug out the corset from the back of my duffel.

"Fuck it," I muttered, running both hands through my hair before heading toward the bar's entrance.

Inside, the place pulsed with energy. Cheers of excitement roared over the music as I shoved my way through the crowd of people that were packed together like sardines, but once I did, I could see why everyone was shouting.

Neon lights flickered, and the thumping beat of music vibrated through the small space. In the center of the L-shaped bar, Astoria and another girl moved in time with each other. There was a glint of mischief in her eyes as she danced with confidence, her movements fluid and alluring. The female behind her had flaming red hair that flowed down her spine as she threw her head back, laughing at something Astoria shouted before she found herself lost in the music's rhythm once again. The crowd was entranced with them.

Across the bar, a woman with dark-blue hair sat with a plastic cup filled with clear liquid in her hand, while a man stood between her legs. He tossed back a shot of dark-colored liquor in one go, grimacing at the taste. A split second later, she was throwing the cup of water in his face with one hand and slapping him with the other. The crack of her palm landing against his cheek sounded even over the roaring crowd. The man stared up at the woman with a mix of admiration and lust. She chuckled before standing up on the bar and making her way over to Astoria as the song changed.

Without even missing a beat, the girls began a rehearsed routine. Their movements sent an electric feeling through the crowd. Astoria backed up to the blue-haired girl, hands running down her hips as she ground down on the other girl. The bar was their stage, and they held every person in this place's attention as they performed.

Astoria bent for a bottle of tequila behind the bar. She raised back up, taking a swig of the alcohol before offering it to the other girls, who stepped away from her to grab a short female by the throat and drag her forward. The girl willingly obliged, opening her mouth as she poured the alcohol down her throat.

Some of the liquid dribbled out of her mouth, over the hand on her neck, and down the front of her chest. The blue-haired girl leaned forward, tongue flicking out, and cleaned up her chest. I chuckled lightly at the scene in front of me. Everything the Knights did, they did well, and I should have known that their bar wouldn't be your run-of-the-mill, small-town dive.

The group outside closed in, and someone behind me shoved forward. I gasped as I stumbled into the back of a muscular man. He whipped around, glaring above my head at whoever stood behind me. "We got a problem?"

"Depends on the next ten seconds," a drunken drawl came from the person.

Hands reached over me and shoved the large man harshly. I ducked in time to miss the punch that swung next, my body getting caught in the throngs of people as they tried to move away from the fight, but there was nowhere to go.

The heel of my boot got caught on someone's foot, sending me flying forward and onto the dirty bar floor. I scrambled on all fours under patrons. Shouts of pain and delight broke over the music. A hand yanked the back of my shirt and dragged me up until my ass was planted on the slick surface of the bar. I gasped, lungs burning for air I couldn't catch in the wave of people. My eyes were trained on where I had just been, watching closely as the crowd trampled the area to get a glimpse of the brawl.

A firm grip caught my chin and tilted my face up, straight into piercing green eyes.

"Starting fights in my bar? What am I to do with you, kitten?"

CHAPTER TEN

kaius

THE BAR FIGHT blurred into meaningless noise. All I could focus on was the woman in front of me.

Acelynn's chest heaved up and down, shallow breaths slipping through her lips as she fought to calm her racing heart. I released her chin, my fingers brushing gently against her skin as I tucked a strand of hair behind her ear. A hitched breath broke through her lips at the movement, eyes glazing over as she focused in on me. But the trance only lasted a second longer before she flinched away with a snarl.

"Don't touch me," Acelynn snapped as her upper body leaned away from me.

I took the movement as a challenge, gripping the underside of her hips, and with one hard tug, I slid her until she was almost hanging off the bar. She tried to squirm away, but it only made her hips drive against mine, the movement causing my cock to harden in my jeans. Our eyes were locked in an intense stare neither of us was willing to break. My mouth twitched into a smile, but the thought I was about to vocalize was cut off by the smashing of glass behind the bar.

“Come on, Karli,” my sister’s voice snapped. There was an edge to it now, half pleading, half furious.

I turned, my gaze leaving Acelynn just long enough to catch the scene unfolding behind her. Karli stood frozen in a pool of shattered glass and liquor, crimson trickling from shallow cuts along her left hand. But it didn’t seem to faze the girl. Her eyes burned with fury instead of pain as they locked on where my hands gripped on to Acelynn’s hips.

Karli’s red hair seemed to glow under the neon lights, making her anger more palpable to everyone surrounding us. I released Acelynn from my hold, letting her slide back just an inch so she didn’t fall forward. My touch didn’t stay away for long as I rested my palm against her upper thigh.

My little kitten turned her gaze over her shoulder and stared Karli down. For a moment, the redhead had the good sense to look scared, but then her eyes filled with the rage that had just been there moments before. She whirled around toward Astoria, shoulder slamming into my sister as she walked past her.

“No, fuck this, Astoria,” she shouted, loud enough to cut through the music blaring from the speakers above. “I am done. Mail me my last check!”

Astoria sighed, dragging a hand over her face as she scanned the rowdy patrons. The fight had ended, but now the regulars were impatient, demanding drinks and attention. Chaos wrapped in cheap cologne, flashing lights, and drunken slurs was where the night was at already.

My sister looked back in my direction and stalked over, fuming. When she reached me, she leaned over the bar top and slammed her fist into my arm. “This is your fault, Kaius.”

“My fault?” I grinned at her, my hand unconsciously tightening on Acelynn’s thigh.

She hissed through her teeth, but I could tell that it

wasn't one of pain. Astoria gaped at me, but I continued to taunt her.

"How was Karli quitting mid-shift my fault?"

"Because you're a man whore!" Astoria screeched, throwing her hands up to get her point across.

I chuckled. "I didn't fuck that bartender, if that is what you are insinuating. And if she had a problem with me pulling your little stray up before someone made her roadkill on my bar floor, then that is her issue."

"I don't believe you," she grumbled, and paused, her eyes lighting up like she'd just had an idea that would most likely cause me another headache. "Ace, you're here. I know you weren't supposed to start until next week, but I could really use a hand tonight."

"Umm..." Acelynn's eyes flickered between Astoria and the crowd. "I feel like this is a lot for a first night."

"It'll be fine. As long as you can identify the alcohol tonight, then you can do it. Just tell everyone we aren't doing anything fancy, and if they give you trouble, Josie will handle it," Astoria said with a lack of confidence that had me covering a laugh with a cough.

Acelynn threw me a withering look, but before she could respond, my sister cut her off with a pleading stare.

"Please, Acelynn. I will get on my hands and knees if I have to."

Astoria dropped to the ground, causing Acelynn to slip from my grasp and jump toward her. She caught my sister by the arm.

"Okay, okay! I'll do it! Just get off the floor. There is glass everywhere, Tori."

From behind them, Nolan appeared with a broom and dustpan. "So she can call you Tori? But when I do it, it's a crime?"

Astoria stood with an icy glare at him. He brought the hand with the dustpan over his heart, shooting her a crooked smile. "That hurts my feelings, Tor."

"Ugh," she snapped, stomping her foot once before shoving past him to help Josie with the line of drinks she was pouring. She turned over her shoulder. "Get your cute ass over here, Acelynn. These drinks aren't going to serve themselves."

I leaned across the bar top into Acelynn, my hot breath brushing up against the shell of her ear. "You heard her, kitten. Get your cute ass over there and serve me a drink."

Acelynn turned her head just enough to let her lips skim mine as she replied, voice sugary sweet and lethal, "The only drink I'd serve you is one laced with arsenic."

"Just how I like them." I grinned widely at her. "Deadly and beautiful."

CHAPTER ELEVEN

acelynn

THE NIGHT BLURRED into a haze of drink orders and blaring music. By last call, I felt like I could collapse where I stood. Every muscle in my body screamed in protest as I made one final trip between the liquor shelf and the ice bucket. I slid a drink down in front of a nameless man just as Astoria appeared at my side. She had her lip pulled between her teeth, nerves practically radiating off her.

"Please don't kill me," she whispered, almost too quietly to hear her.

I turned, quirking a brow in question and bit back the sarcastic remark as I came upon her pale face.

"I think the only thing I'd kill you for right now is if you told me we were staying open for another hour." I winked at her, trying to lighten the mood. She began to pick at the skin by her fingernails, causing my brows to furrow at her. "Astoria, what's up?"

"We...do a last—" The music swallowed her words.

"Huh?"

She sighed, throwing her hands down. "We do a last call dance."

"A *dance*?" I asked, my eyes bugging out of my head.

If she thought I was getting up on that bar to make a fool out of myself, she had another think coming. Astoria smiled awkwardly, and I had my answer. I slammed my hands onto the bar top.

"Absolutely not. You'd have to drag me up there kicking and screaming, Astoria Mordred."

"And the claws have returned," Kaius's amused voice called out behind me.

I spun around to find him leaning against the bar, his smile practically glowing under the neon lights. He tapped a finger on the counter, the metal of his Knight's ring clicking against the wood.

"I guess I was wrong about you, kitten."

"Wrong about what?" I snapped, angling my body toward him.

"I just figured the girl who came flying into the round-table without an ounce of fear, and stood up to their king with a mouth that could get her killed, wouldn't be scared to dance on a bar in front of a crowd that won't remember it tomorrow," Kaius said, his eyes sparkling with an emotion I couldn't quite place. He took a slow sip of his beer and shrugged. "Guess I was wrong."

There was something in his taunts that lit a fire in me. There was no way in hell that I was going to let Kaius think I would back down from a challenge, even if it was over a simple dance on top of his bar. If there was one thing he was going to learn about the true me, it's that I had a stubborn need to prove myself to others. I turned to Astoria. "Is there choreography involved in this last call dance?"

"Not tonight," she squealed before grabbing hold of my

wrist and dragging me toward the end of the bar. Astoria scrambled up the three steps with practiced ease.

I hesitated for a moment. The knots in my stomach were tightening. My gaze traveled back to where Kaius still stood. Nolan was now talking to him, but his eyes were laser-focused on me. He raised his beer in a mock toast before taking another sip from the bottle. That was the last push I needed to clear the steps and make my appearance on the bar's platform.

The stage lights were blinding, and I had to squint to get my bearings. Astoria reached out a single hand toward me to beckon me closer to her, hips already swinging to the beat of a remixed pop song. I took a breath, letting the beat of the music fill me with the confidence I was severely lacking. A kaleidoscope of colors spun over the bar top in waves, the wood glowing beneath our feet. Astoria spun me around once, sending me in front of her and closer to Kaius, watching like I was the only thing worth seeing in the room.

"Loosen up," Astoria shouted over the music. She stepped closer to me, placing her hands on my hips to steer my movements. Her spine pressed against mine as we moved in sync, the crowd erupting with cheers.

A blur of movement to my right caught my eye. The dark-haired girl, who I had learned was named Josie, jumped on the bar a few feet in front of us. Her body swayed with an effortless grace as she threw her head back, hair cascading in wild waves around her shoulders, blue streaks standing out against the dark ink that littered her pale skin as she lost herself to the rhythm. Every roll of her hips was a testament to her way of capturing every eye in this room.

Except for one set. No, that set was on me, and it made the breath in the back of my throat hitch as I continued my dance.

It was an intoxicating feeling to be seen like that. To be admired. Even if it was from someone I'd rather see staring up at me from a body bag. There was still no denying the spark that burned hot between the King of Lovelen and me. Not when I could still feel where his hand had been earlier, the ghost of it on my thigh like a brand. Kaius Mordred was dangerous, magnetic, and far too tempting.

And I couldn't afford to fall for the King of Lovelen.

The song began to wind down when Astoria stopped her to reach behind the bar. I blinked in confusion and looked over my shoulder at her. "What are you doing?"

She popped back up with a bottle of vodka and a matchbox in hand. "Let's give 'em the grand finale, Ace."

I opened my mouth to object, but she was already shoving the bottle into my hands. My head whipped to where Kaius had been standing all night, but he was suddenly nowhere to be found.

"Saturate the top of the bar, but don't fall, and watch for Josie. She'll be pouring final shots."

My eyes flickered between the bottle and the glossy bar. I paused, then flipped the bottle upside down, letting the vodka spill across the wood as I walked. My feet weaved around Josie as she lined up small shots of Patrón in front of a group of waiting customers.

At the far end of the bar, I turned the bottle upright, heart hammering with giddy anticipation. Astoria was at the opposite end now, and I watched as she struck a single match. Her eyes twinkled with excitement as she dropped it. The flames hissed, dancing over the vodka trail as it crawled toward me. Cheers erupted as patrons took their shots just before the fire got to them.

I watched in awe as the flames slithered closer to me.

And then I realized my toes were standing directly in the vodka, and if that flame hit them, I was going to get burned.

Shit.

"Jump," a man's voice called out to me.

I twisted, taking the outstretched hand, and leaping blindly toward him just as the blaze got to me, the heat licking up the back of my legs. I landed hard against the person, stumbling on my feet as I tried to find my bearings. The man's hand anchored at my waist, keeping me from falling on my ass. I sucked in a shaky breath, my mind wandering to how close of a call that was before looking toward who had helped me, to find Nolan standing inches away from me, one hand firmly resting on my hip.

"Are you okay?" Nolan asked, a bright smile shining down at me. He chuckled once as a shadow loomed over the two of us. "Maybe keep the flames to second nights, Tor."

"And where would the fun in that be?" Astoria called down to us.

"Fun? I don't know what your idea of fun is, but mine doesn't include scraping up a freshly crisped Acelynn off our bar top." Nolan shook his head at the girl. "She seems like she would be hard to remove, like mold or some kind of flesh-eating bacteria."

I stepped away from Nolan, hand swatting at his chest at his comment. "Hey, you both love having me around. If you didn't, I would have been sent to that shady motel to fend for myself last night."

"Eh." Astoria shrugged at me as she bent at the knee to come closer to the two of us. "I needed to fix my record when it comes to who I have dragged through here. A stray turned permanent employee is a personal best for me."

CHAPTER TWELVE

kaius

EVEN OVER THE chaos of last call at the Queen's Table, I could hear Acelynn's bright and melodic laugh cutting clean through the noise. She stood in front of Nolan, her smile wide as he said something that made Astoria roll her eyes and throw a crumpled napkin in his face.

My sister hopped down from the bar, grabbing a bottle of dark liquor from the top shelf and pouring three shots. She slid one to each of them before raising her own and launching into a toast that, knowing her, had some sort of sexual innuendo buried in it. The three of them clicked their glasses once before tapping them on the bar top and downing the liquor.

Acelynn's face twisted in immediate regret, violent coughs breaking through her lips. Nolan reached out, patting her back lightly. Any other man in this place laying hands on my new fixation would have had me already halfway through breaking his jaw. But not Nolan. I didn't need to worry about him pursuing her. Not when he had been hung up on my baby sister since we were teenagers. And he knew better than anyone what lines we were willing to cross.

We trusted each other with our lives. Always had. Always would. And we had made that very clear time and time again.

The blade bit into my palm as I dragged it across the skin. Precise but deep enough to scar, because this oath would be lifelong. A permanent reminder of the weight of it. I clenched my fist, letting the crimson pool drip into the rusted metal bowl at our feet. The light scent of rain surrounded us from the passing monsoon.

Across from me, Nolan stood silent. His face was unreadable. He had always looked this way when he was pissed, when he felt out of control.

"This is how we clean house. How we bury traitors, boys," my father had said hours earlier when he decided it was finally mine and Nolan's time to be more than just drug runners for the club. He always expected me to take on his role as president of the Knights of Lovelen and knew who I would choose as my second. This was an initiation, a test of loyalty for both Nolan and me.

"I told you he'd fold," Nolan said through a clenched jaw, voice low.

I didn't respond right away. My hands were still shaking, not from the pain, but from the rage that had coursed through me tonight. And it scared me that I was able to reach that point so easily. How I had been able to turn off my emotions like the flip of a light switch. I had turned into exactly the monster my father had raised me to be tonight.

The betrayal hadn't sunk in fully. Liam. Our own. One of the sacred seven, as they liked to call the club leaders' sons. The ones who would rule for them when they were just dust. We'd grown up together, bled for the cause of keeping peace between the clubs, cracked bones in alleyways when one of us stepped out of line, but now none of that mattered.

Liam had just fucked any idea of peace between our groups to hell. He was feeding intel to the feds. Selling out our drops, mapping out where we had safe houses. Playing both sides, but I had caught him, which meant I had to be the one who delivered the punishment.

"I wanted to believe it was a lie," I finally muttered. "I thought he'd say there was some bigger picture deal happening."

Nolan let out a bitter laugh. "You always wanted to believe in people too long."

"You never believe in anyone."

"That's not true," Nolan snapped, eyes glaring at me. "I believe in you and Vince. Hell, I even believe in Tori when she isn't being such a fucking brat."

"That's why we are still standing," I said, pulling a pack of cigarettes out of my back pocket and placing one between my lips. I offered the box to Nolan, but he waved his hand, uninterested in picking up the habit, as he would say. Lighting the end, I took a long drag before letting the smoke billow into the night air before responding. "We all have each other. If we were truly in over our heads, we know any one of us would go to the ends of the earth to fix it."

I glanced over at him, but he wouldn't meet my eyes. His gaze was locked on the bowl below us that held our mixed blood.

"I didn't want to turn into him," Nolan bit out.

He had always had a fear of becoming the kind of man his father was. And I don't blame him. Lance Bedivere was the type of monster that was created in the darkest corners of hell. He had no regard for human life, and the hundreds of corpses that had been removed from the basement crawl space of the Bedivere family home had confirmed that.

Nolan had been barely six when his father had been sentenced to death. Not that he made it to the electric chair. They had found him dead in his cell only three days after he arrived in prison. I had dragged Nolan back to the club just as Astoria was always bringing strays in. My father must have seen the potential in the young boy, or he knew who his father was, because he didn't fight me when I asked if Nolan could stay.

"You are nothing like your father," I said firmly, but the tension in Nolan's shoulders told me he didn't believe me.

The silence was heavier this time. I knew there was no convincing him, not when he was so far in his head. But I couldn't help but feel the same way as my best friend. I was just a pawn in my father's plan. The prince of Lovelen, silver-tongued and dangerous when necessary. I could handle it, compartmentalize the pain and the shame. I had been forged to carry the weight. To pull the trigger. To slit the throats of our enemies.

"What if it had been me?" I asked suddenly, surprising even myself with the sudden question.

Nolan's eyes snapped to mine. "What?"

"What if I were the one who broke the code? If I had made a mistake like that. Gave something away. Would you have finished me too?"

The muscles in his jaw twitched, eyes not even blinking as he stared me down.

"No," he said simply.

"Why not?"

"Because I would never let it get that far, Kaius." Nolan narrowed his eyes at me.

There it was. That twisted, fierce loyalty we both had for each other. The thing that we never said but always meant. Both of us would bleed for each other, kill without question, cover for the other, even if it meant betraying the very code we had just sworn in blood to. Because that's what you did for a brother.

"I don't need you to protect me," I said, taking another long

pull from my cigarette. The smoke burned my lungs, but at least I could still feel the pain.

Nolan stepped forward, hand still bleeding, voice sharp as razors. "I don't protect you, Kaius. I stand with you. There is a difference."

My throat tightened at the statement. We'd grown up in fire, both of us orphaned in different ways. I had a crown I had never asked for, a legacy soaked in secrets and blood. Nolan had a serial killer father and a mother who had run the second he was behind bars, leaving two boys to fend for themselves. We found each other in the wreckage.

The Knights of Lovelen had molded us. Twisted us into the men we were, but we had shaped each other into something more sacred.

Throwing down the cigarette, I stomped out the ember before offering him my bleeding hand. He didn't hesitate, pressing his palm with mine. Blood smeared between our fingers like war paint.

"No more traitors," I say.

"Only brothers," Nolan answered.

CHAPTER THIRTEEN

THE GHOSTLY MELODY drifted through the quiet, near-empty bar. Astoria had disappeared into the back with Nolan to count the till, and I'd offered to stay behind and clean up the bar for Josie. The last of the empty bottles clattered into the trash can as I swept through the space. Grabbing a cloth from the sanitizer bucket, I started wiping down the bar, working through the sticky residue left behind by spilled drinks and rowdy hands.

"I've got your check for the night," Kaius's voice broke through the silence, low, smooth, and too damn close.

I glanced toward the doorway leading to the back office. He leaned against the frame, one shoulder braced lazily, a white piece of paper stuck between his fingers.

I nodded once. "You could have just added it to the next round of checks."

He stepped from the shadows, coming closer to where I stood. "Didn't know if you would still want to work here after Astoria almost set you on fire."

I didn't look at him. Instead, I focused on a particularly

stubborn spot on the counter, scrubbing harder than necessary. "Nolan saved the day on that. Unless you are rescinding the job offer."

"The job..." Kaius paused. He was only steps away from me now.

I bit my lip, mind spiraling on how working for him could end very badly for me. A sigh slipped through his lips before he spoke again. "It's still yours if you want it, and probably the best one you are going to get in Lovelen. I pay my employees well, Acelynn, and there are no strings attached to your employment. All I ask is that there is a mutual understanding that what happens behind closed doors stays here."

"You mean what your club does?" I said quietly, my hand pausing mid-swipe.

I knew what the Knights were capable of, and that terrified a part of me, even though I had grown up around the life. But my brother, Alec, and my father had kept me at a distance, never letting me see the worst parts of it, never letting me touch what Alec used to call *blood money*. I was probably the most sheltered club daughter to ever exist.

Thinking of my family twisted something sharp in my chest. My throat tightened, but I refused to cry in front of their killer.

Kaius closed the remaining distance between us, his hand resting gently over mine. "Yes. Anything you witness stays behind these walls, Acelynn."

There was a hard edge buried in the softness of his voice. The darkness of the unspoken threat caused the hairs on the back of my neck to rise. I turned my gaze on his. It was blazing with a fire that told me he would do whatever it took to keep his family safe. It was the same spark that was burning me alive as I clawed my way toward justice for mine.

"I understand, Kaius," I said, tone void of emotion.

A beat went by as we just watched each other, both examining the other for the deceit buried beneath our words. I ripped my hand out of his grasp, feet moving back toward the sanitizer bucket.

"Glad we could come to that agreement," Kaius called toward me. The sound of his knuckles knocking against the bar signaled his departure.

"But there is one thing I want in return," I said, peering over my shoulder at the man.

He paused mid-step, but didn't turn to look at me. "Name your price, kitten."

"The club's protection," I announced.

The muscles in his back tensed underneath his dark T-shirt. When he didn't respond to me, I continued on, "I clearly don't have the best track record in this town at not making enemies, and if that doesn't tell you that I might have been running from something bigger in Raleigh, then you're dumber than I took you for."

Kaius finally turned back around to face me, part of his face shadowed in the dim light of the bar. I waited for the killing blow to come, but he only nodded once. "Agreed. We can discuss the particulars tomorrow."

It was just past three in the morning when I finally pulled into my driveway. Exhaustion settled deep in my muscles, but the adrenaline that was still pumping through my veins had me on edge. Cutting the car's engine, I quickly gathered my things and made my way up to my front door. The jingle of my keys rattled against my door as I twisted to unlock it, but I realized it was already open.

My heart dropped.

I always triple-checked that it was locked. Paranoia had become routine. Carelessness got you killed.

I reached into my purse and pulled out the pink can of pepper spray my brother had purchased for me when I left for college. Not that it was going to do me much good if it was who I thought it was.

Slowly, I slipped through the doorway, careful to keep my steps silent. The kitchen was untouched, dishes from earlier still in the sink waiting for me to place them in the dishwasher. But the hallway glowed with faint light from my bedroom.

With every step, my heart pounded in my ears louder. If I were smarter, I would be running in the other direction, but he knew I couldn't resist the temptation of finding out if he had survived the night my brother and father carved his club tattoo from his skin in front of me.

Using the toe of my boot, I nudged open the door. It hit the back wall with a bang and revealed a horrifying scene.

On my bed, centered nearly on the white comforter, was a chessboard. Each piece was coated in fresh blood that pooled beneath the board, staining the sheets below.

But the worst part was the rattlesnake that sat coiled in the center of the game. The reptile was trapped under the glass dome of a cake stand. Metal brackets bolted it to the chessboard to keep it caged, but not calm. It struck at the glass with terrifying precision, fangs slamming against the glass surface in a deadly fury.

I jumped back at the sound of its rattle, a warning of imminent danger. My breathing was coming in short and shallow gasps as I watched the snake continue its endless pursuit to get to me.

A single drop of red rained down from the ceiling,

causing my eyes to slowly travel upward to where a bloody symbol was painted across my ceiling.

A dark red spade. In the middle, scrawled in jagged letters: *Pretty Little Ace.*

Stumbling backward, I crashed into the hallway wall before fleeing from the house. My feet tripped down the front steps, across the lawn, and into the safety of my car.

I didn't need confirmation. My heart already knew the truth.

Logan Reid had survived that night.

I knew he would defy all odds of death to get his hands on me. And when he did, he would ensure that he wiped every record of my existence from the face of this earth.

CHAPTER FOURTEEN

THE CAMPUS *of Saint Aveline's Academy was nearly empty at this time of night. Finals week meant most students holed up in their dorms, high on caffeine and dread for the tests to come. But Logan had insisted we meet in the library, something about the silence helping him focus.*

I leaned back against the hardwood chair. My notes were sprawled out in front of me in a messy pile of color-coded highlights and Post-it tabs. Criminology was never an easy subject for me, but I loved the structure of it—rules, patterns, logic. The idea that even chaos could be decoded if you connect the clues.

Logan pulled back from his own notes, the edge of his pencil tapping rhythmically against his bottom lip. "Okay, pop quiz."

I raised a brow. "I thought we were done with those?"

"If you were going to kill someone." He ignored me, voice soft and casual, like he was asking about the weather. "How would you do it? And get away with it?"

I blinked slowly at him. "That's...not on the exam."

Logan's grin widened, all teeth and charm. Part of the reason I liked him. He gave off an effortless bad boy vibe that I swooned over the first few weeks of us dating. All he had to do was run his hand through his light brown hair and toss a wink of his hazel eyes that sparkled with trouble to get me to fall in love. My brother would have hated everything about him. That is why I kept him a secret.

"Come on, doll. You aced every other question I threw out at you. Why not play a little? Hypothetically."

"Well, hypothetically..." My eyes traveled back to my notes. "You'd need to avoid anything personal. No obvious motive, no connection to the victim. Ensure there are no cameras around and nothing to trace me."

"Smart. And how would you dispose of the body?" He nodded, as if impressed with my answer.

My spine stiffened against the back of my chair. "That's not funny, Logan."

"I'm not trying to be funny," he said with a casual shrug. "You've just got the background for it. I mean, you have been trained to know how people think, what makes them tick. That's a dangerous skill, little Spade."

I hated that nickname. He was the only one at school who ever used it.

"I am studying business, not criminology," I said, voice a little sharper than I meant it to be, but something about his insinuation struck me the wrong way. No one at this school knew of my family's crimes. I just told them they owned an extremely successful mechanics shop, which is how I afforded the high tuition. "This was just a fun elective to fill a requirement."

"Right," Logan murmured, leaning forward. "But knowing how to commit the perfect crime? That's power most people don't even realize they possess."

The air between us shifted, thickening to an unbearable amount that made it hard for me to breathe. I pulled at the sleeves of my cardigan as the library's temperature heated. Something dark flickered behind Logan's eyes, something that I had never noticed before. Or maybe I had just chosen to ignore it.

"You ever hear about that guy who got kicked out of his gang in a small town in Arizona?" he asked suddenly.

My stomach dropped because, of course, I had heard of Liam, but he hadn't just been kicked out of his club. I shook my head no, waiting for him to respond.

"Blacklisted from his whole scene. Word is, he and another guy tried to flip on someone big. Burned bridges with their family name. But I am pretty sure they were killed for their crimes."

I felt like I was going to vomit. This wasn't a random story he had found while scrolling the internet. Not when it was tied to my father and brother, who had spent years burying their dirty laundry that came from the club. No one would dare speak of the execution of club members, knowing the consequences.

"What gang was it?" I asked, heart thudding.

Logan's lips turned up in a devious grin, but he didn't answer me. He just leaned further back in his chair, arms crossed behind his head as he watched me like a cat that had just pinned its prey.

That's when I knew that wasn't just mindless flirting or school banter. Logan had been playing the long game with me. He had known who I was from the moment he had met me at that little tropical dive bar all the college students went to.

And somehow, it led back to my blood.

CHAPTER FIFTEEN

VINCE DROPPED a folder onto the mountain of paperwork I was buried in. It landed dead center, scattering a few invoices as he fell into the chair across from me before I could tell him to get the hell out. I glared at him, jaw tight. I never went to bed last night, and judging by the dark shadows under his eyes, neither had he.

"That's everything I could pull on Acelynn Thorton," he said, jerking his chin to the folder. "It's not much, just some transcripts and old addresses. Personally, I think someone may have forged them."

"You think everyone's documents are forged, you paranoid bastard," I muttered, flipping the folder open.

He wasn't entirely wrong. Inside was a high school transcript from a public school in North Carolina with addresses that lined up with a rundown apartment complex she supposedly grew up in. But there was no trace of her on social media. Not even a dead account. Which was odd, considering everyone usually had at least one account, even if they hadn't touched it in years. My eyebrows furrowed. "Maybe she went by something else when she was younger."

Vince's growl cut through the air. "Don't make excuses for her just because you want to fuck her, Kaius. That's how you get one of us killed or worse, locked up."

I grunted at his comment, knowing I couldn't deny the fact that I was more than just intrigued by my little kitten. My attention on her last night had made it evident to everyone in the club, but no one except Nolan or Vince would have the balls to say it to my face. Not one Knight was brave enough to cross me by pursuing her when she was working at the Queen's Table.

"Keep digging," I said flatly, slamming the folder shut and sliding it aside. "You must be missing something. She knew who we were. That doesn't make her a threat, but I want to know what the hell she was running from in North Carolina before it lands on our doorstep."

"Sure thing, boss," Vince muttered before standing to go.

His irritation rolled off him in waves, but I didn't care. He would get over it, just as he always did when someone new was initiated into the Knights. I made sure to cover my bases with every single person around us, even if they were just working behind our bar.

Still, the gnawing feeling in my gut wouldn't go away. Something about Acelynn Thorton wasn't adding up. It felt different from my typical paranoia. Before I could drown in suspicions, a knock on my office door pulled me out of my thoughts.

"What?" I snapped, slamming the papers against the desk with an audible thud.

The door cracked open slowly, and Acelynn stepped through. Her dark hair was gathered on the top of her head in a messy ponytail. Last night's mascara was smudged under her eyes like she had been crying not long ago. She was still in the same outfit from last night, but now she had on an oversized flannel wrapped tight around her frame. She looked shaken, but not broken.

"Nolan said you were in here." Acelynn's voice was timid. She hovered near the threshold of the room, shifting back and forth between her feet.

I stood, rounding the desk slowly. "What can I do for you, kitten?"

"Remember when I asked for the Knights' protection earlier?" she asked, voice trembling just enough to set the hairs on the back of my neck on edge. Her terrified gaze refused to meet mine.

I frowned toward her. "Yes, and I thought we would discuss it later today?"

Acelynn swallowed hard. "Yeah, I am going to have to cash that deal in early, Kaius."

"Explain," I commanded, expression lasering in on her.

She folded her arms across her chest, pulling the flannel tighter around her front. "Because he found me, and I'm pretty sure he's snaked his way into a club that would actually take him."

"You're saying the guy you are running from tried to patch into the Knights once?" I growled at her, rage beginning to boil over at this. I knew she was hiding something from us, and while this wasn't the worst thing it could have been, it still wasn't ideal.

Shaking her head once, she stepped forward. "No."

Acelynn did not yield to me. Instead, she took another step forward, closing the distance between us until only a breath remained. If my mind wasn't whirling with a thousand questions, I would have been impressed by her boldness.

"No," she countered. Her bright hazel eyes looked at me with determination as she said, "Logan wasn't a Knight when I knew him, but he wanted to be patched into any club he could get into. At one point, he was, which is what I thought got him killed. But apparently, he is back to haunt me from the dead."

CHAPTER SIXTEEN

THREE KNIGHTS STOOD in my bedroom, each one with a different reaction to the scene they were witnessing. Kaius hadn't said much since I confessed everything about Logan. His silence was worse than yelling. It felt sharp, heavy, and made my anxiety claw at my chest like a trapped animal.

"I am not touching that thing," Nolan muttered, nodding toward the coiled snake in the glass dome.

A laugh slipped from my lips, but died instantly when Kaius shot me a warning look. I dropped my gaze, shame washing over me. There was no way I could go to Watson or Parsons about this without Logan finding out. And if he did, there was no telling what he would do to me in retaliation.

Which left me with only one option—asking the Knights of Lovelen for help. And right now, I wasn't even sure if trusting them had been a good idea.

"Vince," Kaius barked out, his voice deep and gravelly. "Get the snake and dispose of it."

Without a word, Vince emerged from the shadows he had

been sulking in like he'd been waiting for orders. He grabbed the chessboard, the reptile thrashing violently against the glass as he stalked out of the room. I shuffled my feet back and forth, bracing myself for Kaius to finally explode. I deserved every ounce of fury he was going to unleash on me, maybe not for what I had done, but for what I hadn't told him yet.

"Logan Reid was stripped of his patch from the Death Dealers two years ago." Kaius's voice was deadly quiet. The control in every word made them even more terrifying.

I could feel his stare burning into me. Tears pooled at the corners of my eyes, but I refused to look at him.

He continued, "We were explicitly told he was dead. So tell me, Acelynn, how the hell is he suddenly back from his shallow grave?"

"I don't know," I mumbled. The truth was slippery even in my own mind. Even the good memories with Logan were now shrouded in darkness if I tried to reflect on them. I swallowed hard. "We met in college in North Carolina. He had this fascination with the club life. Particularly the Knights of Lovelen and the Death Dealers, but I didn't think much of it at the time. Just let it go in one ear and out the other when he started on about it again. Logan graduated a year before me and moved back home to California."

My throat felt like it was on fire as I told the story, because all of it was the truth, one that Acelynn didn't live, but a scared girl who had let him push her around, and that scared me to divulge to the men who had betrayed my family.

Clearing my throat once, I continued on, "Or at least that's what I believed until he showed up at my dorm one day with a fresh tattoo and a story about initiation. It just got worse from there. His anger and outbursts suddenly felt charged by something more sinister. Logan started claiming he was being unfairly treated in the club and had a whole conspiracy on how the leaders were out to get him. That's what got him stripped of his patch."

"Why did you think he was dead?" Nolan asked, gaze full of skepticism.

I shrugged once. "I got a call from someone claiming to be a part of the club that said they skinned his tattoo from his body, and they didn't cauterize the wound quickly enough, so he bled out. Didn't seem to ask for a picture of the crime scene for proof."

"You don't skin a patch off for someone who gets one of your own killed," Nolan snapped this time.

I could feel the blood drain from my face. My feet stumbled back until they hit the wall, forcing me to stay in the room with the two of them.

"I had no idea," I whispered. It wasn't a lie.

When Logan and I had first gotten together, he had been secretive. Obsessive. And I had thought it was fun to be with someone like that. That was before I figured out Logan didn't love me. It was my last name he fell in love with because he understood the power that came with it. When he finally wormed his way into the club, it had become clear to me our relationship was failing, and the anger he felt for everyone involved in the club life that "wronged" him was taken out on me. I grimaced at the memories that flashed across my mind, but as quickly as they came, I shoved them back into their little box.

Nolan exhaled, averting his gaze from me. "Sorry. I shouldn't have snapped at you."

"Nolan," Kaius warned, but his second didn't seem to care much for it as he flashed him a steely look. Reaching up,

Kaius ran one hand through his light-colored hair and then down his face. "You're right."

"Usually am," Nolan replied with a shrug.

I forced down the bile rising in my throat and found the courage to speak again. "I thought he was dead, if that makes any of this any better."

Kaius stared at me, his expression unreadable. "It doesn't. But it was worth a shot, kitten."

I smirked at his pet name. Something about it sent a wave of calm over me. If he was calling me kitten again, that could only mean that his anger wasn't directed at me anymore, but at the man who had painted my ceiling with blood.

Kaius extended one finger, beckoning me forward. "Come here."

I moved slowly, every step cautious as my brain tried to catch up with my movements. When I reached him, Kaius placed his hands gently on my shoulders and turned me, so my back was pressed up against him. Taking one hand, he reached under my chin and tilted it toward the ceiling. "Look closer at the words. See how he capitalized certain letters?"

Kaius kept me locked in place as I stared at the bright red letters above my head. The first word was the only one that had the odd capitalization to it, and as soon as I put it together, I could feel my legs give out from under me. Kaius caught my weight, not letting me crumble to the floor below me.

A whisper left my lips as I spoke. "Prey. He always taunted me, telling me I was his favorite prey to chase."

"And now the prey will become the predator." Kaius's hot breath met my left ear as he spoke. "I'll make sure of it."

KAIUS

Acelynn trembled beneath me, her wide eyes staring up at the blood-slicked words scrawled across her ceiling. Fear radiated off her in waves. I had meant it when I said my little kitten would not become prey to a fallen member. She was mine to chase, mine to protect. And I didn't share.

I let go of her jaw, my fingers reluctantly sliding away from her skin. She made no attempt to step away from me. Instead, she wrapped her arms tightly around her middle, shoulders caving in as if her own bones were too heavy to bear.

Shifting my attention away from her, I turned toward Nolan. "Take Acelynn back to the Queen's Table. Have Astoria set her up in one of the dorms."

She didn't argue. That alone sent a fresh feeling of unease crawling down my spine. In the short time I have known her, Acelynn has always been fire and sharp edges—never silent compliance. Whatever had happened between her and Logan had left fractures she hadn't let show until now. I knew Logan. I knew what kind of chaos he thrived on when he wore the Death Dealers patch. Alec Spade had always described the new initiate as unstable, dangerous, and the reason why I took my seat at the roundtable years too early.

Acelynn moved like a ghost, her steps clumsy and unfocused. Nolan stayed close, one hand hovering over the small of her back in case she became unstable. He glanced over his shoulder at me, a silent promise in his eyes saying *I'll get her home safe.* I didn't need the reassurance. Nolan had never failed me, but the fact that he gave it anyway twisted something in my chest.

As the front door clicked shut behind them, Vince emerged from the shadows again, rubbing one hand over the top of his forearm where two perfect, angry puncture wounds were visible.

I let out a laugh. "Need me to suck the poison from your wounds?"

"Shut up," Vince grumbled at me as he shot me a dirty look, knowing that a rattler's poison would do him no harm thanks to his father's insistence on building immunity to every poison he could find.

Vince's dad had given my own father the idea of using hemlock against our enemies, but neither of us had known that he was sick enough to test his experiments on his own flesh and blood. Vince had survived that hell, and I respected him for it.

His gaze flicked to the ceiling, then back to me. "I told you she was hiding something."

"She had already alluded that she was in danger," I replied coolly. "We were going to talk particulars this afternoon."

"She was with an excommunicated club member," Vince snapped, voice cracking like a whip. It was rare to see him lose his calm, but the moment we stepped into Acelynn's house, he'd been on edge.

It wasn't hard to see why either. Acelynn's home was bare. No moving boxes piled high. No trash needed to be removed from the bin. Not a single nail hole in the wall for decor to show off her personality. Acelynn Thorton did not live in this house. Slept here, maybe. But that was all.

And Vince knew this. He threw a hand toward the red

scrawl above the bed. "Read the damn writing on the wall, Kaius. She isn't who she says she is. That girl is a *Spade*."

"Watch your mouth," I growled out.

My heart pounded against my chest rapidly as the lies I had been trying to convince myself of for over a year threatened to bubble over. Alec Spade's frantic voice echoed in my ears from the night that he was killed by his own father. The night the Spade family went to their graves.

Alec's sister was never around the club life. He made sure of it and forced his father to send her to the most elite schools he could find, where she would be safe. But the time of his father complying with Alec's demands had run out.

The booming sounds of a full bar thudded around the silence in my office. I was buried in paperwork Astoria had tossed onto my desk earlier when my office door flew open, slamming into the wall.

I looked up, coming upon the last man I expected to be walking through the Queen's Table on a Saturday night when it was crawling with Knights.

Alec Spade, the VP of the Death Dealers Motorcycle Club, stood tall in the doorway, his hands shoved in the dark jeans he wore. I leaned back in my chair, reaching down to trace the underside of my desk where one of my many hidden gun safes sat.

"What can I do for you, Spade?" I asked, voice clipped with annoyance.

His chest heaved upward as if he was trying to find the courage to speak. I furrowed my brow at the man. I had never once seen Alec show even an ounce of fear when it came to club business, but now he was practically shaking in front of me. His bloodshot eyes frantically searched around the room on their own, as if his mind was racing faster than he could explain.

"I need to call in a favor." Alec's voice was rough with emotion. I nodded, waiting for him to continue. He stepped fully

into my office, shutting the door behind him, keeping his back to me.

Frowning at the man, I spoke, "The Spades and Knights don't strike deals anymore. Not after the last one went south."

"I know," he whispered. "So that must tell you how desperate I am, Kaius, to come ask the devil for help."

Alec turned back to me and began toward one of the chairs in front of my desk. He slumped down, face falling into his hands as they raked through his long brown hair.

I crossed my arms over my chest. "What is it you need, Alec?"

"I need your help killing my father."

"Kaius." Vince's voice pulled me out of the memory where I damned us all.

The Knights, except for Nolan and Vince, thought the Iron Serpents, a smaller club which had been a thorn in our backsides since the moment they arrived outside of Lovelen, executed the Spades. But it had been my hand that had pulled the trigger that killed Bran Spade seconds after he burned his own family alive in the family home. That night had left scars we didn't talk about, and Vince had never forgiven me for dragging us into it.

"Get a cleanup crew in here," I said flatly, my shoulder connecting with his as I stalked out of the room.

"Don't let the fantasy of pussy cloud your judgment," Vince called toward me. I paused in the hallway as he continued, "We can't afford another devil in our bed. Next time, it'll be *you* choking on your own blood."

CHAPTER SEVENTEEN

acelynn

THREE WEEKS OF SILENCE. That's how long it had been since Logan had made his presence known on my bedroom walls. Three weeks of waiting for the next shadow to be him, the next chill to slide down my spine, the next sign he was still watching me.

I was on edge every second of the day. Astoria had tried to help, dragging me through all the boutiques in Lovelen, forcing me to focus on sequins and leather instead of spiraling. At night, I drown my thoughts by pouring booze for the locals and trying to keep up with the dance routines that Astoria had been coaching me through.

But tonight felt different.

The sun had barely slipped below the horizon when I pulled into the overgrown field behind an old red barn just out of town. It looked forgotten, like time had given up on it. And maybe that was why Parsons and Watson had insisted on meeting here through nothing but a text with coordinates and a time. I had immediately deleted the message the second I saw it, not wanting to leave even a digital whisper of the meeting.

I killed the headlights and waited for a second, watching the dark structure as rain began to tap against my car's windshield. My boots hit the gravel as I stepped out of the vehicle and made my way over to the entrance. My hand brushed against the loose hanging tarps in the doorway.

Cold air wrapped around my arms, biting at the space between my zip-up hoodie and bare skin. I paused, half of me already wanting to turn around, head back to the Queen's Table, and pretend none of this was happening, but the shuffling of feet brought me back to my reality.

Detective Watson appeared first, offering me a light smile and nod. I returned it.

We both had a mutual respect for each other, and if I were only dealing with him, I think this might be easier, but just as my smile appeared, it vanished as Detective Parsons stepped around him.

Shadows covered half of his face in the dimly lit barn. The rain drummed harshly against the roof, adding to the tension that filled the air.

"You better have something big for us today, girl," Parson sneered at me.

I stiffened. He was already irritated, which was never a good sign. The past few meetings, I had been so distracted by the looming threat of Logan that I wasn't able to tell them anything useful. But last night, I got lucky.

The Knights of Lovelen were particularly good at keeping their dirty dealings hidden, but the new initiate had slipped up the other night when I had fed him one too many shots of whiskey.

"Come on, tell me just one secret," I purred at him behind the

bar, leaning ever so slightly against the top so the boy had a good view of my cleavage.

Oscar was the newest initiate for the Knights of Lovelen, and he followed them around like a lost puppy, his big brown eyes begging to learn and help in any way he could. The men completely disregarded the twenty-year-old except for using him as their designated errand boy.

Oscar blushed and shook his head, a few of his sandy-colored curls tumbling into his face. "You know I can't, Acelynn."

"You're no fun," I pouted, sticking my bottom lip out extra to get my point across.

Stepping away from him, I picked up the rag that lay across the bar and started toward another customer, but Oscar's voice called me back. "Wait, there is one thing I might be able to tell you, but you have to promise not to say anything."

A light hiccup came at the end of his sentence, causing a devilish smirk to pull at the corners of my mouth. I turned, watching him from hooded lids, and sauntered back to him.

"What is it?"

Oscar leaned fully over the bar, making it so his mouth was practically on my ear. "We are getting a shipment of Muze at the Excalibur on Thursday."

"The nightclub?" I whisper-yelled back at him.

Muze was a highly addictive synthetic drug that gave the user a temporary euphoric high, but the hallucinations that followed were a dangerous side effect. The paranoia, psychosis, and physical sickness were just some of the milder effects that often plagued users. It was rumored the Knights produced it with a light amount of hemlock to ensure it didn't kill those who partook in it. The feds had been itching to bust the Knights for this operation for years as the drug became more popular in the recreational scene.

Oscar nodded eagerly. "Yeah, it's probably the largest we have had in over a year."

"The Knights will have a large delivery of Muze at the Excalibur tomorrow night," I explained.

Parsons's face lit up like a Christmas tree.

"You are positive about this?" Watson asked, his voice gentle but firm in his questioning.

Turning my gaze to the younger detective, I nodded once. With the confirmation, Watson dug in the front pocket of his uniform, pulling a replica of my spade necklace out for me. It was slightly bulkier than the one around my neck, but not enough to be noticed by anyone but me.

"Here."

He held the necklace out in front of him for me to take. Stepping closer, I brushed past Parsons, who was rapidly typing on his phone, forgetting about me almost instantly after getting the Muze information. I looked up at Watson. "What is this?"

"Safety precaution." He shrugged lightly. "Once the sting occurs, you might need assistance from us. They will begin to be more paranoid. If you are in danger, the spade opens like a locket, and there is a panic button. Just press down on it, and the device will send out a distress call with your location, regardless if you have a signal or not. It'll only take minutes for emergency services to arrive on the scene."

"What if I don't need emergency services and just need one of you to show up?" I asked. The jewelry piece felt like a bomb I was getting ready to disarm in my hands. If I were caught with this or it got accidentally pressed in the presence of the Knights, my cover would be blown. This felt more dangerous than a burner phone, given my recent run-ins with an ex-boyfriend turned deranged stalker.

Watson shoved his hands in the front pockets of his pants. "Then you won't need them, but it's always better safe than sorry. No matter what is happening, if you feel unsafe or need help, press the panic button, and I will be on my way to you."

CHAPTER EIGHTEEN

acelynn

IT WAS JUST past four in the morning. The bar had finally emptied out, and I stood behind the counter, restocking bottles and wiping down surfaces I'd already cleaned twice. All day, my stomach had been in knots from the knowledge of the sting that had gone down at the Excalibur.

Kaius and a few other Knights had left hours ago without a word. Not even a goodbye. Astoria had been clueless to the fact that it was probably the last time she would see them for a long time. When they returned, the energy inside the Queen's Table shifted. The crowd practically split apart as the Knights re-entered, power dripping off Kaius as he passed through the space.

My breath caught in my throat when his angered eyes locked with mine. For a second, I thought he could see right through my façade—through the lies, the betrayal, the panic button disguised as a pendant around my neck. But then he turned, whispering something to Nolan before stalking into the roundtable room. The Knights in the crowd shifted to follow their king.

A cold chill washed over my entire body as I watched those wooden doors slam shut, the bass of the bar's music covering up any screaming that was occurring behind them. Astoria had paused for a moment, eyes watching the same spot as me, before releasing a shaky breath and going back to slicing a batch of limes.

I always wished I had a conscience like my brothers, because maybe this wouldn't feel like acid in my veins, and the guilt of what I had told both of the detectives yesterday wouldn't be making me physically ill. But I didn't. I had my secrets, a hidden panic button around my neck, and a sickening ache that told me I'd made a deal with something darker than I might be able to handle.

Hours passed in a haze before Nolan finally emerged by himself, eyes sharp and unreadable as he lasered in on where Astoria was flipping the barstool chairs onto the tops of their tables. His hand traced her lower back, fingers lightly drawing shapes where her skin was exposed between her pants and cropped shirt. She leaned back into his touch unintentionally, taking solace in the quiet of the bar and Nolan.

I couldn't understand why neither of them took the leap of being with one another when they were both so clearly made for each other. A tinge of jealousy shot through me because I knew in my heart I would never have that. Never be looked at by someone as though I had hung the moon in the sky to shine down on just them. I was hard to love fully. I could give someone my everything, and even then, would it ever be enough?

Shaking my head, I returned to the bar, letting the two of them have their moment, but it was shattered as the double doors of the roundtable flew open and struck the walls behind them. My hand tightened on the knife I had just finished drying before looking up at the man in the doorway.

Kaius Mordred, the King of Lovelen, was staring me down with a lethal smirk that had my blood running cold.

The knife clattered to the floor as I sprinted from behind the bar, my sneakers catching against the worn flooring. I skidded around the corner of the bar in a panic as Kaius lunged forward. Ducking away from his grasp, I increased my speed until I was inches away from the doorway. With both hands, I pressed against the metal door using all my strength to throw it open, but before I could get through, Kaius's hand latched around the base of my ponytail and yanked me back with brutal force.

A scream ripped through me, but the sound only caused him to pull harder. My legs gave out, and suddenly I was being dragged backward across the floor like a rag doll.

Astoria's terrified screams broke through the air, and I could hear Nolan trying to calm her, most likely holding her back from pummeling her brother right now. Kicking my feet out, I began to thrash against him, making the pain in my skull grow more intense. In one quick motion, my body flew up and then slammed down onto the ground.

I heaved hard as the wind in my lungs disappeared, tiny black dots dancing across my vision from the lack of oxygen now flowing to my brain. Rolling to my left side, I curled into myself, a sharp pain in my back now screaming at me.

Kaius's dark figure loomed over mine, power dripping off him in heavy waves. This was the man who haunted my dreams. He was no savior of mine, and in this moment, I knew he would not even bat an eye as he carved into me for his own sick satisfaction. Kaius, ever so slowly, bent at the knee until he was only inches above me.

A pathetic whimper slipped through my lips, causing a ghostly smirk to trace his mouth. He reached out, brushing a piece of hair off my sweaty forehead in an almost tender motion. I tried to scramble back, but he was faster than me, his other hand reaching out to grip the center of my throat. His fingers tightened around it as he flattened me on my back once again and leaned in. We were so close, our noses nearly brushing. I weakly clawed at his wrist, back arching further into him as my eyes rolled into the back of my head.

"Knight got your tongue, kitten?" Kaius loosened his grip slightly, allowing air to flood into me once again.

I heaved in a few ragged breaths, letting the color of the world around me come back with a raging force. Sinking closer, Kaius flicked out his tongue, licking up the trail of tears that had pooled down my face.

He groaned out once, "Sweet little Acelynn, I am going to have so much fun destroying you."

CHAPTER NINETEEN

kaius

A SHUDDER RIPPLED THROUGH ACELYNN, her fear palpable on my tongue. The euphoric taste of her tears was like liquid gold, and it had my mind wandering to what other parts of her tasted like. The little sounds she would make when I hit just the right spot she was begging for. These were thoughts I shouldn't be entertaining, not here, not now. But fuck, it was getting harder to push them down.

I hadn't anticipated for her to run from me, but I knew I had to contain Astoria regardless, which is why I sent Nolan out first. I tore my gaze from the trembling girl beneath me to look toward my sister. Astoria was curled into Nolan, her face buried in his chest as he ran soothing strokes through her tangled hair. She was thinking that I was going to kill the girl right here. Oh, how wrong she was.

"I'm sorry," Acelynn whispered, her voice fractured and raw.

It struck something deep in my chest, and I almost

ripped my grip away from her neck. Her tiny hands were wrapped around my wrist, grounding her to me.

I tilted my head, keeping the mask on even as the voice in the back of my mind screamed at me to let her go. But Acelynn needed a reminder of who she was under the protection of, and how asking questions was going to get her killed the next time. "What are you sorry for, kitten?"

Tears clung to her lashes. "For running."

I hummed low at that. "For running? Is that why you think I have you pinned underneath me?"

Her head bobbed once, no words coming from her open mouth. I licked my lips. "Acelynn, we both know that's not true."

A jumbled mess of pleas began to spill from her lips, but I cut them off with a simple squeeze, just enough to remind her I was in control. Her nails clawed at my arm again. More tears mixed with black mascara spilled down her face. The next time she would look like this for me would be when I slid my cock in her hot, wet mouth, hands tangled in her dark hair as I fucked it. The thought alone had my length hardening, but I shoved down the primal need to take her here and now. I would own Acelynn Thorton in every way imaginable and make her the Queen of Lovelen.

Ripping her from the ground by her forearm, I placed her on her feet and began to drag her through the bar and out the back door. She slammed her heels into the ground, gravel flying in every direction as I forced her stiff body closer to the circle of Knights. They all had their backs toward us as they waited for my instructions. Pushing past them, I brought her upon the scene playing out in front of us. Blood sprayed across the ground, mixing with the dirt, and becoming a muddy mess as Vince laid another punch on the initiate who had sold us out to the cops. His nose sat crooked on his bruised face, and the T-shirt he was wearing was hanging in strips across his body. The fresh inked Knights of Lovelen symbol seemed to glow in the moonlight. Oscar's helpless pleas rang into the night air.

Acelynn tried to pull away from me, away from the horror in front of her, as I locked my arm around her upper chest and held her tight against mine. The crunch of Vince's fist against Oscar's cheek caused her to flinch into me. I gripped the underside of her chin, squeezing just enough that it made her cry out for me.

"Do you see that, kitten?" I spoke calmly. Her body began to shake in fear as I forced her to watch the beating. "This is what happens when one of our own betrays his brothers."

Vince paused his movements. "Come on, Oscar. You were so forthcoming about your theories of who the rat was at the roundtable. But then we saw you cozied up to little Miss Sunshine over there, and you can't remember what you said?"

"Seems like kitten's got his tongue." Nolan stepped up next to me, arms crossed over his chest as he watched the initiate he had just tattooed last night heave on all fours. Kicking out his foot, it met Oscar's stomach with a sickening crunch.

The man howled out, only causing Acelynn to sob louder. "I swear..." Oscar's voice was desperate. "I didn't tell her shit. She kept asking me for my secrets, but I didn't tell her a thing about the Muze shipment. She's just like every other bartender you have at the Queen's Table who is willing to spread her legs if you tip them well."

"Watch your mouth," Nolan snarled at the man, throwing a punch that clipped him under the jaw.

Oscar's head snapped back, causing him to lose his balance and topple into the dirt behind him. Nolan stood over his body and ripped him up by the sides of his torn shirt.

"Astoria is a bartender at the Queen's Table, and if you speak about her like that again, I will cut your balls off and feed them to you. Are we clear?"

Acelynn shivered at the venomous tone Nolan took with Oscar. It was rare that he got this angry during a club issue, but when it came to my sister, any disrespect would set him off. If they both would stop being so stubborn and finally admit they had been in love with each other since we were kids, then maybe this pent-up rage would subside. But then again, maybe it would just fuel it more.

Nolan tossed Oscar back onto the ground before turning and stalking away, his shoulder meeting mine as he did. I ignored the sign of disrespect, knowing he probably didn't even realize he had done it and was going to cool off for a moment.

"Why don't we ask Acelynn about these secrets she so desperately wanted to know?" I called out, releasing her jaw lightly so she could answer my questions. "What did you ask Oscar about during your shift on Monday night, kitten?"

She turned around in my hold, and I could now see just how pretty the gold in her hazel eyes shone in the moonlight. Acelynn began to speak through broken sobs. "Nothing. I served him drinks, and we talked about how busy the bar was that night. I swear I don't know what secrets he's talking about or anything about a Muze shipment, Kaius."

"I know you don't, pretty girl." I smirked, my thumb coming up to brush over her bruised lip. She shivered at the contact, and I didn't miss the fact that she slightly leaned into my touch. "We just needed to show you what happens when someone we trust rats us out to the feds."

Oscar's voice argued my point in the distance, but I

ignored it as I watched Acelynn's face drop in relief at my words. Good, now she understood, even if she doesn't realize that this test sealed her to the Knights for life. Sealed her to me for life. I tucked a dark piece of hair behind her ear before calling out over my shoulder, "Nolan, hold her in place."

Acelynn's eyes widened slightly as Nolan returned and gripped her arms behind her. Her back arched against him, pleading with the man to let her go, but Nolan held firm, making it impossible for her not to witness what I was about to do. I reached into my pocket, pulling out the glass syringe Vince had retrieved for me earlier. Oscar began to scramble backward, but didn't get far as the heel of Vince's boot connected with his chest, pinning him to the ground.

"Hold him still," he barked out the order to the Knights standing behind him.

Ryan and Wes, two of our newest initiates, raced forward. Even though both of their faces were as pale as ghosts from fear, they each willingly held one of Oscar's arms down by his sides. I stepped over Wes, leaning down to grip Oscar by the forehead and pulling his neck taut for me. I chuckled at his screams. "I do not tolerate betrayal of any kind, Oscar. You understood that when you joined the club."

Grinning at the pathetic whimper he let out, I called out to the Knights surrounding me, "We will take it to a vote. Any objections to the punishment of death for Oscar Jameson's crimes against the Knights of Lovelen, including being a double agent for the feds and feeding them information about pertinent dealings?"

Silence from each and every man. The only sounds filling the surrounding air were Acelynn's screaming pleas, but she didn't get a vote on this. I hovered over Oscar. "The jury's out, Oscar boy. Say hi to old daddy dearest for me when you get to hell."

Plunging the needle into the side of his neck, I released the lethal hemlock dose into his bloodstream. I dropped him, watching as his body reacted to the drug as he convulsed against the gravel. A white foam pooled from his lips, and I couldn't help but feel a sense of amusement at the sight. After a minute, he stopped moving, and I knew the hemlock had done its job.

CHAPTER TWENTY

acelynn

I WAS ROYALLY FUCKED.

Nolan released my arms, the loss of his support sending me tumbling onto the dirt-covered ground. My hands hit the ground, sharp rocks biting into my palms, but I didn't care. My body lurched as dry heaves ripped through me, my stomach convulsing from what I had just witnessed—what I had allowed to happen to an innocent man.

Kaius towered over me. "Come on, kitten. Let's get you back inside."

I slapped away his extended hand, rage coursing through me as I stared up at the monster I always knew he was. "Fuck you, Kaius."

"Don't test me, Acelynn. Not here." His voice dropped into a low growl, making the pit of my stomach warm with anticipation of what the power he held could do to me.

I hated myself for the way my body responded to the authority in it. For the way I *wanted* him to use that power to punish me. To *prove a point.*

I had just aided in the murder of a man I had all but sent

to the firing squad, and here I was, falling apart and craving the touch of his killer. Before I could react, his arm hooked around my waist, and I was hoisted up over his shoulder. My fists pounded against his back in anger. Each released another burst of emotion from me until I was screaming, "Put me down."

Kaius ignored my request and started back into the bar. Eventually, my screams gave way to guttural sobs. My body sagged against him, fingers gripping the soft cotton of his shirt, grounding me to him even though he was the last person I wanted to seek comfort in.

I thought I could bury my feelings when stepping into this role, mask them with the rage I felt for the Knights of Lovelen, but I had always been one to show every emotion on my face. Alec had known this, and it was probably why he had kept me so far from the club. Showing any emotion got you or the things you loved killed in their line of work.

The relentless echo of Oscar's haunted screams filled my ears, guilt clawing its way back up until I thought I was going to be sick. Regret consumed me with a force that would have me curled into myself if I weren't being held by Kaius.

The click of a door opening and closing brought me back to reality before Kaius pulled me back over his shoulder and lowered me onto an unfamiliar bed. The mattress dipped under me, sheets too soft for a room so cold. I stared at a chipped panel in the wooden door, willing my mind to disappear into that tiny imperfection. Maybe if I stared long enough, I could escape to some place where none of this had happened. No more painful reminders of my mistakes, no more blood on my hands, no more anything.

"Acelynn." Kaius's soft voice was distant, but I couldn't get myself to respond to him.

Calloused fingertips began to stroke down both sides of my face until they cradled me in their grasp. Bright green eyes met mine, breaking my line of sight to the chipped wood and slamming me back into reality with a raging force with just a look.

I gasped as my heart constricted, pain burning in the center of my chest. It was as if my lungs were going to cave in on themselves. I was a prisoner of my own making to this feeling, and the sick monster toying with my mind relished in my pain. The guilt devoured me, and some sick part of me welcomed it.

Kaius's grip tightened on my jaw. "You need to breathe."

But his words were muffled, buried under the roar of blood in my ears. My breath came in shallow, panicked stutters. Then I was leaning into his comfort to bury myself in his chest, letting out a broken moan. Kaius didn't pull away. Instead, he gathered me into his arms, his hands slipping under my shirt in slow, soothing strokes. I could feel the hot, wet tears gathering in a patch on his shirt, but he didn't seem to mind.

"Shhh," Kaius whispered gently. "I've got you, kitten."

He pressed a soft string of kisses across my forehead. It was such an intimate moment for two people who had barely spent any time with each other, but it felt so right. The gesture shattered me. I didn't deserve his compassion when I was still set on a plan to avenge my family and destroy the very people who had shown me nothing but kindness in times when I needed it.

Even my own flesh and blood had never given me this feeling of comfort. They just shipped me off, thinking it better than having to deal with the overly emotional daughter who unintentionally looked down on them for the innocent blood they carelessly spilled for power. Now, I was no better than them.

"I don't deserve this," I whispered, voice raw and frayed from screaming.

His lips continued their pattern against my forehead. "You're safe."

I let out a deep breath at the statement.

"You're safe," Kaius repeated. "I promise no one is going to hurt you under my protection."

"Why are you being so kind to me?" I asked, voice cracking with emotion that had him tightening his arms around me.

"Just focus on taking deep breaths for me, Acelynn." Kaius smoothed back my hair as he instructed me, "In. One, two, three, four, five. Now out. One, two, three, four, five."

I obeyed his command, wanting this burning feeling to go away. Kaius smirked against my skin. "Good girl. Do it again."

After minutes of repeating the motion, my breathing became elongated and relaxed, my body ceasing from shaking in his arms. We didn't move from our position, though I buried my face deeper into Kaius's chest, breathing in his scent of freshly washed linens with a hint of the inside of a mechanic shop.

It smelled like a home that I had long since buried in my subconscious. Flashes of greased hands and the slight aroma of two-stroke flashed across my mind. I squeezed my eyes shut, begging the images to retreat. They were too painful to remember right now. Kaius continued the soft paths of his hands on my back, and I focused on each stroke as they tracked down my spine.

"I'm sorry," I murmured into the silence, not sure if he had even caught my words. Kaius shifted back, smoothing back the pieces of hair from my tear-streaked skin. My heart began to thud against my chest at a rapid pace, stomach swimming with nervous excitement as I stared at the most beautiful man I had ever encountered. Kaius was heartbreakingly beautiful, golden strands falling into his eyes, expression unreadable.

But the little voice in the back of my mind reminded me I was a liar, a fake, a snake hidden in the grass ready to strike when provoked. Kaius Mordred was not looking at me. He was looking at a carefully curated version of me I knew he would fall in love with. The thought had my heart dropping into the pit of my stomach, self-hatred filling in all the cracks in my heart. I tore my gaze away from his.

"I shouldn't have taken it that far with you, Acelynn." Kaius's voice was strained with regret. Shaking my head at him, I wanted to tell him he should have taken it further than a few bruises. He should have injected me with the hemlock syringe and let the sweet hand of death pull me under. I deserved it. His thumb caught a lone tear. "Look at me."

Forcing my gaze to meet his, I sucked in a deep, rattling breath. "You were protecting your family. I understand that, Kaius."

His brows pinched together. "It doesn't make it right. I should have never laid a hand on you without your expressed consent."

Rolling my eyes. "How do you know I would let you?"

Kaius's eyes darkened as he scanned me over, sending goose bumps prickling across my skin. He moved his thumb down my cheek to rest in the center of my bottom lip. With a light push, he separated my lips, and I unconsciously wrapped them around his thumb, softly sucking against the skin.

He smirked knowingly. "Lucky guess, kitten."

And just like that, reality hit me square in my chest. I jerked away from Kaius, skin flushing with embarrassment and anger at myself. I was not supposed to let myself enjoy the touch of a killer. It wasn't part of the plan, and until I could separate my heart from that fire burning in the pit of my stomach, I couldn't let him touch me like that. When he did, I wanted to be detached, for the act of pleasure to mean nothing to me. But right now, it would mean everything to me.

This wasn't some twisted fairy tale.

I wasn't the broken girl who found safety in the arms of a monster. I was going to be the one who lit the match to the fire, which burned the Knights' kingdom.

And I was falling for the man who would burn with me when it was not a part of the plan.

Kaius's hands lingered in the air where I had been seconds ago. Slowly, he lowered them, understanding in his eyes as he stood. He didn't try to touch me again as he spoke, "You can sleep here tonight."

And with that, he turned on his heel, stalking into the connected bathroom. Maybe that was the kindest thing he could've done for me. Leave me alone with my thoughts, wrapped up in a blanket that smelled like him. Because if he had reached for me again tonight, I might have found peace in the violence that was Kaius Mordred. Then all this scheming would have been for nothing.

CHAPTER TWENTY-ONE

acelynn

A DULL ACHE pulsed behind my eyes as I peeled them open. The space around me slowly came into focus—an unfamiliar ceiling, soft sheets, and the scent of the man who had filled my dreams still clinging to my skin.

My body felt heavy, like I'd been sinking in dreams that wouldn't let go. I turned my head. The spot beside me in the bed was empty and cold. Covers untouched or rumpled, which meant I hadn't been out for very long.

I drifted my gaze toward the open bathroom door. The faint hiss of running water could be heard just beyond the wall. Steam curled into the room like lazy fingers. A dim light cast on Kaius, who stood shirtless in front of the sink, a loose towel slung low around his hips, head slightly bowed as he braced both hands on the porcelain.

My eyes traced the sculpted lines of his back, each muscle flexing subtly beneath his skin as he shifted his weight. His shoulders were broad, built like a man who'd carried more than his share of burdens on them. Strength coiled through every inch of him, but it was the ink that held my attention.

His skin was a canvas of dark, inked art. Tattoos climbed up his spine and shoulders like creeping vines, ancient symbols woven with violent beauty. But the one etched between his shoulder blades stole the breath from my lungs. The Knights' sigil stood out against all the other pieces marring his skin. The cracked holy grail was shaded in just the right way that it appeared to jump from the surface.

The crooked crown hung off one side of the rim like it had been carelessly discarded over the cup. He had no other color through his other tattoos, making the purple hemlocks blooming around the base of the grail stand out even more. Delicate yet fatal, their petals curled up the cup like they were reaching for something just out of reach.

It made the deadly symbol look beautiful and terrifying without even trying.

I continued to admire the art until I noticed something. Underneath the ink, faint, almost hidden by the black swirl of lines, were scars. Pale ridges of flesh, some thin, others jagged, running like ghosts under the Knights' sigil. They were old.

Wounds that had healed over time, only to be buried beneath ink.

I sat slowly, eyes locked on a particularly long scar that ran from below his left shoulder blade to his right hip. "Those weren't from a fight, were they?"

Kaius didn't flinch or look surprised at my sudden question. As if he had known the entire time I was watching him, like he wanted me to see them. His eyes met mine in the mirror. "No."

His voice was a deadly quiet that sucked all the air from the room. I turned, letting my feet rest against the cold floor below the bed. My hands gripped the sheet, pulling it around me as I spoke. "Who did that to you?"

"My father," he said through clenched teeth.

The words hung there between us. I knew it was the reality of the life he had grown up in. Alec was always littered with bruises and cuts from my father. It was something that shouldn't be so normal for me to understand. I stood now, letting the sheet trail after me as I went. When I got to the doorframe, I leaned one shoulder against it, unsure if I was invited into the space. Into this highly personal piece of him, but something in the center of my chest refused to let me move away.

Kaius straightened, running one hand through his damp hair. "My father wasn't the type of man who believed in second chances. Or weakness. Especially not from his children."

He turned toward me fully. The light of the bathroom cast a golden glow across his chest, highlighting every scar, every sharp edge, every dark line etched into him.

"I started to earn these the night I turned ten," Kaius continued, voice even.

He reached out, pulling my hand not holding the sheet up to his chest. My fingers traced over a jagged scar that ran over his collarbone as he continued to speak.

"He said if I ever ran again, he would carve a crown into my back to remind me where I belonged. My being the shithead kid that I was didn't believe him until he did make good on his promise."

My gaze lingered on the reflection of his back in the mirror to the now obvious scar his tattoo covered. He had turned his trauma into something permanent. A badge. A warning. A vow.

"You tattooed over the scars," I murmured, pulling my

eyes back to where my fingers were still absentmindedly running over the puckered skin.

"I didn't want to forget." Kaius's voice was soft, but the emotion behind his words was palpable. I could almost taste it. "But I wanted to decide how those memories were remembered."

Something in me broke in that moment. Not just for the child who had been hurt, but for the man who still carried that pain—layered over with ink, power, and violence he wore like armor.

I smiled lightly up at him. "I thought you were invincible."

Kaius stepped further into me, my back now pressed up against the doorframe. He placed one forearm above me, leaning into me until his lips were just a breath above mine. "I'm anything but invincible."

The hand that was at his collarbone traveled down his chest, letting my fingers barely ghost his skin as I did. When I got to the edge of a scar near his ribs, his breath hitched slightly, but he didn't pull away.

I wanted to hate him, to push him back and rebuild the walls I had let fall tonight. But all I could see was the boy who had survived hell and risen from it with nothing but fire in his veins. It reminded me of my brother, of all the boys who had survived this life.

And I didn't know what scared me more—the fact that suddenly Kaius Mordred made me feel like I was the only person in this world he cared for. Or the part of me that still wanted to destroy him.

CHAPTER TWENTY-TWO

acelynn

THE NEXT MORNING, when I woke, Kaius was already gone, which made it easy for me to slip out of the bar before I was caught by anyone in the club. After the conversation last night and what he had shared with me, I don't think I would be able to face Astoria or Nolan without them assuming something had happened. For some reason, if Kaius had just fucked me, it would have felt less intimate than him baring his trauma to me.

I hoisted myself onto my kitchen counter, the air from the open freezer brushing against my heated skin as flashes of what I would have let Kaius do to me if I hadn't pulled away last night filled my mind.

The image of Kaius's teeth scraping across the most intimate parts of me sent a shudder down my spine. I could almost hear the low growl that would come from him when I whimpered his name. The spoon dipped in the ice cream I had just been eating clattered to the floor, ripping me from my dirty daydream and back to reality.

I was not just a normal girl thinking about the possibility

of sleeping with a normal guy. I was tangled up with the president of the Knights of Lovelen. And I was the poison ready to destroy everything in his life.

The sudden ring of my phone sent me leaping off the counter. I stumbled over myself as I made my way over to my bag. Overturning the gray fabric satchel, the contents spilled across the hardwood floor. Coins clanked to the surface, sounding like bombs detonating in the battlefield in my mind. A lone, half-used lip gloss rolled across the kitchen into the living room, disappearing under the couch, never to be seen again.

My chest felt heavy, lungs refusing to fill with the air they needed. But it was no use, not when the overwhelming surge of fear coursed through me as I remembered the sounds of Oscar's screams. I could taste the metallic tang of blood on my tongue. Tears streamed down my face as I tried to find where my damn phone was.

There was no going back from how I was starting to feel about Kaius. I felt that in the silence when we both lay wrapped up in each other's embrace late into the night. Felt it in the way Kaius had stroked up and down my spine softly, slowly soothing me to sleep. And the worst one of all—I had felt it in the featherlight kisses he had placed against my forehead when he had calmed my fears that had begun to plague my dreams, nightmares slowly disappearing until I was left with one of the best sleeps I'd had in years.

Shaking the bag once again, an unfamiliar cream envelope tumbled out of it. My trembling fingers traced the edge of the closure, picking lightly at where it was sealed, until I finally tore through the paper.

Inside, there were three different Polaroids. The first showed me standing outside the red barn, glaring up at Parsons. I shuffled to the second, my face twisted in a scream behind Kaius as he hovered over Oscar's spasming body. Foam spilled from his mouth like a death rattle captured in time. The third had me freezing in place. It was Kaius and me. He was leaning over me in the doorway, eyes watching me intensely as my hand explored his scarred chest.

Blood rushed to my ears, blocking out the outside world. There was an unspoken passion that surrounded us, the moment so incredibly intimate, leaving me feeling exposed. From the angle of the photo, the image would have had to have been taken from inside the small closet to our left, which meant someone had to have been in the room the entire time or planted a camera. I was going to be sick.

Ripping my eyes away from the photo of us, I dragged them down to the red words that were scrawled out on the white strips of two of the Polaroids. The third was only marked with a single red spade. My brows scrunched together before I slammed down the images to arrange them on the floor in front of me, taking in the full sentence.

MiNE tO haVe.

My mind whirled as I tried to unscramble the capitalized letters just as Kaius had shown me on the night of the rattlesnake. A scream ripped through me when the letters clicked together, and I slammed the bag to the ground, silencing the ringing in my ears.

Venom.

A direct taunt from the poisonous snake that Logan had left on my bed the last time he made his presence known.

Prey. Venom. Prey. Venom.

The words tangled in my throat as I whispered them, trying to make sense of the sick game he was playing. Logan was watching me closely. He had been in Kaius's room recently. My throat constricted at the idea of Logan being that close to me, and I began to gag, but nothing came up. I couldn't stay in this town, not when I was betraying the Knights, and Logan was the wild card that was being unwillingly played. I was either going to be killed by the hands of the man I once loved or the man who was beginning to become my favorite addiction.

Light glinted off a silver key sitting across the room. Wiping the tears that were flowing down my face, I lunged for the set of keys and the photos before sprinting to my car. I didn't lock my front door. What was the point? Logan had already proven he could enter without being detected. I tossed the Polaroids onto the dash, letting them scatter across the surface haphazardly.

Starting the car, I peeled out of my driveway in the direction of Lovelen's city limits. Tonight, Acelynn Thorton would die, and I would don a new identity somewhere that had never heard of the Knights of Lovelen or the Death Dealers. Somewhere I could blend in without feeling the need to constantly be looking over my shoulder. Somewhere safe, Kaius soon forgotten about. We would be a passing regret to one another. Tears burned the corners of my eyes as I selfishly prayed that he would think of me often, maybe even as the one who slipped through his fingers.

The sun spotlighted the "Welcome to Lovelen" sign, and I could almost feel my body beginning to relax at the thought of leaving this cursed town. I was moments away from being free, but a screeching sound began from the engine of my car. Smoke puffed out the sides of the closed hood as it began to sputter and lurch forward. I coasted the car off to the side of the road until it was sitting right in front of the welcome sign.

Slamming my head back against the headrest, I let out a

frustrated scream. Panic clenched down on my chest as I realized I was stuck on the border of Lovelen with no way to contact anyone. Both the burner phone and my cell were lying somewhere in the middle of my living room, and there was no way in hell I was pressing the panic button hanging around my neck—not with the photos I had stashed on my dashboard.

Throwing two of the three images in my back pocket just in case, I searched around for the other one, but it must have slid under my seat during the drive. Whatever. I could get it later. For now, my mind was solely focused on escaping this godforsaken town.

Blowing my bangs away from my face, I leaned down, pulled the lever to pop my hood, and stepped from the vehicle. Smoke billowed from the engine, the smell of burning oil filling the air around me. I cursed under my breath. Of fucking course this would be my luck right now.

The roar of a motorcycle approaching filled the silence as I tried to fiddle with the radiator cap. Hissing, I ripped my hand away from the hot engine as it burned me. The stream of a headlight shone against the side of my car, and I could hear the driver cut the engine.

My hand curled around the lip of the car's hood, anticipating the worst. Right now would have been a great time to have a wrench in my hand. The crunch of gravel sounded under heavy footsteps until I could see a set of dark boots standing right next to me. My heart quickened in anticipation as I waited to find out what they wanted from me.

"Running from us already?" Kaius's dark voice filled my ears.

I peered at him from the corner of my eye.

There was a tinge of a smirk ghosting across his lips.

"And here I thought you weren't scared of anything. Especially the big bad Knights of Lovelen."

Leaning further into the car, I turned to stare up at the man. "I'm not running away, Kaius."

He hummed in amusement, settling a hip against the car. "Mm-hmm, sure you're not."

"I'm not," I yelled at him. A deep sigh escaped me as I tried to regain my composure. "Sorry. I shouldn't have snapped at you."

He lifted a single finger, brushing some of the dark hair that had fallen from my ponytail behind my ear. "Everything all right, kitten?"

"No," I whispered, my hand reaching out to tinker with the radiator cap again now that it was cooler. "Everything in my life is going to shit."

Kaius maneuvered himself around the car, one arm coming over my body while the other one landed onto my hand in the car. I breathed in his cologne of old leather and amber, letting the scent capture my senses. Digging my heels into the gravel, I refused to lean back into him like I wanted to as his words tickled the inside of my ear. "If everything is going to shit, let me help you, Acelynn."

Shaking my head, I bit the inside of my lip. "You can't help me, Kaius."

"I am sure that anything you tell me can't be worse than the things I have done in my life." His voice was a soft comfort I wanted to wrap myself in.

Maybe he could alleviate my Logan problem. He had helped the last time my deranged ex left me a present. But the weight of my duty to find out what happened to my family still made me wary about whether I should trust him. Could one night of vulnerability make up for slaughtering everyone that I loved? No, it couldn't. But if I left Lovelen, I wouldn't be able to find out why Kaius and the Knights had done what they had.

Turning in place, I set one hand on his chest and lightly pushed him back. He stepped an inch away and watched as I reached into my back pocket to grab the two Polaroids. Holding them up like a pair of playing cards, I let him pluck them from my grasp and examine them. "They are from Logan."

"Fuck," he hissed out, eyes trained on the very intimate photograph of the two of us. One thumb came up, stroking the image lightly before he shuffled to the next image of Oscar's execution. Kaius's eyes darkened as he stared at the scene, a flash of regret coming and going quickly, but then he was moving on to the words at the bottom.

"Venom," I breathed out. "The letters spell out venom. He is reminding me that he could hurt me if he wanted to and do worse than just leave a poisonous snake in the middle of my bed."

"I won't let him touch you." Kaius met my eyes, anger for the male responsible shining in them. His words were sharp and clipped, laced with a protectiveness I had never experienced before. I wanted to bathe in that protectiveness. To let it wrap me in its embrace and keep me safe from the world.

I stepped forward into him, and without even a second thought, his hands found my hips. I shivered at the contact, trying to remind myself that I could not fall in love with Kaius. But he had to fall in love with me. It was the only way I could get answers from him.

"I'm not scared of getting myself hurt, Kaius." I rested my hands on his chest, tilting my head back to see him. His grip on my hips tightened, but I continued, "I don't want to get Astoria or any of the Knights killed. I don't think I could live with myself if that happened."

"Logan isn't going to get anywhere near Astoria or you," Kaius assured me.

I scoffed at him and pushed out of his hold. My hands gripped the roots of my hair as I walked away from the overly confident man and toward the welcome sign. Logan was dangerous, and he had just proven he could slip in and out of places he was not supposed to be able to. I turned in a circle, taking in a deep breath. Kaius inched forward but kept a good amount of distance between the two of us.

"Acelynn, you need to trust me. Astoria has someone with her at all times right now. She is protected, and you will be as well."

"He got into your room," I snapped at him. "I guess we should have done a better job of checking for the monster in the closet before you told me your deepest secrets. Don't worry, I'll remember that for next time so that if I don't pull away and you fuck me, it won't be all over the internet the next day."

"Next time?" Kaius's voice was pure sex, and it went straight to my throbbing cunt. I shot him a look that told him to tread lightly, but this was Kaius, and he never bowed out of a challenge. "If I wanted to, I could fuck you over the hood of this car where anyone driving by could see. Then we wouldn't have to check the closet for monsters, and I could let everyone in Lovelen know that you're now mine."

"I would like to see you try," I scoffed at him, my eyes rolling to the back of my head, missing as he prowled forward.

His hand latched around my throat, pulling me back toward him. With his other hand, he reached up and unlatched the hood from its suspended state, letting it slam shut. Kaius's hand released my throat only for him to replace it on the left side of my head, tangling his fingers between the strands and roughly pulling. My body spun around before my back was slammed down against the dirty hood of the car. He shoved my head harder into the metal, causing a strangled cry to come from me.

"Kaius—"

"Shhh, kitten." Kaius's voice cooed from above me, a single finger ghosting across the edge of my shorts. "You asked for this, challenged me for it. Now let me show you what happens when you provoke the King of Lovelen."

My throat bobbed as I swallowed at the silent threat that laced his words. I was already panting, the excitement of getting caught by anyone who drove by making the slickness between my legs grow. He reached down my body, using his free hand to trace the soft skin between my cropped tee and the edge of my shorts, sending electricity shooting through me, my clit tingling with anticipation. Ever so slowly, he dipped his hand beneath the hem of my shorts, popping the button open. My breathing became heavy at his torturous actions. Him. I needed him. Consequences be damned.

Kaius watched me with a hungry gaze that made the heat growing between my legs build to an almost unbearable fire. I groaned out, eyes rolling to the back of my head as his fingers traced the inner part of my thigh. Dear god, this man hadn't even taken my clothes off, and he already had me in the palm of his hand.

Without warning, he ripped my shorts down my legs, the sound of tearing fabric mixing with my heavy pants. My body immediately tried to squirm away at the sudden exposure, but he had me pinned against the car. My hips bucked upward as the pad of his thumb ghosted over my clit.

A dark chuckle pooled from his lips as he continued to tease me. "Come on, kitten. I want to hear you beg for it."

CHAPTER TWENTY-THREE

kaius

ACELYNN THORTON WOULD BE both my heaven and damnation today. My fingers curled around the top of her lace underwear, pulling them fully off her until she was bare in front of me. I had to resist the urge to groan at the sight of her already glistening pussy. The view had my mouth watering. I ran another stroke over her, this time inciting a whimper from her plump lips.

"Kaius..." Acelynn's voice was breathy as she tried to get me to touch her where she desperately wanted me to. I laid one arm over her hips, keeping her pinned to the car.

Acelynn rolled her hips into my leg, desperate moans pooling from her lips as she tried to get any sort of friction. The rough material of my jeans caught against her clit, and the most delicious sounds began to fill the air around us. I wanted more. I wanted everything. A jolt of arousal shot down my spine. This woman was addictive and sweet, and I wanted to devour every inch of her until she was screaming for me to stop.

"You like that, kitten?" I asked, watching as she brought

her bottom lip between her teeth, nodding once at my question. I hummed as I pushed up her top, letting the material bunch under her chin.

Wasting no time, I dipped down and latched my mouth onto one of her exposed nipples, swirling my tongue over the sensitive skin for a few moments before testing her with the graze of my teeth. A shocked gasp shot through her, and she arched further into the feeling. I smirked, finally clamping down on it fully, inciting a scream of pain that morphed into pleasure from Acelynn. We stayed like this for a few moments as I switched to her other breast, giving it the same treatment.

Pulling back from her, I looked down to admire my little kitten all spread out for me. Nipples hard and shiny with my spit, chest heaving up as she tried to catch her breath, and the evidence of just how drenched she had become was coating my jeans. And it was all because of me. My eyes trailed up to Acelynn's face, glazed over eyes and swollen lips meeting my own.

"Fuck," I groaned out. "You look so pretty like this, Acelynn."

Her breath caught in the back of her throat at the use of her full name. The small sound had my cock throbbing within the confines of my jeans, and it was taking every ounce of self-control not to ruin her. Keeping eye contact with her, I reached down and dragged two digits along her soaking folds. My fingers found their rhythm as they rubbed tight circles around her clit.

Our moans mingled together as I pressed down harder, my lips finding their way down her body until I was bent at the knee, inches away from where she wanted me the most. Two fingers spread her wide before I licked up her cunt. Acelynn's hips bucked, and I reached up, holding them down in place. A low groan vibrated against her as I tasted her for the first time. My tongue darted out, swirling around her sensitive bud.

"Oh god," she moaned, the sound catching as I plunged a single finger inside of her.

Acelynn's walls immediately clench around me, causing a growl of pleasure to rumble deep within my chest. Inserting another finger, I pumped in and out of her. Acelynn's hand tangled in my hair, pushing me back to her. A laugh slipped out of me, and I dove back down to latch my mouth around her clit as I pushed back into her harder, curling my hand upward to hit that sweet spot.

She groaned out in satisfaction, hips grinding down harder on me. I was devouring her like a starved man. Devouring as if I were on death row and she were my last meal. Incoherent words began to spill from her lips, and I knew she was close.

I peered up at her, fingers still pumping hard in her as I spoke, "You wanna come, kitten? C'mon, pretty girl. Show me how beautiful you look when you come undone. Come all over my face and fingers. Come for me, Acelynn."

The words were the final thing that had her tumbling over the edge, pleasure overpowering her as she let go. Acelynn's eyes rolled to the back of her head, coming hard on my fingers, a strangled scream of my name ringing out in the desert. I was more than positive the entire city of Lovelen could hear her, but neither of us seemed to care. My fingers kept thrusting into her, tongue licking up every last drop of her release. I watched Acelynn closely as she rode out her orgasm. She had her eyes shut tightly, soft pants leaving her swollen lips as she finally came back down from her high and looked toward me.

I pulled my fingers from her pussy, release coating them.

Without any hesitation, I placed both digits between my lips, tongue swirling around the delectable taste of Acelynn. Her breathing hitched as I groaned in pleasure. She didn't know it yet, but she was mine now. My little kitten could hide in the darkest corners of the world, but it still wouldn't be far enough for me not to find her. Acelynn Thorton was mine, and not even heaven or hell could separate us.

CHAPTER TWENTY-FOUR

MY CHEST HEAVED up and down as he gently released me. I laid both hands on the hood of my car, taking a moment to collect my thoughts. A deep blush began to crawl up my face as I looked around the desert landscape. Kaius's knuckles brushed down the side of my face, and I turned my eyes down, not able to meet his intense gaze.

"Still thinking about running, kitten?" A devious smirk played on his lips.

I shook my head at him. There was still a little voice in my head that told me to run as far as I could from this town, but now, in my post-orgasm bliss, I could see that maybe I could survive this. Maybe the man in front of me wasn't the monster I had molded him to be.

There were still so many unanswered questions that needed to be solved, and I would get them—even if it sent me to my grave. Because if the King of Lovelen wanted to drag me to hell with him, then I would gladly burn.

A feral smirk of my own pulled at my lips. "Maybe."

I let out a squeal as Kaius threw me over his shoulder. He

playfully slapped my still-bare ass as he began walking toward his motorcycle. "Keep talking like that and I will fill that smart-ass mouth of yours until you can't choke out a single word."

Hiding in the muscles of his back, I didn't fight against him. After a moment, we arrived at our destination, and Kaius pulled me back over his shoulder to set me on my feet. Without hesitation, he reached down and pulled up my shorts, buttoning them the best he could manage with the tear in them.

"Those were my favorite." I pouted up at him.

Kaius's hands slipped up to my hips, firmly gripping them until he was lifting me up and setting me on his bike. I spread my legs, inviting him closer to me. His lips hovered over mine.

"I will buy you another pair. Hell, I will buy you whatever you want if you promise not to run again."

My hands skim down the fabric of my jean shorts, noticing both my keys and the Polaroids must still be over by the car. I looked up at him through my lashes. "Can you grab the photos? I don't want to leave those here if you are going to call a tow for the car."

Kaius nodded in agreement before turning to walk back toward the vehicle. He turned over his shoulder. "Go in the side bag. There is a sweatshirt in there."

"Why would I need a sweatshirt?" I asked.

The sun may have been setting, but it was still ninety degrees even in the shade in Lovelen.

"Because I would prefer that your ass wasn't on display for all of Lovelen." Kaius peered down the large gaping hole he had made in my pants.

I gasped, my back turning to him as he chuckled. My fingers worked quickly to unbuckle the strap of the side bag and pull it open. On top was a light gray sweatshirt with maroon block letters that said "Arizona State University" across the chest. Before I shut the bag, my eyes caught sight of a vial of bright purple liquid.

Reality came crashing down around me. I had just let Kaius eat me out in the middle of the desert when last night he had killed an innocent man. A burning cold rage filled the pit of my stomach. I would not let myself be manipulated by him. Not when I had him exactly where he should be to destroy him.

What the hell had I been thinking?

My hands lingered over the vial, my mind wandering to a conversation that my brother had once had with my father when they thought I was asleep on the couch.

"Did you hear? That kid in the Knights has been slowly injecting himself every day with a small dose of rattlesnake venom." Alec's soft voice spoke out in the kitchen where he and my father sat. My back was to them from where I lay on the couch. It was late, so neither of them bothered to check if I was awake before speaking freely.

"He is probably trying to build up an immunity," my father's rough voice answered back.

Alec let out a chuckle. "Is that even possible?"

"Vince has been dosed with so many poisons his entire life by his father that he would probably survive the apocalypse with the roaches."

A shiver traveled up my spine. Poisoning your own flesh and blood to ensure they were untouchable was sick.

They had gone on to talk about things with the auto shop after that, as if they hadn't just revealed that someone was using their son as their own personal experiment. The crunch of boots sounded out behind me. I reacted quickly, reaching forward and taking two of the vials from the pouch.

I needed to become immune to the king's favorite poison if I was going to survive him. Just as Kaius reached me, I began to slip the sweatshirt over my head, letting the two vials slide beneath the sleeve with my hand.

"Ready to go, kitten?" Kaius asked, laying a soft kiss on the crown of my head.

I smiled brightly and turned to face him. Leaning in, I brushed my lips against his. "Are you sure you aren't going to get sick of me?"

"Fat chance in hell that happens, Acelynn."

He slammed his lips against mine, holding both the bike and me steady as he devoured me. My hand gripped tight on the hemlock vials as I smiled into the kiss.

CHAPTER TWENTY-FIVE

kaius

BLOOD SPLATTERED *across the training mat as my fist caught the initiate on the nose. He let out a groan as he gripped his face, fingers beginning to become coated in red as the blood gushed out.*

"I think you broke his nose, Kaius." Nolan chuckled lightly before tossing the kid a towel.

The initiate thanked him, pressing the cloth on his face and moving out of the ring. Nolan stepped up, tapping his knuckles up as he went.

I shook my head. "I'm done for today."

"No, you aren't," Nolan argued, bouncing from one foot to the other. "Something is bothering you, and you need to release that on someone who can actually keep up with you."

I scoffed. "And you think that's you?"

Nolan's face darkened at the challenge. "You know it is."

Wiping the sweat from my forehead, I waited for him to make the first move. Nolan struck quickly, holding nothing back. He had always been impatient in the ring, never giving any thought to his moves until he was halfway through the fight. I blocked the punch, then struck back with a powerful jab to where he left his right side exposed. Nolan coughed out at the impact but continued to charge forward, this time clipping my jaw with his fist. I opened and closed my mouth, retreating backward to avoid his next one. We danced around each other, slipping through each attack. With every punch, the anger I was trying to repress from my conversation with Alec began to rise to the surface again.

The helplessness in his tone had struck a chord in me, and I had agreed to his terms—agreed to marry a woman I had only ever met once. The princess of the Death Dealers, Emersyn Spade, would be mine in a week. I had been no older than thirteen when we had met briefly, but what I did remember of the young girl was her bright blue eyes that held onto every word her brother said to her.

The crunch of Nolan's fist slamming into my cheek broke me from the memory. My head snapped back, and I groaned in pain. Brushing my fingers against where he had landed his blow, I sighed. Nolan stepped closer to me, already unwrapping his hands. "What the fuck is wrong with you?"

"Do you remember Alec Spade's younger sister?" I asked, my voice barely above a whisper. Nolan narrowed his eyes at me and nodded once. "What do you remember about her?"

"That she was too innocent to be a club president's daughter." Nolan laughed lightly. "She was sweet, but she also wasn't around a lot. Her parents sent her off to study in some fancy boarding school. Wasn't she named like Emily?"

"Emersyn," I grumbled.

"That's it." Nolan snapped his fingers toward me, the memories beginning to resurface for him. "Why are you asking about her?"

"Alec needs me to marry her," I sighed, running one hand over my face. "And we have to help him kill his father."

Nolan narrowed his eyes at me. "You? Marry the Spade

family princess? Wasn't the entire point of sending her away to protect her from the big bad monsters in this life?"

"It was," I said, reaching between the ring's ropes to grab two water bottles. Tossing one toward Nolan, he caught it and unscrewed the cap to take a long drink. I let the water calm me for a moment before continuing. "But that was before her father got himself in too deep and the Iron Serpents offered him an out that didn't have him buried six feet under."

"He's selling his daughter to the snakes?" Nolan's water bottle hovered in front of his lips. I nodded once. We both knew that the Iron Serpents didn't deal in drugs or weapons. They hadn't for a long time. Their underground sex ring was highly lucrative, and once someone was in it, they never came back. Well, except for one girl, who had escaped right under their noses and was now under my protection.

Dominic, their club's president, had a new wife every few years, and they all wore the same haunted look in their dead eyes. But catching them in the act was like catching smoke. They moved their location around so many times that tracking them was useless. I had tried. Nolan had tried. Hell, we had even tried to get an initiate on the inside, but that was a dead end as well.

"He used the only thing that would get me to agree." I stared down my second with a burning rage. The muscles in Nolan's jaw popped, the fist holding the water bottle clenching tight around the plastic. Water sprayed across the training ring.

"Alec threatened Astoria and is still walking around here without a bullet between his eyes?" Nolan growled out, the tips of his ears beginning to grow red, but I could tell he was trying to keep his rage contained.

"He didn't threaten her." I crossed my arms over my bare chest. "Alec just used the idea of her against me. Asked me if I were in his position, what I would do to keep her safe. The only way to

ensure that Emersyn is protected is an alliance between the Knights and the Death Dealers."

"And the only way that alliance stays in place is if Alec's father is dead." Nolan stared at me blankly.

I nodded once, letting him take in the information. There had been no roundtable meeting on this, and I knew that he was pissed that I had made the decision without him, even if it would have resulted in the same outcome. It was dangerous for us not to trust each other, but this hadn't been about a lack of confidence in Nolan. There just hadn't been time to fuck around about this deal.

Nolan raised a single eyebrow at me, his lips quirking up at the corners. "Do you think he would prefer to be castrated or poisoned?"

"I was thinking both."

"All of our books are off," Astoria grumbled, fiddling with a pencil as she pored over the numbers on the page.

Her light hair was piled up on top of her head in a messy bun, a stark contrast to the dark clubbing dress she was wearing. Nolan's zip-up was pulled over her shoulders, the sleeves bunched up at the ends to ensure she could hold the bar's books properly. She was swimming in the damn thing, but still tried to tell me it was her jacket when I snapped at her to stop stealing Nolan's things.

"Let me see it." I reached out, not taking my eyes off the marriage contract in my left hand.

It had never been signed by Emersyn Spade, and I still wondered what had happened to her. Alec had left to retrieve her from inside his family home the night of the massacre, but then our entire plan had gone up in flames. Literally and figuratively. If she had been in the home when the fire started, there was no way she would have gotten out. But there was also a part of me that had always thought she might have been the one to start it as a distraction to ensure she could get away.

Her body had not been one of which was identified by the police through dental records, which meant she had either run so far from Arizona that no one knew her name or she was living the hell that her brother tried to save her from. She was the one Spade no one knew enough about, and she could have used that to her advantage. Emersyn Spade had been underestimated her entire life, and that night she could have wanted to prove she wasn't the innocent little angel her family had labeled her as.

Astoria leaned forward, handing the book to me. I didn't miss the wince that passed over her. My brows furrowed as I leaned back in my chair. "Is your shoulder still bothering you?"

Astoria's eyes glazed over, but she clenched her jaw, suppressing her emotions just as we had always been taught to. Shaking her head once at me, she rolled her shoulders back. "No. It's fine."

"Asto—" I began, but a knock on my office door cut me off.

Astoria turned over her shoulder. "Come in."

I rolled my eyes at my little sister. Even if I reprimanded her, it wouldn't matter. Astoria was on another level of being independent, and sometimes it worried me. I set the marriage contract upside down on the desk, leaning back in my chair nonchalantly.

The wooden door swung open lightly, and Acelynn's smiling face peered in. She was in a black leather top that laced up the front with a pair of matching pants. The corset style accentuated her breasts, and if my sister wasn't sitting just a few feet away from me, I would have dragged Acelynn into this room and taken my time untying that top with my teeth. A deep blush began to crawl across her skin as she stood under my stare.

Clearing her throat, she turned her attention toward Astoria. "Josie wanted to know if you had ordered any more cocktail napkins? We are out of them behind the bar, and she couldn't find them in the dry storage room."

"No," my sister groaned out. "Give me five minutes, and I will come figure out what we are going to do."

"Okay," Acelynn said, turning to head out of the room.

I eyed how the leather pants hugged her perfect ass before she retreated from my sight. Astoria stood, hand coming out to smack me across the back of the head.

"Ow! What the fuck, Astoria?" I yelled out, my hand reaching up to feel where her metal ring clipped my skull. There was already a bump beginning to form, and I glared toward her.

"Stop eye-fucking my friend," Astoria attempted to whisper-yell at me, but failed miserably.

I shrugged nonchalantly at the suggestion. She would find out soon enough that I was doing much more than eye-fucking her so-called friend. If I had my way, after we got back to the bar yesterday, I would have spent hours getting to know every inch of her skin. Acelynn was the sweetest drug I had ever taken, and if I didn't have responsibilities, I would still be buried between her legs—an addict seeking my fix.

Astoria's jaw dropped, eyes wide with the sudden realization. "YOU DIDN'T!"

I flinched at the volume of her high-pitched voice. Her mouth opened and closed, but nothing came out. I chuckled lightly. "I don't know what you are talking about, baby sis."

"You slept with Acelynn!" She pointed an accusing finger toward where the girl had just been before standing upright and slamming her hands down on my desk, sending random papers flying across the space.

Rolling my eyes at her dramatics, I stood to match her stance. Astoria waved a finger at me. "I swear on everything that you love, Kaius Mordred, if you run her off, I will cut it off." Her glance downward had me gulping at the suggestion. "Then we won't have an employment issue."

The door swung open again, this time revealing a very amused Nolan. Stepping into the room, he shoved the door shut with his foot. "I hope you know that every single person in this bar just heard that."

"Fucking hell, Astoria," I groaned, running one hand over my temples. That meant Acelynn heard her tantrum, and I am sure she was standing behind the bar, mortified. I would make it up to her later.

Astoria shot me another glare. "I'm serious, Kaius. Don't mess this up."

"I hadn't planned on it," I snapped at her.

Astoria's eyes softened at that, and I opened my mouth to apologize to her, but she cut me off with a small smile.

"You actually like her, don't you?" Astoria's voice was gentle as she spoke.

I nodded once, not really knowing how to articulate the way Acelynn made me feel. It was unlike anything I had ever experienced. One second, I wanted to rip into her for that smart mouth of hers, and the next, I couldn't imagine my life without her. Every thought since she had flown into the roundtable was consumed with her. Her pretty hazel eyes. The little sounds she made when I kissed that spot on her collarbone. And that damn brilliant smile. I could stare for hours and never tire of it. Astoria whipped around to Nolan. "Have you ever seen him like this?"

Nolan shook his head. "Don't drag me into this, Tor."

"Nolan," she shouted, and I could practically see the pouty lip she was shooting at him.

Nolan sighed, throwing his head back like he was praying to whatever force was out there to give him the strength to resist my sister.

"No, I haven't seen him like this." Nolan flashed me a sympathetic smile. I shot him a dark look, causing him to throw his hands up in surrender and begin to back up toward the door. "I'm just telling her the truth. You have been different since Acelynn arrived, and it's refreshing to see you not so grumpy all the time."

"I wasn't grumpy," I protested, settling back down in my seat and casting my eyes downward to the club's books again. "Don't you two have some cocktail napkins to handle?"

The two of them shuffled out of the room, but before the door shut, Astoria poked her head back in with a bright smile plastered across her face. "I really am happy for you, Kaius. If anyone deserves to find someone, it's you."

CHAPTER TWENTY-SIX

acelynn

THE LIGHTS of the bar were making the pounding headache I had behind my eye pulse. I had taken a small dose of hemlock this morning, letting the drug enter my bloodstream little by little. After two hours, I had taken the full tiny vial and had paid the price. My body had rejected the substance, causing intense pain through my limbs and hallucinations of shapes dancing across my ceiling.

I had lain on my kitchen floor, staring at the shadows floating across the ceiling until they finally faded hours later. The entire time, I had the spade necklace clutched in my hand to ensure that if I felt any inkling that my body was shutting down, I could press the button that lay within. But now all I was left with was a piercing pain in my head and the want to sleep off this hangover.

My hands meticulously cut the lime slices for the night, trying my best not to make eye contact with Josie, who had been curiously looking at me since Astoria outed her suspicions of Kaius and my activities behind closed doors. Or not so closed doors if you count the car. The office's entrance creaked open before Nolan and Astoria bounded out of it. I tensed, waiting for Astoria to yell at me for being involved with her brother. Even if we hadn't slept together yet, we were still playing with fire.

"So did we figure out the napkin debacle?" Astoria shoved her hip into mine.

I watched her from the corner of my eye as she removed the ponytail from her bun and let her blond locks effortlessly fall down her back. She had a bright smile on her face, and not a drop of anger rolled off her.

"Uh, yeah. Josie was able to find one last box shoved behind something in the storage room," I mumbled under my breath and set down the knife on the bar top. Turning toward her, "Look, Astoria, I am sorry—"

"There is no need to apologize, Acelynn," Astoria cut me off, hand coming to rest on my shoulder. A teasing smile played on her lips. "I think you are perfect for my brother. You don't put up with his shit, and there is just something about the two of you together. It makes sense. It's almost like magic."

"Don't get all sappy on me," I said, laughter spilling from both of us.

Astoria squeezed my shoulder. "He wanted to see you before we got slammed. Probably wants to apologize for my outburst."

"He doesn't have to do that. We would have gotten caught sooner or later," I said, wiping my hands against the cloth next to the limes. "Are you sure you aren't going to need me?"

She shook her head, lightly shoving me toward her brother's office. "Nope. Josie and I will hold down the fort until you're back. Won't we, Josie?"

"If we must," Josie's sarcastic tone called over her

shoulder at us. She shot me a playful look as if she was in on some sort of joke that I was not. Rolling my eyes, I began making my way back to the office, butterflies dancing in my stomach.

"Oh, wait, Acelynn," Astoria's voice called me back to her. I turned on my heel, her once sparkling eyes now holding a lethal edge that I had never seen before.

"Yeah?"

"The boys had me clean out your car before they sent it to the mechanic in town. I put all your things in a duffel in my room." Astoria's voice was still bright and cheery, which made my stomach drop.

I didn't let the fear pumping through my veins show on my face. If she had found that last Polaroid in my car, that means she knew I was involved in some way with Parsons and Watson. But if that was the case, why wasn't I already six feet under? Why hadn't she ratted me out to Nolan or her brother? She didn't owe me anything.

She continued, "You can grab it after your shift."

I nodded once, shooting her a soft smile. "Thanks, Astoria. I appreciate that."

"It was no problem." She cocked her head to the side, examining. "Us club girls have to stick together. Isn't that right?"

"Always," I said, voice cracking slightly. The blood had drained from my face, and I hoped the dim bar lighting camouflaged that. Before she could say anything else, I turned on my heel and headed toward the office.

Maybe Kaius didn't really want to speak to me. If Astoria had shown him the third Polaroid, then maybe this was a ploy to get me away from the crowd. No one would hear me scream over the bass of the music, and one dose of hemlock wasn't going to save me. If I confessed every sin I had made, every dark childhood horror I had witnessed, would he spare me? Find pity in the poor Spade daughter who just wanted answers. My hands shook as I reached for the brass handle of the door, hesitating for a moment before pushing directly in without knocking.

Kaius's sharp eyes snapped up to mine. They softened in recognition as I closed the door behind me, fingers tracing the lock for a moment before latching it shut. He didn't seem upset. Maybe he didn't know.

"What are you doing?" Kaius's words were rough, drawing me farther into the room until I was standing to his left.

My eyes wandered around the space. I had been in his office only once before tonight, when I asked for his help with the snake, but I hadn't taken in the space that night. The room was painted a dark shade of gray and was illuminated by four low, light gold sconces on either side of the walls. A long, deep brown wooden desk stretched out at the back of the space, and Kaius lounged behind it in a black leather chair.

Two smaller plush chairs sat in front of the desk, and little gold metal upholstery tacks lined the edge of its dark leather. Kaius turned in his chair, hand reaching out to pull me in between his legs and the desk. The room whispered of power. The kind of power I had to dismantle from the inside out. This wasn't only about my family anymore. This was pure survival. There was no world in which I could hide from the King of Lovelen, even if he no longer held the crown.

"Your sister said you wanted to speak to me before we got busy." I peered at him through my lashes.

His brows furrowed slightly, causing me to chuckle.

"I am guessing that was a lie."

"It was." Kaius's fingers toyed with the strings of my top. "But I am not complaining."

Neither was I—not outwardly. But on the inside, I felt the thrill of control slip into place like a blade being sheathed. I hummed lightly. A burst of confidence rushed through me as I eased back just enough to drop to my knees. They hit the hardwood floor in front of his chair, and he arched one brow at my actions but didn't move to stop me.

I reach up, unbuckling his belt before unzipping his jeans and tugging his already rock-hard dick out for me. Wrapping my hand around his base, I gave him one last look before I closed my mouth over his tip, sucking lightly. My tongue glided along his shaft, licking up the generous amount of pre-cum, lubricating his dick with every pass, each stroke and swirl of my tongue calculated. He probably thought this was a repayment for what we did yesterday. But every gasp, every buck of his hips was another way I was getting him to fall into my trap.

Kaius's breath hitched in the back of his throat, causing satisfaction to fill me. His fingers threaded into my hair as I worked my mouth up and down him. His cock was so large, filling my mouth fully, and what I couldn't fit, I had my fingers wrapped around, pumping him torturously slow.

A low groan filled my ears, and I glanced up at him through hooded eyes to find his blazing stare looking back into mine. Keeping my gaze on his, I let my teeth scrape down his soft skin. Kaius threw his head back, silent curses finding their way to his lips.

He pushed my head down, his cock hitting the back of my throat, causing me to gag for a second before he let up. I let him do it once more. It made him think he was in control. Because the more power he felt now, the harder it would hit when I took it from him. "Come on, kitten. I know you can take me fully. Breathe through your nose."

It shouldn't have, but the command turned me on like nothing else, and I found myself submitting to him as he fucked my mouth. Tears poured down my face as he continued to use me for his own pleasure.

"Oh fuck. That's a good girl." Kaius breathed out. His hips bucked in time with his hand's movements, forcing more of his dick down my throat as I gagged and choked. "Look at me with those pretty eyes."

I stared up at him with wide eyes, inciting another moan from him. With one more forceful shove, he came, letting the hot liquid hit the back of my throat. He slipped out of my mouth as I swallowed his cum, the thickness sliding down my throat. Letting him see the devotion he wanted to believe in. Letting him think I was his.

Kaius released my hair, his thumb coming to clean up a string of drool that had landed on my chin. As he swiped upward, I brought his thumb between my lips, circling my tongue around the soft pad of his skin. He groaned, "If you don't stop that, we will never leave this room."

Kaius pulled his thumb from my mouth with a pop, and I smiled up at him. "I wouldn't be complaining."

I stood once again, but before I could get to my full height, he gripped the strings on my top between my breasts and dragged me in for a long kiss. Moaning against his lips, I leaned in further involuntarily, cursing myself for liking the feeling of his lips on mine, but he pulled away.

With a knowing smirk, he quipped, "Clean up your face, kitten, and then get back to the bar. We don't want someone to come looking for us."

CHAPTER TWENTY-SEVEN

KAIUS LEFT me to get cleaned up with a simple kiss to the lips. I smiled as if I were obeying. But inside, I was already counting down the moments I could drop the façade. My fingers swiped at the smudged mascara on my face as I tried to even out my makeup the best I could in the reflection of his computer monitor.

Luckily, it would be dark enough in the bar that no one would truly notice. Stepping back, something crunched under the heel of my boot. I peered down, finding a simple sheet of cream-colored paper. Reaching down, I picked it up, ready to place it on the desk, but the dark inked letters had me frozen in place. It was a marriage certificate. My heart sank as I continued reading.

This certifies
Kaius Julian Mordred and Emersyn Ryan Spade
were united in marriage on
June 18th, 2025

The date of the Death Dealers massacre sent a shiver down my spine. All the other lines were left blank and unsigned. I stepped back, my thighs hitting the edge of the desk chair. My chest felt heavy, like an invisible weight was pressing down on it, suffocating me with its intensity. Every breath in felt like an uphill battle, shallow and jagged, as the air in my lungs refused to enter. My mind was spiraling out of control, a whirlwind of fear and questions tearing its way through it.

Why was my given name placed on a marriage certificate to Kaius? I was never told I was going to be married off, and even though it was not uncommon in my family line of business, Alec would have warned me. Images of the days leading up to the massacre flashed before my eyes, and I tried to scrutinize every sentence he said to me. Every slight tic of his brow or scowl that crossed his face, because there was no way my brother would have hidden this from me.

Settling down in the seat, I desperately tried to find some sort of relief to the burning sensation in my lungs. But it was no use. The walls seemed to be closing in around me, trapping me in a suffocating embrace. My heart pounded in my chest, a relentless beat echoing in my ears. Tears began to well up in my eyes as I struggled to find something to ground me.

It felt like I was drowning on dry land, engulfed by a sea of panic and terror I had never felt before. My hands were shaking uncontrollably as I clutched the armrests of the chair, searching for something, anything, in my memories to anchor me to a reality that made sense. The world continued to spin around me, a blur of colors and shapes that had me wanting to vomit. I was trapped in a nightmare of my own past, and if Kaius knew who I was from the beginning, I might as well have just been a mouse being played with by a cat.

Gripping my hands into fists, I dug my fingernails into my palms, cutting into the skin. The pain distracted me just enough for me to calm my breathing. I had to pull myself together and get back to work because there was a good chance Kaius had never seen what I once looked like. I had done a good job of purging myself from the internet, leaving no trace of the blonde-haired, blue-eyed Emersyn Spade behind. Now I was only Acelynn Thorton, and I had to play the role if I wanted the answers I was owed.

It was a typical Saturday night at the Queen's Table. The bar was packed wall to wall, and I wasn't even sure if it was even in code to have this many people in the space. I had avoided getting up on the bar to dance for most of the night, but it was getting to the point that Astoria was constantly asking if something was wrong. I had tried to put on a brave face, but even Kaius, who was standing with Nolan and Vincent near the pool table room, was shooting me worried glances.

A new country song blared through the speakers, and Astoria shot me a hopeful look that I would join her on the bar. I sighed, knowing we had been practicing this line dance all week, and I was going to have to either get up there to perform or break Astoria's heart. Quickly, I bounded up the steps to the top of the bar, letting Astoria pull me into the middle of it. She knocked her hip with mine slightly before we began the simple movements. I threw my head back laughing as we moved our hips in a circle, spinning once before continuing the footwork we had perfected.

There was something about dancing on this bar that

freed me from every worry in the world. No more thoughts of dead family members or the rival clubs that mowed them down. No more thoughts of being married off or getting caught by your supposed fiancé for betraying him. No more thoughts at all.

Astoria's frightened yell pulled me from the routine, and I looked down to see a drunken man gripping her left ankle. She tried to kick and squirm away from his touch, but he firmly yanked, sending her toppling into the crowd.

"Hey! What the hell are you doing?" I cried out, jumping into the swarm of people after her.

I could hear her still screaming over the music, and I followed the sound of her voice. Two men had her held between them, their cruel laughter drawing even more of a crowd around them. I shoved my way through the mass of people until I was right in front of one of them. Before I realized what I was doing, my fist swung up and clipped one of the men in the side of his face. He spun around, eyes going over my head and to another person behind me. I jumped out of the way just in time as he tackled the other patron, and before I knew it, the bar was in full chaos. Punches and screams rang out in the space. The music was cut short, making it much easier to hear them.

"Astoria," I screamed.

She turned to look at me, eyes filled with fear.

I reached out. "Grab my hand."

She had to slightly jump to lace her fingers with mine, but once I had a tight grip on her, I ripped Astoria forward. She tumbled through the crowd and slammed into me.

"Watch out." Her wide eyes stared at something behind me.

I turned just in time for a woman with a bright orange top to land a hit against the side of my skull. A cry broke through my lips, and the entire room began to spin. Astoria gripped my shoulders tightly as my body started to sway from side to side. I could barely hear her screaming for Nolan or Kaius as blood pounded in my ears.

My eyes felt heavy, wanting nothing more than to fall into the endless darkness that called to me when Kaius's green eyes appeared in front of me, and suddenly, I was in his arms as he shoved through the fight. I snuggled into his chest, breathing in his scent to calm my racing heart. Kaius's angered voice barked out an order to someone, but the words were disjointed in my mind.

"You can't go to sleep, kitten," Kaius's soft tone called down to me.

The only response I could make was a light whine. His hand lightly slapped the side of my face, and I snapped open my eyes to glare at him.

A slight chuckle slipped from his lips. "There you are, pretty girl. Now don't close them again. Keep your eyes on me."

"You're bossy," I grumbled, eyes tracking the space we had ventured into. I was sitting on the side of one of the three pool tables in the game room.

The glass pane windowed doors were shut, closing in Kaius, Astoria, Nolan, and me in the room. He tweaked the edge of my chin, shooting me a quick wink before turning over his shoulder to meet Nolan's gaze.

"I got them." Nolan nodded once toward the door. "Go handle that shitshow."

Kaius looked back at me once before he stalked out the doors. I sighed, lowering myself so I was lying back against the pool table. The thumping of the club's bass shook the black crystal chandelier above me.

"Here," Astoria's voice called over me before a bag full of ice landed in the center of my chest.

I hissed out at the contact it made with my skin before grasping it in my hand and lifting it to the bump forming on my head.

Astoria chuckled. "This is not how I expected the night to go."

"I don't know," I grumbled. "This seems pretty up to par with my current luck."

I turned to look at her, causing both of us to burst out laughing. It was the type of laughter that you could only get with your best friend. The one where it made your stomach hurt because you couldn't stop once you began. I hadn't laughed this way for years, and I had missed it. Astoria was beginning to heal a piece of me long since gone, and I was incredibly grateful for her. Even if she was now in possession of that image, it was clear she wasn't going to use it against me. Or maybe she didn't even find it.

Tears began to collect in the corners of my eyes as we curled into each other, our hysterical laughter filling the room. Hell, even Nolan had joined in with us. And I realized that this is what it felt like to truly belong somewhere. To feel at home.

CHAPTER TWENTY-EIGHT

acelynn

A POUNDING on my door startled me awake. I groaned as the pain in my head intensified as it continued. There were people just leaving for work when I arrived home from my shift. Kaius had fussed over the bump on my forehead for hours, but had reluctantly let me go home after my begging began to become pathetic. He had sent Vincent to sweep my house for any weak spots yesterday, which made it easier to convince him that I could handle going home to sleep and shower.

I turned over, looking at the time on my phone. The light of my phone screen burned my eyes, causing me to squint at the device. The white block letters read 8:00 a.m., which meant I had only been asleep for less than an hour and a half before whoever was banging on my door disturbed me. Maybe they would just go away if I ignored them.

After another minute of the knocking, I threw my blankets from my body and made my way down the hall to the front door. I peered through the peephole to see who was behind the door and came upon Watson.

I slid the lock open and cracked the door. He stood there, uniform crisp and pressed as always. The morning sky was dark from the storm, rain lightly pelting down. A slight chill filtered through the door, causing me to shiver. Watson's eyes flicked over my shoulder, as if expecting someone else to emerge from the shadows behind me.

"Morning," he said, voice too cheery for it being this early.

"Either you're here to arrest me or something worse," I muttered, stepping aside to invite him into the house. The last thing I needed was someone spotting us speaking.

He walked past me, and I shut the door behind us. From the pocket of his dark jacket, he pulled out a small, battered flip phone.

Watson held it out. "Take this."

I eyed the device. "Why do I need another one?"

"The other one was compromised. Don't use it unless you absolutely have to. But my suggestion would be to snap the damn thing and toss it in the canal if you still have it."

I wrapped my fingers around the phone, feeling its weight in my palm. Something in the pit of my stomach told me that Watson wasn't being entirely truthful about the other burner, but I trusted him enough to take the device and hide it better than the last one.

"Thanks for the heads up," I said, slipping the phone into my sweatpants. Watson lingered in the hall, eyes darting to the small window next to the door.

"You ever wonder," he began slowly. "How certain people in this city manage to stay one step ahead of the raids, the warrants, the occasional 'accidental' evidence leaks. Hell, even the occasional breaking and entering?"

I folded my arms over my chest, shoulders shrugging slightly. "Thought they just got lucky."

Watson's mouth curved into a smirk. "It's never luck. It's inside help. The Lovelen Police Department has more cracks than a broken teacup. And I recently connected the dots that every one of those leaks led back to one person. A person who surprisingly has come into quite a large sum of money recently."

"Parsons?" I asked, raising one eyebrow in question. It wasn't a surprise to me. I had suspected it for a while that the older detective wasn't entirely truthful with his quest for the Knights' takedown. Without them in control of most of the territory, they had the final say when it came to the drug distribution.

Watson nodded solemnly. "He takes his orders from somewhere else but is still getting a cut and the power he craves from the leaks. Parsons will wear the badge when it gets him through a door, but the second the badge becomes a liability, he's just another hired gun. He isn't doing the Knights' dirty work, which makes me think he was working for your father at one point and now has switched loyalties to another club. But this mission to destroy Kaius and the Knights has to come from the loss of that big cut he got from the Death Dealers."

My stomach turned at the truth. My father had always had a dirty cop on the inside to ensure they could stir the narrative away from the club when he needed it. But the thought that someone as slimy as Parsons had been that person made me sick.

"And no one else in the department has noticed?" I asked, praying that he would say an internal affairs case had been initiated for Parsons, and his warning was just a precaution.

"They've noticed," Watson responded flatly. "They are either on the payroll too or too scared to make any moves against him. Parsons is untouchable, and he knows it. That's dangerous. It's not just that he's corrupt, but that he is comfortable in being that way. He'll feed you to whatever monster with the biggest check without even blinking."

I nodded once. Maybe it wasn't the Knights who had orchestrated the destruction of the Death Dealers. But that didn't explain why Kaius had been standing over Alec's body that night, taunting him until he put a bullet in his head. Didn't explain the marriage certificate. And most definitely didn't explain why my brother had made me light the damn house up in flames that night.

"Alec," I screamed over the gunfire. My socked feet skidded against the tile floor, praying that the rain of bullets didn't catch up to me. I turned down the main hallway of our home, body slamming into someone's chest. I let out a screech, swinging at the man, but he caught my wrist in his hand.

"Emersyn, hey." A familiar voice soothed me, but I continued to fight against their hold. "It's me. It's Alec."

I froze, eyes finding the matching blue ones of my brother. Slamming one final slap to his chest, I whispered, "What in the fuck is going on?"

"A rival club is trying to patch over the Death Dealers." Alec's gaze traveled above my head, watching for any threat that might come our way. "And they are doing a damn good job at it."

"Who?" My voice shook in fear.

I had heard of this happening to other clubs, and most of the time, there wasn't a soul left to remember them. My stomach dropped as I took in my older brother. Blood and dirt covered his skin, and bruises blended in with the dark ink he had obtained over the years. This wasn't good, and I knew that. Tonight, the Death Dealers would fall.

"The Knights of Lovelen," Alec spat out between clenched teeth. "I asked them for help, not for a damn massacre."

My eyebrows knitted together. "What do you mean you went to them for help?"

"It's not important." Alec's glare landed on me, and a fear that I had never felt when it came to him filled the pit of my stomach. This version of my brother was not the loving and kind man I had grown up with. This was a dark predator ready to take on anyone who stepped in his way. Even the little sister he had always protected.

I tried to dodge Alec as he lashed out, but he caught me by the shoulder, slamming my back into the wall beside us. The gallery walls my father had proudly hung up rattled upon impact. The most recent photo of our family on the beach in Mexico flew to the floor. Glass splintered in the frame, and I couldn't help but notice how Alec's smile didn't reach his eyes in the image.

Alec snapped his fingers in front of my face. "You need to listen to me, Emersyn."

I gulped down the burning acid traveling back up my throat and nodded the best I could toward him. He examined me for a moment longer before speaking. "The house needs to burn. I don't care how you do it, but after tonight, our family home needs to be nothing but ash."

"What about—" I began, but Alec's fist slammed into the wall next to my head, cutting off my question. Flinching away from the collision spot, I stared wide-eyed at him. "The house of Spades will be nothing but a distant memory by dawn."

My stomach churned at the memory. There were so many holes in that night I was still trying to piece together, and every time I thought I might be closer to those answers, something else had me doubting my narrative. But there was one thing I was sure of—I needed to grow my immunity to hemlock, no matter if I was found out. It might be my only leg up against Kaius and Parsons.

"I need something else, but it's not exactly legal," I said, watching Watson for any hesitation.

"None of what we are doing is exactly legal right now, Acelynn. What do you need?" he asked, eyes sharpening as he waited for my reply.

"Hemlock." I didn't bother to beat around the bush. "I would prefer it in liquid form like the Knights use, but I understand if you can only get it in the plant form."

For a second, something unreadable passed over his face, a mixture between concern and calculation.

"I don't think I can get you either. The plant doesn't grow in the desert, and I am pretty sure the only one who has the facilities to do so is Vincent," Watson said.

I cursed under my breath.

He ran a hand over his jaw. "But there has been talk about a basement under the Queen's Table. It's where they keep the supply for when they need it. No one gets in unless they are trusted, and even then, it is rare that you see anyone but Kaius, Nolan, or Vincent emerge from there."

My thoughts flashed back to the first night I met Astoria. She had mentioned the basement and probably didn't think I would think anything of the comment. But it made sense. Where else did they go when they wanted the torture to be long and drawn out? There was no way they could interrogate someone behind the bar without getting caught.

"The Knights stash a lot down there," Watson continued. "If they don't want the world to see it, then it's hidden below ground. Poisons, relics, old records—all the Knights' dirty little secrets stored for their eyes only."

"And you don't know where the entrance would be?"

He shook his head. "No. I have only heard whispers of it from other detectives. But it is somewhere under the bar. The other bunker is in their nightclub, the Excalibur, and I don't think they store even a fraction of their items there in case of a raid."

My fingers drummed against my thigh, mind wandering to the secrets that the basement held in it. I knew I had to get in there to take the hemlock, but maybe there were also answers I needed stored away there too. I smiled devilishly at Watson. "Sounds like a fun field trip."

His eyes narrowed. "If you go looking for the basement, make sure you are alone. I mean, bar completely empty. If you get caught, you might never get back out."

With that, he headed for the door, leaving behind the faint scent of rain-soaked wool and the uncomfortable knowledge that the line between ally and enemy was thinner than I once thought.

CHAPTER TWENTY-NINE

THE ALLEY behind the Queen's Table was quiet as a grave and just as welcoming. Even though the sun was barely up, it already felt like I had stepped into an oven. The air was thick with the stale taste of last night's beer and the sour bite of pee. To the left of the warped emergency exit door, there was an outdoor AC unit working overtime, humming like a sleeping animal. Across from the door was a large industrial trash can that smelled like it hadn't been picked up in weeks.

I kept close to the shadows, even though I knew there were no cameras overhead. I had checked yesterday when I took the garbage out at the end of my shift.

Watson's words still lingered in the back of my mind—*There's a basement. Vince keeps the hemlock stocked in there. Don't get caught.*

I moved farther down the alleyway, coming upon the two stainless steel doors that almost blended into the darkness the brick walls cast over them. The padlock was fresh, the brass clean from the constant handling, which meant this wasn't a forgotten item. Someone had been down here recently. But they weren't there now.

I knew Kaius and Vince were gone for the day. He had told me last night that they had to make a trip down to the border to negotiate the movement of the Muze that was being brought in. It was a larger one than normal, and I knew Kaius didn't trust anyone to handle it but himself. Astoria was with Nolan. They had left for his house to try to get some sort of sleep before coming back here to open the bar later tonight. And Josie...well, I didn't actually know where she was, but it wasn't in the bar or one of the dorms. She had made it clear that she didn't have a room here, but wouldn't elaborate on where she called home.

I slipped the pick from my pocket, the metal cold and familiar against my fingers. Working one end into the lock, I coaxed the tumblers into place until I heard a faint click. A sharp thrill rushed through me as I undid the chains around the handle and eased them open, the hinges moaning in protest until they were just wide enough to slip inside. The stairs dropped into pure darkness.

The air was heavy, cool, and faintly damp. The mix of rust, dust, and something sharper, like leaves or bitter roots, filled my nose. I switched on my phone's flashlight, letting the beam of light carve out a path for me through the dark. I reached the bottom of the stairs. The basement was small, with a long wood workspace table taking up most of the space. Surrounding the table were shelves lined with glass bottles and small jars filled with strange substances. Handwritten labels curled at edges, indicating what was in each container.

Powdered nightshade. Belladonna extract. Snake venom.

My eyes scanned each row, taking in every deadly thing

just in the small space. I turned to look over my shoulder, coming upon another steel door. It was clear that it led into a man-made room. A place where their victims went to die.

Finally, after a moment, I found what I was looking for. Three shelves down, dead center, was a full row of the beautiful purple liquid I was searching for. My pulse quickened because I was coming to realize that this wasn't just about replenishing my supply. It wasn't about building immunity. This was protection. I knew what a lethal dose looked like, and if I needed to protect myself, I had a means to do it.

My fingers brushed against the vials before I began to gather four of them, making sure to take from the back to hide the fact that any were missing from the naked eye. Tucking them into the pockets of my jeans for safekeeping, I made sure they were secure. My skin was itching to get out of here before someone came down those stairs. But I had to see if any of their other sins were hidden here.

I moved toward the metal door behind me, pushing through it and coming into the room of horrors. The walls were pure concrete, and there was a rusty drain in the center of the room. At least I prayed that the color was from rust, but I had a sick feeling it wasn't. A single folding chair sat over top of the drain, the legs bolted into the ground to ensure the person sitting in it would stay put. I gagged at the stench emanating from the room. It reminded me of the smell of burning flesh.

Stumbling out of the room, I scanned the space behind the table, coming upon crates stamped with what appeared to be false shipping labels. As I picked one up, I could hear the faint rattling of loose ammunition. A battered metal filing cabinet, worn from age, was pressed into the corner of the room. It was the only thing that didn't look like it belonged in this place. I moved quickly, ripping open the top drawer. My flashlight's beam caught on something scrawled across the top drawer in red paint.

A spade.

The sight hit me low in my gut, a cold recognition that made my hands clench. I plucked the manila folder out from the crammed space. While this folder was relatively small, others were so full that the seams were splitting. A few of them bore names I didn't know, but all I cared about was the one with my family name. Inside the folder, they were separated by tags. One for me, one for my brother, and one for each of my parents.

I tabbed through them, crime scene photos I had never seen spilling into the beam of my flashlight. Angles of the charred house I hadn't been allowed to re-enter. A bloody handprint was smeared across the white fridge in the kitchen. My mother's fingers were visible beneath a linen sheet. My throat tightened, but I forced myself to flip through every single page. Witness every single image and burn them into my brain. My family's deaths would not be forgotten.

The police reports were riddled with black bars—entire paragraphs redacted. It made my blood boil. What were they trying to cover up? Witness statements had large red stamps across them that read "WITHHELD." At the back of my father's tab, there was a single loose photo.

Detective Parsons was standing in my family's front yard the night of the massacre, a sick smile spread across his face. My chest went cold. It felt like someone had ripped my heart from it. I slammed the file shut, barely registering that my breathing had gone shallow and quick.

A faint creak sounded from the bar above. I froze, every

muscle locking up. Before I could even think, I was racing up the stairs and out of the basement. My movements were sloppy as I shut the double metal doors tight and locked them back into place. Then I fled from the alley, not looking back to see if I had been caught.

CHAPTER THIRTY

kaius

RAIN FELL IN SHEETS, *hammering against the rows of black umbrellas like drumbeats. The Lovelen graveyard was a patchwork of cracked stones and leaning monuments, the type of place where, over time, names were forgotten but the haunted lies never were. I was surprised to see how dark the sky had been when I stepped outside. It wasn't typical for it to rain this hard in early May. But Mother Nature had decided she would mirror the heartbreak that was ripping through the Knights.*

My boots sank into the sodden ground with each step, water pooling in the depressions left by mourners before me. The coffin was deep mahogany stained nearly black. It was already halfway lowered into the grave, the Knights' symbol that was carved into the top standing out as water collected in the divots, as if the symbol refused to let go of the man inside.

Surrounding the grave stood the core of the Lovelen club and their families. Men and women dressed in black, their faces a mask of studied restraint. Some lowered their heads in genuine grief. Others kept their chins up, eyes darting between the living, avoiding the casket altogether. In the Knights, a funeral wasn't just for the dead—it was about taking stock of who remained and who could be next.

Detective Parsons of the Lovelen PD was here. His tan trench coat's collar pulled high against his neck, gaze not fixed on the grave but on Nolan from across the crowd. Astoria clung to Nolan as he held an umbrella over her, not letting a drop of rain touch my sister. Her eyes were transfixed on the coffin, haunted and distant as if she was reliving the events of the past month over and over again. She pulled her injured arm closer, the dark-blue sling blending into her dress.

I moved my gaze back to Parsons. It seemed off that a detective was here at a private funeral, but my father had too much pride in him to have Parsons removed. I caught a flicker of a nod pass between Parsons and Nolan. Too subtle for most to notice, but if I had, my father most certainly did. He noticed everything.

And by the red color creeping up the back of his neck, he had seen the entire thing. Standing tall at the head of the grave, his suit immaculate despite the weather, he didn't bother a second glance at the coffin. His gaze swept the crowd like a blade, lingering just long enough to make the person shift uncomfortably before moving on. When my father's eyes found me through the rain, they held a silent order.

Follow me.

I broke away from the crowd just as the priest had instructed the mourners into the beginning lyrics of a hymn. The background noise faded as we crossed the cemetery in silence, boots crunching on wet gravel until we reached our family's mausoleum.

The structure rose from the far corner of the graveyard like a sentinel carved from shadows, its stone walls weathered from years of the harsh weather conditions, but still its commanding presence remained. Unlike the plain, tilting headstones around it, this structure was built to be remembered—a testament to the wealth, lineage, and a stubborn refusal to be forgotten my father had instilled in the Knights.

Tall fluted columns framed its arched entrance, each etched with intricate carvings of swords, chalices, and swirling lines. Curling ivy and hemlock crawled around the columns like a silent warning to anyone passing by. The door was a heavy slab of wrought iron, its once black surface now dulled to gunmetal. At its center was the Knights' crest. It was sharp to the touch, as if it had been carved to endure long after flesh and blood had rotted away.

The roof was domed and crowned with a weathered statue—an angel with downcast eyes and wings spread wide. Through time and the beating sun, the face had worn into something unreadable.

This was the kind of place that didn't just hold the dead—it kept our secrets too.

As we stepped inside, the air changed. It was cold enough to bite, and the scent of candle wax and old stone was thick. My father shut the door behind us, and the sudden quiet felt heavier than the rain outside.

"You saw it," he said. It wasn't a question.

I leaned against the marble wall behind me, letting the flickering candlelight throw shadows across his face. "Saw what?"

I knew my ignorance would irritate him, but I didn't much care. Not when it came to Nolan. He stepped closer, water dripping off the tips of his suit jacket and pooling at his feet. "There were too many eyes on each other and not on the grave. Too many hands buried in their pockets, like they've got something to hide."

He took a deep breath, slow and deliberate. I didn't dare speak when he was explaining what he observed. My father continued, "The Knights have always had many enemies outside these walls, Kaius, but the ones who will ruin us will come from the inside."

His words were like the sound of a lock turning, a truth that was obvious to all but never spoken. It was unsettling to hear.

"We are an empire built on loyalty." He began to pace down the narrow aisle between the stone crypts. "It is the only thing that keeps the blood from staining our hands. You break that rule, you're not just betraying a man. No, you are betraying centuries of tradition. You're pissing on the graves of every Knight who gave his life for the club. To keep the secrets that continue their legacy."

The way he said it, loyalty wasn't just a rule in the Knights of Lovelen, it was a religion. Something you worshipped over in the dark of your room when you questioned if it was worth continuing on with the club life. Not that I had a choice in leaving. I was born a Knight, and I would die one as well.

My father stopped pacing, his eyes locking on mine. They were hard and unyielding. He made a slow slicing motion across his throat. "Nolan is already dead. He just hasn't realized it yet."

He turned his back to me, studying the nameplates on the wall as though they might whisper advice for him to follow. "There is a rot in the foundation, Kaius. It's slow, but it's spreading. Parsons is too cozy with Nolan, and Nolan's debts aren't to us anymore. Sooner or later, one of them is going to test the limits of the Knights. And when they do..." He let the words hang like a blade suspended in the air.

I didn't let him finish the sentence. The rain was louder when I stepped outside, running cold down my neck and spine. Funerals in Lovelen were never just farewells. They were warnings. I knew it then, standing in that graveyard with my father's voice still echoing in my mind. The Knight we had just buried wasn't the only one fated for the dirt.

CHAPTER THIRTY-ONE

kaius

THE DOOR to the back hall of the bar slammed hard enough to rattle the glassware. Nolan strode in, jaw set, and the veins in his neck standing out like cords.

"It's gone," he said, voice low but tight. "I searched all over that damn room, but the hemlock is missing again. That is a total of ten bottles in less than a week just gone."

I didn't look up right away from the decanter in my hand, finishing pouring the whiskey and setting the glass down on the polished bar top separating us. "Gone? Are we positive?"

Nolan scoffed at me. "Of course, I am sure. You know how Vince is about his supply. He practically counts it every hour."

He dragged a hand through his hair, the stress of this showing on his face. I leaned back against the metal drink fridge. There were no cameras down there or in the alley to ensure there was no digital trail of our victims. Whoever was dipping into our hemlock supply knew this. They would have to be close enough to us to know how to evade us and get into the basement undetected. It could be any one of the Knights.

"You seem way too calm about this." Nolan's brows furrowed. "Vince is about to go on a torture spree to get whoever was touching his precious to squeal."

I rolled the glass in my hand, watching the amber liquid catch the dim light. "I'll handle it."

"How?" Nolan questioned me.

I shot him a dark look, but he didn't back down to me. I inclined my head and raised one brow, the conversation ending in words, but Nolan understood what I would not speak aloud.

I watched as Nolan stormed off, the weight of the situation lingering in the air. The basement wasn't just a vault for our deadly secrets. It was meant to be beyond reach, even for most of the Knights. Whoever had taken the hemlock hadn't broken a lock or left an ounce of evidence of who they were. It was as if they were a shadow that had slipped between the cracks of the wooden door, and that made them even more dangerous than them having the hemlock.

This person had broken the unspoken law that bound us all together. And there was only one man alive who could guide me on how to handle this breach. Only one man who understood how truly dangerous this was for all of us.

Alaric Camberly.

Vincent's father was the only elder alive in the Knights of Lovelen. I only sought him out for advice when we were in dire need. He was older than the oaths of the Knights were written. I hated that I had to speak with him, but it was either that or let the stolen poison turn into a full-out war.

CHAPTER THIRTY-TWO

acelynn

DOSING myself with hemlock was getting easier and easier as the days went by. I was still having side effects, but they were beginning to become manageable, giving me the ability to go about my daily life without having to worry about a sudden hallucination.

But as I got better at swiping the hemlock from the basement, I was beginning to get sloppy, taking too many vials too quickly. I had counted all ten vials I had taken last night. Most of them were still completely full, but it brought me a sense of comfort just to have them.

As soon as my feet crossed the threshold of the bar, I knew something was wrong. Nolan, Vince, and Kaius were standing huddled in the hall between the bar and the back rooms. Vince was clearly upset, face red with anger as he harshly whispered toward Kaius.

I strolled over to Josie, who was restocking the straws and napkins slowly, clearly trying to catch any word from the three men.

"What's up with them?" I asked, taking a seat in front of her.

She shrugged once. "Vince seems to think someone is stealing from us, but I checked the books. Everything is accounted for, so I don't know what he is going on about."

My heart sank, sickness rolling through me. Vince wasn't talking about money from the bar being pocketed. He was discussing the hemlock, and soon enough, they would notice the missing file. I needed to return it as soon as possible.

I gulped once. "That's odd. Everything has been adding up for me as well."

"He gets like this sometimes." Josie rolled her eyes. "Vince is a little neurotic when it comes to the club's things. Money, drugs, hell, probably even sex—Vince has a tab on it."

"Acelynn." Kaius's sharp voice had Josie and me both snapping our heads in his direction. He lifted one finger, beckoning me toward the group.

I stood on shaky legs, slowly walking over to where he stood. When I finally got to the group, Kaius slung an arm over my shoulder, dipping down to whisper in my ear.

"I need you to do something for me, kitten," he purred, voice soft as silk and sending my rational thoughts right out the window.

I didn't dare speak, afraid my voice would give me away.

Kaius smirked down at me. "I need you to go pick up a few supplies from the Excalibur tonight. I already spoke to Pierce, and he will have them pulled for you."

"What is it?" I asked quietly. My eyes wandered over to the two other men in the circle.

Nolan had a passive look on his face, his eyes stuck, glaring at the spot above Kaius's head. Vince looked as if he could burn down the entire city of Lovelen with no remorse.

Eyes burning with a fire that made me want to move closer to Kaius. If he suspected it was me who swiped his precious vials, his self-control was unmatched.

Kaius chuckled once, laying a searing kiss to the crown of my head. "Just a few bottles of alcohol Josie noticed we were out of and some paperwork I left in my office there."

"Okay," I breathed out.

It should be simple enough. Just drive to the nightclub the Knights owned, pick up the package, and bring it back here. There shouldn't be any issues.

The Excalibur vibrated with music, a bass pounding through the floor like a second heartbeat. The air was thick with the scent of sweat, spilled alcohol, and a hint of something floral. Red and gold neon lights shone across the mass of bodies and polished wood. I kept my head down, weaving between the bodies pressed close on the dance floor behind a security guard. I could feel eyes watching me, some curious, others wary, but no one stopped me. This was still the Knights' territory—Kaius's domain—which gave me protection, but not enough to let my guard down.

The security guard rapped his fist against the plain black door in the back, the metal "MANAGER'S OFFICE" sign rattling as he went.

A voice inside beckoned us in. The man in front of me pushed the door open, one hand gesturing for me to go in first. I stepped inside the small office, freezing at the sight before me. A woman was bent over the dark desk, cheek pressed into the wood. A large red ball gag protruded from her mouth, and drool pooled out the side onto the surface below her.

A man stood behind her, dick slamming in and out of her. The movement looked painful as he rammed her hips into the desk. One hand was tangled in her dark hair, red streaks woven between his fingertips. She moaned. It was loud, even through the gag. He ripped her head back, causing her to arch into him. Her eyes met mine, but I knew she wasn't truly seeing me, mind too high on pleasure to notice me.

The man, whom I assumed was Pierce, picked up his pace, thrusts becoming sloppy as he neared his release. I couldn't look away, my eyes staring at how they met each other roughly. My mind wandered to how I would look in the same position with Kaius, how he would make me scream for him under the gag, the pleasure that would rock through me. With one final shove, the man groaned as he came, but it was cut off by the shrill wail of the girl.

Pulling himself out of her, he laid one slap against her ass, grinning at how the skin bloomed red. The gagged girl whimpered as he spoke to her. "You're such a good whore for me. Now don't move while I talk to Kaius's new pet."

The praise had my cheeks flaming red. Would Kaius do the same for me? I don't even know why the thought crossed my mind. I wasn't going to let Kaius fuck me, not like that. But the thrill of the idea did make heat pool in my core. The sound of Pierce zipping up his pants had my attention back to him.

"Acelynn," Pierce greeted me, a sadistic smile pulling at his lips.

He was the kind of man who commanded attention without even a second thought. Dark hair slicked back just enough to reveal his sharply defined features. His high cheekbones and strong jaw were dusted with perfectly maintained scruff. Even with a smile, his lips appeared like they held a secret or two. I was almost taken aback by the piercing shade of pale blue eyes that almost appeared gray in some lights. Pierce was wearing a simple dark T-shirt that clung to his broad shoulders and toned chest. Creeping out the top and sleeves was dark ink that covered most of his tanned skin. I had to stop myself from admiring how perfectly his jeans hugged his hips.

Pierce cleared his throat, and my eyes snapped back to his. "You here for the delivery?"

I squared my shoulders, letting my face show the annoyance I was suddenly feeling for this man. He got off on humiliating women, it appeared, and I wasn't going to act like I was okay with that. "No, I thought I would take my turn next."

He barked out a laugh, waving a finger at me. "Not a chance. Kaius would have my balls pinned and framed on the bar wall if I even thought about touching you."

"Kaius doesn't own me," I sneered at him.

"Maybe not yet." Pierce winked at me, his knuckles grazing the spine of the dark-haired girl.

Now that I was getting a good look at her, she reminded me of Josie, without the tattoos. If this girl dyed her red streaks blue, she would almost be the spitting image of her.

Pierce continued, "But you will soon be begging him to tame you. They always do."

"Just give me the package." I thrust my hand out to him. Pierce moved smoothly, dipping below the girl's legs and reappearing with a small brown box. It didn't look big enough to hold the items Kaius had requested of him. "That's not what he wanted."

"I can assure you, it is." His voice was low and cautious. He slid the item across the desk. I stepped forward, ignoring the girl as I picked up the box. It was slightly heavier than expected, wrapped tight, the edges sharp and unforgiving beneath my finger.

"Best not to linger with that in your possession." Pierce's eyes flicked toward the door. "Take the employee exit just down the hall. It lets you out the back, quieter, and less chance of being seen."

I didn't argue. The music faded as I quickly exited and made my way out the door and down the narrow service corridor. The muffled sounds of the crowd and laughter shrank to a dull thrum, replaced by the echo of my own footsteps on cold concrete.

Pushing open the employee exit, I was hit by the hot, dry night air. There were a few random people milling about, passing around a cigarette, and chatting about the current crowd filling the club. I turned, moving quickly toward where the alley led out onto the main road. Then came the familiar voice, but it was low, sharp, and too tense to be the one I spoke to daily.

I froze in the shadows near a stack of empty wooden liquor crates. My eyes squinted in the dim streetlights' glow, one of them flickering overhead. But even in the darkness, I would recognize her.

Astoria.

She stood with her back partly turned, speaking to a man whose face was swallowed by the darkness, and a hood pulled over her head. Their bodies were rigid, their movements tight and clipped, like a dance neither of them wanted to perform but were being forced into. I stepped closer, careful to keep my breathing quiet. From where I stood, I could only hear fragments of their conversation.

"Not here. You can't just—" Astoria's voice was harsh, but the man interrupted her with a firm shake of his head.

Then, as if she could sense my presence, Astoria glanced sharply over her shoulder. Our eyes locked, and in that instant, something cold and dangerous sparked between us. Like for the first time, she saw who I really was.

Her expression hardened into steel. The man shifted, as if ready to step around her, but she blocked his path effortlessly, her stance unyielding.

"Go inside," Astoria commanded. "Now."

I was frozen, unable to run. My hands clenched around the cardboard box, pulling it closer to my chest. She took a step toward me, her heels clicking sharply against the pavement. The scent of her heavy perfume washed over me, suffocating and intoxicating all at once.

"Acelynn..." Astoria shot me a sickening smile. Voice smooth, but there was a thread of a threat mixed within. "You didn't see anything. You didn't hear anything. And you are not going to mention this to my brother or Nolan."

I raised an eyebrow, daring her. "Or what?"

A slow, cruel smile curved at her lips, but it didn't reach her eyes. Her breath was warm against my cheek as she leaned in closer to speak. "Or I will tell Kaius about the Polaroid I found under your driver's seat."

My stomach tightened, a cold twist coiling inside me. But I forced my face to stay calm, refusing to give anything away. Astoria watched me like a predator sizing up her prey. Then she stepped back, brushing past me toward the door.

She tossed a dark look over her shoulder. "Such a good girl for her Knight. Wouldn't want to ruin that with our little secret."

Then she disappeared through the back door. I clutched the package tighter, its weight suddenly unbearable, as if it contained something nefarious. And honestly, it might.

The night had shifted, darker and heavier now. And I was caught in the middle of something far bigger than was brewing in the shadows of the night.

CHAPTER THIRTY-THREE

acelynn

THE STRONG STENCH *of gasoline filled the inside of my nostrils. I continued my methodical task of pouring another gallon of gas through the home I grew up in. The liquid sloshed across the tile floor, leaving deadly puddles in its wake. Every inch of this place had to be saturated if I had any chance of it burning to the ground like Alec wanted. I stepped into the main kitchen, letting the red container slam onto the ground as I dropped it. My hands dug in my pocket for the box of matches I had found in the drawer of my father's desk, right next to his favorite lighter and pack of cigars in his study. There was a single match in the box.*

One chance to light up the Spade legacy. One chance to change both Alec and my entire lives. I couldn't fuck this up. Pulling open the matchbox, the cardboard creaked as it went, and I came upon my one chance. Striking down hard on the ignition pad, the flame burned quickly. I drew the match up to eye level with me, staring it down as I debated my decision. The heat of the flame began to lick the pads of my fingers, and I sucked in at the sting, drinking in pain as it grew. A single gunshot rang out in the yard behind me as I flicked the match into the gasoline-covered room.

Quickly, I turned, my feet carrying me out the kitchen's back door and into the desert. When I was a good distance away from the house, I turned over my shoulder to watch the fire grow higher and higher as it caught on the accelerant. Then the screaming began.

The little brown package in the passenger seat of Nolan's car felt like a bomb just waiting to be set off. When I was a few blocks away from the nightclub, I veered off into a church parking lot and killed the car's headlights. My fingers brushed against the cardboard as I picked it up and set the box on my lap.

Kaius would know if I opened it, but I honestly didn't care very much. I wanted to know what I was carrying around. The way Pierce hadn't wanted me to linger made me think this wasn't just paperwork left behind.

The rip of the tape coming off the box had my heart skipping a beat. I tossed it aside, peeling back the lid from the box. Inside were the golden gems of Muze. Their almost iridescent coloring seemed to sparkle in the dim streetlights. I reached down, plucking one pill from the container. There must have been hundreds in this tiny box.

I had never done drugs recreationally, not when I knew that addiction ran in my family. Though some may say dosing myself with hemlock could turn into needing to chase that high. But for now, that wasn't a problem. I knew girls who had done Muze in college. They said it made parties more fun as it held them in a euphoric state where everything was neon colors and bubbly personalities. It was why the drug was so popular on the club scene, and when something was popular, it made it lucrative. Kaius knew this. That was why he made sure the Knights were the only ones bringing in Muze, the only ones distributing it.

The pill fell from my hand, landing in the center of the pile. I closed my eyes, took in a shaky breath, and tried to calm myself. Alec had been strung out the night of the fire. I could see it in his dilated pupils and erratic behavior. He had been acting strangely my last few visits, and I had caught him taking something at the auto body shop, but I didn't dare question him. What if that was the reason this all happened? What if Kaius wasn't to blame but Alec in his crusade to get that next high? I couldn't help but feel like I hadn't gotten the full truth from him in the hall.

Maybe my brother had played his final ace that night, and it had burned any answers without hesitation.

CHAPTER THIRTY-FOUR

kaius

THE ROAD to Alaric Camberly's property cut through the part of Lovelen where the shadows clung to the ground thicker than fog. Old, abandoned brick buildings leaned like weary statues, their doorways sealed shut for decades with large planks of wood nailed into the surfaces to keep out the locals. So far, no one had been dumb enough to go searching in them, not that they would find anything truly disturbing on the surface. The real horrors lay in the chambers below, which all led back to the main house.

By the time I reached the iron gates, I could already feel the weight of the man's presence behind them pressing against me. His reputation wasn't a thing of the past. It breathed, like an animal that had never been uncaged, into the cracks of the Knights' every choice.

The gates opened without a sound. He had been watching me from the moment I entered onto the dirt road leading to the house. The drive was long, dotted with random cacti and overgrown brittle bush that bent and twisted like gnarled fingers. At the end stood the main house, three stories of gray stone, its high roof pitched like the blade of a spear.

Heavy oak doors swung inward before I could knock. Maia opened the door, her dark hair perfectly slicked back into a tight bun as always. I smiled down at the live-in nurse. Maia had been around since before I could remember. She was the one who had patched up wounds, fed us just because she knew we wouldn't do it for ourselves, and had been the motherly figure I needed when my own mother had fled from Lovelen, leaving behind her two young children.

When the doctors had told us we needed to keep Alaric comfortable, she had stepped up there too. We all thought he had months to live, but it turns out the old man was even more stubborn than we all anticipated.

I think Maia was the only person in this world who was brave enough to stay and put up with Alaric's shit. She never backed down to his violent outbursts. She just sat there and waited for him to be done with his tantrums. I admired her for that.

"Hello, Maia." I smiled at the woman.

She was probably no more than five feet in stature, but what she lacked in height she made up for in attitude.

"Kaius," she greeted me, pursing her lips at my presence. "He is waiting for you in the study."

"Thank you." I stepped around her, laying a single kiss on her head.

"You look good, Kaius," her voice called to me.

I turned to look at her over my shoulder. She had a devious smirk on her face.

"Does it have to do with that new stray Astoria dragged into your world?"

"Nolan needs to learn when to shut his mouth," I groaned, running one hand over my chin.

Maia chuckled. "Don't be too hard on him. I am very persuasive."

"And we all know it." I shook my head once before heading to the back of the house, where Alaric's study was located. My steps sounded against the marble flooring, each one reminding me I didn't belong in this house of horrors.

The corridors of the old house were like a time capsule of the Knights' history. Photographs of the early days, my father's bright smile shining through the glass as he stood with Alaric, one arm slung over his shoulder in a brotherly way. Before the power got to their head and they were just a band of misfits who wanted to rule the world. Before the greed, power, and money got to their heads.

I stepped through the study's open door, where Alaric Camberly was waiting for my arrival. The room was large, with shelves so tall they needed a rolling ladder to reach the top. The air smelled of leather, cigar smoke, and something sharper, almost medical—crushed herbs and the faint tang of arsenic. Even in the summer heat, he had a fire crackling in the stone fireplace.

Alaric sat in the armchair across from the fire. His dark hair had gone completely silver, patches of it missing from where it had fallen out. Deep creases sat around his mouth and eyes, their marks earned from making decisions no man should make. His shoulders were broad, his posture unbent despite the weight of sickness and age. A thin oxygen tube sat below his nose, one of the only true signs that he was still dying from the cancer he had obtained from his obsession with poisons. Alaric Camberly wasn't just Vince's father. He was the last man you'd ever want to owe a debt to—the last man you'd ever want to betray.

"Kaius," he said, voice low and monotone. Some might

take that as a sign that he was no longer dangerous, but I knew better. "I was hoping to see your face soon."

"I figured it was time." I took the chair opposite him, the leather worn and smooth, the seat slightly too low. Subtle reminders that this had once been my father's seat across from this man. "Figured waiting around wouldn't change anything. I know you still have spies who report back to you."

His steel eyes studied me for a moment before he spoke again. "They aren't spies when they are reporting to a man who gave them the power they have now."

"I assume you know about the hemlock?" I asked, ignoring his jab. He never wanted me to be the leader of the Knights, saying I was too soft for it. Alaric nodded once but did not say anything further. "Nolan and Vince are out for blood. They want names."

A faint twitch pulled at his lips, though it wasn't from amusement. "That hemlock was stored in the basement for a reason. My son is meticulous in accounting for it. The Knights had kept that stock for one purpose and one purpose only—to send a message that leaves no room for interpretation. When something like that begins to disappear, it is not by accident. It is intentional."

"I'll handle it," I said, my voice clipped.

"See to it that you do," Alaric replied, leaning forward to rest his elbows on his knees. Firelight caught the silver Knight's ring on his finger, the grail mark glinting like a watchful eye. "It is best to move the supply soon, even if it is just the hemlock. Missing poison isn't the only shadow moving in our house."

"You think someone is planning something?" I narrowed my eyes at him. I thought in getting rid of Oscar we had smoked out the rat in the club, but maybe he had been working with someone else.

Alaric's gaze held mine. "The Spade family massacre... you remember the official story given, yes?"

I didn't blink. "Yes. I remember."

"The truth rots under it," he said flatly. "The Spades were allies of the Knights, if you could call us that. We both had a mutual respect for each other, but didn't let the other overstep their bounds. They were the keepers of things too dangerous to scatter in the wind—records, names, debts owed by powerful men. When they were annihilated, it wasn't a random vendetta. It was surgical. Someone knew exactly what they wanted, exactly what they were taking. And they thought they would get away with pinning it on the Knights."

I leaned back, keeping my expression blank, but inside, pieces I hadn't known were connected were beginning to shift into place. "You think whoever is taking the hemlock is tied back to the massacre?"

"I think in our world..." Alaric's voice dropped to almost a growl. "Coincidence is a fairy tale for children. If someone is willing to steal from our supply, they are willing to betray the whole order. Maybe even kill to avenge it."

The silence was thick in the air as I watched him take a deep breath before continuing, "And betrayal in our world is a death sentence."

The flames in the hearth popped, sending sparks flying through the air. I didn't move, mind racing a million miles to try to put together who would be willing to risk everything to unravel the Knights. The hemlock wasn't just stolen. It was taken with intent. If the Spades' destruction and this theft were connected, it meant the rot Alaric feared wasn't just under the surface—it was in the bones.

I stood, but the elder Knight's voice cut through the air before I could turn. "You've got your father's fire, boy."

His voice was quieter now, and I could hear the dying man hidden under his words. The one he tried to hide from those of us who visited. Alaric continued, "But fire burns whatever it touches, friend or foe. Choose carefully where you set it."

I turned on my heel, not looking back at the man as I left. But I carried his words with me like a knife hidden in my back. Whoever had taken the hemlock had just moved themselves from a shadow in the corner to a name I'd be writing on a grave.

And I was already thinking about how to dig it.

CHAPTER THIRTY-FIVE

acelynn

THE CLOCK in Kaius's office was mocking me with every tick. I had been waiting for him for over an hour. Nolan hadn't elaborated on where Kaius had gone, just said he was out. He had explained he could get Kaius the package if I didn't want to wait, but I wanted to face the man who had sent me on this errand. Wanted to ask him what the hell was his problem.

I paced another lap around the office space, the thin carpet doing nothing to soften the impatient snap of my boots against the floor. The lamp on his desk threw long shadows across the walls, stretching and shrinking the more restless I got.

The box sat in the center of his desk like it owned the room. If I didn't know any better, I wouldn't think there was anything sinister hidden beneath its lid. But I had seen the caps of Muze piled up in there.

Once I realized what it was, the drive home from the Excalibur felt like hours. Pierce had pressed the box into my hand as if he were handing me a birthday present. So nonchalant that it felt like it was second nature to him. I wasn't about to show up to the King of Lovelen empty-handed.

But now, staring at it in his territory, in his office, I wasn't sure if that was the smart choice.

What was even worse was that my mind kept flashing back to the alley behind the club, to the hiss of Astoria's voice when she realized I'd been watching her. That conversation had been intense, and even though I couldn't make out her words, her tone had been sharp and low. She didn't back down to the man when he argued against her, holding all the qualities a girl raised in the club life should be. Steady and vicious. That was until she saw me. Then her anger had turned to a new target.

The way she had threatened to show Kaius the Polaroid, as if the image was a blade and she was more than happy to twist it—my stomach was still knotted from the altercation. She didn't even have to tell me what the consequences would be if she went through with her threat. I knew it would be bad enough to plant at least a seed of doubt in Kaius's mind, even if I was able to explain my way out of it. Just that doubt would destroy whatever fragile space I had carved out here.

The sound of the bar's entrance opening yanked me back into the room. Footsteps, heavy and deliberate, traveled quickly through the hall. When Kaius finally stepped into the office, the atmosphere shifted. It was always like that with him. He didn't just enter a room. He *claimed* it. He wore a long dark shirt with the sleeves rolled up, letting the ink covering his arms stand out. His eyes swept over me before landing on the desk.

"You've been waiting." His voice was low and unreadable.

I nodded toward the box. "You want to explain to me why Pierce handed me that to deliver at the club instead of what you told me I would be getting?"

"Pierce gave that to you?" Kaius's gaze flickered to it, then back to me, eyes harder now.

"Yes," I hissed, taking one step toward him. "He said that it was what you asked for."

Kaius paused. The silence was sharp. He tilted his head slightly. "I didn't tell him to send anything back with you other than the liquor and paperwork. Which I had assumed was done since Josie is stocking the bar with it now."

"I didn't bring anything other than that back."

He chuckled, shaking his head slightly. "Explains why she is in such a piss-ass mood."

I frowned at him. "Then why—"

"You ask too many questions, kitten. And in my line of work, questions get you killed." Kaius stepped closer.

I gulped, my back hitting the edge of the desk before I realized I had moved. The air felt heavier now, every inch of him towering over me in a deliberate, consuming way.

"You walked into my world, Acelynn, and things have started moving without my permission. That never happened before you. Now you're standing here with a box of Muze, acting like you don't understand what this means?"

Heat flushed through my chest. It mixed with the flicker of unease in my gut. I licked my lips. "Maybe I don't understand your world fully, but I know when someone is keeping me in the dark."

Something flashed in his eyes—a flicker of suspicion, the kind that made my pulse spike. "And are you hiding something, kitten?"

The words cut through me, each accusation closer to the truth than he even realized. My heart beat erratically against my chest, throat going tight as I tried to speak. "I'm not—" My words were lost on my tongue as I rationally tried to think of a response. Because I had almost just confessed, almost given myself away to the deadly man in front of me.

I am not who you think I am.

Kaius's hands came down hard against the desk beside me, caging me in. The heat of his body short-circuiting every sensible thought in my brain. His face was so close now, I could feel the soft drag of his breath, the smell of the whiskey he had drunk earlier that day filling my senses.

"Careful," he murmured, voice rough enough to scrape along my skin. "In this room, secrets have teeth. I know you have claws, Acelynn, but do you have the bite to back it up?"

"You know I do," I replied, voice sharp and laced with a slight bit of seduction. Maybe I could still gain the upper hand in this conversation, steer his focus away from what I was hiding.

For a long beat, we just stared at each other. Kaius's gaze dropped to my mouth, and the air between us turned electric. I could feel the moment his control began to waver—the fraction of a second where he thought about closing the distance. I had him right where I wanted him.

But then he walked out of the room without looking back at me, and I just stood there, pulse still thrumming in my throat, and the phantom heat of his body hovering just over me. What was worse was that I was disappointed that he hadn't kissed me. Yes, we had gone farther than just a simple kiss, but this felt different. This time, I was emotionally invested in his lips meeting mine, in the fact that maybe he could fall in love with me, not the image of the girl I portrayed myself as. This moment felt electrified, and I think he knew that too.

Somewhere deep in my gut, I knew we were drawing near the end of this dangerous game. It was just a matter of time to see who held the loaded gun to whose head.

CHAPTER THIRTY-SIX

acelynn

IT HAD BEEN days since I had last seen or heard from Kaius. I wouldn't say he was avoiding me, but that might be giving myself too much credit. Kaius wouldn't stay away from his own bar and the Knights just because he felt something toward me.

The rush at the Queen's Table had finally bled out into the streets for the night, leaving the bar with the strange after-hours quiet. A couple of regulars nursed the last of their beers in the corner, too stubborn to leave a drop behind, but even their voices were muffled under the slow, melancholy hum of a jazz track dripping from the speakers.

"I'm going to take this out," I called toward Astoria.

The trash bag was heavy in my hands as I yanked it out from under the counter, the bag slick and bulging, like it might split at the seams any second. The smell of sour beer, citrus rinds, and something oddly metallic clung to the inside of my nose. Astoria nodded once at me before turning back to counting the till. To say it had been awkward between us the last few shifts would be an understatement, but there had never been a good time to speak with her. Maybe tonight we could clear the air because, as much as I hated to admit it, I missed Astoria.

I shoved open the back door, bracing against the harsh heat of the night. The alley was still, lit only by a flickering streetlight that buzzed overhead. The dumpster creaked open, and I tossed the bag into its darkness.

That's when I noticed it. At the far end of the narrow alley, the basement doors were swung open. I knew for a fact that none of the boys would just leave that open for anyone to venture into. My feet moved quickly toward the shadowed doorway.

"Hello?" I called out, staring down into the basement's depths, waiting for someone to jump out and ask me what I was doing, but no one came. Crossing the invisible barrier, I took the stairs two at a time, letting the coolness of the underground bunker chill my heated skin.

Everything in me told me to leave. To go back to the bar and pretend I hadn't seen it. But curiosity didn't work like that. I reached up, fingers searching for the string to the overhead light, pulling once when I found it and illuminating the entire space. Nothing looked out of place, all the vials perfectly aligned, and the discarded remnants of something Vince had been working on scattered across the worktable. But still, I couldn't get the gnawing feeling that this was some sort of trap out of my mind.

"What are you doing?" Astoria's high-pitched voice startled me.

I whipped around, facing the girl as she descended the last steps.

"That door was open," I stammered, pointing one finger toward the entryway. "I thought this was maybe another dry storage unit that someone forgot to close up."

"You always seem to be sniffing around where you don't belong." She crossed both arms over her chest as she glared at me. I took her in for the first time tonight. Her light-colored hair was pulled back into a claw clip, a few loose strands framing her face. She didn't look like she had worked a moment tonight, makeup still perfectly intact. She let out a laugh. "You know what? Save whatever other excuse you have for me. That Polaroid told me everything I needed to know about you."

"Enough with the Polaroid, Astoria!" I screamed at her, my patience wearing thin. "Did you ever stop to think maybe I had an explanation for what was in that picture?"

"Careful, sweetheart. Some secrets you can't take back if you dig them up," Astoria sneered at me.

I rolled my eyes at the girl. "Cut the tough girl act."

"Well, go on." Astoria motioned with her hands to continue. "Try to explain away the obvious."

"Like you have any room to talk, Miss 'I'm having secret meetings with strange men outside my brother's nightclub.'" I shot her a knowing look.

Her face became flushed with anger, but she didn't say anything more.

I continued, "I was being questioned about the Knights by those two detectives when that picture was taken. They caught wind that I was now working for Kaius as a bartender and were trying to grill me about what goes on in the bar."

"And what did you tell them?" Astoria narrowed her eyes at me.

"Well, considering I had barely even started working here, there was nothing to tell." I shrugged nonchalantly. Astoria went to speak, but I cut her off. "Even if I did know what I do now, I wouldn't have said anything. I wouldn't betray you like that."

"You mean you wouldn't betray my brother like that?" Astoria grumbled. She stepped back, taking a seat on the bottom step of the stairs.

I stepped forward. "No. I mean, I wouldn't betray you, Astoria. Yes, I am seeing your brother, if you can even call it that, but you're my best friend, Astoria, and that means something to me."

She peered up at me through her lashes. "I am sorry for holding this over your head instead of just asking you. There has been a lot going on in my head, and I might have gotten a tad jealous that my brother has been stealing all your time."

"It's fine," I said, the corners of my mouth quirking up into a small smile. "You gonna tell me what you were doing at the club the other night?"

Astoria's entire face flushed red in embarrassment. "I, uh...I was meeting up with an old fling, but I didn't want you to say anything to my brother and it get back to Nolan."

"Will you two stop skating around each other and finally sleep together?" I joked, throwing my hands in the air.

She groaned, leaning back against the stairs and throwing her head back.

"I mean, seriously, I have never seen two people so in love with each other refuse to admit it."

"You're one to talk," Astoria gasped at me. "My brother and you are sleeping with each other, but can't even admit that they might feel something in their cold, dead hearts."

I barked out a laugh, but it was cut off by heavy stomps coming down the stairs. Astoria shot up from her spot, turning just in time to see her brother come into view.

"What the hell is going on?" Kaius's voice boomed with lethal precision. His jaw was tight, the vein in his temple faintly visible. "You want to explain to me why the two of you are lurking around down here, Astoria?"

"The door was open when we went to take the trash out," Astoria said, her voice sickly sweet as she batted her eyelashes at her brother. "I wanted to make sure nothing was wrong, but didn't want to leave Acelynn up there all alone."

"Alone?" Kaius narrowed his eyes at her. "Next to the bar she works at every night?"

"Well, I mean—"

"Stop," Kaius's voice cracked through the air. We both froze in place, waiting for him to continue. His gaze moved from Astoria to mine, unblinking. "You both are hiding something, and I will not stand here and be lied to."

He spoke like it were a fact, like he could smell the deceit on the two of us. Kaius moved down one step. "And I don't have the patience to play guessing games."

Astoria looked down at her hands, her jaw tightening as if she were fighting back tears. I held the man's stare even as my pulse was pounding, the heat of his scrutiny making my skin itch.

"We were planning a surprise party for Josie's birthday," I said casually.

Kaius narrowed his glare on me, waiting for me to crack under its pressure.

"Her birthday is in a few days, correct?"

"Josie doesn't celebrate her birthday." He cocked his head to the side. "Does she, Astoria?"

Astoria only responded with a meek nod. I sighed, pulling his attention back to me. "Who doesn't celebrate their birthday?"

"Someone who wants to bury their past life," Kaius snapped at me. The venom in his voice made me jump slightly. He didn't give me a chance to respond, jerking his chin toward the doors. "Upstairs. Now."

I didn't speak. I didn't even dare to breathe. Every

instinct in my body screamed that I should flee, yet I remained frozen, tethered by the pressure of Kaius's hand against the small of my back. It was firm, unyielding, yet deceptively gentle—the kind of touch that could control without overt force. My stomach knotted in a mess of nerves, anxiety, and something darker, something I didn't want to name even to myself. Behind us, Astoria stirred, her movement barely audible. The faint scrape of her shoes was the only reminder that I wasn't alone, but I didn't dare draw her attention, not now, not while Kaius's eyes cut through the space like twin blades.

The stairs groaned beneath our weight, each step resounding like a drumbeat that matched the erratic thrum in my chest. I held on to the railing as though it were the only thing keeping me anchored. Kaius moved like a predator in his element, smooth and precise, his dark eyes scanning every inch of the stairwell as if he could see the very secrets hidden in the shadows. Every step I took felt measured against his presence, a silent acknowledgment that nothing, absolutely nothing, would go unnoticed tonight. When we reached the back hall, he paused and turned to face his sister.

"Astoria," he said, voice calm, unwavering, yet edged with authority. "Go wait at the bar. We'll talk later."

She didn't protest, only gave a small nod, her nervous gaze flicking toward me before retreating toward the bar. Through the hallway's small corridor, I caught a glimpse of Josie cutting limes, a mundane contrast to the tension coiling around us. Once Astoria disappeared, it was just Kaius and me. The hallway shrank around us instantly. Every sound—the soft scrape of our shoes, our collective breathing, the distant clink of glasses from the bar—was magnified. I felt exposed in a way I had never felt before. He hadn't touched me yet, not beyond the guiding pressure of his hand, but the air seemed charged with something almost physical. My chest ached in anticipation, every nerve on edge.

"We need to talk," he said, each word measured, simple, but weighted with something heavier than its syllables. Kaius stepped closer, and I could feel the heat radiating from him. "I need to be sure. I need to know you two aren't hiding something from me. Vince has had items taken recently from his private collection. You wouldn't know anything about that, would you, Acelynn?"

"No," I whispered almost involuntarily, voice trembling despite my best effort.

"So you won't have a problem proving that to me." His eyes roamed over my body, scanning slowly, deliberately.

My stomach churned. The thought of being searched, standing completely exposed and at his mercy, should have sent panic surging through me. And yet, I couldn't look away. There was something intoxicating in the calculated danger of his gaze, the way he studied me like I was both prey and a puzzle, all at once. I dropped my eyes, trying to ground myself in the floorboards beneath my feet.

"I understand," I murmured, voice small, almost lost in the charged silence.

Kaius's hand returned to the small of my back, guiding me into his office. The door clicked closed behind us, and the hallway's dim light was swallowed by the shadows of the room. He circled me like a hunter assessing prey. His hand brushed against my shoulder. The contact was brief, ghost-like, yet it sent a shiver shooting down my spine. Every nerve felt alight, every inch of skin aware, buzzing. It was a touch that promised both danger and something far more intoxicating.

"Do you think you can hide anything from me?" His voice

was low, teasing, sharp, the kind that made my pulse pound so loudly it seemed to echo in my ears.

I could only shake my head. My chest rose and fell with shallow breaths. Every breath I took felt like it might betray me. He moved closer, causing me to hold perfectly still, letting him work, knowing that one wrong move could tilt the balance and change everything.

His hands traced the lines of my back, not violently, but with a meticulousness that left me painfully aware of every inch of myself. I felt utterly exposed, vulnerable, and yet, I trusted him to the dangerous edge of reason. The line between fear and desire blurred, shifting like liquid in dim light.

"Strip," Kaius commanded, and the word fell over me like a lash.

I obeyed, trembling, hands fumbling to lift the loose band tee over my shoulders. The fabric slipped silently from my fingers to the floor. My shorts followed in a slow, deliberate motion, leaving me in nothing but a simple black thong. His eyes devoured me, causing goose bumps to crawl across my skin. Even though he had seen me before, something about this—the intimacy, the control, the heat—made it different. Dangerous. Thrilling.

"You've got nothing," he murmured, almost to himself, low and resonant. His gaze lingered, studying, drinking me in. "But you were reckless."

A shaky breath escaped me. My legs trembled under me, though I couldn't tell if it was from fear or arousal. His eyes darkened, unreadable and intense, pressing into me with palpable heat.

"You'll stay out of the basement," he said sharply, voice final, decisive. "Or next time..."

The threat hung unsaid, but I understood perfectly. The

memory of his hand brushing along my back, the quiet cadence of his voice, both commanding and intimate, would linger long after tonight. I nodded, eyes lowered, acutely aware that he was still watching, measuring, memorizing every movement, every subtle quiver. Silence stretched, dense, thick, electric. Then, his fingers lifted my chin, drawing my gaze to meet his. The heat in his eyes was intense, a flame licking at the edges of my self-control. His touch ghosted down my front, skimming over skin that burned under the brush of his fingers, before dipping between my legs. Kaius shifted my panties aside, and without any warning, he shoved two fingers into my already wet pussy.

A gasp escaped me, my back arching into the door as I stepped back into it. But he didn't let me get far, following my movements until my spine pressed against the hard surface, eyes rolling back as the rhythm of his fingers intensified. With his free hand, he lifted one of my legs, changing the angle and finding a spot that had my muscles quivering, heat filling my core with an intensity I couldn't deny. A moan slipped past me, helpless and raw, as his lips brushed against the shell of my ear.

"You're never going to go snooping again, are you, kitten?" His voice, hot and low, caused me to shiver.

"No," I breathed, shaking my head. "I swear I won't."

"I'm not sure I believe you." His chuckle was deep as his thumb moved in perfect rhythm with his fingers over my swollen clit, teasing me mercilessly. He added a third finger, pumping in and out of me rapidly, each stroke bringing me closer to the edge.

"I'm so close," I gasped, voice strangled, caught between shame and desire.

"Hmm," he hummed, pulling my face up to meet his. His

eyes locked with mine, unrelenting, a grin tracing his lips before he pulled his fingers free, slapping a hand down against my cunt. I jolted, a whimper of disapproval escaping me.

Kaius's smirk was cruel and knowing as he brought his fingers to his lips, taking his time to taste me, before speaking. "Sorry, kitten. Only good girls get to come. And you have been far from that today."

Before I could protest, he shifted my leg back to the ground and moved me away from the door before exiting the office. I was left trembling, hot, wound tight, a storm of need and frustration coursing through me. My chest rose and fell rapidly, every muscle alive, every nerve screaming.

Slamming my head back against the door, I groaned out, "Fuck me."

CHAPTER THIRTY-SEVEN

kaius

"WE ARE DOING A BONFIRE TONIGHT," Astoria said as she strutted into a booth in the corner of the bar.

Acelynn sat in the chair to my right, legs resting over mine as she shared the space. She was absent-mindedly scrolling on her phone, trying her best not to twitch as my hand rose higher onto her thigh with every stroke. I knew she was still mad at me for the stunt I had pulled the other day in my office, but at least she was talking to me again. I turned my gaze up from the bar's books to look at my little sister.

She shook her head at my glare. "No arguing. We haven't had any fun recently, and it is making all of you grumpy."

"I am a ray of fucking sunshine, Tor," Nolan said as he breezed past her to sit to my left.

She shot him a look but didn't scold him like she typically did.

"A bonfire sounds fun." Acelynn peeled her eyes from her

phone screen. "But won't someone notice if we light up the field behind the bar?"

"Oh, sweet innocent Acelynn," Nolan cooed after her, reaching across to pinch one of her cheeks.

She swatted at his hand, retreating closer to me. I slung one arm over her shoulders, pulling her into me.

Nolan continued, "We don't light up the field behind the Queen's Table. The Knights take our party out to the middle of the desert near the old airplane hangar."

"There is an old airplane hangar?" Acelynn perked up at the idea.

I chuckled. "Yes, we have been going since we were teens. Started out as a way to hide our partying from our parents, but turned into somewhat of a tradition, you could say."

"And no one will bother us there?" She peeked up at me, hazel eyes wide and full of wonder.

"Not if they're smart," Nolan scoffed. He leaned back against the booth, kicking both feet up to rest on the table.

Astoria and I moved at the same time, pushing his legs off the furniture. He toppled over sideways, landing in a heap of himself next to me.

My sister smiled at me. "So is that a yes?"

"Yes, we have to show Acelynn how the Knights truly party," I said, shooting her a smile. She began jumping up and down, clapping at the confirmation. "Just make sure you flip the closed sign on this time. We don't need a repeat of the last bonfire."

"That was Nolan's fault." Astoria glared at the man beside me before flipping her hair over her shoulder and walking away to prep for tonight's festivities.

Nolan straightened up. "How come it is always my fault when it comes to her?"

"You are an easy target." Acelynn smirked at him.

"Astoria knows you could never truly be upset with her, and she uses that to her advantage."

"I could be upset with her," Nolan scoffed.

Rolling my eyes at my best friend, I began listing moments that he should have been upset with her. "How about the time Astoria shaved off your left eyebrow when we were sophomores in high school because you ate the last piece of cake? You didn't even yell at her. Or the time she ran your car into a telephone pole because she was reapplying lipstick, and you laughed. I swear my sister could murder your favorite person in the world and you would ask if they deserved it."

"Well, Astoria is my favorite person in the world, so that doesn't really make a lot of sense," Nolan blurted out. The second the words slipped from his lips, the tips of his ears tinged red, and he bolted from the booth.

Acelynn and I shared an amused look before going back to our tasks we had been doing before my sister interrupted us.

CHAPTER THIRTY-EIGHT

THE DESERT HAD its own kind of silence.

Even with the Knights' laughter breaking across the open air, it felt like something vast and watchful was just beyond the horizon, always listening. The night sky stretched for miles, making me slightly dizzy as I stared at it too long—an endless ocean of black velvet pricked with icy, silver stars.

The abandoned airfield was the perfect setting for a bonfire, secluded from prying eyes, making it perfect for the Knights to let loose. This place was a graveyard of metal and history. Rusted World War II airplanes lay crooked in the sand like wounded beasts left to rot. Their bodies were streaked with layers of graffiti—acid-bright tags, skulls with melted eyes, and curses in thick black paint. The artwork bled together, a hundred different hands trying to leave their marks on something long since forgotten.

The largest wrecked plane hunched in the shadows beyond the bonfire's reach. Its broken windows gaped like hollow eyes, and in the flickering light, it almost looked alive.

The Knights had claimed the open space between the

wrecks, building a fire so big it could probably be seen for miles. Flames leaped high, spitting sparks that vanished into the night. Nolan and two others were feeding it hunks of wood, their faces glowing red from the heat. Surrounding the fire were three beaten-up sofas, torn and worn from sitting in the sun. I didn't dare sit on them, not knowing what might lie in their cushions. Someone had dragged an old speaker out here, its sound warped and crackling as the music flowed through the open summer air.

Astoria was draped across a folding chair near the fire, long legs crossed at her ankles. She smiled brightly at the story one of the men was telling. I stayed on the edge of the group, boots scuffing the sand. The heat barely reached me here. My arms wrapped tight around myself, though it wasn't just the chill of the desert night that made me hold on. Something about the empty stretch of land and the silent hulks of planes made the hair rise on the back of my neck.

That's when I felt him.

Kaius didn't need to announce himself to me—he never did. His presence was a pull all its own, dragging me into his orbit no matter how much I fought against it. I caught the faint, smoky scent of him before he spoke, laced with the clean bite of whiskey on his breath.

"You're hiding," he murmured, voice low enough that it vibrated against the side of my neck.

"I am not," I said, keeping my eyes trained on the fire. "I'm observing."

Kaius stepped closer. I could feel the heat of his body press against my back. "Watching is boring. Come on."

His hand brushed against my wrist, his touch light at first, then curling around it with purpose. That simple touch burned more than the fire did. Kaius led me away from the others, weaving between the wrecks until the voices and music dimmed, swallowed by the echo of the wind whistling through jagged metal.

Dropping my wrist, he stepped up into the largest plane before turning to help me in. From up here, the wings stretched out like broken arms, the tips dipping into the sand. The graffiti inside the cabin was older, faded into a ghost of colors. The smell of rust and gasoline clung to the air.

Kaius's hand slid to my waist, pulling me into him, the rough brush of his jacket against my bare arm causing me to shiver. His other hand braced against the cool, dented metal beside my head. I could hear the low, steady cadence of his breathing, feel the heat rolling off him in waves.

"Better?" he asked, his mouth just inches from mine.

I wanted to say no. I wanted to tell him to go back to the fire and leave me in peace. But instead, my gaze locked with his, the space between us heavy and charged, like the air right before a lightning strike.

His lips dipped closer. I could taste the faint burn of whiskey. My own lips parted, the pull between us snapping tight until it hurt.

An earsplitting scream ripped through the desert. We jumped apart, turning to see the landscape below us lit up, and it wasn't the fire the Knights had set. It was farther out, beyond the circle of the wrecks, maybe a quarter mile or so away. At first, I thought someone had set another blaze, but then I saw the shape—perfectly symmetrical lines crisp on the dunes in the distance. A massive spade, flames licking the edge, the center black against the burning sand.

The Death Dealers mark. My family's mark.

Every muscle in my body locked up, my lungs forgetting how to work properly. The world seemed to tilt on its axis, pulling me toward the symbol as if it were a black hole.

Kaius stiffened, his head turning toward it. "What the hell..."

My stomach dropped as the wind shifted. It carried a sharp, oily stink of whatever accelerant they had used. The flames hissed and roared like they were laughing at me.

"It's him." My voice cracked before I could stop it.

Kaius's head snapped back to me, eyes narrowing. "Logan?"

I bit down hard on my tongue, tasting copper, trying my best to choke down the tears before they could escape. The promise he had made when I left him rang in my skull, the constant threats that looked over me in Lovelen, every word dripping with the certainty that I would be his once again, no matter whose protection I was under.

Kaius's grip tightened on me as I swayed on my feet. "Acelynn..."

But I couldn't look at him. My eyes stayed locked on the spade, the flames climbing higher into the night like a warning. Like a countdown.

CHAPTER THIRTY-NINE

acelynn

THE BONFIRE SMOKE STILL clung to me, woven into the fibers of my clothing and tangled through my hair like a ghost that refused to be shaken off. Even after the drive home, it lingered—dry, acidic, and tasting faintly of the accelerant that had burned the sand dunes.

It made my stomach roll. The smell of fire reminded me of my family home burning to the ground. But the night was over, and the Knights had gone into a full investigation of who could have burned the spade into the sand. I had snuck out of the bar before Kaius could stop me.

The moment I stepped into the front hall of my home, something felt off to me in my gut. The space was too quiet, and I could see the stove light in my kitchen shining into the living room. I had never turned that light on. The metallic tang of adrenaline coated my tongue before I even touched the doorknob. My fingers tightened on my keys, slotting one between my knuckles like a makeshift blade. Old habit.

Stepping further into the house, I finally caught the scent

of another. Cologne—deep, woodsy, and expensive—the kind you smelled on men who thought money made them invincible. It didn't belong here in my makeshift home.

When I finally turned the corner, I came upon a man leaning against my kitchen counter like he owned the place. My blood ran cold as I stared down the only living elder the Knights had. Alaric Camberly, the father of the poison maker of the club. A skill passed down from him to his son. I remember when he would visit my family home to speak with my father. His voice could cut through you like a knife, even when he was smiling. And right now, he was smiling, though it was the kind that made my skin crawl.

He traced a finger over the granite countertop, slow and deliberate, like a predator deciding just how much fun it wanted to have before it made its kill. "Hello, Emersyn."

I couldn't breathe, the air from my lungs vanishing just by a single name. A name that didn't belong here. Not anymore. Not *ever*.

"I think you have me mistaken for someone else," I managed to say, forcing my voice into something flat and dismissive.

Alaric's smile widened by a fraction. "No, I don't think I do."

The sound of my heartbeat was so loud it drowned out the hum of the fridge. My palms became damp as my nerves rose.

"You've gotten very good at hiding in plain sight," he continued, his tone casual, as if he were making small talk with an old friend. "I almost believed the story myself. The Spade family wiped out. The Death Dealer's king and his precious princess, both gone in the flame. So tragic."

The word *tragic* rolled off his tongue like a joke. The walls seemed to press in around me. I wanted to step back, but doing so would mean retreating, and I had spent way too much of my life running from men like Alaric.

"I'm not sure what you think you are doing here," I said, turning my head to the side to examine him further. "But you need to leave."

Alaric ignored me, instead reaching into his coat pocket and pulling out a Ziplock bag. Inside were five vials of hemlock. The same bag I had buried inside the wall of the fireplace, where a loose stone could be pulled in and out. How he was able to find it so easily made my vision blur.

My chest tightened. "Where did you—"

"I got curious," Alaric cut in smoothly, rolling one of the vials between his fingers. "Curiosity can be...dangerous. You've been keeping secrets, Emersyn. Risky ones. Imagine what Kaius would think if he knew you were lying to him the entire time he was between those pretty thighs."

The way he said Kaius was like he was taunting me. Alaric moved around the counter to come stand in front of me. He chuckled, shaking his head as I didn't take the bait. "You're going to tell me why you are here. Why the daughter of the Death Dealer's leader is hiding under the Knights' protection. And if you're persuasive, maybe I will keep your little secret between us."

My fingers curled into fists. "And if I'm not?"

Alaric's smile vanished, now replaced with a sharp and hungry look. The shift was instant. His hand shot out, clamping down around my throat. He slammed me back into the wall hard enough to rattle the picture frames above me. My ears rang from the impact. I clawed at his wrist, my breath catching as his grip tightened, cutting off air.

"You should have stayed dead," Alaric snarled, the elder's

calm demeanor cracking into rage. "Because the second your father's enemies find out—"

I didn't let him finish his sentence, my knee coming up hard and slamming into his ribs. The blow stole his breath, and he loosened his grip just enough for me to wrench free. I crawled toward the kitchen. My legs felt wobbly as I stood on them, using the counter to balance as I rounded it. I went for the drawer by the stove without thinking. My fingers closed around the black handle of a chef's knife that was kept in there. The steel gleamed under the yellow light.

Alaric lunged, catching a fistful of my hair and yanking my head back so hard white dots began to dance in my vision. Pain flared sharply across my scalp, but I spun with the pull, shoving the knife upward with both hands.

The blade landed home beneath Alaric's ribs. A sharp intake of breath, and his eyes went wide—not with fear but with shock. It was as if he hadn't considered I'd fight like this. His body jerked against mine. Hot blood welled around the knife, running over my fingers in a thick, sticky stream.

I yanked the blade free, and the wet sucking sound it made turned my stomach. Alaric staggered back, one hand pressing against the wound, crimson running between his fingers and onto his white shirt in seconds. He tried to speak, but the words were caught in his throat, breaking apart in a wet cough.

After a moment, he went down, hitting the tile floor hard, legs curling in on himself before going still. The smell of iron was sudden, overwhelming, clinging to the back of my throat until I thought I would choke on it.

I didn't move for a long time. My breath came in short, ragged pulls as my hands trembled in front of me. The knife clattered against the tile when I finally let go. My palms were slick with Alaric's blood.

I turned back to the motionless man in front of me. Alaric Camberly, Vince's father, was dead on my kitchen floor.

The home was silent except for the faint hum of the refrigerator. The smoke from the bonfire was still in my hair, but now there was something else clinging to me, heavier and far more permanent.

CHAPTER FORTY

kaius

THE BONFIRE WAS nothing but smoldering ash by the time we arrived back at the old air hangar. The wind was pushing the smoke into thin, broken wisps that disappeared into the night. Nolan, Vince, and I now stood in the same sand where laughter and music had carried only hours. Now it was silent. Dead quiet, except for the restless hiss of the wind crawling over the sand dunes.

And at the center of it, carved deep into the earth like a scar, was the spade.

The fire's glow hadn't done it justice. Seeing it now, without any distractions, it was impossible to ignore how deliberate it was. Blackened sand formed the sharp, cruel lines of the symbol, standing out against the pale landscape.

I crouched low, running a hand over the hardened surface. It was still warm beneath my palm. Whoever did this hadn't been gone long, and they had known we were out here tonight of all nights.

Nolan came to stand beside me, his shadow cutting

across the symbol. His face was grim, mouth set in a tight line. He matched my position, studying the burn like it might speak if he stared long enough.

"This wasn't some stupid kids," he finally said, voice flat. "This was precise. Whoever set this wanted us to get the message."

"Accelerant," I muttered, already cataloging the details in my mind.

The scorch pattern was too clean, the black edges uniform. Someone had poured fuel with purpose across the dune. Someone who knew what they were doing.

Vince paced just beyond us, his boots dragging through the sand, restless energy radiating off him like heat waves. His eyes flickered between the symbol and the rising dunes behind it. Vince was sharp and unsettled tonight, something both Nolan and I knew was a recipe for disaster. Vince finally turned his attention toward us. "Are you saying this was staged before we even arrived here tonight?"

"We would have noticed someone pouring gas through the sand." I stood, brushing dirt from my hands. The desert stretched out endlessly around us, moonlight catching the shifting sand, and yet the symbol seemed to pull all the light into itself, dark and heavy.

Nolan's wary gaze met mine. "Then the question isn't how. It's who."

Vince gave a sharp, bitter laugh, raking both hands through his hair. "We already know who. You think anyone but the Death Dealers would use that mark?"

The name hung heavy between us. I felt it in my chest, that old, familiar weight pressing down. The Death Dealers were gone. Broken. Buried with the Spade family massacre. And yet here we were, staring at proof that ghosts don't stay in their graves in our world.

"Don't jump to conclusions," I warned, though my jaw was tight. "We don't know anything yet."

Vince turned on me, eyes flashing, grief and fury tangled in every word. "Don't act like I am just making up wild theories here, Kaius. That symbol doesn't show up out of nowhere. Whoever put it here wanted us to see it. Wanted us to know they're still out there."

"Or someone wanted us to think they are," Nolan countered, his voice calm, measured, but I could see the tension in his shoulders, the way his hands curled into fists at his sides. His eyes were slightly glazed over, and I knew from years of watching him decode our problems that he was trying to pinpoint the exact moment someone slipped up tonight. A simple lie, a strange twitch in their body language, anything that could tell him who had done this.

The three of us stood there, the wind pulling at our clothes, the charred spade like a wound at our feet.

My gaze snagged on the faintest detail—tiny footprints along the edge of the dune, almost lost to the shifting sand. Smaller. Lighter. My chest went tight. Acelynn had been out here tonight, right in the heart of this chaos, her energy off as she watched the fun filtering around the bonfire. I had thought it was the anxiety of being so exposed to our antics, but could it have been nerves for what was to come?

For a second, the thought struck hard and cruel. Could this act have been hers? It would have been easy for her to slip away from the crowd when we had first arrived. We had left my sister and her out by the planes to get more firewood. It was the perfect amount of time for her to douse the sand with gasoline.

The idea clawed at me. Acelynn had slipped into our world too easily and asked too many careful questions. She had shadows in her eyes that I hadn't been able to place. And wasn't that exactly the kind of twisted fate that haunted men like me? That the one person I wanted most was the same person destined to tear me apart?

But then I shut it down. No. Not her. She was reckless, sharp-tongued, and stubborn as hell, but she wasn't this. Acelynn wasn't fire in the sand or blood in the dark. She was the one thing in my world that I hadn't yet corrupted.

I forced the thought down where it belonged—deep, buried, and snuffed out before it could grow roots.

I let the silence stretch, forcing my breath to become steady. I couldn't afford Vince's impulsiveness or Nolan's doubt—not now. I had to see past the fear, past the shadows of the past clawing their way back for revenge.

Finally, I spoke. "Whoever did this knew what they were doing. They had access to accelerant, they had time, and they wanted to send a message. That narrows the field."

Nolan's eyes met mine, sharp. "Knights or Dealers."

I gave a single nod.

Vince swore under his breath, pacing again, fists clenched at his sides. "If it's the Dealers, we should be preparing for war. Whoever survived has been strategically moving themselves across the board in plain sight. They could even be getting help from inside. If it's one of ours..." He shook his head, jaw working. "That's worse."

The air felt colder suddenly, the night heavier. My gaze dropped back to the spade, and for a moment, it wasn't just burned sand I was looking at. It was a memory. Fire and blood. Screams swallowed by smoke. Gunshots ringing out in the night air. The ruin the Spades had left behind.

I shoved the memory down, burying it as deep as I could.

"This isn't random," I said, my voice low, final. "Someone's trying to drag the past back into the light. We find out who, and we end it before they get the chance to make a killing blow."

Vince broke the silence, voice cutting sharp. "It's her."

I snapped my head toward him. "Watch your fucking mouth."

"You know I'm right," Vince pressed, his tone low, dangerous. "Acelynn was here. How is it that she knew so much, so fast, about us? Because I sure as hell wasn't having midnight chats with her. So tell me you haven't thought the same thing."

Anger burned up my spine, hot and uncontrollable. I took a step toward him, fists clenched so tight my knuckles cracked. "You think I don't notice everything she does? You think I wouldn't know if she was playing the Knights? If she was playing me?"

Nolan shifted between us, tension sparking like a live wire, but Vince didn't back down. His eyes narrowed, daring me.

"You're blinded by Acelynn," he said, almost a growl. "And that'll get all of us killed."

I closed the space between us until my words were nothing but a hiss through my teeth. "Say her name like that again, and I swear I'll make you eat those fucking words."

For a moment, the only sound was the wind shrieking over the sand. Then Nolan shoved at both our shoulders, breaking us apart.

"We don't have time for this shit," he snapped. "Whoever's behind this, we'll find them. But right now, we move. All of us."

I kept my glare locked on Vince a heartbeat longer before I tore it away, swallowing the rage threatening to split me open. But inside, the doubt I'd buried clawed to the surface again, whispering the same cruel thought I refused to believe. What if it really was her?

Neither Nolan nor Vince said another word. But the look in their eyes told me they were thinking the same thing I was.

The Spade family wasn't finished with us. Not by a long shot.

CHAPTER FORTY-ONE

THE KNIFE, slick with blood, lay on the floor in front of me. I couldn't look at it anymore. Couldn't look at *him,* sprawled out on my hardwood in a grotesque slumped-over shell of himself. Alaric's face was frozen in a half-snarl, half-question he hadn't had the chance to ask me.

My breath came in sharp and shallow spurts, tearing up my throat. The coppery tang of blood clung to the back of my tongue, stronger than it should've been, like it wanted to seep into me. Alaric's blood spread across the tile in widening veins, dark and syrup-thick, tracing the cracks of the grout until it brushed up against the toe of my boot.

My fingers trembled so badly I had to curl them into fists to stop the shaking. If I didn't get control of myself, I'd fall apart.

And if I fell apart, Kaius would see through me.

The Knights would know.

Emersyn Spade.

The name rattled against my brain like a curse. Alaric had spat it at me like venom before he lunged, before instinct—

or desperation—took over and ended him. The truth was out now, at least in his mouth. If Kaius found this scene...I'd be finished.

No more pretending. No more Acelynn Thorton. No more revenge plot that was spiraling horribly out of control. Unless I made sure the story told itself before anyone else could tell it for me.

My eyes darted wildly around the room. The wreckage of the fight wasn't enough. There wasn't adequate evidence to suggest a *struggle*. I needed more. I needed a scene. A script. Something to bury my crime under layers of chaos and hysteria. Something that painted me as the victim who had no choice but to kill the deranged man in my home.

I staggered to the kitchen table, shoving hard until the legs screeched across the floor and tipped onto its side with a crash that made me flinch. The sound reverberated through my bones, loud enough to feel like a warning. I went further, yanking the drawers and cabinets in the kitchen open, like he had been rummaging through them, searching for something before I made it back home. Silverware spilled across the floor in a clattering rain. I ripped a picture frame from the wall, glass shattering as it hit the ground. My fingers dug into the couch cushions, shredding them apart until feathers and fluff rained down onto the living room floor.

My body carried me from room to room, destroying everything in my path until there was nothing pristine left. But it still wasn't enough.

The reflection in the darkened window of me didn't match the stage around her. Face pale, smooth, and unmarked. I didn't look like a victim.

I pressed my lips together until they hurt and seized the broken lamp lying among the mess. My arm shook as I pressed the jagged brass edge against my forearm and pulled. Pain flared instantly, a searing line of fire, hot and wet. My breath hissed through my teeth, but the sting anchored me. It had to *look* real.

I raised the heavy lamp base and slammed it against my cheek. The burst of pain nearly dropped me to my knees. My ears rang. My vision blurred with tears, but when I blinked them away, the redness and swelling across my cheek was exactly what I needed. I struck again, lighter this time, enough to bruise, but not break. Then I slapped myself once, sharply, the crack echoing in the silent house.

When I looked in the window again, the woman staring back almost scared me. Dark hair wild, face blotched and bruising, blood on her arms and cheek. A trickle of crimson trailed down from the corner of my lip. My hand traveled up to the collar of my shirt, pulling until the fabric gave way and ripped down the middle. A long tear now made the shirt hang awkwardly off my body. Now she looked like she'd fought for her life.

My stomach twisted at what I was doing, but I pushed it down, shoved it into the same locked place where I kept every other horrible truth.

And then remembered the one thing Kaius couldn't find in my possession. *The hemlock.* My eyes snapped to the Ziplock bag Alaric had found still lying on the countertop. He'd confronted me with it, the evidence of who I really was. That was the thread I needed to spin this whole lie into something believable.

I lunged for the bag, heart hammering, and flung it against the ground near Alaric's body. The vials shattered, spraying shards of glass and sticky liquid across the floor. The smell hit immediately—sharp, bitter, poisonous, curling in the air like smoke. I coughed, covering my mouth with my arm, then crouched near Alaric's body.

With careful, shaking hands, I dragged the glass into his palm, cutting deep into his skin, and smeared his blood across the broken vials. I pressed one jagged piece against his wrist until the crimson ran and dripped, mixing with the poison, the story writing itself in every drop.

The elder Knight turned traitor. Twisted by hemlock. He attacked me, and I had no choice.

I bit down on the inside of my cheek until I tasted blood. Tears streamed down freely now—not all of them forced. Because part of me knew how far this had gone, how deep I was burying myself.

I was making it impossible to turn back.

I staggered to the corner of the room, sliding down against the wall, and let my head fall into my blood-smeared hands. I needed Kaius now. Needed him to come running, to see the chaos and the blood and the girl who looked shattered.

Not the girl who'd done the shattering.

With hands that tremored too violently to be faked, I dug my phone from my pocket. Blood smeared across the screen as I tapped his number, nearly dropping it twice before the call connected.

It rang once before he answered. His voice was clipped, low, already suspicious. "Acelynn?"

I sucked in a jagged breath and let it out in a sob that cracked like lightning. "Kaius...oh god! Kaius, I need you! Please, please, you have to come. He broke in, and I didn't know what to do. I think I killed him..."

My voice tumbled over itself, frantic, unraveling in panicked gasps. I dragged my fingernails down my cheek to make the sobs more ragged, let them claw out of my throat until they didn't sound staged at all.

"I'm bleeding. I can't...I can't do this. I don't know what to do."

"Where are you?" His tone sharpened, steel beneath the demand.

"My house," I choked, letting the sobs convulse through me, raw and broken. "Kaius, please hurry. I'm so scared—"

I let the phone slip from my hand, let it clatter against the floor beside me, so he'd hear the muffled sobs through the speaker. My cries cracked and fractured, the sound of someone spiraling.

A woman at the end of her rope. A victim.

I pressed my hand against my burning cheek, against the stinging cut on my arm, and let myself sink into the role I'd built out of blood and lies.

Because when Kaius came through that door, he couldn't see Emersyn Spade.

He had to see a broken girl who needed saving.

Even if no one could save me now.

CHAPTER FORTY-TWO

kaius

ACELYNN'S VOICE still echoed in my head, broken through the phone, raw with panic. I'd heard screams, confessions, lies, and begging in my lifetime, but this had cut straight through me like a razor. She hadn't sounded like Acelynn, not the sharp-tongued, fire-eyed woman I knew. She'd sounded small. Shattered. Afraid.

The desert night was quiet when I pulled up to Acelynn's place. Too damn quiet. The air pressed down heavily. Even the crickets were silent, as if the whole stretch of neighborhood knew something was wrong before I did.

I killed the engine and stepped out, gravel crunching under my boots. My hand went instinctively to the gun holstered in the back of my waistband. Habit. Preparedness. Paranoia. Call it what you want.

The house loomed dark, one window glowing faintly where the curtain didn't quite shut. The front door was cracked open, tilting on its hinge like someone had forced their way in. I pushed it with two fingers, the wood creaking as the shadows inside swallowed me whole.

The smell hit me first.

Blood. The iron tang coated my nostrils before I even spotted the source. It tangled with something else—sharp, bitter, poisonous. A scent I was all too familiar with. Hemlock.

I stepped inside slowly and deliberately, letting my eyes adjust to the wreckage laid bare under the moonlight filtering through the blinds. The place was chaos incarnate—chairs overturned, drawers gutted and scattered, the coffee table split down the middle like it had taken a boot to the spine. A vase lay shattered against the wall, its water soaking into the rug, petals trampled underfoot.

It looked like a struggle, but it was too neat in its destruction. The kind of scene you'd set if you wanted people to think you'd fought tooth and nail for your life. I filed that thought away, teeth grinding against each other as I crossed the room.

And then I saw her.

Acelynn was crumpled against the far wall, a mess of tangled hair, torn clothes, and fresh bruises already blossoming across her face and arms. Her skin glistened with sweat, streaked with blood that looked half dried, and half smeared from her touch. She was shaking, shoulders curled inward like she was trying to fold herself small enough to disappear.

A few feet to her right lay a body.

Alaric.

A knife wound under his ribs was visible even where I stood, crimson pooling thick beneath him in large puddles. His hand lay outstretched in broken glass, hemlock vials shattered around him, the acrid stench of the poison biting at the back of my throat. The old Knight's eyes stared wide and glassy at the ceiling, fixed on the nothingness of death.

My jaw locked. A hundred thoughts surged and rattled in my skull, but I shoved them down into silence.

"Acelynn," I said, voice low, flat, carrying across the room like a knife dragged on stone.

Her head jerked up. Her eyes were swollen, red-rimmed, brimming with tears that clung stubbornly before spilling over. The look on her face nearly made me pause—terror, relief, desperation all bleeding together in one wreck of expression.

"Kaius..." Her voice cracked, raw as her body shuddered. She pushed herself up and stumbled across the chaos until she collapsed against me, her sobs breaking loose as if she'd held them back just for this moment. "Kaius...I didn't mean... he came at me. I didn't know what to do."

Her words twisted, choking out half-sentences and shredded fragments of excuses. Her fists clutched at my shirt, smearing blood across the black fabric as if marking me with it, binding me to the scene.

My arms went around her, almost against my will. The instinct was older than reason—hold, steady, protect. Her pulse thrashed against my wrist where her throat brushed it, wild and unsteady, the beat of someone on the edge of collapse.

But my mind never stopped moving.

Alaric. Here. Dead.

Her story—an attack, a break-in, a fight for her life.

The wreckage matched the tale well enough, but there was something in it that sat too neatly. No overturned bloodstains in places they shouldn't be. No spatter where there should've been panic. Everything angled just so, every break plausible.

It was staged. I'd bet my life on it.

But when I tilted her chin up, forcing her eyes to meet

mine, what stared back was chaos of a different kind. Her gaze swam with tears, wide and frantic, pleading with me not to look too closely. Not faked. Or at least not all of it.

"Breathe," I ordered, low and sharp, trying to cut through her hysteria. "Start from the beginning."

Her lips trembled. "He broke in. I was alone, and he knew that. I think he knew about me—" Acelynn's words broke off, panic flaring before she caught herself, biting down on the rest like it had burned her tongue. Her eyes flicked away too fast. A lie. Or at least, not the whole truth.

My grip tightened on her chin, forcing her gaze back to mine. The softness in me burned away, leaving nothing but iron. "No skipping. No pretty lies. Sit."

She froze, confusion and dread fighting on her face. When I pointed toward the overturned chair by the table, my tone allowed no argument. "Now."

Her legs wobbled under her as she staggered toward it, the scrape of wood against tile loud in the silence as she righted it and sank down against the cushioned top. She clutched her hands together in her lap, knuckles white, eyes darting anywhere but my gaze.

I stayed standing, a shadow over her. "From the top, Acelynn. Every detail. If you hesitate, if you feed me some half-truth, I'll know. And then the Knights will know."

Acelynn's chest rose and fell too fast, panic stealing the air from her lungs. "Kaius, please, I didn't—"

"Don't." My voice cracked like a whip. She flinched. "This isn't about begging. This is about survival. Yours depends on how you answer me."

Her throat bobbed as she swallowed, tears welling again. "He came at me. He knew my name. He said...he said something about owing blood. I grabbed the knife. I didn't think, I just—"

Her voice splintered, trembling into sobs. I watched her every twitch, every pause, the way her eyes flickered left when she lied to me. Fear radiated off her in waves, but not all of it was from Alaric's attack. Some of it was directed toward me. The thought of what I might do if I didn't like her answers consumed her. And maybe that was exactly what she needed to feel.

Acelynn had gotten too comfortable in the club. Thought some pretty little tears and blood-covered white lies would just be swept under the rug. But not this time. This time, she had to answer not only to me but to the Knights for her crimes against one of our own.

"Enough," I snapped, letting the silence around us hang. I stepped forward, bending at the knee to look her in the eye. "You're safe now. He can't touch you."

But even as I said it, I stared past her at Alaric's body, unease burrowing into my gut. Safe from him, maybe. But what about being safe from her? The little bit of doubt that I had earlier on the sand dune was beginning to crawl back to the surface.

Her small frame shook against the back of the chair. My hand reached out, catching her jaw in my hand. Tilting her face to meet my eyes, her tears stilled. For just a heartbeat, her breath hitched between us. So close I could feel the heat of it, could almost taste the salt of her tears. A flash of anger glinted in her eye, and in that moment, I knew she was more dangerous than Alaric had ever been. The elder Knight had known something about her past, and she had slaughtered him to keep the secret. But the small voice in the back of my head told me that it wasn't true, that Alaric had attacked her in a crazed moment, thinking she was a ghost from his past. It wouldn't have been the first time something like that had occurred, but Vince had always been fast enough to stop him.

I leaned closer, letting her see the cold in my eyes, letting it cut through her hysteria like the truth she couldn't dodge. My voice dropped to a near-whisper, each word a knife pressed to her throat.

"You have Knight blood on your hands." I let the weight of it hang there, iron and final. "Now you have to pay that debt."

The silence that followed was heavy, suffocating. Her tears stilled. Her breath caught sharply. The blood between us—Alaric's, hers, mine by proxy—sealed the moment like a pact.

And for the first time, I realized just how far gone we both already were.

CHAPTER FORTY-THREE

acelynn

THE ROUNDTABLE ROOM reeked of smoke, sweat, and something heavier, like judgment. The kind that clung to the walls, to the eyes that pinned me down from every angle.

I sat in the chair facing the two double doors, my legs trembling beneath me. No matter how I moved, I could not force them to still. My palms pressed flat against the polished wood, sticky with sweat I couldn't scrub off, no matter how hard I rubbed them into my shirt.

Kaius sat across from me, broad shoulders tense beneath his jacket, eyes unreadable. Nolan leaned lazily in his chair to Kaius's right, but there was nothing casual about the sharp flick of his gaze as it swept over me, dissecting every twitch, every shallow breath. Vince paced the length of the room, restless, his fists clenching and unclenching at his sides. He hadn't looked at me since we'd cleaned up the mess.

The mess.

Alaric's blood was gone from the floor of my house, his body no longer sprawled in glass and poison. But I could still feel it on my hands, under my nails, seared into my skin like something that would never wash off. The silence stretched until it felt like it would crack my ribs open. Then Kaius leaned forward, folding his hands on the table. His voice was low, steady, heavy enough to pin me in place.

"You have Knight blood on your hands." He'd said it earlier, in the wreckage of my home, and he said it again now like a verdict.

My throat tightened as the words echoed off the stone walls.

"That's not something we can ignore."

I swallowed hard, trying to steady my voice. "I told you, he attacked me. He came into my house and—"

"And you killed him." Nolan's voice sliced clean through mine, calm and lethal. "Doesn't matter how. Doesn't matter why. A Knight is dead. That blood debt doesn't just vanish."

I flinched, my fingernails scraping against the shallow grooves of the table.

"What are you going to do to me?" My voice was small, raw.

Vince finally stopped pacing, his shoulders stiff as he turned to face me. His eyes were a storm—dark, furious, grieving in a way I couldn't quite name. "You murdered my father, Acelynn. The only living elder who was left of the Knights. You killed him in your house, and now you need to prove that you aren't against us, prove that you are not a Spade playing both sides, because from where I'm standing, a whole lot of shit has gotten fucked up since you waltzed in here. Prove you are who you say you are, Acelynn. That's all we are asking of you."

The sound of my name—or rather, the *wrong* name—on his tongue made my stomach turn. *Emersyn Spade.* Daughter of the Death Dealers' leader. The girl who'd died in the family massacre. Or should have. My chest tightened. "What do you want me to do?"

Kaius's gaze sharpened, carving right through the trembling mess of me. "Tomorrow night, a shipment comes through the border. Muze."

The word itself was poison, the drug whispered about in every back alley, the one that had ruined more lives than fire and steel combined. "We've already paid, but the delivery requires a face-to-face drop. A lump sum, no mistakes."

Nolan leaned in, smirking faintly, but his eyes were all steel. "That face is going to be yours. You'll drive down, hand off the money, and bring the shipment back to the club. Clean. Simple. No questions."

My blood went cold. Delivering Muze wasn't just some errand. It was a test. One misstep, one second of hesitation, and they'd decide I wasn't proving loyalty. That I was proving guilt.

"And if I don't?" My voice cracked before I could swallow the weakness down.

"Then we'll know," Kaius said flatly, "that you're not with us. And if you're not with us, Acelynn..." His eyes burned into mine, cold enough to freeze bone. "You're against us."

The room pulsed with silence, the air too thick to breathe. I nodded. Slowly, then faster, like if I agreed enough times, it would drown out the sound of my heartbeat slamming against my ribs.

"Fine," I whispered. "I'll do it."

None of them smiled. None of them eased. Because this wasn't a victory. It was a leash.

By the time I left the roundtable, I could still feel the weight of their eyes clawing down my spine. The nausea in my gut was so sharp, I nearly doubled over in the hallway. As soon as I shut the door of my car, I dug into my pocket for my phone. My hands shook, fumbling over the screen until it rang through.

"Watson," I breathed when he picked up, my voice hushed but hard with urgency. "I need you to do something for me."

A pause on the other end. Then his voice responded, low and cautious, "What is it?"

I pressed a hand against the steering wheel, grounding myself, because if I didn't, I might spiral into the panic waiting just under my skin. "Tomorrow night, I need Parsons distracted, out of the way. Do whatever it takes. I can't explain why. You are just going to have to trust me. Can you do that?"

Another beat of silence, then Watson exhaled slowly. "Yes, I can handle that."

The call ended, but the dread didn't. Because this wasn't survival anymore.

It was war.

CHAPTER FORTY-FOUR

acelynn

THE HOUSE still smelled faintly of bleach. Even after the Knights' cleanup crew had scoured it top to bottom, I could smell it—the chemical sharpness clinging to the air like invisible ghosts, trying too hard to erase the violence that had stained these walls. No matter how many times I blinked, I still saw Alaric's body on the floor, his blood dark and tacky under the weak light of my kitchen. My throat clenched with the memory of his eyes in that final moment, shocked that I had been the one to end him.

But the Knights hadn't let me sit with that. They had dragged me into the roundtable room, made me stand beneath the unyielding weight of Kaius's stare, Nolan's suspicion, and Vince's hollow silence. And then Kaius's words had cut me open like a blade.

You have Knight blood on your hands. Now you have to pay that debt.

I couldn't shake it. Not in the way Nolan's hand had lingered near his gun the whole time I spoke, not in the way Vince hadn't looked at me once. But most of all, not in the way Kaius had said it. Like a sentence, not a warning. So now here I was, wearing bruises I hadn't earned honestly, wearing a mask I couldn't take off. I slid into the driver's seat of an unmarked sedan with a trunk full of cash Nolan had dropped off earlier. They hadn't trusted me with this job. They had dared me to survive it.

The desert landscape bled out in every direction, endless and hollow. Driving at night felt like steering through the underworld, headlights carving out fragile tunnels of light in a sea of black. The road stretched on and on, cracked and narrow, as if it might collapse beneath me and swallow me whole. My hands gripped the wheel so tightly, the leather began to cut into my palms. The engine's low hum was steady, but underneath it I could hear my own pulse hammering.

Every so often, I checked the rearview mirror, half-hoping, half-dreading to see headlights cresting over the hills. If Nolan and Vince had decided to tail me, maybe this would feel less like a suicide mission. But the mirror stared back empty, the desert swallowing me whole. My mind wandered to Logan. Logan, with his wolf-smile, his endless cruelty hidden behind charm. The ghost of the man who had once called himself mine. If anyone could light a spade into the sand, it would be him. Now that he knows I'm alive, it's only a matter of time before he buries me himself. And if he knew I was alive, then I might as well just bury myself in my own grave. My knuckles tightened further as I shoved the thought down, trying to refocus my thoughts.

Kaius hadn't given me a choice. If I wanted to prove I wasn't an enemy, I would drive this money down to the border and bring back the Muze shipment without flinching. No excuses. No stumbles. And so here I was, the perfect little pawn, driving straight into hell. The first sign of the border meeting point was the smell.

Smoke drifted on the wind, acrid and greasy, the kind of smoke that clung to your clothes and followed you home. Then came the faint glow, pulsing weakly in the distance—an oil-drum fire eating away at the night. My stomach twisted as I approached, headlights spilling across rusting fences and half-collapsed gates. This was natural land that wasn't technically owned by any governing official. The chain-link fence sagged under barbed wire, and the leaning concrete walls looked like they hadn't been touched in years. A no-man's-land. The kind of place where you could bury a body and no one would ever find it.

Two SUVs sat just beyond the fence, engines growling low, their shadows huge in the firelight. A few men lounged against them, silhouettes sharp and restless, guns gleaming faintly at their sides. Not Knights. That much I could tell instantly. Knights carried themselves with a rigid soldier's weight. These men were looser, cockier—sharks circling blood.

I slowed, my tires crunching over gravel. The men straightened, attention snapping toward me. One peeled away from the others, stepping into my headlights. He was broad, his jacket heavy with patches stitched in symbols I didn't recognize, but the smirk on his face was universal. A predator's grin.

"You must be the delivery girl," he said, voice thick with amusement.

I swallowed hard, forcing myself to keep my tone level. "I'm here with payment."

He tapped his knuckles against the hood, like I was a toy he was considering buying. "Cute thing like you, running

Knight errands? Didn't think they trusted outsiders with the good stuff."

My skin prickled. "The money's in the trunk. Count it if you want."

He motioned lazily to his men. They moved like jackals, yanking open the trunk, dragging out heavy duffels stuffed with cash. Zippers hissed, and one of them whistled low.

"Plenty," he said.

The leader didn't look at the bags. He just watched me with amusement. His grin sharpened. "And in exchange..."

He snapped his fingers. The second SUV opened, and a crate was hauled out and dropped onto the dirt. The wood creaked under the impact, reinforced by metal bands, stamped with a single black word burned deep into the grain: Muze.

The scent hit me immediately—chemical, sharp, bitter as poison. It made the back of my throat ache.

I kept my face blank. "Deal's done. I'll take it from here."

The man chuckled, shaking his head. "No handshake? No drink for the road? You Knights are colder than rumors say."

I didn't move. Didn't flinch. "Just business."

His eyes lingered on me, longer than I wanted, longer than I could bear. His smirk thinned into something else—something quieter. Hungrier.

"You look familiar," he said softly. "Got family around here?"

Ice slid down my spine. My pulse thudded hard in my ears.

"No," I said flatly.

For a breath, he just stared, as though peeling me open, layer by layer, like he could read the name etched into my bones. Spade.

Then, just as suddenly, he grinned again. "Fine. Run along, delivery girl."

The crate was shoved into the trunk. The slam of metal rang out too loudly in the night.

I got behind the wheel, every muscle stiff, every nerve stretched taut. As I pulled away, I felt his eyes burning into the back of my skull.

Only when the firelight faded behind me and the desert swallowed me up again did I let myself breathe. But the air came in shallow, ragged gasps, and the knot in my chest didn't ease.

Because I knew tonight hadn't ended anything.

It had only begun.

The drive back felt longer, the desert darker, the crate heavier, as if the Muze itself was pressing against the air, leeching poison into the car. My fingers itched where they touched the steering wheel. My throat ached with the chemical tang that seemed to bleed from the back seat.

Every bump in the road sent a jolt up my spine, but worse was the silence. With every mile, I felt more certain I was being followed, even if the mirror stayed empty. My mind spun with images of Logan, of Death Dealers waiting just out of sight, of Kaius's cold gray eyes if I returned with even the smallest mistake.

By the time the lights of the city glowed on the horizon, my whole body was trembling. Not from fear anymore. From exhaustion. From the weight of everything I had to carry.

And from the certainty that the Knights hadn't sent me out here to succeed.

They had sent me out here to prove I could bleed for them.

CHAPTER FORTY-FIVE

kaius

Got it.

THE TEXT from Acelynn flashed across my phone's screen. Two simple words typed fast enough that she hadn't wasted time with punctuation. She had successfully obtained the Muze.

Not that I hadn't already known.

The tracker I had planted beneath the driver's seat had told me everything I needed tonight. Every turn she'd taken, every unnecessary stop, every time she hesitated for longer than I liked. Her path lit up for me like a thread through the dark. If she'd been compromised, if she'd even thought about betraying me, I'd have known long before this message.

Still, seeing her words, raw and real, untied something in me I hadn't realized was knotted. She'd pulled it off. She was safe. And she was coming back.

The Queen's Table hummed with its usual nightly buzz around me. Vince sat near the end of the bar, slouched but alert, fingers tracing the lip of his glass without ever taking a drink. His eyes weren't really here—lost somewhere far and cold, like always—but he noticed everything. Astoria leaned over the counter, bright laughter snapping like sparks as she teased Josie, who flicked lime juice at her in retaliation. Nolan stood sentinel, back to the wall, arms folded across his chest, scanning the room with the unyielding stare that had earned him the reputation among the Knights.

It was ordinary, in the way nights in our world ever could be. Familiar. Steady.

Then the doors slammed open.

The music died on a strangled note. The chatter cut to silence so thick you could hear the hum of the beer cooler behind the bar. Every head turned.

Detective Parsons filled the doorway like a bad omen, his badge flashing gold under the dim lights. His smirk was wolfish and hungry, flanked by a tide of uniforms that spilled in behind him. Detective Watson trailed just a step back, not grinning, not smirking, just grim, his eyes cataloging the room with quiet calculation. The air shifted instantly, heavy as a storm about to break.

"Evening, folks," Parsons called, spreading his arms like he owned the place. "Why don't we all make this easy? Line up nice and pretty against that wall."

No one moved at first. My Knights didn't bow to anyone.

Then one of the uniforms snapped the action of his rifle with exaggerated menace. The sound cracked the silence. Patrons muttered, cursed under their breath, and chairs scraped across the floor. Slowly, uneasily, bodies shuffled toward the wall.

I didn't move until I had to.

Two officers closed in, postures stiff, weapons at the ready, like they were herding a wolf into a cage. They weren't wrong.

"Against the wall," one barked, voice breaking with nerves.

I stood, smooth, deliberate, swirling the last of my drink before setting the glass down with a quiet clink. I didn't look at them. I looked at Parsons. And when his smirk widened, I knew exactly what this was.

The pat-downs began, rough, impersonal. But Parsons didn't delegate Astoria. His hands skimmed her waist, too slow, too deliberate. His fingers pressed into the curve of her hip, lingering, sliding lower than protocol demanded. Astoria stiffened, lips peeling back from her teeth in a soundless snarl. Beside her, Josie flinched as another officer shoved too close, searching places he didn't need to search.

Nolan broke.

"Get your filthy hands off them," he snapped, stepping forward with a suddenness that made the room jolt. His shoulder rammed Parsons back a step, shoving the man's grin askew. Everything detonated at once.

Guns lifted. Officers shouted. The bar erupted with panicked movement, a half-scream from one of the patrons, Astoria cursing loud enough to cut glass.

Parsons staggered, then laughed. Actually laughed, like this was the game he'd been hoping for. "What's the matter, Knight? Don't like a little police work?"

"Police work?" Nolan's voice was sharp enough to draw blood. "That's what you call putting your hands on women who never asked for it?"

His fists curled, knuckles whitening until the sound of his bones popping carried over the noise. I saw the moment Parsons decided. His grin widened, and he snapped his fingers. "Arrest him."

Officers swarmed Nolan, grabbing his arms, wrenching them behind his back. He didn't resist at first, not until they slammed him face-first into the floor. Then he roared, thrashing like a chained animal, boots kicking hard enough to shake the floorboards. Astoria screamed his name. Josie shoved against the officer holding her, desperation in her voice. Vince didn't move, didn't blink, but I saw the twitch of his jaw, the way his hand flexed like he was inches from pulling a blade.

I stepped forward, and the word that left me was quiet, but it ripped through the chaos like a lone bullet. "Enough."

Half the room froze. The rest caught the tension a beat later, silence folding in on itself until all that remained was ragged breathing, Nolan's snarls, and Parsons's ugly laughter. The detective turned toward me, smug as sin.

"Your boy assaulted an officer," he said smoothly. "That's jail time."

I tilted my head, letting my silence stretch until it bit. "From where I stood," I said softly, "I saw a man defending his own from a dog who doesn't know when to keep his hands to himself."

Watson's jaw ticked, the faintest crack in his mask. His gaze flicked to Parsons, then me, then away. He wasn't here to protect us—but he wasn't blind either.

Parsons leaned in, eyes glittering. "Careful, Mordred. You really want me to drag all of you out of here in cuffs tonight?"

Behind him, Nolan cursed through clenched teeth, still straining against the metal around his wrist. Astoria trembled with fury, chest heaving. Josie was pale, pressed so close to the wall with vacant eyes that told me she had disappeared inside herself, disappeared into the memories that haunted her. Vince finally moved, shifting his weight, his eyes dark as midnight storms. The whole room was a hair trigger away from war. I smiled. Just enough to show teeth.

"You've made your point," I said, voice smooth and cold.

I stepped closer until only Parsons and Watson could hear me. "But understand this, Detective. Lay another hand on one of my own, and I'll remind you what happens when the Knights stop playing nice with your department."

For the first time, Parsons's grin faltered. Only a flicker. Then it was back, brighter, sharper, dangerous. He leaned close, the stink of gin clinging to his words. "You're not as untouchable as you think, Mordred."

Then he straightened, smirk flashing wider for the room as he dug into his coat pocket. Paper crinkled. My gut went cold before he even unfolded it.

"This little dance," he said, waving the sheet, "was just foreplay." He snapped it flat, holding it up so every Knight, every patron, could see the bold header across the top. "Search warrant. Signed and sealed."

The uniforms shifted, anticipation rolling off them like heat. Parsons's voice dropped, venom threaded with delight. "By order of the department, we're turning this place inside out."

Watson's gaze cut to me once more. Apology didn't live in his eyes—but warning did.

Parsons dropped the warrant on the bar with a slap of finality. "Hope you've been keeping tidy, Mordred. Because now we get to see what your precious Queen's Table is really hiding."

Then the search began.

CHAPTER FORTY-SIX

acelynn

THE STREETS around the Queen's Table were too quiet. Normally, even before I stepped out of my car, the bar pulsed with sound, bass rattling the windows, laughter spilling into the night, the kind of energy that made the air feel alive. But tonight, when I killed the engine and climbed out, there was only the static ring of police radios and the scattered sweep of red and blue lights bouncing off the brick façade. My stomach dropped. Something was very wrong.

I slammed the car door and moved fast, my boots crunching over gravel as I came around the corner. That was when I saw them—the wall of uniforms, bodies in dark Kevlar and navy, blocking the entrance like a barricade. Each of their faces was set in the same hard lines. The glint of badges hit my eyes like polished steel.

The knot in my chest twisted until it hurt. No. Not tonight. Not after everything I'd risked to prove myself to him. I shoved past the first two officers who reached for me, ignoring the bark of "Ma'am, stop!" and shouldered into the bar with a force that was fueled by panic.

What I saw froze me cold. The Queen's Table was chaos. Tables overturned. Bottles shattered. The scent of spilled vodka mixed with sweat and fear. The usual haze of neon had been cut through with harsh flashlight beams, every corner probed and exposed. And pressed against the far wall, hands raised, were the Knights.

Nolan was already cuffed, a red welt rising along his cheekbone where someone had slammed him into the ground. He was seething, straining against the officer gripping his arms like he'd bite his way free if he could. Josie's jaw was clenched, her posture rigid with humiliation, while Astoria's lips twisted in a snarl every time Parsons brushed too close. Vince...Vince was stone. He leaned against the wall, motionless, but his eyes were sharp enough to cut glass, following every twitch of movement in the room.

And Kaius...

He wasn't against the wall. He stood at the center of it, not restrained, not cowering, though three officers circled him warily, hands hovering over their holsters. His presence filled the bar like gravity. His face was carved from shadow, unreadable but dangerous, a man holding back a storm with nothing but his will.

At the eye of all of it was Detective Parsons. His grin was smug, self-satisfied, the kind of smile that thrived on power. He looked like he'd already won, like tearing this place apart was just child's play before the final strike. Detective Watson stood just behind him, silent, steady, and watching everything. Unlike Parsons, there was no glee on his face. Just calculation. I knew this was his doing because I had asked for a distraction, and he delivered.

My voice cracked through the air, louder than I intended. "What the hell is going on?"

Every head turned. Parsons's grin stretched wider when his eyes landed on me.

"Well, look who wandered in," he drawled, striding forward. "The prodigal girl herself. Couldn't resist a party, huh, Acelynn?"

My skin crawled hearing my name in his mouth in this capacity. We were both playing our roles, and I knew he was going to take immense pleasure in drawing it out in the most painful way possible. I forced myself to plant my feet, even though my pulse was slamming in my throat. "You have no right to be here. This is harassment."

"Harassment?" Parsons cocked his head, eyes dragging over me in a way that made me want to scrub my skin raw. He gestured broadly at the mess of his officers' flipping stools and rifling drawers. "No, sweetheart. This is called police work and is what happens when rats run wild in my city and think they can hide in shadows forever."

Behind him, an officer slammed open the back door and disappeared through. I knew where they were going, and I just prayed that what they found in the basement wasn't going to send every one of us to jail. I mean, herbs and files weren't illegal...

Another officer ripped through crates behind the bar, tossing glass aside like none of it mattered. The sound grated like nails on my nerves. I took another step closer until I was breathing in the sour stench of his cologne. "Police work usually requires evidence. A warrant. Actual probable cause. Do you have any of that, Detective? Or are you just here to play thug in uniform?"

The smile twitched. Just a flicker, but I saw it. A crack in the smug mask.

He bent down until his mouth hovered by my ear, low enough that only I could hear. "Careful, sweetheart. We both know how to play this game. That smart mouth might earn you a set of cuffs again. Maybe even your own cell this time. I'd love to see how well you hold up under questioning with all your new knowledge."

The words were slick with threat, coiled with promise. My chest burned, but I refused to let him see the fear. I raised my chin, spitting fire back at him instead. "You don't scare me."

And that was when Kaius moved. The shift was subtle—just a step—but it carried the weight of an earthquake. The officers around him stiffened, hands hovering closer to their guns. But he didn't look at them. His eyes were fixed on Parsons.

"That's enough," he said, and the words rumbled low, lethal, like a warning before the kill. Even from across the room, the warmth of it washed over me. It made my heart thump against my chest. I turned my gaze on him, heat pooling in my core at his intense stare. God, even when I was furious at him for what he made me do tonight, I still wanted him to show me just how unhinged he could be with me. The thought had my cheeks flushing slightly.

"You don't threaten what's mine," Kaius continued, voice still low, but sharper now, honed with years of practice. "You don't touch her. You don't even breathe her name unless I say so. Do you understand me, Parsons?"

The air in the room constricted. For the first time, Parsons's grin faltered. He straightened slowly, eyes flicking between me and Kaius, measuring, calculating. "We'll see how clear things are once we finish the search."

Just as I thought the entire room was going to combust into flames, officers stormed in from the back door, and the chaos truly began. Their boots pounded against the hardwood floor as they tore through the hall.

"There is nothing there," Watson's voice called out over the grumbles of the other officers.

Parsons's eyes flashed with anger before he tore off in the direction of the basement. I followed after him, not caring that I was being screamed at to stop. When my feet finally landed on the final step, I came upon an entirely different space than what I had seen just a day earlier. The basement was empty, scrubbed to sterility, just rows of liquor bottles, bags of ice, and cleaning solution. The table was bare, no trace of anything illegal left behind. No Muze. No vials. Nothing but a stage that smelled of alcohol and smoke. Even the filing cabinet, which had sat in the corner, was now gone.

I watched Parsons's face as the reports trickled back—empty, negative, cleared. His jaw tightened, his smirk stretched thinner, like a mask starting to crack under the weight of its own lie. Watson took the papers from one officer who was reporting the scene around us, scanning them quietly. His expression barely shifted, but when his eyes lifted to meet mine across the room, something flickered. Relief. Regret. A warning. I couldn't tell.

Watson handed the report to his partner. The silence dragged as Parsons processed defeat, eyes scanning over each and every word on the white sheet of paper. Finally, with a sound like a growl, he shoved the report back into Watson's chest and turned on me.

"This isn't over," he snarled, jabbing a finger into my chest. His eyes found mine last, sharp and venomous. "One of these times, they are going to slip. And when they do, I'll be there to watch them burn."

The venom in his voice should've rattled me. Instead, something wild rose up in me, sharp and reckless. I smiled, slow and sweet. "Looks like tonight isn't that night."

The words hit him like a slap. His eyes narrowed to slits, but before he could strike back, Kaius strode down the stairs and stepped in front of me, a wall of steel and shadow.

His voice was quiet, absolute. "Get out of my bar."

And for once, Parsons obeyed.

The officers filed out, leaving wreckage in their wake—shattered glass, overturned tables, and the stench of smoke and tension still clinging to the air. Only when the last badge had disappeared through the door did I let my shoulders sag, breath trembling out of me. Kaius turned slowly, his eyes landing on me, and for a moment, the room felt too small to contain him. But I knew I wasn't free to go, not when I still had to prove that the Muze was securely obtained. Proved that I was on the right side of the Knights.

CHAPTER FORTY-SEVEN

acelynn

THE BAR FELT HOLLOW after the raid, like the life had been sucked out of it and only shadows remained. Broken chairs lay scattered like bodies on the frontline. Shards of glass glittered across the hardwood, catching the dim bar light in sharp flashes. The air reeked of spilled liquor and sweat. A haze of dust still drifted down from where shelves had been knocked askew. Even though Parsons and his team were gone, their presence lingered like a bad taste.

I moved carefully across the wreckage, my heart still pounding from the confrontation. Astoria was pacing near the pool tables, her face pale with fury, lips pressed into a thin line. Josie leaned against the bar as Vince examined the bruises already darkening her wrist from Parsons's rough grip. Nolan's absence was a raw, gaping wound. They'd hauled him out in cuffs, his rage echoing even as the flashing lights swallowed him whole. I'd wanted to tear after him, to scream, to claw Parsons's face open with my nails. But I'd stood rooted to the floor, knowing that one wrong move could bring it all crashing down.

Kaius hadn't said a word since the police had cleared out. He stood at the bar like a statue, shoulders squared, the weight of responsibility hanging off him as if it had been carved into his bones. His silence pressed heavier than any threat Parsons could've made.

I thought about leaving him to his brooding, but something in the tension of his jaw told me he wasn't finished—not with me, not with tonight. So when he finally moved, I followed.

The night air outside was damp and heavy. Sirens still echoed faintly in the distance, their wails bleeding into the dark city streets. My pulse quickened when Kaius strode straight to the car I'd left behind earlier, his long strides eating up the pavement. Without a word, he ducked down, slid his hand under the driver's seat, and pulled out a small black tracker.

My blood froze.

He turned it in his hand, the faintest smirk tugging at his lips before his eyes cut to me.

"Next time you think about running off with something that dangerous," he said, voice low and sharp, "remember that I'll always know exactly where you are."

"What the hell are you talking about?" I asked.

The sting of humiliation and anger hit me square in the chest. Heat burned up my neck, and for a second, I could barely breathe. He'd been watching me. Every move. Every turn. Every mistake. But it didn't make any sense that he thought I was running. I hadn't strayed from the directions given. It had been a straight shot.

"There was a moment on the drive back." Kaius flipped the device up in the air, letting it fall back into his hand once before continuing, "You hesitated, sat at that four-way stop for too long. I assumed you were debating on running for it.

It would have been so easy to just leave, even though I'll always find you, kitten."

I wanted to claw the smugness off his face. Instead, I stood there in glaring silence, watching as he strode over and popped the trunk. The Muze was still there. Safe. Untouched. Relief flooded me, leaving me momentarily unsteady. At least Parsons hadn't found it.

Kaius shut the trunk without another comment, brushing past me like I wasn't worth his time tonight. He didn't even glance back to see if I was following. The sting of that cut deeper than the tracker. I followed anyway.

The Queen's Table was quieter now, the remaining Knights cleaning up the wreckage. Vince and Josie whispered near the booths. Astoria had disappeared to one of the dorms, I assume, and the air hummed with the kind of silence that came only after disaster. But Kaius didn't stop to speak to any of them. Instead, he kept walking, all the way back to his office. I quickened my pace, not letting him close the door before I slipped through at the last moment.

The room was dim, lit only by a single lamp that cast shadows across the cluttered desk. Maps, ledgers, half-burned cigarettes, a knife, a revolver—chaos laid out with deliberate intent. The faint smell of smoke and leather clung to the space. It was him in every way—commanding, dangerous, suffocating.

I spun on him, anger spiking hotter now that we were alone. "You put a tracker on me?"

Kaius didn't even flinch. His hands braced against the desk, his gaze unwavering. "You were sloppy tonight. I had to make sure you didn't do something stupid."

My jaw dropped. "Sloppy? I just walked through a goddamn police raid without getting caught, and you're calling me sloppy? I did your fucking dirty work and picked up your drugs to prove to you I was loyal, but I'm just a girl who can't handle herself? Screw you, Kaius."

His gaze snapped to mine. "You walked into a raid like a lamb into a wolf's den. Parsons could've gutted you just to get to me. Do you have any idea what kind of target you painted on yourself tonight?"

The heat in my chest exploded. "So...what? I'm just supposed to sit pretty and wait for you to give orders? Hide in your shadows while you play king of the goddamn world?"

The corner of his mouth tilted in a smug, infuriating smirk. "If the crown fits."

The sound of my palm slamming against his desk cracked through the air. "You arrogant bastard."

My voice trembled, not from fear but from the sharp edge of rage. "You think you own me because you pulled me into this world? Because you make me feel—"

The words caught in my throat. I bit them back, choking on their truth. But he saw. Oh, he fucking saw.

His eyes darkened, hunger breaking through the mask of control. "Because I make you feel what, Acelynn?"

The air between us shifted, sparking dangerously. My heart hammered in my chest, each beat dragging me closer to something I wasn't ready to name.

"Because you piss me off so badly, I could scream," I snapped. "Because every time you open your mouth, I want to put my fist through it. And I hate you for making it so difficult to hate you. Because—"

My voice cracked, softer now. "Because I can't tell if I want to kill you or..."

He closed the distance like a predator striking. One hand slammed against the wall beside mine. The other seized my chin, tilting my face up until his breath mingled with mine.

"Or what?" he demanded, voice low, dangerous, unraveling.

My breath hitched. My whole body burned. "Or kiss you."

He didn't hesitate. His mouth crashed against mine with a violence that stole the air from my lungs.

It wasn't sweet. It wasn't gentle. It was fire meeting gasoline, the explosion of weeks of fury and restraint ripping loose in one brutal kiss. His hand tangled in my hair, the other clamping against the small of my back, dragging me forward until I was pinned between him and the wall.

I clawed at his shirt, yanking him closer like I hated him, like I needed him, like both urges would tear me apart if I didn't let them out.

The kiss was raw, messy, teeth and tongues clashing with the desperation of two people who didn't know how to want quietly. He tasted like whiskey and smoke, like danger, like everything I shouldn't crave and everything I couldn't stop.

By the time we broke apart, gasping for air, my lips were swollen, my pulse a thunderstorm in my veins. His forehead rested against mine, his breath ragged, his hands still gripping me like he didn't know how to let go.

And God help me, I didn't want him to.

The silence that followed was deafening. My chest rose and fell in sharp bursts, and all I could think was how much I hated him. How much I wanted him. How much those two things were becoming the same.

I pulled slightly, though my body screamed against it. His eyes followed me, dark and heavy, and I could see the war raging in him as clearly as I felt it in myself. Without another second, I dove back in for his lips.

CHAPTER FORTY-EIGHT

acelynn

THE MOMENT his mouth claimed mine again, I forgot how to breathe. Dear god, he already had me unraveling, panting for him like I was starved. No kiss in my life had ever stolen from me like this, demanding more than I thought I could give. It wasn't just his lips against mine. It was submission. It was a surrender I didn't realize I was capable of until I found myself chasing every flick of his tongue, every drag of his teeth. There was no fight left in me. Only the instinct to obey, to follow wherever he led, until I was reduced to nothing but his praise. Kaius pushed us back until the backs of my legs hit his desk.

The scrape of his calloused fingers hooked around the lace at my pants, tugging them and my underwear down in one slow, deliberate pull. The air hit my bare skin, and heat rushed up my chest, shame and exhilaration twisting together. My eyes caught his. They were hungry, restrained, reverent, and feral all at once. It was as if he were holding himself back from devouring me whole. He didn't groan, not fully, but his throat bobbed, the sound low, caught between awe and possession.

And it was me—I was the thing unraveling the King of Lovelen.

My mouth watered at the realization. His touch skimmed over me again, and this time I couldn't hold back. A whimper slipped from my lips, helpless and needy.

"Kaius," I gasped, the sound broken, stripped of pretense.

His hands gripped my hips, lifting me up and onto the wooden surface. My voice barely existed between the sharp edges of my breathing, but I knew he heard me. He always heard me.

His hand was merciless in its patience, dragging me further down the desk until I was sprawled out on the surface, my spine arching and my thighs trembling around the deliberate wedge of his knee. The rough denim scraped my skin, holding me open, forcing me to give him room. My hips jerked, rolling into his hand, into anything that might relieve the aching, molten tension swelling inside me. The pad of his finger found me, brushing against my clit, sending my voice shattering into the air. A raw, primal moan clawed its way out of me, echoing off the walls of his office. The sound didn't feel like mine. It belonged to him, given freely. My body begged for more before my mind could catch up.

A jolt raced down my spine, pulling at something I didn't want to name—addiction, maybe. Because he was a drug, this man. One taste and I was gone. Kaius leaned down, lips mapping fire down the column of my throat, teeth scraping over that tender hollow where neck met collarbone. Each nip and lick was a brand, claiming me in invisible ink. His hand trailed up, bunching my shirt, until in one decisive rip the fabric was gone. My gasp caught, but I barely had time to react before his mouth closed over my nipple. Heat licked up my chest, his tongue circling, teasing, before the sting of his teeth made me cry out. Pain spiked, sharp, then bled instantly into a dizzying rush of pleasure. I arched, desperate to give him more of me, letting him mark what he wanted. His smirk dragged against my skin as he switched sides, his lips slick, teeth merciless. A scream tore from my throat, but it cracked into a moan that echoed too sweetly.

When he finally pulled back, my chest was flushed, damp, glistening from his spit. My breath came in harsh, uneven gasps, and he looked at me like I was something rare. Something he both owned and admired. My nipples peaked from the chill of the air, hardened and sensitive, while wetness from between my thighs smeared across his jeans where our bodies brushed.

And it was all because of him. Because of the man I should have wanted to kill.

His gaze lifted from my body to my face, and the weight of it nearly buckled me. His lips, swollen and red, curved into something dark and reverent.

"Fuck," Kaius groaned, the word drawn out like he was choking on it. His eyes softened even as hunger clouded them further. "You look so pretty like this, Acelynn."

The use of my full name snapped through me, sharp and intimate all at once. It had always sounded different on his tongue, but this time...this time it was heavier, intimate enough to make my pulse stutter. I had no chance to reply before his hand slipped down again, sliding through my wet folds with practiced ease. I was soaked, ruined for him already, and the way his fingers circled my clit made my moans blur with his.

The pressure built, tighter and tighter, until it felt unbearable. He lowered himself, his lips trailing down my body, until he was kneeling between my spread thighs. Two fingers parted me, exposing me completely, before his mouth descended.

The first stroke of his tongue had me bucking up, a gasp ripped from me. His hand clamped down on my hips, holding me still, anchoring me in place as he groaned against me. The sound reverberated straight through my core. He devoured me shamelessly, tongue teasing, swirling, plunging deep, until my thighs shook against his shoulders.

"Oh god," I moaned, the sound broken as he thrust a finger inside me. My body clenched hard, sucking him in, and his growl vibrated against my clit. Another finger joined the first, stretching me, pumping in and out with a merciless rhythm.

My hands dove into his hair, pulling, guiding, but he was relentless, laughing low and dark against my skin before dragging his tongue across me again. The curl of his fingers hit something inside me that made my vision blur. I ground harder against him, desperate for release, for anything that could break me open. Words tumbled from me, incoherent, lost in the sounds he tore from my body. And then his voice cut through, raw, commanding, devastating.

"Eyes on me," he drawled against me. "If you close them, then I stop. Do you understand, kitten?"

I responded with a soft mewl, which had him pulling away. His movements halted, causing me to snap my gaze to him. He had one eyebrow raised in question. When I didn't respond quickly enough, he began to pull his fingers from my pussy.

"Yes," I screeched. Kaius paused, pumping one into me as I continued. "I'll keep my eyes on you. Just please don't stop."

Kaius let out a low chuckle. "My sweet girl is so greedy."

His pace started again, this time rougher and faster than

the last. I fought the sensation of closing my eyes. Never taking them off him as he dove back down to my clit. That was all it took. The image of Kaius Mordred worshipping the most intimate part of me sent me tumbling over the edge. The tension snapped, unraveling into a tidal wave that crashed over me, violent and blinding.

Pleasure tore me apart as I screamed. The King of Lovelen's name ripped from my throat, echoing against the walls of the club. I didn't care who heard. I didn't care about anything but this—him, me, the fire consuming us both.

My body shook as my release flooded his hand, his mouth, greedy as he licked, sucked, took every drop I gave. He didn't stop, not until I was trembling, wrung out, my eyes rolling back as the last spasms shuddered through me. When I blinked myself back to reality, his gaze was already on me, watching me closely.

His fingers slipped free, coated in my slick. And then, slowly and deliberately, he brought them to his mouth. He moaned around the taste of me, his tongue curling around his digits like he was savoring something rare. My breath hitched, my chest rising and falling, unable to comprehend how a man could look so devastatingly sinful doing something so obscene.

Kaius Mordred may have been the devil incarnate, but he was also the salvation I had been looking for in a world full of darkness that would soon consume me, and there was no way in hell I was running from him. Not when I was this close to finding out answers.

His fingers popped free of his lips, wet and glistening. "I warned you," Kaius said darkly, his voice a low growl that curled heat down my spine. His eyes locked on mine, full of fire and promise. "Once I start something, I see it through to the end."

His hands clamped down on my thighs, spreading me wider across the desk, until there was no room for hesitation, no escape.

"Now bend over the desk," he ordered, his voice edged with sin and hunger. "Because I'm not done with you yet."

CHAPTER FORTY-NINE

kaius

MY LITTLE KITTEN COULD RUN, hide, claw, and snarl at me all she wanted, but none of it mattered. She could bury herself in the darkest parts of this world, beneath the filth of back alleys or the shadows of crumbling cathedrals, but it wouldn't be far enough. I'd still find her. Acelynn Thorton belonged to me—body, mind, and whatever tattered thing she called a soul. And there was no force in this world that could keep us apart after tonight.

The air in my office was thick with tension, her scent clinging to the walls, a mix of adrenaline, fear, and the sweetness of her arousal. Acelynn stood slowly, back to me, her palms braced against the edge of the desk as if she could anchor herself there. My eyes tracked every subtle shift in her, from the rise and fall of her chest to the tremble in her shoulders. I closed the distance, my knuckles brushing down the center of her spine. She shivered beneath the touch, letting out a sigh she probably hadn't meant for me to hear. That small sound ignited something primal in me, something I could no longer contain.

My hand tangled in her dark locks, and with a sharp pull, I forced her down over the desk. She let out a startled shriek that melted into a breathless moan, the sound filling every crack of this dim-lit office. The sharp press of her hips against the wood made her gasp again when I pinned her there, grinding the hard length of my cock against the heat of her pussy. She tried to twist her head, to speak my name, but I shoved her cheek harder into the desk. The wood groaned under the pressure, her voice breaking into a strangled cry.

"Kaius—"

"Shhh, kitten." My voice came low, coaxing and cruel all at once, the growl rumbling from somewhere deep in my chest. My free hand traced the bare line of her shoulder blade, teasing her with the faintest brush. "You asked for this. You challenged me for it. And now I'll show you exactly what happens when you dare to play games with the King of Lovelen."

Her throat bobbed, swallowing back fear—or maybe anticipation. She turned her eyes to me, and even in the soft light, I caught the flicker there. The defiance was still alive in her, but already smothered by the weight of desire.

Her breath came fast, uneven. The slight pain I'd given her only made her wetter. I could smell it, could feel it radiating from her body, slick heat beckoning me like a damn siren. I dragged my hand lower, slow, deliberate, over the curve of her waist and down the smooth plane of her belly until I reached the dip of her hips. The twitch in my cock nearly drove me mad.

I needed her. Consequences be damned.

Stepping back just enough, I slid my knuckles over the curve of her ass, letting them ghost down to the puckered hole just beneath, earning a bitten-off moan from her lips. Her body betrayed her with every touch, every drag of my hand. My belt came loose with a sharp metallic clink, and I slid down my zipper. My cock was already rock hard, pulsing, my hand stroking it as her whimpers filled the air like a hymn to my sins.

Her eyes locked on the motion, pupils blown wide. Her tongue darted out, wetting her bottom lip, a silent plea written all over her expression. I leaned over, pressing closer to her trembling body, and guided the thick head of my cock against her folds. She was drenched, soaked enough that pushing inside was no challenge.

"Fuck," I groaned as her tight heat closed around me. The grip of her pussy nearly undid me then and there, clenching down so sweet and perfect like she'd been made for me.

I pulled out slowly, savoring the drag of her walls around me before slamming back into her with a punishing thrust. She cried out at the stretch, a broken sound that bled into a sob as her body gave in. I spat on her slick cunt, watching the glisten of it coat her folds before I smeared it over her with my hand. She tried to push back into me, desperate, needy, and I gave her no warning as I slammed into her again, harder this time. Her body clutched at me like it didn't want to let go.

Her hands scrambled over the desk, clawing for something to hold on to, the wood creaking under the strain of my pace. I gathered her hair in one hand and yanked, dragging her spine up against my chest, forcing her to feel every brutal thrust.

"You're so wet for me, Acelynn," I snarled against her ear, my lips brushing her skin.

Her eyes rolled back, head falling against my shoulder as I drove into her relentlessly. The sound of flesh meeting flesh echoed loudly in the silence of the office. My hand slipped around her, fingers trailing down her stomach until I found her clit. I rubbed tight, ruthless circles, sending her unraveling even faster.

She was gone within seconds, a cry of my name breaking from her lips as she came undone around me. Her pussy clenched hard, milking me, and the flood of wet heat against my cock pulled me under with her. My thrusts grew erratic, sloppy, until release tore through me with a guttural groan.

When I finally pulled out, she collapsed forward, palms braced against the desk, chest heaving as she tried to catch her breath. The room smelled of sweat, sex, and sin. My hand brushed down the line of her spine, coaxing her to look at me. Her eyes were glassy, lips parted, cheeks flushed in the aftermath.

"Still hate me, kitten?" I asked, smirking as I bent close enough for her to feel the heat of my breath.

She shook her head, too dazed to form words. A feral smile curved her mouth. "Maybe."

Acelynn's defiance was like gasoline to an open flame. My hand landed with a sharp slap on her ass, her skin flushing pink beneath the blow.

"Keep talking like that," I growled. "And I'll put that mouth to better use until your attitude is in check."

CHAPTER FIFTY

acelynn

THE MORNING LIGHT poured through the curtains in slow, lazy stripes, spilling golden across the sheets tangled around me. For the first time in what felt like forever, I hadn't woken to fear or nightmares, but to warmth. My body still hummed with the memory of his touch, the bruising strength of his hands, the heat of his mouth on mine.

Kaius.

Even just whispering his name in my head sent a shiver rolling down my spine. The night had been fire and chaos, violence and tenderness, all wound together until I didn't know where one release ended and the other began. I'd fallen asleep against his chest, listening to the steady rhythm of his heartbeat, letting it lull me into the kind of peace I hadn't believed I was allowed anymore.

But morning was cruel. Morning reminded me that the world outside his arms was still waiting for me, claws sharpened and ready. It reminded me that I still didn't have answers to what happened to my family that night, and he was the only one who could give them to me. I knew that if I revealed myself, told the truth of my original intentions of being here in his bar, all of this would shatter. I wasn't meant to have happiness like this in my life. Time and time again, the universe reminded me of that.

It made me think some people are just meant to suffer through life and be the lessons for others that lead them to true happiness. Some type of fucked-up karmic siren that gets dropped into people's lives. That's why I had told Kaius I needed to go home to grab a few things earlier. I needed space to think through whatever this was.

I dragged myself out of the warmth of my bed, each step heavy as I padded into the bathroom. My reflection in the mirror almost startled me. I looked undone. My lips were still swollen from his kisses, my neck marked in deep, dark bruises I couldn't hide even if I tried. I looked...claimed. A shaky laugh slipped from me as I reached for the drawer, pulling free a packet of makeup wipes. I wasn't sure if I wanted to erase the evidence or cradle it close like proof that, for one night, I hadn't been broken.

The wipe brushed over my lips, smearing away the remnants of Kaius's mouth, and something inside me ached. My reflection stared back at me, fractured by the faint light, as though she wasn't sure who she was anymore. Acelynn. Emersyn. The liar. The traitor. The girl who had kissed her enemy like he was salvation. I pressed harder, trying to scrub myself clean.

And then the world shattered.

A violent crack exploded through the mirror as my forehead slammed into it, spiderwebs of broken glass splintering around my reflection. My breath caught, a scream choking in my throat as shards cascaded into the sink. Hot pain bloomed across my skin, followed by the slow slide of blood down my temple. Before I could stagger back, a hand fisted in my hair and yanked me away from the sink so hard my spine arched. My body collided with the bathroom counter, the edge biting cruelly into my ribs.

"It's been too long since I've heard that sweet scream."

The sound of his voice froze my blood.

Logan.

I thrashed, but his grip only tightened, dragging me backward, out of the bathroom, and into the bedroom where the golden morning had suddenly turned suffocating. His strength hadn't faded with time. If anything, he was harder, crueler than before. He threw me onto the bed, the mattress caving beneath the impact, and his weight followed instantly, crushing me. His knees pinned my hips, one hand capturing both my wrists above my head with ease. I writhed, kicking, but he only laughed, leaning over me like a nightmare made flesh.

My heart screamed inside my chest, beating so fast I thought it might break free. "Logan...please—"

He pressed a finger to my lips mockingly, smearing my blood there as though silencing me was some kind of game. His hair was buzzed close now, his scar deeper in the daylight, twisting around his eye until he looked more beast than man.

"God, you've been busy," he sneered, eyes darting to the bruises on my throat. His grip tightened painfully on my wrists. "Didn't take you long to find someone else to keep your bed warm. Thought of me at all while you spread your legs for the King of Lovelen?"

My stomach knotted, shame and fury clashing in equal measure. "You don't get to ask me that. You don't own me, Logan. You never did."

The slap came so fast I barely saw it. My cheek split with pain, the metallic taste of blood blooming across my tongue.

He tilted his head, almost admiring his work, before dragging his thumb down the mark he'd left.

"Still got that fire," he murmured darkly. "That's why I picked you in the first place. That's why you'll always be mine, Emersyn."

That name. It cut deeper than the slap. My chest squeezed, every breath sharp and burning.

"That girl is dead," I rasped, teeth gritted against the tears threatening to break. "She died in that fire with her family. You killed her."

His laughter filled the room, cruel and endless. "You think flames can erase what you are? What you owe me?"

He leaned closer, lips grazing my ear. "You were supposed to bring me something real. Something I could use to tear those bastards down. Instead, you're in their king's bed. Are you really that stupid?"

"I wasn't supposed to bring you shit. I don't work for you," I hissed, spit flying onto Logan's face through my clenched teeth.

Logan raised an eyebrow at me. "But you work for Parsons, right? And Parsons works for my boss, so by association, you do work for me."

Anger flared even through the terror, reckless and wild. "I'd rather burn with Kaius than rot with you."

His hand slammed down against the pillow beside my head, making me flinch. His eyes blazed with something unhinged, his grin crazed.

"Careful, doll. I'll start thinking you've forgotten who holds the strings." His voice dropped lower, more venomous. "You bring me something on the Knights. Soon. Or I'll carve reminders into that pretty skin of yours that even your king won't want to touch."

A sob shook free of my chest, half terror, half fury. He

pressed a mocking kiss to my temple, soft, revolting. "Remember, betrayal is punished by death. I'll be watching, little Spade."

And then he was gone.

The silence he left behind was deafening. My body curled in on itself instinctively, arms wrapping tight around my stomach, as if I could hold myself together by force alone. The sheets beneath me were tangled, stained with blood from my brow, my cheek burning where he'd struck me. I couldn't move. I couldn't breathe. For one night, I'd felt bliss. For one night, Kaius's arms had made me believe I could be something more than my past, more than Logan's puppet. Now the illusion had shattered because Logan was right about one thing.

He wasn't going to stop watching me. And sooner or later, I was going to have to choose—betray Kaius or burn for him.

CHAPTER FIFTY-ONE

acelynn

THE KITCHEN SMELLED FAINTLY *of garlic and roasted chicken, the leftovers of dinner clinging to the air. A single bulb flickered above the table, its yellow light casting sickly shadows over the linoleum floor. I sat with my elbows braced against the wood, pencil in hand, trying to focus on the half-finished homework in front of me. The numbers swam, my handwriting uneven from how tightly I was gripping the pencil. All I could think about was the folded paper burning a hole in the bottom of my backpack.*

A history test that had a huge sixty-four written out on the top.

Not the worst thing in the world. Kids failed tests all the time. But to me it felt catastrophic, as though it spelled out in red ink just how inadequate I was. It had been sitting there all Thanksgiving break, taunting me from its cage. Alec would have told me to shrug it off, reminded me that school was only one part of my life, and grades didn't define me. Alec always knew how to make failures feel like they didn't matter.

But Alec wasn't here.

It was just me and Dad.

He sat across from me, the newspaper stretching wide in his hands. A cigarette smoldered between his fingers, curling smoke into the air. His glass of whiskey sat untouched, but his gaze flicked over the newsprint without really taking anything in. The silence pressed heavily, like the whole room was waiting.

"Emersyn," he said suddenly, his voice sharp enough to cut.

I jumped. "Yes?"

"Bring me your schoolbag."

My blood ran cold. I looked toward the bag slouched against the counter, its zipper half open. The test was inside, folded, and hidden. My first instinct was to lie, to say it was in my room, to buy myself time. But his tone left no room for excuses.

"Yes, sir."

The scrape of my chair against the tile echoed too loudly as I stood. My legs felt weak as I crossed the room, kneeling to unzip the bag. The paper was there, wedged between notebooks, and I pulled it out with shaking hands. When I turned back, he was already watching me.

"Give it here."

I stepped forward, setting it on the table. He didn't look at it at first—just at me, his eyes flat and cold. Then slowly he picked it up, unfolded it, and studied the grade circled in red.

"Sixty-four."

My voice cracked. "It was a hard test."

"Hard?" His voice was deceptively calm, almost quiet. "Is that what you tell yourself? That life is hard, so failure is excusable?"

"No, I—"

The slap came before I could finish. His palm connected with my cheek in a crack that reverberated through the kitchen. My head snapped to the side, tears springing instantly to my eyes. I gasped, my hand flying up to cover the hot sting. I turned slowly back to him, my vision blurring. He had never hit me before. Never.

"D-Dad?" My voice trembled, disbelief choking me.

"You listen to me." He leaned forward, his voice suddenly thunderous. "Failure is not an option for a Spade. Do you hear me?"

My heart hammered so hard I thought it might break. "It's just a test—"

His fist slammed down on the table, rattling the ashtray, making the lightbulb above sway. "It is not just a test. It is proof you do not understand who you are. Proof you don't understand the code."

"The...code?" I whispered, wide-eyed.

"Yes." His gaze bored into mine, terrifying in its intensity. "The Spade family code. Family before all. Debt must be repaid. Betrayal is punished by death. That is who you are. That is what you will live by."

The words struck me harder than his hand had. My mouth went dry.

"I don't—"

"You will learn." He shoved the paper aside, scattering pencils and notebooks across the table. His hand shot out, gripping my chin hard enough to bruise, and forcing my eyes up to his, his voice a growl. "Say it. Family before all."

I shook, the words catching in my throat. "F-Family before all."

"Again!"

"Family before all!"

"Debt must be repaid."

"Debt must be repaid."

"Betrayal—"

The door banged open.

"Dad!"

Alec's voice cut through the room. He strode in, still in his practice hoodie, sweat darkening his collar. His eyes locked on the way Dad's hand gripped my chin, on the tears streaking my cheeks.

"What the hell are you doing?" Alec demanded, shoving his backpack down.

"Teaching her," Dad snapped, his hold tightening. "She needs to know the code."

"She's a kid!" Alec pushed forward, his body sliding between us. He shoved Dad's hand off my face and planted himself in front of me like a shield. "You don't teach her like this."

Dad's nostrils flared. "You want her to end up soft? You want her to get crushed when the world shows its teeth? I won't have it. She needs to learn."

"Not like this," Alec hissed, his fists tight at his sides. "You can't just hit her."

"She failed." Dad's voice was ice. "And a Spade does not fail."

"She failed a test," Alec snapped. "Not the family. Not the code. School doesn't matter."

For a moment, I thought Dad might hit him too. The air was thick with it, his fury radiating in waves. But then, with a sharp breath through his nose, he snatched up his glass of whiskey and stormed out of the kitchen, muttering curses under his breath. The front door slammed a moment later, leaving silence in his wake. I sat frozen in my chair, my cheek still burning, tears dripping down my chin. My whole body shook.

Alec crouched in front of me, his hands gentle on my arms. His face softened when he saw the redness on my cheek. "Emmy...hey. Look at me."

I blinked at him, chest heaving. "He...he hit me."

"I know." Alec's jaw tightened, his voice breaking. "I know. And I'm sorry."

"I didn't know about...the code. I didn't even know—"

"Shhh." He pulled me against him, his arms wrapping around me tight.

I buried my face in his hoodie, sobbing into the sweat-soaked fabric.

"You're okay. I won't let him do that again."

"But what if I fail again?" My words cracked apart with fear. "What if I—"

"Then I'll take the blame." Alec leaned back just enough to look me in the eye. His expression was fierce, protective, older than his years. "You hear me? I'll take it. I won't let him break you."

"But the code—"

His mouth twisted. He hesitated, then lowered his voice. "The code is real. And yeah, one day you'll have to know it, even if I want you nowhere near the club life. But you won't learn it like this. Not from him. Not tonight."

I searched his eyes, desperate. "So what do I do?"

"For now?" He brushed a thumb across my damp cheek. "You keep your head down. Go back to school after the break and continue with your studies. You try. You fight for yourself. And when it gets too hard..." His hand squeezed mine. "You come to me. Always."

I nodded, clinging to his hand like it was the only steady thing in the world. The kitchen was still heavy with smoke and anger, but Alec's presence cut through it, anchoring me. He couldn't erase the sting on my cheek or the words Dad had forced into me, but he made them feel less suffocating. And that night, as I lay awake in bed, those words looped endlessly in my head.

Family before all. Debt must be repaid. Betrayal is punished by death.

The code. I hadn't asked for it. I hadn't even known it existed until tonight. But it had been carved into my bones the night I was born, and I would have to abide by it if I wanted to survive in this world.

The family code haunted me in dreams. Not whispered, not chanted, but *commanded*. My father's voice was sharp, brittle as glass, breaking the silence of my dreams. He stood behind me as I kneeled at that old kitchen table, reciting lines I didn't understand, each word scraped across my tongue like barbed wire. *Family before all. Debt must be repaid. Betrayal is punished by death.*

Even after months of trying to bury those nights—bury *her*—Emersyn still bled through.

I woke in tangled sheets, my heart hammering against my ribs like it was trying to break out of me. Sunlight leaked through the cheap curtains, cutting the room in half with sharp golden lines. For a long moment, I lay there completely still, afraid to move, afraid that if I did, Logan would be standing in the corner of the room with his crooked smile that always promised pain. But he wasn't. Not yet.

I was alive for now, and that had to be enough.

CHAPTER FIFTY-TWO

acelynn

THE HUM of Astoria's car filled the silence as we sped down the highway. The desert rolled endlessly on either side, flat, wide, and blinding under the afternoon sun. My seat belt cut across my chest like a shackle, reminding me with each bump that no matter how fast we drove, I couldn't outrun what waited behind us.

The faint smell of Astoria's vanilla lotion clung to the leather seats. A half-drunk cup of coffee sloshed in the cupholder, its bitter scent fighting with the sweetness. Normally, I found comfort in these things. Familiarity. The simple markers of a happy life. But today everything felt warped—too bright, too sharp, like staring at the world through broken glass. Astoria's voice filled the space, rapid and bubbly. She was retelling the plot of the latest dating show she had been watching, words tumbling too fast, as though if she stopped speaking, the silence would swallow us whole. I stared out the window, watching the desert shimmer. My reflection stared back at me, pale and haunted, lips pressed thin as if they could hold back the tide of everything I hadn't said.

"Acelynn." Astoria's tone snapped through the hum of the car radio. "Are you even listening?"

I blinked, dragging my gaze from a cactus outside. "Yeah," I lied softly. "The guy picked the Kansas girl, then changed his mind. Isn't that against the rules?"

She huffed, sharp and humorless. "Producers don't care about rules. They want drama."

Drama. The word made my stomach twist. Logan wanted drama too. Only his was blood and violence and ruin. A week had passed since he'd cornered me, his voice thick with promises of what he'd do if I didn't cooperate. A week of sleepless nights, of weighing lies against truths that could get me killed. He wanted to destroy the Knights. A mission I had been trying to get myself to complete for the months I had been around them. But, damn, did each and every one of them make it difficult for me to hate. Or maybe that was just my heart not allowing me to fall into the darkness it was destined to inherit from my DNA. I knew now that if I gave Logan anything that could hurt any of the Knights, it would destroy me. But if I didn't...

I pressed my nails into my palm until they left little half-moons. I needed to hear Kaius's voice. I needed to anchor myself to him before I drowned.

"I need to call Kaius," I murmured, pressing my fingers to my temple. The words slipped out before I could stop them, raw and desperate. My hand reached out, ready to disconnect my phone from the CarPlay I had been using to stream my music.

The vehicle slowed at a red light. Astoria's hands froze around the wheel. Her grip turned bone-white, the tendons in her hands standing out like wires.

"Kaius?" she repeated slowly, dangerously.

"Yes, you know, your brother?" My voice trembled. I couldn't look at her as I ripped off the giant bug-eyed sunglasses that covered my face to see the car's screen better. "I have to tell him..."

But I didn't know what. That Logan had found me? That I wasn't Acelynn at all but Emersyn Spade? That I'd been lying every day of my life since the night Alec died? When I finally glanced at her, her eyes were knives.

"You have five seconds," she said, her voice soft, lethal. "To tell me why your eyes look like Alec Spade's."

The name hit like a gunshot. My breath stopped, my chest collapsing in on itself.

My lips moved before my brain could stop them. "Because Alec Spade was my brother."

Astoria's chest rose sharply. For a second, a crack appeared in her mask, grief flickering raw in her expression. But it was gone as fast as it came, replaced by stone.

"Continue."

"Tori—"

"Don't," she hissed, "call me that."

The light above us turned green. A car honked behind us, swerving around with an angry horn blast, but Astoria didn't flinch. She was coiled tight, jaw clenched, waiting.

Tears blurred my vision, the desert outside smearing into colors. "That night—I didn't know what Alec was planning. I swear to god, Astoria, I had no part in it. I didn't lie about that to you. Not after that first night. You're all I've had."

Her breathing was uneven, but her eyes stayed merciless. "Does he know you are still alive?"

The words were a death sentence. Because I couldn't tell who we were talking about. Kaius or Alec. Which was stupid since I saw my brother on the morgue table, saw that his chest never rose or fell with life. But then again, Parsons had been the one to show me my dead brother, the same detective who was so clearly playing both sides. If Logan or Alec or whoever the hell was above them orchestrated this, then it had all been for nothing. I was again just a pawn in their chess game, being moved around to gather information for them. But how would Astoria know this?

"Who?" I asked, voice deadly quiet.

Astoria's face lost all its color, realizing her mistake the moment I demanded a name. She shook her head and turned back to the road. She accelerated quickly, not caring about the speed limit. I watched the speedometer climb past eighty-five, and my stomach dropped.

"Astoria," I shouted at her, but she didn't even acknowledge me, muffled words spilling from her lips as she pressed harder on the gas pedal. I began digging through my purse, not caring if Kaius found out who I truly was. "I am calling your brother."

Before I could dial Kaius's number, a text appeared on the car's Bluetooth CarPlay.

"Josie says..." The robotic woman's voice filled the cab of the car. My heart thudded in my chest. Josie had never texted me. I didn't even think she had my number. "They know. Get out while you still can."

The message sent shockwaves through my body. My eyes turned slowly to see Astoria's tear-filled ones staring back at me. I could practically see the wheels in her head turning as she debated her options.

"I'm so sorry," Astoria choked out. Her entire body was practically vibrating in fear. I knew there was nothing I could do the moment she made up her mind. "I can't let you leave."

The car lurched violently as Astoria jerked the wheel. Tires shrieked against asphalt. My body slammed sideways, the seat belt cutting into my collarbone like a razor blade. The horizon spun. Sky, sun, sand, and asphalt whirled end over end as the car flipped. Metal screamed. Glass exploded. Coffee and blood and dirt swirled together in a storm. My scream was ripped from me, swallowed by the thunder of destruction. Then everything went still.

CHAPTER FIFTY-THREE

acelynn

FLAMES LEAPED *across the kitchen floor with ravenous hunger, consuming everything they touched. The fire hissed and roared as it spread, curling up the walls, catching on grease-stained dish rags and shelves cluttered with cooking oil. It was beautiful in a terrifying way, wild and merciless, like a living thing tearing its way through the legacy of Spade Manor.*

The heat hit me in a wave, searing my skin. My eyes watered as I stumbled back, coughing, the flames growing faster than I had imagined. Within seconds, the house was alive with fire, every crack and crevice lit up with destruction.

Then came the sound that shattered me. A single gunshot cracked through the night outside, sharp and too close. My entire body jolted. My head whipped toward the kitchen door, panic surging in my veins. More shouts followed, muffled and violent. I could hear boots on gravel and the clang of metal being tossed.

I didn't think. I just ran.

My legs carried me through the smoke-filled kitchen and out the back door, heart slamming against my ribs like it wanted to escape. My socked feet slipped on the slick tile, but I didn't stop until I burst out into the desert night, gasping for air that was no longer poisoned with smoke.

The chill of the air bit at my damp skin, but I didn't slow down until I was halfway across the yard. Only then did I turn, my chest heaving, to look back. The house was an inferno. Flames licked skyward, painting the night in shades of orange and red. The roof began to collapse in on itself.

And then I heard it—screaming.

Not the kind born of surprise or fright. This was agony. People were still inside. Trapped. My hands flew to my mouth, bile rising in my throat. I hadn't thought. God, I hadn't thought about who else might have been caught in Alec's orders. My body trembled as the voices carried into the night, raw and broken. My fingers curled into fists, nails biting my palms as the truth settled into my bones. The Spade legacy wasn't just burning.

I was burning with it.

CHAPTER FIFTY-FOUR

acelynn

WHEN I FINALLY CAME TO, I hung suspended in the wreckage, the seat belt biting into my ribs. The world was upside down, blood dripping from my temple and sliding into my hair. I sucked in a ragged breath as my vision wavered in and out of focus. My forehead burned from where the airbag had hit me. The only thing I could focus on was the sound of the blood dripping from a cut in my hairline as it pinged against the roof of the car. Every part of me throbbed in pain, but at least I was awake and aware.

"Astoria," I croaked out. My body tried to jerk forward to release the iron grip the seat belt had on me, but it was no use with how it was locked in place. Astoria groaned out in response to me. I turned my head to look at her. She was slumped motionless beside me, hair wet with blood, her chest barely moving. Panic surged, raw and consuming. "Astoria, wake up. Please, you can't—"

My voice cracked into a sob as I stretched my hand toward her. My fingers found hers, limp and cold, but I still gave them a squeeze to remind her that even if she had made a mistake, even if she hated my guts, I was still here. That I wasn't going anywhere.

The crunch of boots against broken glass approaching caught my ears, and I ripped my hand out of hers. My fingers gripped either side of the seat belt as I yanked at the device. My eyes scanned the area around me until I caught sight of Astoria's purse. I leaned forward, gritting my teeth against the pain shooting through me as I tried to get into the front zipper pocket. My hand yanked it to the side, and I dove down deep until the cool kiss of metal touched my skin.

Just as my fingers wrapped around the blade, a figure leaned in through the shattered driver's side window. A masked figure crouched next to Astoria, knife flashing silver. Before I could react, he sliced her seat belt. Her body crashed hard onto the roof of the car in a heap on itself. The figure reached into the car, ripping her out effortlessly through the window. Astoria's body scraped against twisted metal, blood streaking across the dirt as they went.

"No!" My scream tore through the silence, wild and raw. I clawed at my seat belt, blood-slick hands slipping against the button. The more I fought, the tighter it seemed to hold me—a restraint, a trap.

"I told you, doll," Logan's deep voice called out to me, but in my panic, I couldn't pinpoint which side of the car he was on.

I placed one of my hands against the roof and reached down to the clicker, slamming my palm into the release over and over again until finally the device gave way with a snap. I tumbled down, glass biting into my palms and knees as I scrambled through the broken window. The desert sun burned overhead, blinding and merciless. Dust and blood coated my tongue. I could feel my body beginning to shut down with every movement, but I had to get out to Astoria.

The black tar burned against my skin as I made it fully out of the passenger side.

Logan stood tall, the mask gone, his smile crooked and cruel, the kind of smile that always promised suffering. He had Astoria by the arm, her head lolling to the side, eyes half-shut and dazed. She looked broken.

My stomach dropped. Logan crouched low, his shadow falling across me as I pressed back against the wreck. He leaned close, his breath hot, his eyes glittering.

"I told you if you didn't make yourself useful," he murmured, his smile widening as he ran a finger along my jaw. "I'd make you useful."

The sun blazed overhead, but all I felt was the ice in his words. And for the first time, I realized, he hadn't just found me. He had been waiting. Watching. Every step had been planned. The crash hadn't been fate. It had been the trap snapping shut. And I think Astoria had a hand to play in all of it.

CHAPTER FIFTY-FIVE

kaius

RED and blue lights reflected off the twisted metal of my baby sister's car like some grotesque carnival. The silver frame, once sleek and polished, was bent in on itself, caved like a crushed ribcage. Glass littered the asphalt in glittering shards, but it wasn't the glass that turned my stomach. It was the blood. So much of it. Smeared across the hood. Spattered along the pavement like careless brushstrokes. Thick enough that the metallic tang crawled into the back of my throat.

Nolan shoved past me with the recklessness of a man who didn't give a damn about protocol or boundaries. His voice cracked as he screamed Astoria's name. It rose above the shouts of officers and the distant wail of sirens. He sounded half-feral, like his soul was tearing free from his body. I didn't call after him.

My eyes scanned the chaos instead, cataloging every face, every weapon holstered at a hip, every badge into my memory. If the bastard responsible for this was still here, if he thought he could hide in plain sight, I'd find him. But the other car, the one that had crashed into hers, was gone. Not abandoned, not overturned, not even parked across the way. Vanished, like it had never even been here. I ducked under the yellow tape, ignoring the way the crowd shifted to make space for me. Fear followed my shadow. It always did when in public.

"This is a closed crime scene," someone called out.

I lifted my gaze to find Detective Watson barring my path. Young, sharp-featured, with eyes that had already seen too much. The kid barely looked old enough to shave. His voice wavered at the edges, but his stare didn't falter. To his credit, he didn't step back when I turned my full glare on him. Smart or stupid, I couldn't decide.

"That's my little sister's car," I said, my tone as cold and flat as the blood drying on the pavement. I didn't need to raise my voice to make it dangerous. I only had to nod toward the silver four-door to drive the point home.

He didn't argue. Just crossed his arms over his chest, the way a man does when he wants to look like he still has control.

"But you already knew that," I continued, "seeing as you let Nolan storm in without giving him any grief."

Something flickered in his eyes, but instead of flinching, Watson let out a humorless chuckle. "Everyone in town knows Astoria Mordred is Nolan Bedivere's. Only an idiot would try to stop him right now."

I ran a hand over the stubble on my jaw, fighting the urge to bare my teeth. "You got a point there."

"She wasn't on scene when we got here," Watson went on, his voice calm and calculated. He wanted me to know he wasn't rattled. "Witness says she was taken."

My gaze snapped to his. "Witness?"

Astoria had left the bar alone and hadn't mentioned

picking anyone up to run her simple errand of dropping the bar's funds off at the bank. Josie had been kicking a few of the newer Knights' asses in a game of pool when Nolan had gotten the call. I should be mad they called him instead of her own brother, but the way Nolan had raced out of the bar without a second glance back at us, I knew Astoria would never be unprotected.

Watson gestured with two fingers toward an ambulance parked off to the side. Its back doors were open, spilling a wash of sterile light onto the asphalt. Three officers stood like bodyguards around a woman small enough to look breakable, her shoulders draped with a thin blanket. Her dark hair was matted with blood, sticking to her scalp in crusted strands. She spoke softly to a female officer, her posture trembling like a half-broken thing. As if she could feel eyes on her, the woman turned over her shoulder to meet my gaze.

Blue eyes met mine. Too blue. Terrified and sharp, cutting straight through me. I'd seen them before, staring out of another face, another time. The same shade as a dead Spade brother, who had once betrayed Nolan and me, turning our perfect plan into a ruin of blood and ashes.

My hands curled into fists, nails biting into my palms. It took everything in me not to lunge at Acelynn, not to cross that stretch of asphalt and drag her by her hair until she was screaming on the floor of my basement. I could almost taste it—the copper bite of hemlock on my tongue, the image of her eyes dimming as the poison worked its way through her veins. But the thought sliced deeper than it should have. Every heartbeat was a sharp pain, tearing through the part of me as every moment she lied to my face flashed through my mind. That hollow ache, that fury that had no place to go.

And I knew the truth. No matter how I tried to paint her

as the enemy, no matter what name she wore, I couldn't kill her. Not when she was the one who had already started piecing me back together from the inside out. My mind dragged me backward, years ago, to the Spades' house—their suffocating walls, their polished lies, their rot dressed in velvet.

I'd stormed out of the meeting room where my father and Alec's were deep in negotiation. While the Knights exclusively dealt in the distribution of Muze, the Death Dealers dabbled in multiple different drugs that were just as addictive and much more deadly. Muze for powder. Distribution for territory. Both leaders so smug, convinced they were protecting their children when telling us to scram from the table when negotiations got serious. It was almost comical. I was the next president of the Knights. Alec would take the throne of the Death Dealers. Every deal they cut would be ours to carry. They thought they were shielding us from the dirt when really, they were burying us in it. Turning the corner, I stopped short at the sight in front of me.

Emersyn Spade. The princess of the Death Dealers was perched precariously in the opening of a laundry chute. Her small frame strained as she used all her body weight to shove at the jammed door, trying to wedge it closed with all her strength. I leaned against the wall across from her, an amused smile toying at my lips as she continued to struggle.

"What the hell are you doing?" I asked, letting a laugh slip from my lips as she shrieked, nearly falling backward.

She glared at me, arms crossed, as though the posture could make her look fierce instead of like a kitten puffing itself up. Emersyn craned her neck out of the chute, eyes darting like she expected a shadow to come for her. I turned to look in the direction she was. "Who are you looking for?"

"My brother," Emersyn grumbled, casting her eyes down to the ground. She scooted all the way forward, letting her legs

dangle out of the chute. They swung back and forth, hitting the wall with a light thud each time. She bit her bottom lip, peering up at me with an innocent look. "Please don't tell him I was spying on the meeting."

"Is that what you were doing?" I let out a low chuckle.

Emersyn shrugged her shoulders.

I shook my head. "I won't tell Alec anything."

She shot me a bright smile. "Good, because if you do, then you would have to protect me from him."

"Oh, is that so?" I cocked an eyebrow at her.

Emersyn nodded once. "Yeah, or the guilt would eat you alive. I mean, I know you are like some big bad president in the making, but imagine looking back on your life, remembering you got the Spade princess murdered by her own brother."

This girl was funny and a breath of fresh air from all the bullshit people that normally accompanied a visit to a rival gang's home. I stepped forward, my height still towering over her, even with her sitting in the laundry chute. Emersyn leaned back casually so she could crane her neck up to meet my gaze. I had just met this girl today, and yet it felt like I had known her my entire life. Our quips flowed off each other like we were seasoned in each other's humor.

"And what if I don't care if your brother kills you for doing exactly what I assume he said not to?"

"You do." Emersyn smirked up at me.

I narrowed my eyes at her. "Do what?"

"Care." She leaned back on her hands, turning her head to the side and examining me further. "And if you don't now, you will later. Don't you know, Kai? The knight always saves the princess in the end."

I had thought of that moment every damn day since I was thirteen. And then years later, Alec Spade stormed into my office, begging me to save his baby sister. As much as I had wanted to fight it, to deny him, that memory haunted me. Her voice. Her smirk.

The way she had made the world feel lighter in those few minutes than most people could in a lifetime. No other human had ever come close, not until Acelynn. Now, standing in the wreckage of my sister's car, staring into those too-familiar blue eyes, I realized the truth I'd been running from.

She had betrayed me, played me like a game of chess. And I would have to put a bullet between her eyes for it.

CHAPTER FIFTY-SIX

acelynn

KAIUS'S STARE was a weapon in itself. His eyes cut into me with a sharpness that made my chest ache and made my bones want to splinter under the weight of it. It wasn't just anger in his expression—it was disappointment, betrayal, devastation, all wound together in a look that should have made me crumble to dust on the spot. That should have sent me running for the hills, screaming for distance between us.

But I didn't run.

I couldn't.

Something in me was tethered to him, as dangerous as it was, as wrong as it felt to even crave the invisible string when his gaze promised ruin. My eyes burned, the sting of unshed tears threatening to break through, but still I refused to look away. I held his stare, even as my vision blurred, even as the weight of my guilt sank deeper and deeper into the hollow pit of my stomach.

Kaius stepped away from me as though my very presence was poison, and his voice ripped through the air, low and commanding, calling Nolan's name like an executioner summoning the gallows. I flinched at the sound, not because it startled me, but because of the finality in it. There was no softness left in his tone, no trace of the boy I'd glimpsed in him once, no hint of the man who had promised—if only in subtle looks and half-kept words—that I was safe in his presence.

Then he turned from me.

He stalked back toward his truck, each heavy step echoing like a verdict. When the engine roared to life, it drowned out everything—the chaos around me, the faint voices calling orders, even the frantic rhythm of my own blood as it pounded in my ears. The sound was deafening, a wall of fury and decisiveness that seemed to swallow the world whole. I lifted my hands, raking them back through my tangled, matted hair. The strands caught between my fingers, pulling at my scalp until it burned, but the pain was nothing compared to the storm in my chest.

I tilted my head back, eyes finding the endless stretch of sky above me. Blue. Beautiful. Cruel. The kind of day that should have been filled with laughter, sunlight, and freedom. Not this. Not me standing in the middle of it, suffocating under the weight of choices I could never take back. My throat tightened, a bitter laugh bubbling in my chest but dying before it could escape.

I was a dead woman walking.

Every step I had taken since lighting that match had carved me closer and closer to the grave, and now it loomed before me, wide and waiting. And the truth—the truth that settled cold and sharp in my gut—was that I didn't care. Not really. What was the point of fighting for a life I never wanted in the first place? Death felt less like an ending and more like a release. Maybe it was selfish. Maybe it was cowardly. But the thought of closing my eyes and letting it all stop—the guilt, the fear, the constant weight of being both pawn and betrayer—was a kinder fate than the hell I had been born into.

I clenched my fists at my sides, nails digging into my palms until my skin threatened to break. I wanted the pain. Needed it. At least it reminded me I was still here, still breathing, still paying the price for the choices I had made, because there was no one else to blame.

Not Kaius. Not Nolan. Not Alec. Not even my father.

It had been me.

I was the one who had lit the match. The one who had taken a single flame and burned my entire life to ash. And now, standing beneath that endless, indifferent sky, I finally understood what it meant to be both executioner and condemned. There was no forgiveness for what I had done. Not from the ones who had burned. And not from him.

The red taillights of the King of Lovelen's truck blazed like twin embers against the desert sun. I stood rooted where I was, watching as they grew smaller and smaller, cutting down the trail of asphalt until the vehicle swung hard to the right and disappeared from sight. A tug at my arm snapped me back to the present, a sharp jolt against the road-burned skin that made me hiss. My head snapped sideways to glare at the paramedic hovering beside me, his latex-covered hand still reaching as though I were some fragile thing about to fall over.

I ripped my arm out of his grasp, eyes narrowing. "Don't touch me. I'm fine."

He gave me a flat, irritated look, the kind men gave when they were used to being listened to. His partner hovered near the open ambulance doors, clipboard in hand, tone softer but no less grating. "We should really take you in to get checked out. Shock, concussion, broken bones—all things that you might be suffering from but just aren't feeling them yet."

"I said I'm fine." My voice cracked like a whip. "I'm not going to the hospital. I don't have time for that."

For the hundredth time, I bit down the scream of frustration crawling up my throat. They weren't listening. No one ever listened.

"If she doesn't want medical attention, let her go." The first paramedic muttered the words like they tasted bad in his mouth, his disapproval heavy, judgment clear in every clipped syllable. His tone implied I was reckless, difficult, and ungrateful.

It made my blood itch and my fists curl. I tore the blood pressure cuff from my arm and let it fall in a heap at his feet.

My boots hit the pavement a second later, a jolt of pain spiking through my ribs as I hopped down from the ambulance's metal step. A groan escaped before I could bite it back. My muscles screamed, the accident already leaving its mark, unseen bruises flowering beneath my skin. But I ignored it. Pain was just another language my body had learned to live with.

I pushed forward. One step, then another. My shoulder clipped a body in the crowd, hard enough to jolt me. The man I struck turned, his plain suit marking him for what he was before I even caught the shadow of his badge. Detective Parsons.

"That's a long walk home," he called after me, smugness dripping off his words like oil.

I didn't slow down. Didn't give him the satisfaction of eye contact.

"I'm not going home," I muttered, more to myself than to him. But he heard.

"But aren't you, though?" he drawled, his tone mocking, taunting.

The words were barbed, but it was the smirk in his voice that made my blood spike hot in my veins. My steps faltered. My spine stiffened.

Slowly, I glanced back at him over my shoulder. His mouth curved into a crooked, knowing grin. "You're the double agent turned triple agent. Tell Kaius I said hi when he fucks you tonight. I'm sure he'll love hearing my name fall from your lips as he's buried in that tight cunt."

The words landed like a slap, sharp and humiliating. My jaw dropped, breath catching in my throat. "Excuse me?"

I turned fully now, facing him. He stood with his head cocked to one side, his eyes dragging lazily over me, slow and deliberate, like he was peeling me open with just a look. His smile didn't reach his eyes. It was something darker, uglier, a predator's grin that made the hair on my arms rise despite the summer heat. I forced myself to stand tall, to plant my boots onto the pavement and not squirm, not give him what he wanted.

A low chuckle rumbled from his chest. "What's the matter, doll? Hit a nerve?"

His voice dropped lower, meaner. "Alec was right. You're just a two-timing whore who can't see farther than how wide her legs can spread."

My heart lurched, my pulse skidding. For a split second, the air was punched out of my lungs. Alec's name on his tongue was an obscenity, a violation that ripped me open more than anything else he could have said.

He didn't know my brother. He couldn't have. This man didn't deserve to even breathe Alec's name into the air. He was just repeating whispers from its messenger, twisting information into something jagged and cruel. Because no matter how much I told myself he was lying, no matter how many times I repeated in my head that I hadn't betrayed Alec, that I was fighting tooth and nail to set things right for the Spades, for our family, the words found their mark. Doubt always did.

And there was only one person alive who could have known that. The same person who took sick pleasure in taunting me from afar. My throat burned, but I swallowed it down, locking my jaw so tight it ached.

The detective's grin widened as if he could sense the wound he'd opened. He winked, a mocking little gesture that turned my stomach. "Better run along, doll."

I held his stare for a moment longer, daring myself not to flinch, not to show him an ounce of the fear and fury churning inside me. Then I spun on my heel, boots grinding against the pavement, and walked away before my trembling hands betrayed me. But his words clung to me like smoke, pungent and suffocating, following me with every step.

CHAPTER FIFTY-SEVEN

acelynn

THE LIGHTS of the marquee sputtered to life just as the cab rolled to a stop in front of the Queen's Table. Crimson bulbs flickered against the fading dusk, bleeding their glow across the cracked asphalt like a warning more than a welcome. I shoved a handful of crumpled bills into the cabbie's hand, murmuring a thanks before stepping out into the evening air.

The parking lot stretched before me, deserted, empty but for my own shadow. A low hum of music pulsed from inside, seeping through the thick wooden door as if the bar itself was alive and breathing. The melody was distorted, rock and rage in equal measure, its bass line carrying across the gravel, making the ground vibrate beneath the soles of my boots.

Every step forward crunched against the loose stones, loud in the silence of the evening air. My stomach coiled tighter with each footfall. The Queen's Table wasn't the kind of place you entered without reason, and tonight, my reason might just be the noose tightening around my neck.

I stopped before the door, pressing one palm against its

weathered surface. The wood was cool beneath my hand, the vibrations of the music running through it and into my skin, crawling up my arm like static. I drew in a shaky breath of desert air, thick with dust and the faint sting of exhaust fumes, and forced my emotions down, locking them away. If I carried them inside with me, I'd already be dead.

With one push, the door groaned open, and I stepped into the lion's den.

Darkness swallowed me first. The overhead lights had all been cut, leaving only shadows to stretch long across the room. The glow of the neon sign above the bar, Queen's Table in jagged red, spilled across the hardwood floor like fresh blood. The air was hazed with smoke, curling tendrils that clung to the rafters and slid low to the ground, smothering every breath I tried to take.

Kaius sat in the center of the dance floor like it had been carved out just for him. A single chair, his throne, bathed in the dim neon wash. Smoke curled upward from the cigarette between his fingers, and every drag lit his face in brief flashes of firelight, throwing his sharp features into cruel relief. Power wasn't something he wore—it was something that poured from him, an invisible shroud that filled the room.

The music roared from unseen speakers, the bass so heavy it rattled the glass bottles lined on the shelves behind the bar. The sound thudded through my bones, syncing with the frantic pace of my heartbeat. I shivered, though not from the cold. It was him. Always him.

My lungs stung as I inhaled, the bitter nicotine-laced air sinking into me until it burned. I hated the way it felt, the way it clung to my clothes, my skin, my hair. But some broken part of me savored it too—because it was his. Because this room, this suffocating atmosphere, was an extension of him.

A silhouette in smoke and sin that I couldn't look away from.

His eyes lifted to meet mine, glowing like embers through the haze. He didn't smile. He didn't need to. The weight of his stare was enough to make me feel stripped bare.

Then, through the smoke, his hand rose. Just one finger extended, curling inward in a gesture that was equal parts command and dare. His voice slid through the pounding music like a viper striking, low and mocking. "Don't be shy now, kitten."

The words scraped across my skin. My body betrayed me, feet moving before my mind could argue. He drew me in without effort, his gravity inescapable. Each step closer tightened the noose I'd willingly slipped around my own neck.

My chest heaved, breath shallow, heart hammering so violently I thought it might burst free. The rational part of me screamed to turn, to run, to get as far from him as possible. But I knew the truth as well as I knew my own name. If I ran, he'd catch me. And if he caught me, I'd die the same death.

So I walked forward. The smoke thickened, wrapping around me like the embrace of something ancient and merciless. My boots whispered against the floor until the tips of mine brushed the edge of his. Inches. That was all that separated me from the King of Lovelen, from the monster cloaked in a man's skin.

He didn't move. He didn't need to. The threat radiating from him was enough to make my body lock in place, waiting for the strike. And I would take it, because there was no part of me that didn't deserve it. I had lit the match. I had burned the legacy. I had opened the door to this life. My brother knew it before he died. Kaius knew it now.

Hell, deep down, so did I.

"Alec!" My throat was raw from screaming, the sound splintering like glass in the night air.

Panic clawed up my chest, choking me. I had done what he told me. I had lit the fire. I had watched our family home turn into a glowing pyre against the darkness. He had failed to mention that people were still inside. I had assumed it was abandoned. But as the flames climbed higher, a shadow had moved. Someone had been in there. And they were screaming for help.

I sprinted forward, lungs tearing against the smoke. My feet slid in the loose dirt as I reached the edge of the home. Heat licked at my skin. From the upper bay window, a figure forced itself out, stumbling into the open air before gravity claimed it.

"No, no, no—"

Their body slammed against the shingles with a hollow crunch, then tumbled down the roof like a rag doll, hitting the ground in a heap that made my stomach heave.

I dropped to my knees beside them, the gravel biting into my skin. The smell hit me first—burnt flesh, sharp and metallic, turning bile into acid at the back of my throat. They whimpered, a sound so faint it broke something inside me. Tears blurred my vision as I hovered uselessly above them, hands trembling, desperate to touch but terrified of doing more damage. Their skin was blackened, charred beyond recognition, features melted into something inhuman. And then I saw it.

Beneath the wreck of burned skin, the glint of silver embedded in flesh. A small charm, glowing faintly in the firelight. A spade. The world collapsed inward.

"Mom?" My voice fractured, a sob torn from my chest as I clutched at air.

Her eyes—the same ones that my brother and I shared with

her—fluttered open. Blue. That same impossible shade of blue that had always been my safe place. They found mine, soft even in agony, the kind of look that once made monsters under the bed disappear.

"Please, no, please—" My words fell apart. My breath came in panicked gasps as hers rattled into silence.

She drew in one last, shuddering breath, and then...she was gone.

I screamed. A sound so animal, so feral, it didn't feel like it came from me.

But grief didn't have time to settle its claws, because rough fingers seized my arm and yanked me upward. My head whipped around, fist flying on instinct. My knuckles cracked against a skull, and a grunt of pain echoed back at me. The grip only tightened.

"Hit me again, Emersyn..." Alec's voice was a razor dragged slowly over my spine. My brother. My blood. And yet nothing about him was familiar anymore. His tone was a weapon, stripped of warmth, sharpened into something cruel. "And I'll bury you next to Mommy Dearest."

Fear iced my veins. This wasn't my Alec—the one who used to sneak me candy, who shielded me from Father's rage, who once swore he'd protect me from everything. This was something else. A beast. A wolf with its teeth bared, and I was the rabbit caught in its jaws.

"Sorry," I whispered, broken, hating myself for the weakness but unable to stop.

He spun me so I was facing him fully, fingers digging into my jaw until pain flared white-hot down my face. His blue eyes glowed with fury and something worse—amusement.

"I gave you one job," he hissed, the words hot against my skin. "And you can't even follow instructions."

"I did—" My voice cracked.

His hand clamped tighter, forcing a cry from my throat.

"I told you to burn this place down and run." He wrenched my face toward the blazing inferno behind us. "Does standing here look like running, little sister?"

"No," I sobbed, the word catching on a jagged edge in my chest.

Alec shoved me hard. My feet tangled with the body on the ground—her body—and I fell, wrist twisting under my weight as I collapsed against her. My mother. Burned, gone, the last light in her eyes finally fading away, leaving behind a hollow stare. I let out a raw, guttural scream that tore through me like shrapnel.

"Tell me what to do, Alec!" I begged, voice hoarse, hands shaking as I pressed them into the dirt. "Please, I'll do it right this time. I promise!"

He crouched, bringing his face level with mine. His expression softened, not with compassion, but with a twisted kind of pity that made me want to vomit. His smirk curved like he was about to tell a joke.

"Tsk, tsk, tsk. I believe you, Em," he said, voice low, taunting, almost playful. "But you already fucked up our plan. How am I supposed to trust you won't deviate again?"

"I won't," I swore, tears streaking hot across my cheeks. "I swear it."

"Swear?" His smile widened. "Promises are dangerous little things, sister."

Another sob racked me, and I dropped my gaze, unable to withstand the sharp light of his cruelty. But Alec wasn't finished. He hooked two fingers under my chin and forced my face up until our eyes locked. His grip was bruising under his power.

"Then promise me this and only this, Emersyn Spade," he murmured, voice velvet over steel. "You will be the downfall of the Knights of Lovelen after tonight. I want them erased. Wiped from

the earth...or rotting in a cell until they choke on their own breath."

His fingers dug deeper, forcing me to nod, though every part of me screamed in terror.

"Can you do that for me?" he asked, deadly calm.

And in that moment—broken and blood-soaked, the ashes of my mother at my knees and my brother's demand like a knife at my throat—I didn't have a choice.

I whispered, "Yes."

Even though the word tasted like betrayal.

"We were to be married," I blurted out, the words spilling from my lips without thinking. Kaius lowered his cigarette, his eyes examining me as I fidgeted under his stare.

"Yes." His voice cut through the room, clipped and void of warmth, as though he'd rehearsed detachment for centuries. He leaned back in his chair, casual but dangerous. "Your brother insisted that I marry you to ensure you were kept safe, but from what I can see, you have taken care of yourself quite well, Emersyn Spade."

"Don't call me that," I snapped at him. "That girl died on the day you murdered my brother."

"I never murdered your brother." Kaius tilted his head, a predator scenting weakness.

I took a step back, desperate to put space between us, but his hand shot out, impossibly fast, gripping the back of my thighs. The heat of his touch burned through the denim. My body went rigid. "Not so fast, kitten."

"I saw you kill him," I spat, though my voice wavered. The memory clawed at me—the sound of the gun, the hollow ache in my chest, the world collapsing. "I *felt* it. The shot ripped through me too."

His thumb moved lazily against my thigh, featherlight, maddening. "Did you?" Kaius's voice was softer now, almost cruel in its calmness. "Or were you hallucinating? When you lit up your family home, did you even know what was behind those doors? What lived in your walls? It wasn't insulation, I can tell you that much."

"No," I breathed out.

Kaius stood, unfolding his tall frame until it towered over mine. The air around him seemed to shift, grow heavier, denser, as though the weight of his presence alone might crush me. His hand dipped behind his back, and I knew what was coming. I closed my eyes, bracing myself, and refusing him the satisfaction of seeing fear in me. Cold metal pressed against my temple. A shudder ripped down my spine, my breath becoming shallow and ragged.

"Look at me, Acelynn." His voice was velvet over steel, soft but commanding.

Against my will, my eyes flew open, colliding with the storm of his green gaze. They weren't cruel the way they should've been. They were fractured, wounded. A devastating sadness flickered there, a mirror of my own. "There was Muze in your home, and when you lit that damn place up, the entire place became a biohazard. There was no way you didn't get a contact high being that close to the fire. I didn't kill your brother that night. I simply put him out of his misery."

"That doesn't change anything." My teeth ground together.

His gaze drifted above my head, as though the weight of what he carried was too heavy to meet me. Rage, grief, and exhaustion swirled together on his face. I slammed my hands against his chest, forcing him to see me, to hear me.

"No, you don't get to feel sad for anything in this situation. My family is dead because of the Knights. What? I wasn't a good enough power play for you?"

"I wasn't marrying you for power." Kaius's gaze snapped back to me.

I rolled my eyes, my fury rising. The barrel of the gun dug harder into my skull, making stars burst in my vision. "But you, coming into this bar, into my club with the sole intention of fucking us over, cannot be left unpunished."

"Then punish me, oh powerful King of Lovelen," I hissed out at him. "If it weren't for today, you would have never known who I was."

Kaius's grip trembled, and he leaned closer, whispering, "I knew."

I refused to look away from his bright green eyes as the conflicted emotions he was feeling flashed through them. Hurt. Anger. Heartbreak. Each one was more devastating than the last as they continued to loop through his mind. The tears that had moments ago burned my lash line were now streaming down my face, but it didn't stop me from lifting my chin in defiance at him as I waited for the end to come.

I would not beg this man for my life, not before and not now that I held feelings for him. The gun shook slightly with his next words. "I knew, Acelynn. From the start, I knew you were using us for your own gain, whether that was protection or something else. No one strikes a deal with the Knights without an underlying bit of selfishness. But I had no proof. Vincent called it, and I told him that he was paranoid. I let my guard down as you captivated every single one of us. I let myself fall in love with you."

"Do you think I had a choice?" I bared my teeth at him. The silence around us stretched thin, and I took the opportunity to reach up toward the hand that held the gun. His finger rested loosely on the trigger, and I curled my own over his in the small space. "I never had a choice in this, Kai."

The nickname slipped past my lips before I could stop it. His entire body flinched. I don't know why I called him that. I never had before, but there was something so familiar to it when it rolled off my tongue. I continued my speech. "I was sitting in an interrogation room and was given two options: rot in a jail cell for the murder of my family or become their informant. That was it. I chose survival."

His dark eyes narrowed on me, fury raging in them, but I continued. "I don't regret what we have or meeting any of you because somehow, in the most fucked up way, this healed me. I was so angry when I came to this bar with the mission of destroying everything you held dear, but then I met each of them, and I couldn't help letting them in. So no, I don't regret coming here and taking from each of you."

Kaius leaned in, the ghost of his lips tracing my bruised ones. "But you do have one regret. I can see it in your eyes, kitten."

"Yes." I sucked in a shaky breath, my words brushing against his. "My one regret is losing it all because I was so blinded by a promise to people who never loved me. My family wanted to marry me off, use me, control me. My own brother was more interested in destroying you than in my safety in the end. I never felt loved by them, but didn't know that at the time. I thought loyalty was a form of love, but it's not. I now know how a real family loves, no matter if you are blood, and I'm sorry for destroying that."

I curled my finger around his tighter, my eyes never leaving his as I squeezed down on the trigger and waited for the world to fade away from me.

CHAPTER FIFTY-EIGHT

kaius

THE HOLLOW CLICK of the empty chamber echoed in the silence between us, louder than thunder. Acelynn froze, waiting for the end that would never come. I'd never loaded the gun in the first place. With a sharp curse, I tore the barrel away from her temple and shoved it back into my waistband. My chest heaved with rage I didn't know how to direct—at her, at myself, at the fucked-up world that had landed us here.

"Have you lost your damn mind?" I roared, my voice cracking through the quiet.

She didn't flinch. Didn't even blink. Those icy eyes locked on mine like she'd already made peace with death, like I hadn't just offered her a second chance at breathing. Acelynn lashed out, palm landing its blow on my cheek. My head snapped sideways from the force of it, the sting sinking bone deep. Before I could recover, she was on me, fists hammering against my chest. Blow after blow, all the fury, heartbreak, and grief she had buried clawed its way out of her.

Her sobs tore through me worse than her fists. Raw,

jagged, and full of the kind of pain you don't recover from. I let her hit me, let her rage pour out until I couldn't take it anymore. My hands shot forward, catching both her wrists in an iron grip.

"Enough," I growled, yanking her against me.

She didn't fight me this time. Her body crumpled, collapsing into mine like she was finally too tired to keep carrying the weight of it all. I pressed my face into the crown of her head, breathing her in, holding her like I could shield her from the past, from the truth, from me.

"Let it out, kitten," I murmured, softer now. My voice vibrated against her hairline, my lips tracing over her skin like a prayer I didn't deserve to say.

I don't know how long we stood in that spot as Acelynn released all her pent-up emotions from a lifetime worth of lies. She may not know the full extent of them, but there was a part of her soul that was tired of being in the dark. Acelynn was finally feeling everything she had repressed. And I was honored to be the man to hold her through it all. My lips traced her hairline again as her sobs bled out into broken hiccups, her breathing evening out against my chest.

Her voice was hoarse when it finally came. "I have to leave Lovelen, don't I?"

The right answer was yes. The good answer. The one that a King of the Knights should give, to protect the club, to protect what was mine. But the truth? The truth was, I wanted to chain her here forever, consequences be damned.

"Yes." The word left me flat, void of all the emotion clawing inside my chest. "But not until you find what you lost for me."

She pulled away, slow, deliberate. My arms ached from the loss. Watching her walk toward the door felt like someone was dragging barbed wire through my ribcage. I knew down to the marrow of my bones I'd never hold her again. Never find someone who would fill this gaping wound, this hole she tore through my heart, and is leaving me with. I knew this would change me, making me just as cold and heartless as my fucking father.

"You will be the bargaining chip that is used to get my sister back. Logan wants you. We all know this, and I will be ready to hand-deliver you to him when he calls."

The color in Acelynn's face drained, but it had to be done. I had to make her never want to return to this bar. Make her hate me. I stepped forward, hand latching around her throat and squeezing just enough that a squeak left her lips.

I smirked. "And if you manage to slip your way out of this one, I don't want to ever see your fucking face in my town again. You are officially out of cards, Emersyn Spade."

She paused at the doorway, one hand braced against the frame. Her head dipped, just enough for me to see the tremble in her shoulders. When she finally spoke, her voice cracked. "Will you answer one question for me before I leave, Kaius?"

"Anything."

Her eyes found mine, broken and fierce all at once. "Why would you agree to marry someone you had never met? For all you knew, I could've been a raging bitch. Or worse, not your type."

The corner of my mouth twitched despite myself. "You are definitely neither of those things."

A dark chuckle slipped past my throat before I let the truth bleed out. "We did meet, Acelynn. Once."

Her brows furrowed, confusion flickering through her grief.

"You were maybe eight. I was thirteen. It was at a club meeting at your family's home." My voice drifted, memories surfacing like ghosts. "I'd been begging my old man to let me sit in on a meeting, and he finally caved. But really? All it amounted to was me and your brother getting tossed out of the room so our fathers could talk behind closed doors."

A faint shadow of a smile tugged at my lips, though it never reached my eyes. "But I remembered you. Even back then. You had this stubborn little fire in your eyes that reminded me of every trouble I wanted to start but couldn't because my dad would have my ass scrubbing the bar floor with a toothbrush if he caught me. I couldn't forget that night."

I let the words hang there, heavy and unspoken. Because the truth was simple. I hadn't just agreed to the marriage for business, for power, for some twisted idea of her safety. I'd agreed because deep down, I remembered the girl with fire in her eyes, and I'd been a fucking fool to think I could ever burn her out of my system.

The whizz of a football cut past my ear, close enough to clip the side of my head. Alec had overthrown the ball again by a mile. I rolled my eyes, biting back a curse. He couldn't throw straight to save his damn life. With a sigh, I started jogging after it, only to stop short when a small hand lifted the football toward me.

"You are supposed to catch it when he throws it," she quipped at me.

I just stared down at her in wonder. Her blonde hair was now pushed back in a plastic headband that was similar to the tweed skirt she had on. A matching jacket hung open, revealing a white blouse underneath. But what really caught my attention were her bright blue eyes. They matched Alec and his mother's, but there was something about hers that seemed to stand out. Maybe it was the mischievous glint that shone brightly for me, but I knew that I would never forget them.

"Emersyn," Alec's scolding voice called out behind us. "You

know you aren't allowed to be out of your room when the clubs are here."

"You're not the boss of me, Alec," she snapped at him, shooting him a fiery glare.

Alec shoved past me and towered over his younger sibling. Emersyn lifted her chin in defiance, challenging him to do something. I had to hold back a laugh as I watched the interaction. This girl would make a brilliant club president. Too bad for the fact that only men were ever patched into the clubs. Misogynistic bastards.

"Go in the house now," Alec growled at her, his hand coming down to lightly shove her shoulder in that direction. She scoffed at him, which only angered the boy. "Now, Emersyn."

Emersyn threw down the football, and it bounced a few times before landing directly in front of my feet. She crossed her arms over her chest, standing her ground against her older brother. He reached out this time with two hands and shoved her. The girl stumbled backward but didn't fall over. I opened my mouth to say something, but the crack of Alec's nose rang out over my words. Emersyn was shaking out her hand as Alec clutched his face in pain. She turned her gaze to me, shrugging lightly before making her way back into the house.

"I don't remember that," Acelynn whispered, voice so faint I almost thought she was speaking to herself. Her lashes were wet, eyes downcast as though she were afraid of what she might see if she looked too closely at me. "Why don't I remember anything from my childhood that doesn't include Alec being a great older brother?"

The question hit like a knife in the ribs. I dragged my tongue across my lips, searching for words I wasn't sure she wanted to hear.

I murmured finally, my voice low, steady—like I could soften the truth if I kept it calm. "It could be your brain protecting you from reliving the trauma that occurred when you were young."

Her brows pinched together, deep lines creasing the delicate space between them. She was clawing through the fog of her past, desperate for scraps of memory, but every time she reached too far, I could see the pain strike her.

"You said...interactions?" she asked, tentative, like a girl testing the ice of a frozen lake. I only nodded once. Her gaze drifted somewhere past me, inward, chasing shadows. Then, suddenly, like a spark catching dry kindling, her eyes lit. "The laundry chute."

A ghost of a smile tugged at my lips. Of course she'd remember that. The one moment carved into both our childhoods. A memory I'd kept buried in the quiet corners of my mind. I gave her the smallest nod, confirmation without words. For a long heartbeat, she just looked at me. Really looked, like she was peeling back the years of heavy armor piece by piece. Her eyes, glazed with unshed tears, held mine with a weight that was almost unbearable.

"I'll be your bargaining chip to get Astoria back since I am currently out of cards to play." Acelynn's words were a mere whisper. She held my gaze. "Logan is predictable. He will come for me sooner or later. Wait for my call, then try not to get killed when saving your sister."

Then, slowly, Acelynn stepped back. Her hand found the door, pushing it open, the night air spilling in around her like an escape she wasn't sure she wanted to take. I wanted to stop her. Wanted to drag her back into my arms and lock the door behind us. But my boots stayed planted, heavy with the truth of what I had done, what she had done. And how it was about to destroy us both.

CHAPTER FIFTY-NINE

acelynn

A GIRL STARED BACK at me through the glass of my back door. Her dark hair clung in wet strands to her face, rainwater dripping off the ends and bleeding into the neckline of her shirt. Mascara streaked down her cheeks in jagged lines, the ugly remains of tears that had long since dried. Her skin was pale, her lips chapped, her eyes hollow. She blinked once, slowly and mechanically, the way a doll might. No expression. No soul. I hated her.

A burning anger rose sharp and hot in the center of my chest, spreading until it felt like my ribcage might crack from the pressure. How could she be so calm when my entire life was falling apart yet again? Doesn't she care at all? Hot, burning tears filled my eyes, and I swallowed a sob that threatened to escape me. How many more blows could a person take before they simply allowed the next one to take them out? How many more times would I feel completely and utterly alone in this world?

Kaius's words still echoed in my skull, cold and final. He

had demanded I leave Lovelen, as if exile was the only mercy he could give me. I knew it was the right choice, for him, for me, for whatever fragile peace remained, but some dark, twisted part of my soul rebelled against it. That part of me wanted to stay. Wanted to fight him. Wanted to force his hand until he put me down like the traitor he believed I was.

The scream ripped free before I could stop it. It tore out of me raw and violent, slamming against the glass door and rebounding back through the room in sharp echoes. It sounded like someone else's voice, animalistic and broken.

I spun, hands searching blindly for anything to throw. My fingers caught on the smooth neck of a white vase sitting pretty and useless with its bouquet of long-dead flowers. Without thinking, I hurled it. The porcelain smashed against the wall, exploding into glittering shards that rained down like angry stars.

Somewhere between the shattering and the silence, I blacked out. When I came to, I stood in the middle of a ruin. The once-perfect living room had become a war zone. Picture frames hung broken and askew, their glass teeth glinting in the low light. Canvases were ripped wide open, gaping wounds of fabric exposing drywall. Feathers drifted lazily around me, torn free from pillows I must have gutted in a frenzy, each one falling soft and weightless as if mocking the storm that had birthed them. Glass crunched beneath my boots, mingling with shards of fake fruit spilled across the floor.

The rage bled out of me all at once, leaving only the hollow ache. My knees buckled. The impact cracked through me, bone meeting hardwood with a sick crunch, but I barely felt it. My body toppled sideways onto my hip before curling inward, instinct pulling me into the smallest shape I could make. Bringing my knees to tuck to my chest, my arms wrapped around them tight as I rocked back and forth like a child desperate to self-soothe.

But the storm didn't quiet. My body shook violently, shivers tearing through me like aftershocks. And then came the memories—flashes of color and sound, too vivid, too sharp. The truth I had buried clawed its way out of the dark.

The massacre. The blood. The screams.

They roared back in Technicolor, flooding my mind, drowning me until there was nothing left but pain.

The King of Lovelen stood over a body still smoking from fire, the charred scent clawing through the night air until it stuck in the back of my throat. My stomach twisted at the sight of the figure sprawled out on their stomach, arms bent at awkward angles beside them. The flames had chewed through skin and fabric alike, leaving blackened ruin in their wake. My eyes landed on the hoodie, once black, now torn and blistered, but the bleeding spade symbol across its back still screamed through the chaos. My heart stumbled inside my chest. It was the same one Alec had pulled on earlier tonight before everything went to shit.

I crouched lower, pressing myself into the shadow of a pallet stacked high with boxes, their ink-stamped logos glowing in the fire. The sharp edges of wood dug into my thighs, but I didn't move. I had to stay out of sight if I had any chance of surviving. My gaze traced the cartons, examining each label for a clue to what could be contained in there. Then it caught on one of the sides. Someone had tried to scribble out the letters, but they hadn't done a good enough job. Through the lines, I could make out the letters: Muze.

My eyebrows pinched together in confusion. The Spades had control over the ring that filtered an assortment of drugs into the state, which caused some tension between the other clubs and us.

The only drug we didn't touch was Muze, which was the Knights' domain. So why the fuck were the Death Dealers' markings stamped on every single box stacked around me? Why had my brother walked back into the flames when he knew damn well I was waiting outside?

A pained moan broke through the silent desert. It rattled against my bones, freezing the breath in my lungs. I slapped a trembling hand across my mouth to keep the cry from spilling free. Nolan Bedivere prowled in the dirt like a starving predator, circling the body and his king with the kind of smile that wasn't born of joy but of something far fouler. A twisted grin stretched across his lips as he tossed a short blade into the air, catching it again with ease. The firelight kissed every dried bloodstain along its silver edge, making the steel like the stars above us. Behind him, the house smoldered, windows coughing smoke into the desert sky.

And in the shadows just beyond was Vincent Camberly. I had never seen him before, not up close, but rumors whispered themselves through the clubs like prayers and curses alike. How he had poisoned his own mother with the same venom his father had fed to him. His dark hair swayed in the wind, catching stray embers in strands like threads of fire, though his eyes never left the scene unraveling in front of him. Silent. Patient. The kind of stillness that made your soul itch.

"Got ourselves a crispy one, don't we, brothers?" Nolan crouched, blade dancing in his fingers before dragging it across charred flesh.

The figure screeched out, trying their best to avoid the knife, but they didn't have the strength to fight back. A gasp spilled from me, and the three Knights' heads snapped in my direction.

My spine slammed into the rough wood of the boxes, splinters biting through the fabric of my shirt and into my skin. I pressed my shaking palm harder to my mouth, covering my nose and lips, and willed myself to disappear. To smother every trembling sound before it gave me away.

"Probably just a stray kitten that wandered too close to the show," Kaius Mordred's voice deep rumbled around me.

I had heard him speak before. Not to me. Never to me. Always in passing, his words dripping from his mouth like slow, heavy drops of rain in the middle of a storm. I had hidden on the roof above my father's study during meetings, watching shadows move below, greedy to gather scraps of truth about the Knights through the always-opened window.

I had told myself it was curiosity. But every time he spoke, warmth bloomed deep in my chest like a secret I wasn't supposed to hold. The same warmth I felt now. I had asked my mother what that meant not that long ago, and she had responded back with a certain firmness that had me cataloging the conversation away to remember.

"If you feel that, my sweet Spade..." Her eyes were as bright as the stars that night. "Never let that person go. Hold on to them because they are the one who sets you alive and makes you a better version of yourself. And if you feel you are going to lose them, fight like hell to keep them."

A shudder ran through me as the feeling grew hotter as Kaius's voice dragged me back to the present, harder, darker. "Do you have anything to say for yourself?"

Slowly, I turned back to watch the scene. Nolan was still bent over the body, eyes tracking down it to find anything that might jump out to get him. The figure on the ground coughed out something wet and broken in response. No words, just a body that should not have still been alive.

Kaius held out his left hand to Nolan. The silver blade from earlier was laid in the center of his palm at the command. Bending down, he gripped the ruined ankle and ripped it up to him. The awkward angle Kaius had the man's leg in had him screaming and squirming, but he held him firm in place. The knife rested between Kaius's teeth as he rolled down charred denim. Under the fabric, the skin was a bright and bubbly mess of flesh, but you could still see the dark ink of a tattoo. My heart stopped.

My breathing picked up under my palm as panic started to overcome me. A hand of cards was fanned out across the skin, each one labeled with a different suit in the deck. And there, at the edge of ruined flesh, was an ace of spades, my mother's and my initials etched across the top and bottom.

Alec. The boy who told me to run. Who laughed at this hell-hole. Who swore he'd never be caught dead this close to Muze. And yet here he was. Dying. Burned. Tears slicked my hands where they covered my face, sliding down skin too fast for me to stop.

"Hold him for me," Kaius grumbled around the blade between his teeth.

He handed off the leg to Nolan before removing the knife from his mouth and bringing it down on the skin below the tattoo. The cut wasn't clean. It never could be. The sick sound of tearing flesh mixed with choked screams filled the air with a noise that would never leave me. I couldn't watch anymore, biting down on my fist as bile rose so fast up my throat, I nearly choked on it.

It felt like hours before the sounds stopped and a loud thump hit the desert floor. Slowly, I turned back to see what was happening, finding the chunk of skin was now lying in a heap next to Alec's bloody leg. Red liquid oozed, spilling in a heavy river that turned the desert into a paste of mud and crimson. Kaius wiped the blade across his light-washed jeans, red streaks staining pale threads like war paint.

I knew what was coming before Kaius even reached into the waistband of his pants and retrieved the black gun. The dark metal winked dangerously at me in the moonlight as he stepped around Nolan and stood directly in front of Alec's head. My brother weakly lifted his skull from the dirt, eyes locking on Kaius with a defiance that I could practically hear him say, "If he is going to kill me, I am going to look him in the eyes as he does it."

Kaius lifted the gun until the barrel was inches away from Alec's forehead. "My father once told me that it is not the birth of a person that defines who we are, but what they hold in their heart. The actions they take to ensure those they love are never harmed again. And I won't let you hurt her or anyone else again."

The click of the safety releasing rang out through the night air. My breath caught in my throat, but I didn't dare move an inch. Kaius cocked his head to the side, a dark grin coming across his face. "You shouldn't have shown your hand so soon."

The sound of the gunshot was sharp and unmistakable. It cut through the air like a thunderclap, momentarily drawing out all the other sounds around me. A reverberating echo lingered in the back of my ears, and I watched as Alec's head fell into the dirt underneath him. I spun away from the scene, eyes burning with tears as fear coursed through my veins. Each inhale was a struggle as I fought against an invisible force gripping my lungs. I slammed my eyes shut, trying my best to piece my thoughts together, but only one repeated itself like a metronome.

Kaius Mordred, the King of Lovelen, had killed my brother right in front of me.

And I swore on the ashes at my feet, on the blood seeping into the dirt, that if it was the last thing I ever did, I would paint his perfect town in his blood.

"Poor, sad little Spade."

The voice slid out of the shadows like a snake coiling around me. My stomach clenched as I turned, eyes narrowing on the figure at the kitchen table. Logan sat in the farthest chair, posture lazy, one finger tapping a slow, mocking rhythm against the glass surface. The overhead light didn't touch him, his face cloaked in the kind of darkness I'd never been able to outrun. But I didn't need to see him. That voice had been burned into me years ago, stitched into every nightmare, every broken promise.

"What do you want?" My words were clipped. I didn't rise, didn't give him the satisfaction of rattling me. My fingers skimmed the back pocket of my shorts. From where he sat, he couldn't see my subtle movement as I withdrew the phone and hit call on the first name in my call log. "You got what you wanted. I've got nothing left—no fight, no cards to play, not even a single family member living. So whatever this game is, Logan, end it. Enough with your riddles."

"Stop the pity party, Emersyn." He spat the name like venom.

My gaze flicked down to his arms, rage bubbling hot under my skin at the sight of the tattoos inked into his flesh —all three club symbols. A spade. A knight. And now, a serpent. He wore them like trophies, a collection of broken loyalties he never even earned. Logan took what he wanted, and without even an initiation, he had decided he was now a member of all three clubs. Which only meant one thing: he wanted the power of them all. To rule them as one, and he would slaughter anyone who got in his way. He followed my stare, grinning wide enough for the moonlight to catch on his teeth. "Tell me what you want, doll. One wish. I'll grant it. What's your desire?"

The answer throbbed inside me, unspoken and dangerous. There was only one man I wanted, one man whose forgiveness I would bleed for. But Logan would never have that piece of me, not when he'd already carved out too much. So I said the only thing that mattered, the only truth I could offer without giving him more of myself. "I want you to let Astoria Mordred go."

Logan chuckled, low and cruel, shaking his head. "And why would I waste such a perfect bargaining chip? The Knights dance on her leash, and I'm the one holding it."

"Use me instead." The words were out before I could stop them. My pulse jumped, but I forced myself to keep going, steady and certain. "Take me. I'll be your bargaining chip. You'll have everything you want—the Knights on their knees, me at your mercy, and revenge wrapped in a perfect, pretty little bow."

Logan leaned forward, his shadow spilling longer across the table. "And what good are you now, Acelynn?"

He hissed my new name like it was poison, and I almost laughed. He thought it was tainted when Emersyn was the name that had damned me. Logan's eyes narrowed. "You torched your leverage with the Knights. You're worthless."

"He'll come for me." My voice stayed flat, even as bile rose in my throat. I knew they were listening to every word, and just the thought of him hearing this made my heart skip a beat. "Kaius will come. And then you can kill him. Isn't that the dream, Logan? The Knights burned to ash and me ready to be your submissive pet."

He studied me, the silence long enough that my heartbeat sounded like gunfire in my ears. Finally, Logan slid a hand into his jeans pocket and pulled out a burner phone. Tossing it across the table, he nodded once. "Prove it."

I reached down, ending the call on my phone and sliding it under a broken lampshade. My legs wobbled as I stood, but I forced them forward. The burner felt like ice in my palm as I flipped it open and dialed the one person I knew would answer an unknown number in the hopes that Astoria would be on the other end.

My shaky hands lifted the phone to my ear, and I listened as it rang, once, twice, and then a familiar voice called out to me over the line, "Hello?"

I swallowed hard, forcing my tone to steady. "Nolan. Meet me at the border of Lovelen where the old, abandoned barn sits. I...I think I know where Astoria is."

CHAPTER SIXTY

acelynn

THE WIND TORE across the lot, cold and biting, carrying the scent of rain and gasoline as the storm crept closer. Heavy clouds swirled like a living thing, black and swollen, as if the sky itself were bracing for bloodshed. I stood there with my hands shoved deep into my jacket pockets, pulse thrumming as I waited for Nolan and Vince. Anxiety churned in my gut, not fear, never fear, but a taut wire pulling tighter with every second. Every flash of lightning lit up the horizon like the world itself was warning me to turn back. But I couldn't, not with Astoria's life hanging in the balance.

The low rumble of two motorcycles cut through the wind, the sound pulling me back into the present. My spine stiffened. I only had moments before Nolan and Vince reached me. Moments to pull myself together and shove down the panic clawing at my throat. They needed information, a plan, a leader—not a girl cracking apart at the seams.

"Should we keep calling you Acelynn, or would you prefer Emersyn? Maybe Ms. Spade?" Nolan's venom dripped like acid as he called out to me. I rolled my eyes and forced myself to face him, meeting his fury with my own resolve.

"Call me whatever you want," I said, crossing my arms over my chest, leaning on my right hip. "But if you want to get Astoria back, not in a body bag, you're going to listen to me."

Nolan lunged forward, his fury breaking loose, but Vince was faster. His arm shot out, catching Nolan around the waist and hauling him back with practiced strength. He pointed one finger at the angry man.

"Calm down," Vince barked, his tone taking no argument. "She's right. If we have any chance of getting Astoria back, we need her."

Nolan's chest heaved, his breathing rapid as his eyes darted like a trapped animal's. My anger softened, twisting into something far more dangerous than rage—sympathy. I moved past Vince, reaching out before I could second-guess myself. My hand found Nolan's, fingers curling around his. To my surprise, he didn't try to pull away.

"We will get her back, Nolan," I whispered, holding onto him like I could anchor us both. "I promise you."

His shoulders slumped, breaking under the weight of that promise, and I caught the shimmer of tears in the moonlight. He tried to hide it, but grief always finds its cracks. My thumb stroked the top of his hand soothingly as he gathered himself enough to speak.

"Don't make promises you can't keep," he rasped, voice heavy with the kind of pain that leaves scars.

"I'm keeping this one." I tilted my head until I caught his wandering stare, refusing to let him escape mine. "Do you hear me? This is the one I'll die for if I have to. Astoria is coming home, and then you're finally going to tell her how you feel."

He scoffed, grasping at denial like it was his last shield. "I don't know what you're insinuating."

"Give it up, you stubborn bastard," Vince cut in, a rare smirk tugging at his lips. "The entire town of Lovelen knows you're in love with her. Hell, probably the whole state. It's pathetic at this point that the both of you keep dancing around each other like you haven't been crazy for each other since you were children. Why do you think no one in the club ever touched her?"

I couldn't stop the laugh that tore out of me, wild and sharp. "Because you would send them to an early grave if they did."

Vince chuckled, the sound rumbling low in his chest. For one fleeting moment, even standing on the brink of war, we weren't enemies. We were just broken people holding onto scraps of our humanity in a world full of darkness. But Nolan only rolled his eyes, digging deeper into his fortress of denial. "You both don't know what you're talking about. Astoria and I are just friends. That's all we'll ever be."

"Friends don't look at each other the way you two do." Vince clapped him on the back as he strode past, hair whipping in the wind. "But fine, keep lying to yourself."

When Vince turned back to me, the humor drained from his face, replaced with the grim steel I was used to. "What's the plan?"

"Logan came to visit me after—" I inhaled sharply, my throat closed on Kaius's name, grief and longing choking me. I forced myself to continue on. "He was waiting in my kitchen. I...I agreed to a trade with him."

"For Astoria?" Vince's brow rose, skepticism heavy in his stare. "What could he possibly want more than her? She's leverage enough to bring the Knights to their knees. Especially Kaius."

"Her," Nolan said, his voice low and bitter as he pointed directly at me.

The words stabbed through me, sharp and merciless. My gaze fell, shame clawing at my insides. They thought Kaius would save me, but I didn't deserve saving. Not after my betrayal. Not after Oscar. Not after everything.

Vince swore under his breath, dragging a hand over his jaw. "So Logan uses you as bait. And then what? We're supposed to kill him for you? Clean up your mess even though you stabbed the Knights in the back?"

"No." My voice cracked like a whip. "Logan is mine."

Nolan tried to reach for me, his voice gentling. "Ace—"

"No." I recoiled, fire rising in me, refusing comfort. "He doesn't get to haunt me for years, crawl out of the grave to torment me, take Astoria from you, and then die at someone else's hands. I want to be the one to end him. I want him to look in my eyes and know it's me who sends him to hell, where he's always belonged."

My chest heaved as panic surged, my vision tilting, the storm spinning above me like it had crawled inside my ribcage. My hand clawed at my chest, nails raking over skin already raw from too many nights doing the same. Vince stepped in, grounding me with both hands on my shoulders. His stare locked onto mine, hard and unyielding. "The shot is yours, Acelynn."

His words cut through the storm, steady as steel. "And we'll be there every step of the way."

Something inside me loosened, the panic ebbing like the tide. For a moment, I wondered if Vince had always been the quiet voice of reason in the Knights, or if this rare glimpse of humanity was something he gave sparingly, like a precious gift.

"I betrayed you all," I whispered, shame rising again.

Vince only shrugged, dropping his hands. "We all fuck up once or twice, Ace. All you really did was stir the pot. You weren't a very good informant, if we're being honest."

"I got Oscar killed."

"No." Nolan's voice, solid and sure, pulled me toward him. His gaze was steady, if tired. "Oscar was feeding the feds information long before you gave the tip about the Muze to whoever you were being blackmailed by, and you weren't the first source who told them there would be a drop that night. Kaius and Vince found the documentation of everything he was letting slip. You didn't get that boy killed."

The weight that had been festering in my chest for weeks lifted, just enough for me to stand straighter. Oscar had been his own breed of snake in the Knights. He had dug his own grave.

"Then it's time," I said, voice firm again. "We get Astoria back. And we put Logan in the ground where he belongs."

As the three of us faced the storm together, I could feel it —the shift. Nolan and Vince weren't just men anymore. They were Knights, dangerous and resolute, their presence rolling off them like the wrath of the sea. And me? I wasn't running anymore. If the Knights fell tonight, it wouldn't be because of my hand. It would be because fate had finally come calling.

CHAPTER SIXTY-ONE

acelynn

MY JUDGE, jury, and executioner stared me down from the swinging tarps of the red barn. The storm broke over the countryside like a verdict. Thunder rolled low across the sandy stretch, and every flash of lightning illuminated the sagging red barn I once used as the stage for my greatest betrayal. It loomed in the distance, tarps flapping like gallows cloth in the wind. My chest tightened because I knew if ever there was a place to meet my reckoning, it was here.

The man in the doorway stood utterly still, black clothing swallowing the light around him. Combat boots grounded him, a cavalier tactical vest strapped across his chest, every detail precise and lethal. The skull-shaped mask he wore caught the flash of lightning, its bone-white grin smeared with grime and rust, as if death itself had stained it. His eyes, hidden behind blacked-out lenses, still seemed to glimmer with a predatory sharpness. A gloved hand lifted. Two fingers curled toward me in a slow, deliberate beckon.

My pulse thudded in my throat, but I forced in one last

gulp of night air before stepping forward. The gun Vince had pressed into my hand earlier dug into the bone of my hip with each step, an iron reminder that violence was the only language I had left. The masked figure retreated with a single step, melting into the darkness as if the storm had swallowed him whole. I reached the barn doors. Every nerve in me screamed to run, but instead, I pushed forward, eyes darting into the yawning black inside.

"You made it." The voice snapped the tension like a whip.

I jerked left, coming nose to nose with Logan. He stood with his arms crossed, a maroon shirt clinging to him like it had absorbed the storm's humidity. My gaze snapped back into the barn. Emptiness was the only thing left where the masked man had just been.

"Did you deliver the message?" Logan's tone was bored, almost lazy.

"Yes." My voice wavered, betraying me. "Where is Astoria?"

"Alive," he drawled, as if her survival was an inconvenience to him. "And if you want her to stay that way, you'll behave."

My stomach sank at the comment. Logan turned his back, sauntering deeper into the barn, and I followed him despite every instinct telling me to bolt. I must have looked like some pathetic stray trailing behind him. At the far end of the barn, a crude table was littered with bottles and glasses. Logan's hands shuffled, producing two shot glasses filled with a liquid that gleamed a pale purple color under the fractured shafts of moonlight breaking through the roof. He offered one to me.

"I'm good," I snapped, forcing my hands into my back pockets, rocking on my heels like defiance alone could shield me.

His eyes narrowed. "Either you take the shot willingly, Acelynn, or I'll unhinge that pretty jaw and force it down your throat."

I didn't move. I wanted him to see that I still had something left, some shred of control. His lips twisted into a smirk. "Break another one."

At his command, the sound of snapping bones followed by an earsplitting scream that matched Astoria rattled the barn's metal framing.

"Stop!" The word ripped out of me as I lunged forward, yanking the glass from his hand.

My lips sealed around the rim before I could second-guess, and I threw the liquor back. The vodka burned, but the taste was wrong. Too smooth. Too masked. Poison dressed as fire. I flung the glass to the ground, letting it shatter at my feet. There was hemlock in that shot. And he thought it was going to kill me. Too bad he didn't realize I had been dosing myself for months now. But what he didn't know would only kill him in the end. Logan downed his own shot and licked his lips, savoring.

"Ready to listen now, doll?" he asked. I wobbled on my feet, letting it appear as if the world was tilting from under me. My stomach rolled as the drug slid through me. Even with the dosing, the hemlock still gave me slight side effects, fogging my limbs and dulling the edges of my panic. Still, I nodded to his question.

"Good." His smile stretched wide, a shadow's grin.

I stepped back, but collided with something solid. My breath froze in my chest. Before I could scream, a hand clamped down over my mouth, fingers crushing my cheeks and yanking me backward. My skull smacked against the ground with a crack that left stars dancing in my vision.

Laughter rolled over me. Not Logan's. A new voice,

darker, harsher. "You promised me you'd burn the Knights for good. Yet here I am, cleaning up your failure because you couldn't resist crawling into Kaius's bed."

I blinked through the haze. The masked man loomed over me. The terrifying skull mask was closer now, the paint mottled with rust-colored flecks I now knew were dried blood. The chiseled mask sat flush against his face, and I could see now that he was wearing full blackout lenses to blend in with the body paint around his eyes. He cocked his head slowly, like a predator examining prey that had already lost. Lifting myself into a sitting position, I scooted myself back just enough to kick out. The heel of my foot caught him in the balls, but he didn't even flinch. A growl ripped from his throat as he seized my hair at the crown of my head, wrenching me off the ground.

"Stupid bitch," he hissed.

I thrashed out, kicking and screaming against his hold, but the drug slowed me, dragged me down into my own body. He slammed me back onto the concrete, and the impact forced the air from my lungs, my chest burning as I tried to pull back the oxygen I had just lost in through my nose. Pain shot up my ribs. The masked man straddled me, knees digging into my hips, his weight crushing. The gun in my waistband bit deeper into my hip.

Logan's laugh slithered across the space. "You're only making this harder, doll."

Two hands wrapped around my throat, squeezing until fire roared in my chest. My back arched, nails clawing uselessly at his forearms. Above me, Logan's face leaned close, the presence of pure evil surrounding me in my fading vision.

"Since you love that fucking Knight so much, you can go down for his murder. We will make it a real Romeo and Juliet story." Logan's words were distorted as his knuckles traced my cheek. The masked man's thumbs pressed into my windpipe harder. "One poisoned, the other killed by his own hand. The news is going to eat that up."

Dots swam over my vision, my chest heaving up for a breath it was desperate for, but I knew would not get. I resisted the urge to shut my heavy eyes as I let my hands slide from his forearms. With all the remaining energy I had left, I lifted my trembling hands to the masked man's face, into the crease between his eye and the mask.

In one swift motion, I ripped it free in one desperate pull. The man recoiled, tearing his hands from my throat. Gasping and coughing, I pushed myself backward, my eyes locking on his face. Recognition hollowed me. Horror rooted me in place so much that I didn't see Logan's fist until it cracked against my cheek. Pain blossomed, the spray of blood warm and metallic coated the front of my white shirt.

"Enough," the unmasked man snapped. But Logan wasn't done. His boot drove into my ribs, knocking me onto my hands. My arms shook under the weight of my body. "I said enough!"

"She ruins everything!" Logan's voice cracked, frenzied. "She couldn't even save her best friend without fucking it up."

Logan crouched low, face inches from mine, spittle flying as he screamed, "Do you see any Knights here? You promised they'd come, but no one's coming. No one was ever coming for you, Emersyn. You should have burned that night, but your brother couldn't stomach the guilt long enough to send you back in."

"What?" I heaved out, my mind racing as it tried to make sense of his words. They were coming out long and jumbled, as if they were bouncing around my brain at a hundred miles per hour.

Logan sneered. "Oh, come on. You're not stupid. You never were, even if you played the role of dumb little sister like a pro."

I shook my head, dazed. "I don't know what you're talking about."

The back of his hand landed a blow to the other cheek. "You don't remember? You're the reason this all started. You couldn't keep your nose out of the business."

"The Muze." The word slid from the other man's mouth, and my blood froze. I refused to meet his gaze, staring at the concrete instead.

"You stumbled onto the shipment," he said, his tone deliberate, accusing. "The one meant to blackmail the Knights. The Death Dealers wanted control. Wanted to force a patch over. But you..." His boots scraped closer. "You found it first. You walked in on your father inventorying the product, and that was the moment he decided you were a liability."

I froze in the doorway of the shop's mechanic bay, the heavy stench of oil and steel mixing with something far more poisonous. My gaze swept over the table where my father and several of his men hunched, counting out small purple vials into neat little rows. The overhead light flickered, casting a sickly glow over their hands—steady, practiced, and far too comfortable with the trade they were dealing. My stomach lurched. This wasn't the first time I'd stumbled into something I shouldn't, but tonight, it felt different. I shuffled back a step, desperate to disappear before anyone noticed me. But it was too late as hands gripped the back of my shirt, yanking me into their body. I tried to squirm from their hold, but it was no use.

"Naughty little Spade," a voice whispered, slick as venom against my ear.

My spine went rigid. I'd know that voice anywhere. Logan. He wasn't supposed to be in my father's inner circle, not here, not in this place that had always been tainted, but at least had belonged to blood. His breath ghosted hot across my skin. "What are we going to do with you?"

"Get your hands off her." My brother's voice cut through the air. Logan dropped me instantly, his hold falling away like ash through fingers.

I staggered forward and craned my head, catching sight of Alec skulking from the shadows. His scowl was carved deep into his face, arms crossed, jaw tight enough to crack. Relief flooded my chest in a single shaky breath.

"I won't say anything to anyone," I blurted.

"You're damn right you won't," my father snapped. His voice was fire, molten and unyielding, and when I whipped my head toward him, his face was tinged a dangerous red. Anger radiated from him in smoldering waves. "You won't get the chance to say anything."

Cold fear cut through me sharper than the chill of steel. I had always feared him, but this version of my father—the calculating one, the executioner dressed in flesh—was something else entirely. My gut twisted, and before I could stop myself, I stepped back closer to Logan, as though his presence offered protection. But Logan would never save me. No, he would throw me to the wolves and smirk while they tore me apart, savoring every scream.

"Alec," my father said, his voice low but commanding, accompanied by a harsh nod in my direction. My brother moved toward me slowly and purposefully. The sight of him advancing snapped something loose inside me, and I bolted. My shoes squealed across the concrete as I slid around a metal table, narrowly dodging grasping hands that shot out to catch me. My father's voice rang

out, ordering them not to touch me, but the words were muffled, drowned by the pounding in my ears.

I risked a glance over my shoulder, my hair whipping across my face, desperate to gauge Alec's position. He wasn't there. He had vanished from my line of sight. And then I was airborne. The ground ripped away beneath me as Alec's arms caught me mid-run, hurling me like a rag doll across the bay. I slammed into a card table with bone-rattling force. Plastic cracked, buckled, and split beneath me before giving way entirely. The table collapsed with a deafening snap, and I spilled onto the floor, gasping, my ribs screaming in protest.

Groaning, I clawed my way onto my hands and knees, crawling clumsily toward freedom, but Alec was faster. My shirt tore with a sickening rip as he wrenched me up by the collar and slammed me against the hood of a car. The vehicle bowed in the middle under my weight. His grip locked my arms above my head at an angle so tight I could already feel pins and needles flooding my fingertips. I kicked, twisted, but his weight pressed down, crushing me into place. His forearm dug into my ribs, each breath harder to take than the last.

"No!" I screamed, my voice ripping from my throat, but it did nothing. Alec had me caged. Out of the corner of my eye, I saw my father approaching. He circled us like a hunter, the blade of a knife twirling casually against his finger. Each step was measured, deliberate, like a countdown as he circled the two of us. He stopped on my left, crouching low, and pressed the tip of the knife into the hollow of my throat. I swallowed against the blade, my eyes darting up to Alec's face, searching, pleading for anything. To beg my father for mercy, for the love he should have been giving his children instead of this twisted version he believed it to be. My face begged for the brother I thought I still had to step in. But he refused to meet my gaze.

"I had plans for you, Emersyn," my father murmured, his voice slick with mockery.

I focused on Alec's freckles instead. Those scattered flecks across his skin, so faint you had to be close to see them. They had once made him look younger, softer, almost innocent. But innocence didn't live in his eyes anymore.

"Just fucking kill me if that's your plan," I spat, teeth grinding through the words. At that, Alec flinched at my words. I tilted my head into the blade, welcoming its sting as I locked eyes with my father. My chin lifted in defiance.

"I mean, clearly all of this"—my gaze flicked to the drugs, to the men, to Alec's hand restraining me—"is more important than your own flesh and blood."

"Emersyn," Alec warned, his grip tightening painfully around my wrists.

I snorted at his caution and bared my teeth at both of them. "DO IT!"

The hood rattled violently beneath me as I bucked against Alec's weight, fighting with everything I had left, not caring anymore about the blade rubbing into my skin. But my father ripped the knife back at the last second. The edge kissed my skin, leaving behind a delicious sting. His eyes glittered with amusement as he leaned in closer, his breath heavy with smoke and rot.

"Maybe killing you would do me more harm than good, little Spade," he whispered, the tip of his knife grazing my jaw now like a lover's touch. "No. I have other plans for you."

Alec Spade stood only inches away from me, close enough that I could see the uneven ridges of the burn scar stretched across the right side of his face. It was raw, angry, and still healing, but he was very much alive. Black streaks of body paint smeared around his eyes gave him the look of something feral, but when he plucked the blackout contacts from them and tossed them to the floor, it was just my brother again. My brother, with those same piercing blue eyes that haunted me. Tears stung at the corners of my vision as I forced the words out, my voice shaking but sharp.

"You didn't go to Kaius to help me, did you? All of this..." I swallowed hard. "It was never about saving me. It was about tearing down the Knights."

Before Alec could answer, a slow clap echoed to my left. Logan. The sound of his palms smacking together wormed under my skin like maggots. My teeth clenched. Without thinking, my hand reached behind me, fingers curling around the grip of the gun I'd kept hidden. In one motion, I drew it and leveled it at him.

Logan smirked, smug even with a barrel aimed at his chest. "What are you gonna do, Emersyn? Shoot me?"

The corner of my mouth twitched. "Yeah. Something like that."

I lowered the barrel and pulled the trigger. The shot ripped through the air, the recoil jolting up my arm. Logan's scream followed immediately, raw and panicked, as he staggered back, clutching at the blood pouring from his leg. He collapsed onto the dirt floor, scrambling backward on his ass. My legs were shaking, but I stepped over him until the muzzle of my gun hovered just above his forehead. He flinched when the hot metal grazed his skin, shrieking like a cornered animal.

I chuckled low, dark. "Want to try asking me another stupid question?"

The blood from his thigh wound spread fast, staining his shirt crimson. His eyes darted wildly, pleading now, lips trembling as he begged for his life. But I leaned in, pressing the gun harder to his skin, savoring the way he shuddered beneath it.

"You know, Logan, you've never been the brightest. If you

had any damn sense, you would've realized something by now." My voice dropped to a hiss. "The Knights are already waiting for my signal."

His teeth chattered, breath coming fast. "W-what's your signal?"

Before I could even form a word, pain lanced through the side of my neck. A sharp sting and then fire flooded my veins. My gasp tore out of me, strangled and desperate, as liquid heat rushed into me like poison. Alec's hand fisted in my hair, yanking my head back against his chest as the needle stayed buried in my skin. I could hear the faint hiss of liquid emptying into me. My brother's voice was soft in my ear, too gentle for what he was doing, as if he were calming a child.

"Shhh..." His breath ghosted against my temple. "Don't fight it, baby sister. You'll only make it worse if you do."

I wanted to scream, to claw at him, to tear the syringe out, but my body betrayed me. The hemlock slithered through me like wildfire, setting every nerve alight. My vision fractured, reality splitting at the seams. The shadows of the barn peeled into shapes, strange glowing colors bleeding across the beams like stained glass. Everything was too bright, too loud, and slipping out of reach.

My knees buckled, and Alec guided me down as if I were fragile glass, lowering me to the dirt with a care that made me want to vomit. He had done this to me, and yet he was trying to be the caring brother I once knew. The gun slipped from my hand, clattering to the floor. A sudden crack split the air as it discharged on impact, the sound ricocheting off the walls.

Logan's scream echoed around me. Through the kaleidoscope haze, I saw him flinch, clutching himself as if the sound alone had shot through him. Then he scrambled, wild-eyed and pale, until he found his legs and bolted through the side door of the barn. A fleeting satisfaction curled through me. I'd meant for that gunshot to end Logan's life, but Kaius would hear it. He'd come just as it had been planned. But even as the thought flickered, another wave of fire rolled through my body, stealing my breath. He'd be too slow this time, and when he arrived, he would be met with a dead girl and a ghost he had thought he had rid himself of standing over her.

Every twitch, every breath, burned. My body felt alive and dead all at once, nerves lit like a thousand watts of Christmas lights wired wrong. A groan broke from me when I tried to move, my head lolling to the side against the dirt.

"You promised me!" Astoria's voice cracked like glass, frantic, breaking through the buzz in my ears. "You promised, Alec! If I did what you asked, you wouldn't touch either of them!"

Her words blurred, fading into the swirl of colors, echoing like they were spoken underwater. I couldn't hold on to them. Couldn't hold on to anything.

"Oh, don't worry. We have plans for you, little darling," Alec taunted her, causing tears to burn hot against my lashes, and through the blur, I forced my gaze up. Alec was still there, looming around me now, completely ignoring Astoria's hysterics. Those familiar blue eyes emptied out, hollow as stone. My lips trembled as I fought the weight pressing down on me.

"We've only got...minutes now," I whispered, my voice cracked and thin. "Before I'm dead."

The tears finally spilled, hot against my temples. I dry heaved as my body began to try to eject the poison coursing through it. "So tell me, Alec...why? Why are you so willing to kill me, your own sister, now, when you could have avoided this all that night and ended it then?"

CHAPTER SIXTY-TWO

kaius

THE DESERT WAS QUIET TONIGHT. Only the low rumble of thunder echoing off the canyon walls broke the silence, each crack rumbling like a warning. Vince, Nolan, and I crouched in the shadows a few yards from the red barn Acelynn had walked into ten minutes ago. But it felt like she had been in there for hours. We were waiting for two gunshots, the signal that Logan was dead, and my sister could be pulled out of whatever hell he had put her through. Nolan hadn't stopped pacing, the sand crunching under his boots every time he turned back.

My gaze snapped off him at the sound of the first gunshot. Silence followed, heavier than the storm pressing down on us. My pulse thundered harder as the seconds ticked by. There was always the chance the sound meant everything had gone wrong, that when I stepped inside, I'd be walking straight into my worst nightmare. But this had been Acelynn's plan. Reckless. Insane. But I had let her run with it. The seconds dragged, and even Vince, who was always steady as a rock, shifted uneasily. I closed my eyes, breathing in a lungful of dry, storm-tainted air. Come on, kitten. One more shot.

The second crack split the night. My eyes opened. Nolan flashed me a grim smile. "It's showtime, boys."

We stalked forward, moving quietly downhill, shadows gliding through sand and brush until the barn loomed before us. Nolan vanished around the left side of the building while Vince took the right. They would take care of Astoria while I dealt with whatever cleanup Acelynn needed handled.

Two voices drifted out of the half-open door, pulling me in. I edged close, fingers brushing the grip of my gun, listening.

Acelynn's voice was off. There was a slight slur to her words. "Start talking."

Then a ghost from our past answered. "You were never going to live a normal life, Emersyn."

Ice slid down my spine. Alec Spade. The son of a bitch I had buried in fire and ash. I edged inside, eyes locking on the sight before me. Acelynn was laid out on the ground. She was as white as a ghost, causing the blue in her veins to stand out. There was a glazed overlook in her eyes that I only saw when Vince dosed a person with hemlock. The thought had my stomach dropping. If she had hemlock in her system, there was no telling how long she had left.

"We gave you the illusion of a safety net when we shipped you off to those fancy schools, but you were always going to be a bargaining chip, whether it was with the Knights or another power move our father wanted. It's the exact reason you were born." Alec loomed over her, taking slow steps toward her, calm, predatory, his voice soaked with venom.

"I don't believe you didn't try to protect me," she whispered, shoulders slumping slightly at his words. "You, out of everyone, were the biggest advocate for me getting away from the club. What changed?"

"I tasted power, little Spade." Alec raised his hands up in an *oh well* motion.

Acelynn's gun lay to her left, just far enough that she wouldn't be able to reach for it without him noticing. Bruises bloomed across her face, stark in the moonlight. My jaw clenched hard enough to crack teeth. The shattering of glass in a back room had Alec moving in a blur toward her, his arm clamped around her throat, twisting her against him. Acelynn's body was limp in his hold, dangling awkwardly off the ground as he forced a gun beneath her chin like a grotesque puppet show.

I stepped from the shadows, weapon raised and sighted square at his head. Acelynn bucked against him, throwing her head forward into his nose. He laughed, red teeth gleaming, his grip iron. The hit hadn't had enough strength in it to do any real damage.

"Look at that, sister," Alec sneered. "Your knight in shining armor, here to save the princess."

Her cry cut through me as he jammed the gun harder into her jaw. My aim wavered on her instead of him as he lifted her up and against his chest, using her as a human shield against me. Rage burned hotter than the storm overhead. There was no way I had a clean shot with her like that.

"Let her go," I demanded. My voice was steady, even if my hands weren't. My gaze never left Acelynn. She was shaking, dirt and blood streaked across her skin, nails clawing at his arm. I wanted to promise she'd be okay, but I couldn't lie to her. Not here. "Once you let her go, we can do all the talking in the world."

Alec only smirked. "I rather like the current position we have."

I tighten the hold on my gun. "Who did I kill that night if it wasn't you?"

"A prospect." He spat truths twisted in poison. That the burned body we had found hadn't been him, just some prospect, and I had fallen for his illusion. "I knew my baby sister was going to be a weak spot for you the second your face dropped when I came to ask for your help. I added my signature tattoo to his leg and made sure he would burn in the house just enough to be unrecognizable."

His nose brushed the side of Acelynn's face before he caught my eyes again. His tongue flicked out as he licked up the side of her face. She screamed at the contact, body convulsing in fear. Alec's dark chuckle filled the barn. "She is on hemlock right now, so I could convince her of just about anything, like I had the night of the massacre."

"You drugged your own sister that night?" I growled, the pieces finally falling into place.

Acelynn's skewed view of what occurred the night of the Spade massacre made more sense now. But it wasn't hemlock that he used then. I turned my head to the side. "It was with Muze, wasn't it?"

I tensed under his smirk as he spoke, "My little sister has been microdosed with Muze since she was old enough to speak. It was a preventive measure my father thought would help us when we shipped her off to the Knights. Guess he didn't take the same precautions with hemlock."

"Let. Her. Go." My voice broke sharp as a whip, gun trembling now with the fury I could barely contain. "This is between us. You want power? Kill me and you'll have it."

Movement behind Alec caught my eye, and I could see Vince's figure hidden in the barn's shadows. He was holding the same position as me, gun raised and aimed directly at Alec's skull. I made the play, dropping to one knee and sliding my gun across the floor. Raising my hands, I baited him. "Come on, Alec. I'm the reason you did all of this. If you kill me now, you have a right to the Knights' presidential seat. You have the power."

Alec laughed, blood and spit spraying Acelynn's face as he yanked her hair, forcing her to look at him. She sobbed against her brother's hand as he stroked the gun along her cheek. "Look at that. The King of Lovelen, ready to die for you, little Spade."

"He's not dying today," Acelynn hissed at him.

In one brutal motion, she slammed her head into his again, this time with more power than before. His nose crunched, and blood gushed down his face. Alec dropped his hold on his sister, a hand coming up to clutch his face. I leaped to my feet, hands lunging for the gun I had abandoned, but before I could get my hands around it, Acelynn had picked it up and leveled the barrel at him. Blood streaked down her own forehead, but her hand was steady.

"What are you going to do now, Em?" Alec taunted, grinning through blood. "Shoot me?"

"I shot Logan," she hissed. "You think I won't kill you?"

My fingers brushed against her lower back, ensuring she knew I was behind her, no matter what she decided. Alec snarled, "Look at you. A Knight's little slut."

"Queen," I corrected, pressing my lips to Acelynn's throat, never looking away from him. Her pulse was steady, and I noted that she no longer looked like she was floating from the drug in her system. But I continued, taunting her brother as my lips continued their trail. "The new Queen of the Knights."

The gunshot cracked like thunder. Alec screamed, buckling as the bullet tore through his arm. He buckled in pain, weapon clattering to the floor. Acelynn stepped forward, planting the heel of her boot into his wound, grinding down until he howled. I watched, half in horror, half in awe at her actions. She leaned down, voice ice-cold. "Hope it was worth it, Alec. Because it was for me."

"Fuck you." He spat blood, words coming through choked breaths.

"Say hi to our father." Acelynn cocked the gun back, placing the barrel just a few inches away from his skull. "Make sure to tell him that the little girl he raised for slaughter destroyed every Spade he ever loved more than his own family."

Alec laughed through his bubbling chest. "You'll never outrun it. You are still a Spade, no matter what you say. The blood that runs through your veins is the same as mine."

"That's where you're wrong." She smiled, cruel and lethal, before the sound of the gunshot ricocheted off the metal in the barn. Acelynn stood over him, chest heaving, blood on her face, and gun steady in her hand. Her voice was quiet, but it filled the barn, final and absolute. "I'm a Knight."

CHAPTER SIXTY-THREE

acelynn

SILENCE HUNG in the air as I watched the light drain from my brother's eyes. Alec's body jerked once, then stilled, his chest sagging under the weight of death. For a moment, everything inside me went silent too. No rain against the barn roof, no thunder rolling in the distance, no Kaius shifting nearby—just me and the monster I had grown up loving.

There were so many questions still lodged in my throat, a thousand things I had wanted to scream at him, demand of him, beg him for, but the chance slipped away with his last breath. All I could do was watch. Watch as the boy who once held my hand during storms, who taught me how to fight, who used to sit on the edge of my bed after our parents' screaming matches and whisper promises that we'd always survive together, faded into nothing but a corpse at my feet.

My chest heaved violently, guilt laced with rage, grief, and a hollowness that could never be filled. I had killed him. Not just the monster he had become, not just the soldier poisoned by his cruel upbringing, but my brother. My blood. I raised the gun again instinctively, hand trembling as a shadow shifted in the corner. My finger itched against the trigger.

A warm hand closed around my wrist, lowering it with careful strength. "It's just Vince."

I didn't resist as Kaius slid the weapon from my grasp. My eyes tracked Vince instead, desperate for an anchor in the storm brewing in my chest.

"Astoria?" My voice cracked, hope and panic cutting through the numbness.

Vince's hand caught my arm when I tried to lunge forward. "Nolan already has her. She's beat up pretty bad, a few broken fingers, but she'll live."

Relief punched through me so hard my knees nearly buckled. I nodded, unable to find the words to thank him. Vince stepped closer, rough palms cradling my face, examining me like I might break apart at any second. His eyes softened briefly, then he let me go.

"You were the thief swiping from my collection, weren't you?" he said, voice practical, clipped. I could only nod at him, so tired of hiding anything. He chuckled once. "Well, good thing. Those doses of hemlock you were taking probably just saved your life tonight. It should be fading, but if you start feeling off, I'll give you something to burn it out faster."

I nodded again. My body still buzzed with a strange, electric hum, but I wasn't sure if it was the drug or the grief —or both. Vince moved around me and clapped Kaius on the back. He exchanged a few low words with him, then disappeared out the front of the barn, leaving the wind and rain to howl through the torn-open doorway.

I stared after Vince, my eyes catching on the tarp flapping

in the storm. For a second, the scene blurred, and I wasn't in this barn anymore—I was back there.

Blood. It painted the dirt, seeped into it, creating a messy paste, and turned the air metallic and heavy in my lungs. I remember falling to my knees, my hands slipping in the warm, sticky pool spreading beneath what I thought was Alec's body. Now I could see the difference between him and the prospect he had set up for death. The body in my arms was younger, barely out of boyhood, but already carrying the weight of a man. His eyes had been open, glassy, his mouth slack in the way death left people unrecognizable. I remember screaming my brother's name, pressing my hands against wounds no hands could fix, shaking him, begging him to wake up.

"You promised me," I had sobbed, voice raw. "You promised we'd always survive together."

Detective Parsons had found me like that, a broken girl clutching the body of her brother amid the carnage of my family home. He pulled me back, his arms iron bands around me as I kicked and clawed to get back to Alec. Detective Watson hovered nearby, face grim, whispering something about trauma, about shock. None of it mattered. My nails raked Parsons's arms as he lifted me, carried me out of the yard while I wailed so hard my throat shredded. My tears soaked through his shirt, my body convulsing with grief I didn't understand how to live through. I ended up in the back of his squad car, hands cuffed in front of me as the two detectives talked just outside the vehicle.

The memory burned as it slipped away, dragging me back into the present—the smell of rain, gunpowder, and Alec's corpse not so different from that night. Only this time, it had been my finger that pulled the trigger.

"Acelynn." Kaius's voice dragged me out of the spiral. It

was softer than I deserved, his knuckles brushing down my cheek.

I sucked in a shaky breath. "I'm sorry."

The words tumbled out before I could stop them. My skin burned with shame, but once the floodgates opened, I couldn't close them. "I'm sorry for ever thinking you were a monster. You were the only one who...who didn't ask me to bleed for them. And I doubted you anyway. You were right. About Alec. About me. About all of it."

Kaius gripped my chin, forcing me to meet his eyes. His voice was steady and sure. It grounded me. "There's nothing for you to be sorry for, kitten. You've consumed my every thought since I was thirteen years old. I'd walk through fire and ruin to get to you, and I'd do all of this again if it meant finding you at the end of it. You are my salvation, Acelynn Spade. The one thing in this world I'd trade my crown for. I love you. Always have."

Tears spilled over, blurring my vision, but I leaned into him, whispering his name like it was the only prayer I knew. "Kai."

Without hesitation, I crushed my lips against his. Kaius seized me instantly, his mouth claiming mine in a bruising kiss that left me gasping. One of his hands slid to cup my face possessively, holding me there as if he could consume me whole. I leaned into him eagerly, craving more, needing more than just this kiss. Pulling back, my voice was a command that trembled with hunger. "You called me a queen earlier. Get on your back, Kaius, and show me how you worship your queen."

He arched a single brow at me but obeyed, lowering himself with deliberate slowness, first to his knees and then to the ground, settling back on his hands. His eyes burned with hunger, watching me with predatory patience as if I were the one putting on a show for him. I wasted no time. My fingers slid down, unbuttoning my jeans and tugging them off along with my underwear. Kaius's gaze darkened as he drank me in, leaning back fully now as if daring me to take what I wanted. Dropping to my knees, I straddled his thighs, my skin alive with fire where it brushed against him. My hands moved quickly, unzipping his jeans and freeing his already hard cock. I gave him a few slow pumps, savoring the way his groan rumbled through his chest, deep and guttural.

Kaius's hand shot up, gripping my face and dragging me down into another fierce kiss. His mouth was hot, demanding, and it made my pussy clench tight around nothing. His lips brushed mine as he murmured, "The clock's ticking before the cleanup crew arrives, kitten."

"And?" I lifted a brow at him, my challenge clear.

I moved forward, lining him up with my aching core and sinking down onto him carefully. A low moan spilled from my throat as my body stretched around him. Kaius groaned, his hips bucking to bury himself fully into me. His teeth nipped at my lower lip, tugging me back into another kiss as I tore at the buttons of his dark shirt. The fabric gave way under my hands, buttons scattering across the floor. I shoved the ruined shirt from his shoulders, too far gone to care about anything but the heat burning between us.

My palm pressed firmly against the center of his chest, guiding him down until his back hit the ground. Both of my hands found purchase above his head where a dark pool of blood had collected. The liquid squelched between my fingers, warm and slick, coating my skin. Pulling from the kiss, I straightened up, dragging my bloodied hands down his abs, marking him with the crimson streaks. Marking him as mine.

I began to move, rolling my hips in slow, deliberate

motions as pleasure pulsed through me. A shaky moan escaped as Kaius's hand reached up, his thumb pressing against my clit in rough, relentless circles that made me shudder.

"Kaius..." My voice broke in a breathy protest as he met my rhythm with hard, punishing thrusts. My lungs burned, my body surrendering every ounce of control to him.

He sat up, stealing another kiss, his mouth devouring every sound I made. Then, with brutal swiftness, he flipped us. My back hit the ground, and his hips slammed into mine, each thrust harder than the last until my eyes rolled to the back of my head.

"Fuck, you're gorgeous," he muttered against my skin, his blood-stained hand trailing up my stomach and shoving my shirt over my breasts. His head dipped, lips wrapping around one aching nipple as he began to toy with it. A sharp whine tore from me as his teeth grazed, then bit, and my pussy clenched tight around him. His mouth lifted slightly, voice ragged and commanding. "Come on, kitten. Let it go."

It only took a few more thrusts before I shattered, crying out his name as release tore through me. My body trembled, clenching tight around him, dragging him over the edge with me. His pace faltered, growing sloppy as he groaned, chasing his own release before spilling into me. Our breaths tangled together in the aftermath, ragged and heavy. Slowly, Kaius pulled out of me, pressing a single kiss to my forehead.

A soft smile curved my lips as I looked up at him, the chaos around us forgotten. "I love you too, Kaius."

He brushed his knuckle beneath my chin, tilting it up with a teasing smirk. "Oh, yeah?"

"Yeah." I bit down on my bottom lip, playful even in the haze of exhaustion. "And I'm glad you kept your end of the bargain of being the knight who saves the princess."

"You didn't need a knight to save you." Kaius's nose brushed against mine, voice low and steady. He pulled me flush against him, eyes burning into mine. "You saved yourself, kitten."

CHAPTER SIXTY-FOUR

kaius

THE DIM HOSPITAL light sent a weak yellow glow over Astoria's body. Her tiny frame seemed to be swallowed by the bed, blonde hair spilling like a halo across the thin white pillow. An IV line dripped antibiotics and painkillers into her veins, keeping her sedated and comfortable. Acelynn stood across from me in the corner of the room, trying to shrink into the shadows, but she was failing.

Her eyes were glassy, fixed on the rise and fall of Astoria's chest like she wasn't sure if she trusted it to keep going. Bruises darkened her face, yet she'd refused all treatment, hell-bent on laying eyes on Astoria with her own. Even unconscious, my little sister was stubborn. She twitched, trying to yank out the oxygen tube, but Nolan caught her wrist before she could rip it free. Nolan chuckled at her motion, standing slightly leaned over her and pulling her hand down to rest at her side.

"Stop laughing at me," Astoria rasped, her voice husky from the hours of screaming Alec had wrung out of her.

Nolan's laugh died instantly. He leaned close, brushing

his knuckles against her hair. Astoria squinted at me, causing me to step back to flick off the harsh overhead lights, leaving us in the softer wash of the emergency overhead lighting.

"Better?" I asked.

Astoria gave a small nod, wild eyes darting between me, Acelynn, and finally settling on Nolan. Relief softened her face as she reached for him. He caught her hand, squeezing tight.

"My brain feels funny. Like it was scrambled and then deep fried," she mumbled, her eyelids heavy.

"You need rest," Nolan murmured, bending to kiss her hairline. His hand smoothed back the baby hairs sticking to her damp skin before cupping her cheek.

She shook her head slightly, lower lip trembling. "Just don't leave me alone, Nolan."

"Never, princess." He kissed her forehead again, inciting a contented sigh from Astoria's lips.

But before the meds could pull her fully under again, I stepped closer, folding my arms over my chest. "Not yet. You and I need to talk."

Her gaze snapped to mine, face draining of the little color it had. The flicker of guilt glinted in her green eyes. Nolan turned toward me, his lips drew back in a grim line, a pulling at his lips. "Kaius—"

"No." My voice cut him off, low and sharp. He didn't get a say in this. Right now, I wasn't coddling my little sister for her wrongdoings. Acelynn shifted uncomfortably as I continued, "We're not doing this shit later. She talks now."

Astoria's throat worked as she swallowed, her hand tightening around Nolan's. "I didn't mean for any of this to happen. It was all me, though. I tipped off the feds about the night Oscar was killed because I knew Acelynn would blame herself. He told me she would blame herself, and he wanted her to be on edge."

Her eyes filled with tears as she looked toward Acelynn. "It was me who broke into your house. Logan told me I needed to draw the symbols and leave the weird, cryptic note on your wall. Before I left, he planted the snake. And the Polaroids...I planted the camera in Kaius's room and followed you to get the other images. I never found the photo in your car. It was just another way they wanted to fuck with your head. I thought if they continued to taunt you, you would run and stay away. I regret it. I regret every single thing that I did for them. It not only hurt you, but it got you arrested that day, Nolan. All I was trying to do was protect you. Protect all of you."

Nolan's jaw clenched. "Protect me? By setting me up to rot in a cell?"

The tears began to fall down her cheeks. Astoria looked down at their hands. "You don't understand. Alec threatened to kill you all. Logan was his errand boy who made sure I didn't stop doing their dirty work. Alec said if I didn't play along, if I didn't feed them information, they'd put you in the ground. I thought if I kept them focused on me, if I gave them just enough...I thought I could keep you safe."

Acelynn stirred in the corner, her voice breaking. "Astoria..."

I cut her off with a snarl. "Don't you dare romanticize this."

Stepping forward, I leaned down over the hospital bed, getting eye level with Astoria. "You think handing our people over to the wolves makes you some kind of savior? No. It makes you their fucking pawn."

Her breath hitched, tears spilling. My voice dropped to a lethal whisper. "You tipped the feds. You sold out Nolan. You kept secrets while Alec broke your bones. And for what? Because Logan pointed a gun in your face while hiding behind his leader? You put us all on the board. And now he's still out there, breathing. Do you understand what that means? He will come back. He will make this personal. And when he does, the blood will be on your hands first."

A broken sob broke through her lips. "I didn't have a choice."

"There's always a choice," Nolan snapped, but his grip on her hand didn't loosen. His anger warred with the softness in his eyes, his voice cracking as he added, "You should've trusted me."

Her lips trembled. "I was trying to save you."

"Save us?" I let out a low laugh, cruel and humorless. "No, Astoria. You played right into Alec's game. You thought you were smart enough to outwit him, and look where that got you. Flat on your back, broken and bleeding, while Logan's still out there free. You didn't save anyone. You damned us all."

Silence weighed heavily over the room. Nolan lowered his head, pressing his lips once more to Astoria's hair, even as his shoulders shook with restrained rage. Astoria's sobs quieted into soft hiccups, shame sinking her deeper into the mattress. And in the corner, Acelynn's hand found mine, her grip trembling, as if she already knew Logan's shadow wasn't leaving us anytime soon.

The door creaked open, dragging me out of the silence. Detective Watson slipped in, the weight of his badge dragging at his shoulders. His eyes swept the room, lingering on Astoria's swollen face, then catching the way Nolan still hadn't let go of her hand as he glared daggers at the detective.

"You weren't supposed to be here this long," Watson

muttered, shutting the door behind him. "Hospital staff talk. And right now, the last thing I need is whispers about certain faces showing up on security footage. Visiting hours are over."

"Then stop wasting time," I snapped. "Say what you came to say."

His jaw clenched, but he pulled a worn manila folder from under his arm. He dropped it onto the bedside table, letting the contents spill—a handful of fake IDs, driver's licenses, and credit cards. All Astoria's face, all different names. Acelynn sucked in a sharp breath. Nolan stiffened.

Watson folded his arms, tone clipped. "I want the truth, Astoria. How long have you been running with these?"

Her mouth opened, closed, her face pale. "I-I don't know. Months. A year. It started with Logan. He said it was the only way to stay invisible, to keep you guys guessing. I didn't think—"

"Didn't think?" I cut her off with a growl, stepping closer to the bed. My shadow swallowed her fragile frame. "You didn't think while you painted a target on all our backs? While you let Logan tie strings around you and dance you like his little puppet?"

Her tears started again, streaking her already bruised face.

"Kaius," Nolan said, his tone breaking. "She's been through enough."

"Not nearly enough," I snarled, dragging my gaze back to Astoria. I grabbed one of the IDs, flicked it between my fingers before dropping it onto her chest like a piece of evidence. "You keep secrets from me again, and you'll wish Alec was the one you had to deal with."

Her sob turned into a sharp, choked breath. Watson cleared his throat, clearly itching to get out from under the tension choking the room. He gathered the rest of the IDs, his gaze flicking to me, uncertain. "She's got heat on her from more than just Logan. Feds don't like being made fools of. You need to decide quickly what role she plays in all of this. Otherwise, she won't make it to the end of the week."

Nolan's voice broke. "She's not going anywhere. She stays with me."

Astoria squeezed his hand weakly, clinging to him like a lifeline. I let the silence hang, then turned my head toward Acelynn. Her eyes were wide, unreadable, searching mine for something she couldn't name. I gave her nothing but steel.

"You're going to help me find him, Astoria," I said, my voice flat and final. "Logan. His boss. Anyone who touches this family again. You're done hiding in shadows, little sister. You're going to help me burn them out of every hole they think they can crawl into."

Her lips parted, a protest trembling on her tongue, but I cut her off before she could breathe it into existence. "This isn't a choice."

The room fell silent again, broken only by the beep of the machines monitoring Astoria breaking through.

I couldn't have pried Nolan from Astoria's side even if I tried. His fingers were welded to hers, his lips pressed against her temple as though his touch alone might shield her from the shadows still clinging to the night. She'd finally cried herself to sleep, her chest rising in slow, steady breaths that were too fragile for my liking. I let them have their peace, for now. I tipped my chin toward the door, a silent command. Acelynn caught the cue, her eyes flicking from Astoria's sleeping form to me. She hesitated a beat before slipping from the room, her steps falling into place behind mine.

The hallway stretched empty, its fluorescent lights buzzing low and sickly against sterile walls. Except Detective Watson was still there. He leaned against the far wall like he'd been carved into it, arms folded tight, gaze sharp on us the moment the door latched shut.

"I wanted to talk to you about something else," he said, pushing off the wall, his voice low, gravel roughened by too much coffee and not enough sleep. "But it got a little intense in there."

Acelynn stiffened behind me. Without thinking, her hand found mine, her fingers lacing tight like she was tethering herself to the only thing that still felt real. I squeezed back once, firm enough for her to feel it. A promise without words.

"What else can we do for you, Detective?" I asked, my voice flat as stone, monotone on purpose.

Men like Watson were always testing boundaries, trying to gauge how far they could push. I wasn't about to give him anything but calm steel. He lifted a plain manila folder between two fingers.

"These are your new documents," he said. "You're officially Acelynn Thorton, if that's who you choose to be. All you need to do is sign."

Acelynn shuffled from behind me, her brows drawn tight. "I don't understand."

Watson's jaw worked, like he wasn't thrilled to be the messenger. "Parsons has a heart, even if he is a slimy bastard. He skipped town this morning but left this on my desk. Though I don't think that's the last time we will see him."

My brow arched, waiting for more.

Watson obliged. "Doesn't take a genius to connect the dots between the barn fire last night and your sister ending up in that hospital bed. While the body inside hasn't been officially ID'd yet, Alec Spade's wallet was found in the bushes outside."

"Alec?" Acelynn's voice trembled, soft but deliberate. She let the shock bleed into every syllable, her expression practiced innocence. "I don't understand what this has to do with me."

"Nothing." Watson smirked at her like he was in on a joke only he understood. Then he shrugged one shoulder and held the folder out.

I plucked it from his grip before flipping it open. Rows of fresh identification stared back at me—licenses, credit cards, paperwork. All with Acelynn's face. All under the name Thorton. I lifted my eyes to him.

"Just know," Watson said evenly, "you never existed to us. No trace of you being an informant. And all charges tied to Emersyn Spade? Dropped. She's a ghost. You are getting a clean slate."

Acelynn edged around me, her eyes wide, lips parting like she wanted to say something, but no words came. She shut her mouth, nodding once instead, stunned silence draped across her shoulders like a too-heavy cloak. I extended my hand toward Watson. He narrowed his gaze at it for a beat, suspicion flickering. Then, reluctantly, he clasped mine, his grip firm but not unbreakable.

"Thank you," I said, quiet but final.

He let go, straightening the lapel of his jacket like he'd just touched something unclean.

"Don't mistake this for a free pass," he warned. "This doesn't change the fact that your little criminal kingdom is still under my watch now that I have taken lead of the department."

A slow smirk curved my mouth. “Wouldn’t dream of having it any other way, Detective.”

CHAPTER SIXTY-FIVE

kaius

RED and black streamers swooped down from the rafters of the Queen's Table, twisting together in a display that looked almost too cheerful for a place that thrived on shadows and blood deals. Confetti-filled balloons littered the floor, popping under boots as people moved through the space, making it damn near impossible to walk without slipping on glitter.

It was over the top, but that was Acelynn. She'd insisted on throwing a welcome home party for Astoria after the hospital finally let her out. A week, they kept her. Too long if you asked me, but even longer if you asked Nolan. He'd practically been glued to her side, looking like hell every time I saw him.

Acelynn was still carrying the weight of guilt for what happened, still replaying the moment she'd dosed herself to keep Logan and Alec from snapping Astoria's fingers one by one. My sister had told her a hundred times that she was forgiven, but guilt was a tricky thing. It clung, even when no one else blamed her. Even when my sister should be the one groveling at her feet for all the insanity she had put Acelynn through the past few months.

"Kai." Acelynn's voice cut through my thoughts.

I looked up to see her balanced on the bar in a short black dress that barely covered her ass. Every time she reached higher to tape another set of streamers, the skirt rode up, giving me a perfect view of the red lace underneath. I hummed low in my throat, dragging my eyes up to meet her bright blue ones.

"Can you grab me another roll of tape from the office?" she asked, trying to look innocent but knowing damn well what she was doing to me.

"I've got a better idea," I said, stepping forward.

I caught her hand and pulled gently, guiding her to sit on the bar. Her legs parted instinctively, and I moved between them, pressing my mouth to hers in a kiss that started soft but could've easily become more if I let it. She leaned into me eagerly, lips chasing mine, but I pulled back just enough to let my mouth trail down her neck. She groaned out my name, her small hands pressing against my chest in a weak attempt to push me away.

"Kaius..." she breathed, voice breaking into a whine when I nipped at her throat. Finally, she shoved me back with more force, pointing toward the office with a narrowed glare that didn't fool me for a second. "Tape. Now."

I lifted my hands in mock surrender, smirking. "Okay, okay."

Her exasperated smile followed me as I slipped into the office. I'd barely gotten my hands on the roll of tape before I heard the creak of the front door and a voice I hadn't realized I'd missed until it echoed through the bar.

For a week, the Queen's Table had felt like a body without a heartbeat. Now, hearing Astoria's voice float through the place again made the bar stir back to life. I stepped out of the office, leaning against the hallway entrance to watch her.

She looked fragile, too pale, and way too thin, but she wore her mask well. Nolan hovered close, every inch the loyal shadow. And Acelynn...my kitten practically launched herself into Astoria's arms, hugging her like she was welcoming a sister of her own. I don't know how she was able to forgive her so easily. Truth be told, I was having a hard time getting past my anger with my little sister.

Astoria smiled, returned the hug, and for a moment, anyone watching would've thought everything between us was healed. That was the point. But I knew better. Astoria and I weren't on the same page, not yet, not after everything. We were still fractured, still keeping our distance in ways no one else would notice unless they looked too closely. For now, though, we'd play the game. Smile for the regulars at the bar and pretend the cracks didn't exist.

Just as we always had in times like these. If the club saw the divide between us, they would begin to talk, and I couldn't have them choosing sides when we still had Logan ready to retaliate at any moment.

Acelynn's eyes met mine over Astoria's shoulder. A small smile tugged at her lips, one that steadied something in me. No matter what name she kept—Acelynn Thorton, Emersyn Spade, or anything in between—she was home. Mine. And I'd burn this bar, this city, and every last one of my enemies to keep her safe in the chaos that came with being tied to me.

CHAPTER SIXTY-SIX

acelynn

THE SOFT CLINK of pool balls filled the room as I lined up my shot against Kaius. I wasn't half bad, even if I'd sworn up and down that I'd never played before. Maybe it was luck, or maybe it was the fact that his eyes on me made me want to show off. Everyone else had either gone home or retired to bed hours ago after the party for Astoria, leaving just the two of us in the quiet glow of the bar.

I heard his pool stick settle against the table and felt him come up behind me, his presence a warmth I'd come to crave. Without hesitation, I leaned back into him, resting my head on his shoulder. The faint scent of smoke and leather clung to his shirt, grounding me. His lips pressed to the crown of my head, soft and unhurried.

"I love you," I whispered, and I meant it with every shattered, jagged piece of me. He smiled into my hair, and though he didn't say the words back, I could feel it. It was in every time he touched me, every time he looked at me like I was both a sin and salvation.

I, Acelynn Thorton, loved Kaius Mordred. The thought

still startled me sometimes. But the name Emersyn Spade still carried Alec's shadow, Logan's cruelty, all the fractures of a family that had tried to own me, break me, bury me alive in blood and obligation. And yet here I was, whispering love into the darkness with the man who should have been my ruin.

Maybe I should shed that name already, let it die with the people who'd carved scars into me. But changing it felt like surrendering a war I hadn't finished fighting. Spade was a curse, but it was also proof I'd survived. Still, when I thought of the future, I couldn't help but wonder...would I keep carrying it like chains if I chose to revert back to it, or would I take the alias I had used to hide behind for so many months and finally let myself be remade fully?

I turned in his arms, letting my back rest against the pool table. He caged me in with his hands, bracing them on either side of me, that small smirk tugging at my lips before I even spoke. "I think I would like to pick up where we left off earlier."

His answering growl was pure sex. "I would very much like that as well, kitten."

In one smooth motion, he lifted me onto the table. This time, I didn't resist when he stepped between my legs. His fingers ghosted up my thighs, goose bumps breaking across my skin at the slow, deliberate trail he left. I shivered, knowing exactly where this was going, my breath catching as his hands slid beneath my dress.

When his fingers hooked into the sides of my red lace panties, the same ones I knew he'd been eyeing all afternoon, I didn't hesitate. I lifted my hips for him, watching as he stripped them from me with deliberate slowness. My heart pounded when he placed them in his back pocket with a smug little smirk.

Heat bloomed in my cheeks, but before I could protest, his lips crashed against mine. The kiss began soft, coaxing, but quickly turned demanding. His mouth claimed mine with a dominance that left no room for me to pretend I wasn't his for the taking. Our tongues tangled, my attempt to take control swallowed by the inevitability that Kaius never yielded. A sharp bite to my bottom lip sent a cry spilling into his mouth. My body arched into him, the friction between us a torture in itself.

His fingers crawled up my thigh in slow, deliberate strokes until they were at my pussy, ghostly touches teasing me until I was trembling. I writhed under his touch, a broken sound escaping me as he finally pressed inside. Two fingers filled me, the pace ruthless enough to steal the air from my lungs. My head lolled back, vision blurring, until his grip tightened at the base of my hair.

"Eyes on me, Acelynn, or I stop." The command snapped through my fog. My lashes fluttered as I struggled to obey, but instinct betrayed me, dragging my gaze toward the ceiling with every wave of pleasure. He paused, fingers buried deep, grip in my hair turning iron hard.

"What did I tell you, kitten?" Kaius's voice was a growl, thick with promise.

"Keep my eyes on you," I gasped, forcing myself to focus, to anchor on the sharpness in his stare.

"Good girl."

His pace resumed, faster now, a third finger stretching me wide. I moved with him, hips grinding down to meet each thrust of his hand. The world narrowed to this—Kaius's eyes on me, his hand commanding my body like no one ever had, the chaos inside me unraveling into something raw and unholy.

"That's it, Acelynn," he coaxed, voice rough with hunger.

"Ride my fingers like it's my cock. I want to hear you screaming by the end of this."

His fingers curled against that sweet spot inside me, thumb pressing hard circles over my clit, and the dam broke. Pleasure ripped through me, my voice shattering in a scream of his name as my body convulsed. I collapsed into the crook of his shoulder, shaking, his hand never faltering until the last tremor eased. Only then did he ease his fingers from me, smoothing down my tangled hair with a tenderness that undid me more than his roughness ever could.

I forced my eyes open, meeting his gaze, my voice raw. "I always thought you would be my damnation, Kaius Mordred. But that couldn't be further from the truth." Our lips brushed. My whisper carried on a breath that trembled with both exhaustion and certainty. "You are my salvation. The reminder that I don't need to right the wrongs of the others in my life to be loved. I can be loved with every fucked-up piece of me, and you'll be there to catch me if one day I shatter."

His mouth crushed mine again, pushing me back against the table, swallowing the small giggle that slipped from me, a sound I never thought I'd find in myself again, not after Alec's betrayal, Logan's cruelty, or the endless fracture of Astoria's pain.

But somehow, in this ruin, Kaius had found me. And in a world built on revenge, this time it had given me the one thing I hadn't dared to dream of. Him.

epilogue one

ASTORIA

"DO YOU HAVE THAT ONE, TORI?" Acelynn's voice rang over the rowdy crowd. I turned toward where she pointed to a young redhead lingering at the end of the bar. Her eyes were wide as she drank in the sight of the Queen's Table on a Saturday night. Poor thing looked like a lamb wandering into the lion's den.

"Yeah, I got her," I called back, though Acelynn was already halfway down the bar, taking an order from another patron. Typical, never waiting to see if I could handle things because it was just expected of me.

I rolled my eyes and made my way to the redhead. "What are you doing here, Penelope?"

"I am old enough to drink, you know." She shot me a glare. Her hair seemed to glow under the neon lights. I laughed under my breath. Sure, she was technically old enough, but there was no way this was about legality. This was rebellion—sweet, trembling rebellion against her father, the sheriff of Lovelen. If he even sniffed out that his precious daughter had stepped foot into the Knights' bar, let alone ordered something, he'd have her locked in her bedroom until she turned forty.

"Okay." I leaned into the bar, giving her a crooked smile. "What can I get you?"

Penelope's shoulders sagged, lips pulling into a pout as she realized I might have been right in my question. "A water is fine."

I sighed softly. Poor girl. She wanted to be wild, wanted to rebel, but fear still gripped her too tightly. She couldn't even commit to one harmless drink, too scared of her father's wrath. Leaning closer, I lowered my voice to something conspiratorial. "How about I make you a Shirley Temple and you can just say it has vodka in it? No one will ever know."

Her eyes lit up, wide and hopeful. "Really?"

I nodded and went to work, stirring the grenadine and soda together. Setting the glass down in front of her, I caught her fumbling for her card. I shook my head. "It's on the house. Go have some fun tonight, Pen. You deserve it."

"Thanks, Astoria." Penelope smiled at me like I'd just handed her a ticket to freedom before slipping back into the crowd. I straightened, only to catch sight of one of the prospects returning from taking out the trash. I snagged him by the collar before he could disappear again. His eyes widened like I was about to string him up in the alley. "Did you see that little redhead who was just at the bar?"

He nodded quickly. "Yes, ma'am."

"Ew. Don't call me that." I wrinkled my nose. "Just make sure all the Knights know that no one in this bar is to mess with her tonight."

"You got it." He was practically trembling under my grip. I shoved him back, and he scurried away like a terrified child.

I snorted. It was rare I got to pull rank on any of them, but when I did? Damn if it didn't stroke my ego.

I turned, picking up a wineglass to clean. My eyes lifted, just scanning the crowd until they landed on a sight that turned my stomach to ice. Nolan Bedivere, leaning down over some petite blonde at the doorway of the pool room.

I froze. My pulse thundered in my throat. He reached up, brushing a strand of her hair behind her ear like it was the most natural thing in the world. She giggled, high and fake, but it didn't matter. The sight alone was enough to shatter something raw inside me.

The stem of the wineglass shattered in my hand before I realized how hard I was gripping it. The sharp crack silenced those nearest as glass rained onto the counter in glittering shards. A few drops of blood welled across my palm. Nolan's head snapped toward me, eyes meeting mine across the bar. His face drained of color, knowing I had caught him flirting with that bimbo.

"Hey, I got this." Josie appeared at my side with a broom, glaring daggers at Nolan before turning to me. "Go clean up."

I set the base of the broken glass down behind the bar and stalked off. My hands slammed against my dorm room door, the blood coming from the tiny cuts on my hand smearing against its white surface. The door didn't even slam fully shut as Nolan slipped through the crack.

I ignored him as he called out to me, determined not to give him any attention as I stormed into the bathroom. Dipping down, I opened the cabinet and shuffled through the products until I came upon an old first aid kit.

"Astoria," Nolan called out to me again.

Slamming the first aid kit down on the counter, the latch broke, and the contents exploded onto the bathroom floor.

"What, Nolan? What could you possibly want from me right now?"

"What is your problem?" he growled, taking one step toward me until my back was pinned against the counter.

A bitter laugh clawed its way up my throat. "Really? Are you trying to intimidate me into talking? Because that's not going to work on me."

His hands braced the counter on either side of me, caging me in. "I'm not trying to intimidate you, Tor. I'm trying to get you to talk to me instead of throwing a tantrum and breaking glass."

"A tantrum?" I scoffed at him. "That's what you think this is?"

"I didn't think I'd have to spell it out for you, but yeah. You're acting like a brat right now."

The word sliced deep. Deeper than I wanted to admit. Because maybe he was right. Maybe I was nothing but the spoiled princess of the Knights, throwing fits, betraying the only people who had ever trusted me, and still I dared to demand more.

I shoved my palms against his chest. "Get out."

"Not until you tell me what's wrong." Nolan held his ground.

"You. That's what's wrong!" My voice broke into a scream. "I almost died, and you confess your love for me at my hospital bedside, and then just ignore me. It's been three months! Three months, and this is the only conversation we have had alone. Then you flirt with a knock-off clone of me in my bar!"

His head bowed, shame flickering across his features. "Tor..."

The nickname ignited every bitter wound inside me. My hand snapped against his cheek with a crack that echoed off the tile. Tears burned behind my eyes, but I forced them back. "You don't get to call me that anymore, Nolan. You lost that privilege the second you decided I wasn't worth chasing anymore."

I shoved past him, shoulder colliding with his chest. This time, he let me go. But his voice followed, raw and low, jagged enough to slice straight through me. "I can't trust you, Astoria. Not after what you did."

The words tore me open more than any rejection could. Because they were true. I had betrayed him. Betrayed the Knights. Betrayed myself. I raced out of the room, turning right and stumbling out the emergency exit. The heavy door clanged shut behind me. Cool night air hit my face, but it did nothing to calm the storm inside. My back slid down the rough brick until I hit the pavement, knees buckling beneath me.

Sobs racked through me, violent and unrelenting. I pressed a shaking hand to my face, the sting of the tiny glass cuts reminding me of the chaos I couldn't seem to escape. Where had I gone wrong? Where had I lost him? Nolan, the boy I had loved since I was five years old. The boy who once swore he'd always choose me. Now I was nothing but the girl who had betrayed him, and the woman he no longer trusted.

epilogue two

THE STUDY REEKED of smoke and secrets. Old candle wax dripped in hardened rivers down silver holders, pooling onto the scarred mahogany desk where maps, coded letters, and ancient ledgers of my family lay open, taunting me with their tales. Shadows bent unnaturally against the walls, crawling across shelves lined with iron-bound tomes and relics stolen from centuries of bloodshed.

The door creaked open. Logan entered, his swagger gone, his shoulders hunched like a beaten dog. The bandage at his temple was stained, the split in his lip barely clotted. His boots scuffed against the stone as he dragged himself forward, his limp from the bullet in his leg that he had been rid of weeks ago still prominent. When he got in front of me finally, he dropped to his knees in a pathetic heap, like I would have sympathy for him if he looked the part.

I let the silence strangle him for several breaths. His shallow gasps filled the space like the rattling of a cornered rat.

"You've failed me," I said, my voice soft enough to force

him to lean forward, but sharp enough that each word cut into him like glass. The tap of my nails against the desk seemed to set him even more on edge. Logan's palms pressed flat to the floor.

"Please, just give me another chance." His voice shook. "Emersyn—she's cunning, but I can get her back under control. I swear I can. I'll finish what Alec started. What you started before him."

I rose from the chair slowly, letting the weight of my presence speak louder than my words. "Control?"

The edge of my coat dragged across the wood floor as I moved toward him. "You couldn't control a half-dead girl in a barn. You couldn't control Alec. And worst of all..." I crouched down until my face hovered close enough that he dared not breathe too loudly. "You couldn't control yourself."

He flinched, but his eyes snapped upward, desperate. "It was Alec's fault! He pumped her with too much hemlock. He—"

"Enough." The single word cracked like thunder through the room. Logan choked his protest off, his chest heaving as silence slammed down between us. His lips quivered, but he didn't dare move. I straightened, circling him like a wolf deciding whether its prey was worth the effort of tearing open.

"Do you have the faintest idea what your failure has cost me? Every move I make against the Knights must be exact. Precise. My plans do not have room for incompetence." I paused, letting the weight of my words drag through the air. "You've been sloppy, predictable. And now the Knights are watching us closer than ever. They are aware of an enemy on the horizon."

Logan lowered himself further until his forehead nearly brushed the floor. His voice cracked. "I can prove myself. Just please don't cast me aside. I've given everything to this cause."

I bent low, my sharp nail hooking beneath his chin, forcing him to meet my gaze. "That's the problem. You've given everything you are...and it still isn't enough. You are nothing, Logan. A disposable card in a stacked deck. And you are out of plays."

His eyes burned, wet and frantic. His lips trembled around words that barely scraped free. "Please don't kill me."

I let my smile flicker across my mouth, a thing devoid of warmth. "Kill you? No. Death would be too much of a kindness for you. And you haven't earned that."

I released his face with a snap of my wrist, sending him sprawling onto his side. He stayed there, trembling, as I returned to my desk. The map of Lovelen sprawling across the surface glowed in the dim candlelight, each territory marked, each Knight stronghold carefully circled. The greater game was still intact. Logan's incompetence had delayed my hand, nothing more.

Fingers brushed over the map as I spoke the words that sealed his fate—not his death, but his purpose.

"Let the Spade girl play her little games." My tone was almost amused now. "We still have the darling under our thumb."

a look at book two:

OUT OF MOVES

The Darling

Returning to Lovelen might be what finally destroys us both.

Months on the run have worn me down to something unrecognizable. New name. New life. Same ghosts. I thought I'd escaped the city and the boy I once loved—until he found me and dragged me home. Now the Knights watch me like vultures, and he looks at me like I'm the betrayal he can't forgive.

But I destroyed everything to keep him alive. As the past claws back and buried secrets splinter open, I can't ignore the truth: he still unravels me with a single touch, even if he swears he'll never trust me again.

The Knight

Astoria Mordred ran from me once. She won't get the chance again.

Bringing Lovelen's Darling home reopened every scar she left behind. The Knights want answers, and I've been charged with pulling them out—no matter how deep they're buried. But Astoria isn't the girl I knew. She's hardened, haunted... and still capable of shattering me.

When an old enemy returns, all sharp edges and whispered threats, I know she's hiding something lethal. And when the truth breaks, I see how long she's been bleeding for me.

Loving her could break my oath. Saving her could cost my life. But losing her again would destroy me.

AVAILABLE APRIL 2026

acknowledgments

Thank you so much for joining me in Acelynn and Kaius's story. Writing their journey, their trauma, their pain, and the scars they carried was deeply healing for me. My hope is that in reading it, someone out there felt a spark of recognition, comfort, or even the first steps toward healing of their own.

When I began this book, my own life felt like it was stuck in limbo. Each day blurred into the next, weighed down by a job that drained me and by people whose motives for keeping me around weren't always kind. But through all the chaos and hurt, I was able to pour myself into something creative—something that gave the pain purpose.

And for that, I want to thank the people who helped make this possible:

Mom and Dad, thank you for always supporting my grand ideas and never telling me that something was too big to dream.

Elijah, the one person who is always there for me, even when I was not fully myself. Thank you for sticking by me through all the craziness, and we can just remind ourselves that "it's probably your brain" when everything seems too dark to conquer. I wouldn't want to hire Etsy witches to read our prophecies and scream "King Jullliannn" at anyone but you.

My editor, Ellie Folden, for help making this book the

best it can be! Sorry for all the grammatical errors you found. I hope some of them made you laugh!

Kayla Ireland, you are a rockstar. Thank you for answering all my silly first-time trad author questions!

To the Love N. Books team! Working with all of you has been such a dream come true as I venture into the traditional publishing realm!

And to you, my beloved readers! Thank you for supporting me through every book I have ever written and for showing up at events and telling me just how much my characters impacted you. I don't think you will ever understand how much that means to me. Your support has kept me going when I thought about giving up and putting this dream to rest. I love you eternally.

Allison Aldridge is an Amazon bestselling author from Arizona who currently resides in Georgia. With a love for all things that have to do with storytelling, she continues to be an active member of the online book community. When she is not writing, you can find her watching hockey with her family or talking about her newfound fictional crush that has appeared in her life on her social media accounts. Allison graduated from Arizona State University with a Bachelor's in English with a concentration in Literature.

www.allisonaldridge.com

www.ingramcontent.com/pod-product-compliance
Lightning Source LLC
LaVergne TN
LVHW040214110826
845146LV00005B/1281

* 9 7 9 8 8 9 5 6 7 7 5 9 9 *